THE DEVIL AND THE MIDWIFE

KRISTINA SUKO

WELL LOVED BOOKS

Well Loved Books

All rights reserved.

Copyright © 2025 by Kristina Suko

Cover Design by Kristina "Kina" Mickahail-Giblin – @picturetincture

Interior formatting and design by Kristina Suko

The characters and events portrayed in this book are fictitious. Any similarity to real persons, living or dead, is coincidental and not intended by the author.

No portion of this book may be reproduced, or stored in a retrieval system, or transmitted in any form or by any means, electronical, mechanical, photocopying, recording, or otherwise, in any form without written permission from the publisher or author, except as permitted by U.S. copyright law.

For permission requests, please contact Kristina Suko at wlovekristina@gmail.com

Published by Well Loved Books

A QUICK GUIDE TO SCOTS

In this book, you will find a variety of Scots words and phrases. I am not an expert, but I have hopefully done justice through my research on common phrasing and Scottish terminology. There will also be some archaic terms, important to the era of the story. I've done my best to list them all below.

Arisaid - the women's version of a great kilt, approximately 9 yards of double wide fabric draped around the skirts, able to pull over the head and shoulders with ease to protect from the weather.

Bairn - a baby

Bannock: an oat-based flatbread, similar to American biscuits, or British scones.

Blaeberries: a native berry much like a blueberry

Blaigeards: scoundrels

Blether: chat

Breist: the Scots spelling of breast

Chyrurgion: an archaic term for surgeon, particularly one who treated skin diseases, hernias, gallstones, and other surgical needs including the delivery of stillborn babies.

Coos: Highland cows

Crowdie: a soft Scottish cheese, similar to cream cheese.

Ken/kent: knew, known

Dinnae/cannae/wouldnae, etc: did not, could not, cannot, would not... you get the picture!

Dinna fash: don't worry

Doaty: slang for stupid

Glaikit: also slang for stupid

Haud yer wheesht: shut up

Howdie: a midwife

Leine: a shirt made of linen, usually with long sleeves with an opening at the neck. The opening could be round, collared, or vee-shaped.

Maffle: waste time

Mo ghràdh: my love/my dear

Muckle gab: big mouth

Nattered: gossiped, chatted

Numpty: yet again... slang for stupid. And perhaps a little dense.

Stram: a big, clumsy, lumbering man

Throws: an archaic term for contractions in labor

Trews: tight pants, think a mix between tights and breeches.

Quaich: a cup from which whisky is drunk. Used in weddings to indicate trust.

Walloper: an idiot, someone who hits someone

Wain: child

Weskit: a waistcoat/vest, worn over a shift, with sleeves that tied on, or a jacket.

the DEVIL and the MIDWIFE

For my mother, who encouraged me to chase my dreams. This book wouldn't be here without you.

THE VILLAGE HOWDIE
Caitriona

Scotland, 1720

Caitriona Irving had long ago decided a young woman's personal happiness could not be contingent upon marriage or man. Men were unreliable, uninventive, unruly. Disappointing at best and destructive at worst. By the age of twenty-seven, she had decided to forsake her duties as the only child of the Irving clan, give up the naive dream of finding a match and building a family, and pursue making her own way in the world.

The shining experience of her thirtieth delivery as the new Howdie of the Village of Brae proved it further: she did not need a man to be happy. She only needed herself. She only wanted to *be* herself.

Which was why, as she sat in the corner of a hazy little cottage nestled into the highland hills, jotting down the latest birth details in her record-book, the sudden arrival of her best friend Maeve brought with it a rather large shock.

"There's a man at yer house and he's brought loads of carriages with him," Maeve said, her brazen entrance shushed by the gaggle of visitors in the single room cottage.

Caitriona leapt from her seat and grabbed Maeve's arm, throwing apologies over her shoulder as she dragged her friend out the door.

"Are ye daft, woman?" she demanded, cheeks flushing with indignance. The village may have been close-knit, but even Maeve knew not to interrupt when Caitriona was delivering a bairn. "I am in the middle of—"

Maeve waved a hand and clucked her tongue. "We've all heard by now, a bonny wee boy for Eilidh and Donald, aye? I kent ye'd be done by now." There was not an ounce of shame on her impish face. The woman had never lost her mischievous tilt, despite having children and a husband to care for. In fact, she'd passed on the trait to her dark-haired offspring, both of whom crowded around Caitriona's skirts demanding treats.

Swatting her hands in the air affectionately, Maeve shooed them away, and the two went to a patch of daisies bobbing in the early morning mist. "Yer mother's in a right tizzy. Nearly lost my head to her claws, she was so frantic. Though I cannae say whether she was excited or worried. With your mother, it's hard to tell."

Bemused, Caitriona glanced toward the village in the distance. Beyond, hidden by the hills, was Irving manor. An estate that had once been grand, and now crumbled at the edges. "And the carriages? Who do they belong to?"

Maeve shrugged. "I dinnae ken, yer mother wouldnae let me stay t' see their owner. She near scared my heart out o' me chest when she found me lingering on the steps of the manor." Pursing her lips, Maeve's bright eyes were wide, but the mirth lingered in her waggling brows and exaggerated movements. "Wouldnae want tae be on the wrong end o' a stick with yer mother." She mimed whacking someone with a broom.

Shaking her head, Caitriona brushed stray red hair from her forehead and smoothed her skirt over her hips, a smile on her lips despite the apprehension lurking in her chest. "I'll just take care o' the last things inside." She turned and ducked back into the cottage.

It was a simple room, with a fire pit in the center as was most common in highland cottages, a bed near the blaze to keep both mother and child warm, and the new bairn's grandparents settling into the low chairs by the fire. A gentle lullaby came from the bed, where Eilidh nursed her baby. Tea sat brewing beside her, a concoction of herbs for any pains the new mother might feel, and Caitriona's special balm for breastfeeding mothers was in a jar nearby.

Though dirt floors were underfoot, the space was clean, full of family, and warm.

There was little left for Caitriona to do but go home.

She had hoped to catch up on sleep when she left. Midwifery was not for the faint of heart. Many a night had been spent awake by the side of a laboring mother, sacrificing her own rest to bring new life into the world. She could not fathom what it might be like to do this with a family of her own to care for; in fact, she was glad of her spinsterhood. Her own ruined reputation afforded her freedom to do what she liked without censure.

Or rather, without *too much* censure.

Caitriona was lucky to be the daughter of the Laird. It was her one stroke of good fortune. Being rather tall, as fiery in nature as her hair might suggest, and ample of figure, Caitriona had lost in the natural lottery of what was in fashion. To add to it, she had a father who encouraged her to think for herself, a wealth of rumors following her, and an inclination to study the natural world which had led to her being far too well-read for her own good.

Her mother often chided her for furthering her spinsterhood. But Caitriona could not help what she loved. Being outdoors, learning to defend herself, and riding her favorite mare on trews were chief among the offenses she committed weekly.

And, of course, following her heart into midwifery. The profession itself was scandalous enough, especially as she had not obtained her license from the parish and could be tried as a witch or denounced as a strumpet by any man who felt threatened by her presence in the birthing room.

It was all nonsensical, of course. She might know more about a woman's anatomy, pleasure, and pain than a man — she was, after all, a woman — and her knowledge of natural healing was superior to the local chirurgeon. But she was not a witch, nor a bawd.

The risk to her reputation and the loss of sleep was all worth it, to Caitriona. Delivering babies and healing the women who bore them fulfilled her in a way nothing else had. And at the end of it was home and bed, like a safe haven for her weary limbs.

But now, the thought of home brought disquiet, a shadow cast over the otherwise happy morning.

Settling the new parents with short, succinct instructions on what to do should any worries arise, she let herself out. The soft chatter would have been music to her ears as she left if she weren't preoccupied with Maeve's ominous news.

Outside, her friend chased her children around in circles, raucous laughter filling the soft air. She had never stopped being playful, and Caitriona loved her for it. She was a wonderful mother. As Maeve swooped her daughter Lillian into her arms, nuzzling her neck to make her squeal, Caitriona pressed a hand to her chest.

An ache hid there, buried beneath the years of making do with her circumstances. Despite her best efforts to set aside the yearning for a family and children, it still reared its head from time to time, unexpected yet familiar. Like an old broken bone, healed over but still twinging with the change in weather.

She shook it away, plastering a smile on her face when Maeve looked her way.

Midwifery was her life now. And that was more than enough. It was her life's calling.

"Ready to face the devil, then?" Maeve quipped, and then, clapping a hand over her mouth in mock shame, she corrected, "I mean, yer mother?"

A snort escaped Caitriona. No matter her mood, Maeve always knew how to make her laugh. Basket in hand, Caitriona shook her head. "Ye're incorrigible," she reprimanded. But affection warmed her heart, softening the anxiety that pressed against her ribs.

"Or perhaps it's the devil come in the carriages," Maeve mused, her penchant for drama unchecked. "They're all black."

Caitriona lifted a brow. "Black?"

"Aye, inky as the night." Maeve waved her hand in the air. "Dark as a dungeon. Sooty as the devil's soul. Anyway, somethin' is afoot."

There was only one thing this could mean, and Caitriona was loath to admit it. Instead, she answered in jest, "I dinnae think my dowry is enough to tempt such a prestigious figure as the devil."

"What a match that would make," Maeve mused, her lips twitching. "The devil and the midwife. He ushers them out, ye bring them in."

They both chortled, and Maeve laced her fingers with Caitriona's in an old familiar way as they strolled down the path. The gravity of what waited lifted, just a little.

Despite the heavy clouds mottling the sky with streaks of white and gray, it was a pleasant day. Mist kissed Caitriona's cheeks as they walked down the road, her free hand trailing over the damp leaves of a nearby hedge. Flowers drank in the moisture from the drizzle.

Ahead of them, Maeve's two bairns giggled and squealed, stopping at a fence to reach their little hands toward the Highland cows, who watched them with lazy regard, their shaggy manes covering their eyes and their horns catching damp droplets.

Their calves were fluffy and curious, bouncing toward the children to nuzzle their proffered hands with velvety noses. It was a pleasant walk through the rambling hills to get back home. Or it would have been, if trepidation had not grown in Caitriona's stomach with every step, settling like an overcooked bannock, hard and bitter.

Caitriona was well aware her lack of a husband was affecting the Irving estate. Their clan was small now, their lands dwindling from years of war and age and, subsequently, the rents were no longer enough to pay for the restoration of the vast rooms of the manor. Her beloved attics, where she had spent dusty days reading as a young woman, were full of rot. The roofs leaked; the nursery had long since been boarded off when its ceiling fell through.

As the only child of her parents, Caitriona had been their token for an alliance with a new clan. A larger, more thriving, and most importantly, wealthier clan. Much to the despair of her mother, Caitriona had instead fallen in love with a man who left her reputation in shambles.

Still, Moira Irving was an optimistic woman, and the years had softened the rumors circulating about Caitriona's sordid love affair. Ever the romantic, Moira Irving spurned the idea of spinsterhood, bemoaning her daughter's pursuit of midwifery, and clinging to hope. Would it not be lovely to have a husband, she said. A man to take care of her, to feed and clothe her and shelter her in the storms.

As if Caitriona were a bairn herself, and not the woman who delivered them.

Her mother meant well, but it chafed at Caitriona's temper. She was well past marriageable years and very settled into her life here. She had learned to be content delivering the babies of the village. Part of her hoped her father would somehow find an alliance with another clan on his own *without* promising his daughter's life away to a man she did not know or love.

Mounting the last hill on their way, she and Maeve looked down over the village of Brae. Though small, there was a bustle of life here. Built of stone and clay, the houses were all in a low, straight line, their thatched roofs dark with mist and their chimneys loosing lazy lines of smoke into the air. A few women gossiped outside the butcher, skirts picking up the mud of the street, and she smiled as she approached them. From the solitary school, small voices repeating lessons could be heard.

Fingers still twined as though they were children again, she and Maeve traversed the distance to the manor, the constant chatter of Maeve's children filling the silence. Caitriona had to shorten her stride, her height giving her an unfair advantage in speed, but she was used to it. Years of friendship had imprinted the familiar gait into her subconscious. It was as natural to her as breathing.

Despite their physical appearances being night and day — or rather, dawn and dusk, as Caitriona's bright red hair was often compared to a sunset and Maeve's blue eyes resembled the clear sky in the morning — the two women had been inseparable since the day they'd met. Even marriage on Maeve's part had not changed their friendship.

In fact, Caitriona had delivered Maeve and Craig's bairns, Lillian and Davie.

A sudden thought occurred to her. Maeve was oddly breathless for such an easy walk, and looking...fuller than usual. While Caitriona would never presume upon the state of a woman's womb, she'd seen that look before on her friend. Twice.

"Maeve, why were ye at the manor?"

Maeve tucked a strand of dark hair behind her ear, having taken off her kerch to re-tie it, and clicked her tongue. "I was lookin' for ye, why else? Fer my own purposes, ye ken?" As if she were speaking of something mundane like the weather, Maeve shrugged. "My terms havenae come in a wee while now, and my breists ache somethin' awful."

Caitriona grinned. "I knew it! When did ye bleed last, then?"

Biting the inside of her cheek in thought, Maeve answered, "Three months ago, I suppose." She rolled her eyes then. "And I've had the most unnatural cravings, Cait. Why, t' other day I looked at my own husband and wondered what it might be like to —" She glanced around and lowered her voice. "— to bite off a piece of his buttocks."

Struck with mirth, Caitriona squealed with laughter, causing Maeve's children to turn and stare. "Ye didnae!"

Maeve snorted. "Aye, I wanted to, but of course I didnae actually do it."

A bubble of humor swelled in Caitriona's bosom as they entered through the gates of Irving manor and stalled in the shadow of the tall archway. A wide courtyard spread before them, and Caitriona shook her head, pulling her friend into a hug. "Well, may Craig survive unscathed. 'Tis common for women to crave unusual things when with child, Maeve, but a piece of his — the poor man." She pealed with laughter again, unable to keep her mirth contained.

Maeve's eyes twinkled. "He deserves it, the glaikit fool, 'tis his own sorry hide that got me with child again." She rubbed her back. "Ach I love them, but birthin' a bairn isnae for the weak."

Caitriona nodded, the old ache ever-present, reminding her she would never truly know what it was like. Ignoring the twinge in her heart she counted the months in her head. "An autumn babe, then?"

Nodding in agreement, Maeve said, "And ye'll be deliverin'?"

"Of course I will!" Caitriona squeezed her friend's fingers. "Blessings on ye, Maeve. 'Tis grand news."

But she could not linger over the news for long. Exclamations of awe rang through the air as Maeve's children wandered through the courtyard, exclaiming over its unusual inhabitants. Maeve let out a low whistle as well. "Nae as grand as these carriages. Have ye ever seen so many black horses?"

Dread crept into Caitriona's limbs and she trailed behind Maeve with leaden feet. In front of Irving manor, where the once-grand staircase was now worn and mossy, the pristine carriages shone. There were two of them, each pulled by magnificent inky horses, who tossed their manes with pride as Caitriona and Maeve passed. Bustling up and down the stairs were several footmen hauling trunks, boxes, and baskets filled to the brim.

A shot of alarm ran through Caitriona when she recognized her own trunks being ferried down the steps. The men carrying them were not from the Irving clan.

Stepping through the wide-open doors of her childhood home, Caitriona found utter chaos. Beneath the dark wood beams of the grand foyer ceiling, Moira Irving was shouting orders at the men who came in and out and flapping her hands at the maids as everyone around her hurried to do her bidding.

"Ach Elaine, this willnae do!" Moira muttered, fussing at the lid of another of Caitriona's trunks, which would not close. Throwing open the lid, she pulled a wrapper out, followed by a shift Caitriona did not recognize, and a quilt which had been part of her trousseau.

"Mother?" Her heart threatened to beat its way out of her chest as she stood surveying the mess. Pottery, jewelry, books, and clothes were being shoved out of sight and carted away over the worn wooden floors, and one of the men even stood on a ladder, taking down Caitriona's favorite tapestry.

It had a unicorn on it, surrounded by flowering trees, a reference to old legends and stories Caitriona had grown up reading. Caitriona watched him struggle, wondering dazedly where the tapestry would go. It had hung in their foyer Caitriona's entire life. "What is happening?"

Moira was a short, round woman with red hair like her daughter and full cheeks which were prone to flush pink with excitement. "Oh my dear, you're finally here!" Moira reached out to her daughter and clicked her tongue. "Ye're a mess!" She dusted a hand over Caitriona's dirty apron and surveyed her mud-stained hem. "Ye must bathe immediately, and change."

Caitriona scowled. "What is all of this?" she demanded, ignoring her mother's fussing.

Moira looked around them. "Oh, I'm packing up yer things, of course! But ye really must go and change."

"Why?" Conscious of the afterbirth staining her clothes, Caitriona clung to her birthing basket and tried to ignore the claws of dread closing around her throat.

With a flutter of her fingers over the triangular white kerch covering her hair, Moira glanced down the hall toward her husband's study. "Ach well we cannae have him see ye in such a state!"

The door to Hamish Irving's library was closed, but an unfamiliar voice seeped out, setting Caitriona on edge. "No, mother, I want to ken why ye are packing up my things?"

Moira let out an airy laugh and clasped her hands beneath her chin, beaming. "Och child, did we nae tell ye? Ye're to be married! And yer betrothed has come to collect all your belongings and settle them at his castle — his *castle,* Caitie girl! — before the wedding next week."

"Next week?" The words hit Caitriona like a shovelful of dirt being thrown over her grave, burying her in dread. Though she still ached from time to time for a family of her own, this was not how it was supposed to happen. Not now. She was happy as the village Howdie. Delivering babies was her true calling.

And sure, Caitriona had envisioned a future for herself in which she someday found marriage. A love match, perhaps, later in life. A pairing of souls with a man who did not mind a woman with a full and busy life, who loved her for who everything she was, including the midwifery.

But an arranged marriage?

She shook her head to clear the roaring of her ears. If Maeve had not stepped forward to gently hold her arm, she might have dropped to the floor in shock. Everything whirled around her and she steadied herself against her best friend, fighting for a breath.

Oblivious, Moira closed the distance between them and patted Caitriona's cheek affectionately. "Yes my love, married! Finally, I can see my beautiful daughter become a bride. Och and we can finish the wedding gown we started when...well. No need to talk about yer past now." Without pause, Moira took her daughter's arm and shoved her toward the stairs, where a maid waited with towels and soap in hand. "Now go on and bathe. We cannae present ye to him lookin' like this."

"Wedding gown?" Caitriona's brain was two steps behind in processing what her mother had said.

Her mother had begun counting the trunks, tucking bits of cloth in here and there as she went. "Aye, and he arrived today to settle negotiations for the Irvings to join his clan. He needs a wife ye see, and yer dowry is our land. Which means all those wings we've shut off from rot will be fixed! Yer beloved attics can be saved, finally." Moira closed the lid of a trunk and dusted her hands together. "Didnae father tell ye?"

He needs a wife. Still struggling to get her lungs to expand, Caitriona shook her head. "Ye're…trading me to fix the attics?"

Moira hummed, her smile a bit strained. "Ach no, love. Not *trading* ye. Ye'll be a wife, the lady of yer own house! 'Twill be a grand marriage, he's rich as the king. I could have sworn we told ye at some point."

Maeve, who was trying to keep her children out of the trunks in the room, piped up, "Is he from a neighbouring clan?"

Moira shook her head. "Well, I am nae too sure, to be honest. Hamish has dealt with it all, I didnae think to ask…"

One of Maeve's children began to whine, and she took both their hands. "Will she be able to tend to the women here still, do ye think?"

Dazed, Caitriona looked from her mother to her best friend. "I have to deliver Maeve's bairn in the autumn."

Moira blinked. "Do ye, now? Well, blessings on ye and yer family, Maeve! 'Tis a day full of grand news is it not?"

No, Caitriona thought. *It isn't.* But Maeve was carting her youngest onto her hip, and squeezing Caitriona's hand goodbye. "I must away, Craig will be wonderin' where I am by now."

When Caitriona began to shake her head, Maeve tugged her close. Low enough that Moira could not hear, she said, "Ye ken I'm always here, if ye need me." There was a smile playing about her lips, though her gaze was concerned. "I ken a good bog where a body willnae be found."

Caitriona laughed, but it was watered down, forced through the thick air that pressed in on her. "I'll be fine," she replied.

"Of course," Moira said, coming closer to slip an arm around her daughter's waist. "We'll all be grand!" She waved Maeve off, fondness in her gaze.

The door closing behind Maeve echoed through the now-empty foyer and snapped Caitriona out of her daze. "I dinnae ken what ye or father have promised, but surely 'tis nae so settled?"

Moira cleared her throat. "Yer father's been receiving letters from the Laird for weeks now. Ye'll be quite taken care of, my darling."

A thrum of anger rushed through her. "For *weeks*? And ye've said nothing?"

"I'm sure I did. Well anyway." Moira waved her off, giving her another little push toward the stairs. "Dinna fash about it, Caitie girl. He's got quite the estate. And a castle! I think ye'll be quite happy bein' his wife."

"I dinnae want to be *anyone's* wife," Caitriona snapped. Her blood was boiling now, and as the last of the trunks was carted away her voice echoed off the walls of the foyer. "I thought I made that quite clear."

Moira lifted a finger to her lips, eyes worried. "Hush girl! Ye'll scare him off with that temper! And what with the trews and the hunting and the fighting with the stable hands. Really, Caitriona, ye should have spent a bit more time learning how to manage an estate."

In the wake of her heart — and her reputation — being in ruins, Caitriona had done everything she could to forge her own path over the years. Unintentionally, she had made herself quite unmarriageable. She had settled into spinsterhood with aplomb, learning to defend herself with a short sword, track and kill animals for food, and having the village seamstress make her trews of tartan wool, which she wore with pride much to the dismay of her mother.

But now, she was glad she had ignored propriety. Perhaps it would save her from this awful situation. No man wanted a wife who would rather spear a hog than plan a supper menu. "Mother," Caitriona said, clenching her fist into the folds of her arisaid, which draped over her skirts. "I willnae be pawned off like this. Ye cannae—"

"Ye've already been promised," Moira cut her off. "And ye'll do as yer father sees best."

Fury roiled in Caitriona's chest. "I am nae a helpless young miss any more, mother. I'm nearly thirty, and I have a profession. A *life* here. I cannae simply uproot myself for…for a man I dinnae ken!" She did not want to know which aged Laird they had promised her to. There were a few clans known for their rich lairds, and most of them were well into their sixties. Her father's age.

A softness entered Moira's gaze. "I'm sure ye'll come around, my dear. Marriage isnae so bad as all that, is it?"

Her stomach roiled, but she clenched her teeth and refused to cow herself. "Perhaps not, but I will not be marrying anyone."

She had taken a step towards the stairs when a deep voice cut through the room.

"Ye seem confident about that."

"Ah, Laird Macnammon! How lovely of ye to join us!" Moira's voice was cheerful.

Caitriona froze, heart pounding, back to the room. She could have laughed at how close Maeve had been with her jest about the devil's carriages.

Rhys Macnammon, Laird of Calhoun Castle and leader of the Macnammon Clan, was one of the wealthiest Lairds in Scotland — and one of the most feared in war. He had spent three years roaming the continent, fighting battles and gaining a reputation, and upon his return had incited a clan war which had ended in spilling the blood of his own uncle.

Since then, his reputation had only grown. The rumors surrounding him were unsavory, and he did nothing to quell them. He seemed to lean into the assumptions, building a character so renowned it was impossible to identify truth from fiction.

And they called him The Devil of Calhoun.

A CLAN DIVIDED

Rhys

Three Days Earlier

Rhys Macnammon did not want a wife.

Sitting on the dais of his great hall before his clan, he was only half-listening as Ewan Burns and Fyfe Darrow squabbled over the lines of their land. Instead, the letters sitting on his desk from Hamish Irving on the matter of his spinster-daughter and a potential match loomed, and his mood grew darker at every turn. A wife would disrupt the comfortable rhythm of his days. She would meddle and prod and nag, changing the order of things. Changing the order of *him*.

The idea of wedding again, after his first marriage had ended in disaster, was about as appealing as stripping nude and jumping into the north sea. Upending his habits for a woman? Unthinkable now. Closer to forty than thirty, Rhys was no longer an eager young lad ready and waiting for love. He was settled.

He did not *need* a wife.

Remaining a widower by choice, Rhys had spent the last ten years in solitude. Had his clan and his lairdship not been threatened, he would have continued on forever. He was content alone. Things ran the way he wanted them to. There were no risks.

But the foundation of his clan ran upon the strength of the Macnammon line. Currently, his Lairdship was being questioned by none other than his cousin, Berach Macnammon, who'd gotten it into his head that he would be a better Laird. The latest argument against Rhys's position was his bachelorhood and childlessness.

He had not yet informed the clan of his decision. Not even Callum, his best friend of over twenty years, knew of his correspondence with Hamish.

Anger fissured through him like fire devouring dry wood.

He did not want a wife.

"Ye're a nyaff and an eejit, Ewan Burns, and ye need tae keep yer coos on yer own land." Fyfe had his finger in Ewan's face. His dark blond hair fell over his face, tangling with his beard, and his cheeks were beginning to go red with anger.

Ewan narrowed his dark eyes. "Haud yer whisht, ye old numpty. Ye wouldnae ken whose land ye were steppin' on even if 'twas written on the ground. My coos are right where they should be, it's *yer* coos breakin' down my fences and makin' a mess of my wife's garden."

"Och ye mean the weeds growin' in that sorry pile o' dirt on *my land*? Ye're talkin' pish." Fyfe scoffed. "'Tis a wonder ye survived the winter with what little ye grow to feed yer family."

Rhys surveyed the two men, standing toe-to-toe in the wide hall, where the clan had gathered. Some were there to present him with their arguments and receive his just judgement. Some were there to present wider issues or ask for help. And some were there for the entertainment.

Squabbles like this only served to turn his mood blacker.

The room was warm and hazy from the blazing fires in the hearth, where a fireplace as broad as three men and as tall as one was surrounded by a stone mantle and several older men dozing off in their chairs.

Smoke rose up to the ceiling, where the dark wood hammer-beams arched and curved in shadows.

Lush tapestries hung on the walls to further insulate the room, their mythical scenes a reminder of the daydreaming he'd done as a boy, staring at the woodland scenes and imagining life in such a place. Three windows on either side of the hall were hidden by deep red curtains, and at this time of day all of the candles were lit. Even Ewan and Fyfe had a warm glow about them, arguing though they were.

Shifting in his seat, Rhys caught the eye of Callum, who raised an eyebrow and grinned. Not only had Callum been by his side since they were lads, but he now also oversaw the stables, and his wife, Jenny, was the housekeeper and cook. The pair had the kind of love Rhys knew he would never find. It was deep and forgiving, overlooking all hurts, loyal to the end.

Unlike his own past marriage, which had ended in betrayal, and then death.

"A pox on yer coos *and* yer wife!" Fyfe spat, bringing Rhys back to the present. His face was as red as the flames in the hearth.

Rhys grunted. It was time to end this argument. But before he could speak, Ewan wound his fist back and punched Fyfe square in the face. In three seconds' time, the men were at each other's throats and Rhys lurched from the dais. Out of the corner of his eye, movement flickered; Callum was headed toward them as well.

Grabbing the farmers by their shirts, Rhys hauled them apart with relative ease. He was a big man, years of keeping active evident in the breadth of his shoulders and grip of his hands. It was not hard to separate the two. But Fyfe was incensed, and swung a wild fist around his Laird, hoping to catch Ewan upside the cheek.

Shoving Ewan toward Callum who was ready to catch the man by his arms, Rhys turned to deal with Fyfe. At the same moment, Fyfe's uncontrolled jab met an unintended target: Rhys's right cheekbone. The sharp slap of knuckles against flesh echoed through the now-silent room.

Several emotions flickered over Fyfe's face, the first being shock, the second being regret, the third and final, fear. "I didnae mean tae — that was meant fer — ye ken I'm sorry Laird I —" His eyes were wide as he uttered a string of unintelligible half-apologetic words, horror registering as a trail of blood slid down Rhys's cheek.

"Enough," Rhys snapped. Turning to glare at Ewan, who was properly cowed, he jutted his chin. "Ye're a pair of numpty-headed windbags, and ye deserve each other. Squabblin' like a pair o' old marrieds ye are. If I have tae hear one more word about coos and gardens I'll throw the lot of ye into a cell and let ye pick each other to death."

Both men nodded, shoulders dropping, all the fight leaking out of them.

"Now apologize and be done wi' it. Might as well join yer lands and let the coos roam where they may seein' as how they like each other so much." He swiped the blood from his cheek and glowered. "Ye could learn a thing or two from yer livestock on how to live peaceably."

Ewan cleared his throat. "Aye well, that's just what my Mary said." He shot a glance at Fyfe, and his warm brown eyes crinkled at the corners.

Fyfe stroked his coarse blonde beard and eyed his nemesis for a moment. But he could not keep the grin at bay. Holding out his hand, he grasped Ewan's forearm in a truce. "I didnae need that sorry pile o' dirt ye call a garden anyway," he said, but his tone was good-natured. "Truth be told I'm a wee bit afraid o' what yer lassie might do tae me about those fences."

Ewan slapped Fyfe on the back and laughed. "Aye they'll mend and Mary'll be none the wiser. How about some ale, then?"

As if the entire argument had never happened, the two men ambled toward the back of the room and the next clansman stepped up to Rhys to present his issues, this time with his neighbor's son, who had been caught stealing kisses and then some from the man's daughter. There was talk between the fathers of settling on marriage, and protests from the young man and woman over whether this was desirable.

Rhys pitied the young couple.

At least, he mused, this young man and young woman knew each other. At least their fathers were giving them some semblance of a choice to wed, though their disapproval was strong against any choice *but* a wedding. At least, when the decision was made between the younger folk to go through with marriage, a shy sort of contentment passed between them.

They had a say in the direction of their future, and Rhys envied them the luxury of choice.

It went on like this for another hour or two, until Rhys's mind was fuzzy and his patience was low. The fires were beginning to die out, and most of the clan had drunk enough ale to lose interest in the proceedings of justice being performed. Little pockets of laughter, song, and even a few halfhearted dances created a low hum in the rafters.

Rhys had decided to end it for the night when one last clan member stepped forward, alone.

"My quarrel is with ye, Laird Macnammon." Alasdair Munroe stood with his hands folded before him, eyes clear and a small furrow worrying between his brows. His tone was respectful, but his words incited a gasp in the room.

Callum, who had settled in a seat near the dais, scowled. "What could ye possibly have against the Laird?" Usually easygoing, Callum was deep in his cups and his fierce protectiveness of his friend sprang to the forefront.

But Rhys stayed him. "Go on, then, Alasdair."

Taking a deep breath, the man continued. "Ye say ye wish to prove yer loyalty to the clan. But we're bein' whittled down around the edges, and 'tis the folk like me and Graham and Malcom yonder who suffer the most. We've lost half our sheep in the last six months alone, Laird. My dogs have gone missin', and Malcom's had a spell o' trouble with his pigs bein' lured off where they shouldnae be. And Graham's daughter —" He cut himself off, the hush around him tangible as everyone waited for Rhys's response.

Graham Macnammon's daughter had been attacked and nearly taken, and though the young woman insisted she was unharmed, she'd never quite been the same.

Alasdair swallowed, his internal struggle belied by the roughness in his tone. "When will ye take action against the man? What will ye do to protect the outliers like us?"

Studying the men before him, who had begun to nod in agreement with Alasdair, he scrubbed his face and sighed. "I ken 'tis not easy, livin' at the edge of the clan lands, bein' open to attacks more than most. I will send men to patrol the areas where ye see the most activity."

From the back of the room, a disapproving voice piped up. "Aye and when will ye stop yer mafflein' and take a wife?" The accusation he was wasting his time came from Keir Begbie, whose gray beard and missing eye gave him a fearsome countenance his jolly personality did not match. It was a bold statement, but Keir had known Rhys since he'd been a bairn, and his loyalty was steadfast.

Several hoots and jibes filled the room.

"Ye're nae gettin' any younger," Keir continued, encouraged by the vocal agreements being thrown his way. "How do we ken ye're nae gonna up and run off again?"

After his first wife had died, Rhys had done his best to run his clan while drowning under the waves of grief and anger. Her duplicity had run deep, and he'd been blindsided. And there had been reminders of it everywhere. In the gardens where he'd planted roses for her, unaware of her wandering heart. The stables, where her favorite horse greeted him every morning after taking her mistress to another man's bed. The empty seat beside him on the dais. Where she'd been a doting wife, on the surface.

So he'd left. For three years, he'd roamed the continent, taking out his grief in wars for lands that did not belong to him, slaking his rage in battle, known for his ruthless fighting and dogged survival. He'd become the Scotsman who could not be killed. The beast of the battlefield. The Devil of Calhoun.

When he had returned, Rhys had been a different man. Gone was the young man eager for life, ready to take on the world, forgiving slights without a thought. In his place was a stoic Laird, who ran his clan with an iron hand and did not tolerate dishonesty.

In his absence, dissent had begun. Taking over while he was gone, Rhys's uncle, Murdoch Macnammon, had spread more rumors about him. Painting him as a wife-killer, a debaucher, a man who had abandoned his clan not to recover from deep grief, but to slake his bloodthirsty nature.

It had taken a war with his own uncle to restore his place as Laird, and he'd spent the last seven years trying to rebuild his clan's trust. His cousin Berach, furious at his father's death and greedy for his own power, had begun to stir up dissent again. Berach wanted to be Laird. Demanded it, as his right, for the years his father had held the title.

Shoving his fingers through his hair, Rhys regarded the curious, expectant faces before him and sighed. He was nothing if not loyal to his clan. They deserved more than empty words and insubstantial reassurances.

"And if I take a wife, will ye be satisfied?" He addressed the room, but Alasdair was the one to nod.

"And a wain!" Keir shouted from his place, his tone full of mischief. Chuckles rippled through the room. "The Macnammons are nae the kind to leave a family."

"Aye," Alasdair agreed. "Nothin' but death herself could take me from *my* wife and son."

To his surprise, Callum murmured his approval. "It would give Berach less hold over the clan, ye ken."

Rhys met his friend's thoughtful gaze, noting that his wife, Jenny, was nodding along.

"If ye had a son, ye might win back some o' the eejits who left ye." Angus Begbie joined the conversation. Keir's brother, the man who had trained Rhys to fight, and the one he consulted for solid battle plans, Angus was a solid presence in Rhys's life. He trusted the man implicitly. "I ken several of 'em left because at least Berach has ties here, with his own wife bein' in the family way."

The letters on his desk came to mind, and he stood. "Then it will be done."

Ripples of surprise washed through the clan. Beside the dais, Callum's mouth dropped open, his brows raised comically high. But Rhys did not explain further. He'd had enough of discussing his future with the clan. If they demanded he marry again to prove his willingness to settle down, then he would. With reluctance, and on his own terms, but all the same. He had spent far too many years giving his mind, body, and soul to the security of his clan to lose it over something as arbitrary as not *wanting* a wife.

After all, he did not have to want her in order to be married.

"Callum, ready the carriages. Jenny, instruct the maids to make up the suite next to mine." He was already moving across the room, the clan parting before him to make way. "We leave tomorrow to fetch a Lady for Calhoun Castle."

His Rumored Past

Caitriona

"We're so pleased ye've come, Laird Macnammon!" Moira chirped, hands whisking over her own skirts to brush away invisible wrinkles. "It must have taken ye days!"

"Two days," he answered. But the Laird was not paying attention to her mother.

Instead, his eyes dragged over Caitriona from head to toe, taking in the mud at her hem, the blood on her apron, and the bare skin at her neck. In her rush to get to Eilidh's side, Caitriona was dressed casually, in her shift, petticoats, and stays. Her arisaid had been haphazardly tucked around her petticoats as an overskirt, and hung off one shoulder.

Though her clothes were fine for everyday wear, she was far too casually dressed to be meeting her future husband.

She heated under his gaze.

Rhys Macnammon was every inch as large as the rumors said. A man of considerable height, with wild black hair falling to one side in a mess of waves, his black leine pulled tight over his broad shoulders, and his dark tartan trews encasing thickly muscled legs.

A scar ripped through his right eyebrow, puckering the skin. Piercing blue eyes met her own.

There was no kindness in his gaze. Instead, brow furrowed, he said, "*This* is your daughter?"

Straightening her shoulders, Caitriona lifted her chin. She would not be cowed.

Moira scuttled to her side. "Ach, I apologize for her appearance." She flushed pink, and gave Caitriona another subtle push. "Caitriona is just going up to change. She's...ah ...well. She's had an accident."

Caitriona snorted. "I've just delivered a—"

Her mother cut her off. "Her mare was foaling. Caitriona always did love the animals, ye ken."

It was an outright lie to save Moira from the embarrassing admission that her daughter was a village Howdie. A woman holding a common job, which could be construed as witchcraft, and which had already done even more damage to her already bedraggled reputation.

The Laird came closer, brow raised with clear disapproval. "I see." He did not break his gaze, and heat crept over her skin with pinpricks of anticipation.

She had never been self-conscious. Though ample in figure, she carried herself with pride, confident in her height and curves despite her mother's constant comments that she should make herself smaller. She was at eye level with most men, a fact she used to her advantage. But as her betrothed closed the distance between them, she had to tilt her chin up to meet his eyes. It was a small thing, and despite herself, she flushed.

"And do ye deliver...*foals*...often?" His eyes flicked to the basket still clutched in her hand, where herbs and tinctures rattled, and her book of accounts nestled.

"Och no, 'twas just a curiosity!" Moira was still trying to push her up the stairs, but her efforts were for naught.

"I am occupied with my pursuits almost daily," Caitriona said, ignoring her mother. "And they take up most of my time. I apologize for any inconvenience to ye, Laird Macnammon, but I willnae be marrying *anyone*."

Something lit in his eyes, just for a moment. It was a flash so quick, Caitriona almost missed it. Curiosity.

"Caitriona!" Moira gasped, stepping between them. "Ye'll do as ye're told, and that's what! Please forgive her, Laird Macnammon, 'tis only exhaustion and shock. She'll be happy to accept yer offer."

Annoyance rippled over the Laird's face at her interruption, and he opened his mouth to say something, but Hamish Irving ambled out of his study just then and his calm voice broke through the tension between them. "Well then, Macnammon, I see ye've met my daughter."

A handsome man still, Hamish was in his middle sixties with graying hair and a plethora of wrinkles around the green eyes he shared with his daughter. Moira fluttered to her husband and took his arm, her smile strained.

"I have." Rhys did not elaborate his thoughts.

"It's settled, then." Hamish took his daughter's hand, and clasped it together with the man before her, content.

Shock rushed through Caitriona at the touch of Rhys's hand against hers. His skin was hot, palm rough. The strength that rippled through him was undeniable, lending credence to the rumors that he killed men with his bare hands. And yet, his thumb skated over the backs of her fingers lightly, sending a tingle of pleasure up her arm that ran straight through her.

It threw her off balance, and she took a sharp breath. Her skin was traitorous. "It is *not* settled," she snapped. Jerking her hand away, she tried to forget the sensation he'd wrought just then.

"Caitriona!" Moira chided her.

Hamish cleared his throat. "Of course it is, Caitriona. Laird Macnammon, I apologize for my daughter's overreaction."

She wanted to scream. Her father, who had always encouraged her to speak her mind and defend herself, was stifling her protests. Giving away her very future. He patted her shoulder as they stood there, and the barest glint of remorse was in his eyes.

More to his daughter than to her betrothed, Hamish said, "I hope ye'll both come to be happy with time."

"She'll be very well taken care of, Laird and Lady Irving." Rhys's eyes were locked on her, but his words were directed at Hamish. "As will ye all. 'T'would be a pity if ye were attacked while the estate is so vulnerable. I'll send my men at once for yer protection, and we'll begin restoration as soon as we can."

Caitriona jerked at the subtle threat. If she did not accept this, her family's clan would be wide open to danger. Laird Macnammon's reputation could protect her family. Very few would trifle with those whose alliance was with a clan so strong.

Anger frothed like waves in her breast, tearing through her limbs and demanding release. She was being backed into a corner. "But what's in it for you?" she said, unable to keep the fury from her tone. "Ye've won enough clan wars to be rich as the king, and they say ye have a dearth of women and bastard children at yer disposal. Why, then, does the Laird Macnammon, the Devil of Calhoun himself, want a wife?"

Hamish blanched. "Caitriona, enough! 'Tis how it's done. Ye've had yer freedom long enough, and now ye must marry."

But Rhys held up his hand, silencing her parents. "If I may have a word?" When no one moved or spoke, he sent a pointed look to her father. "Alone."

The command brooked no arguments.

Moira's mouth dropped open, but Hamish looped an arm around her waist and pulled her away. "Come, my darling. We'll let them speak. They are, after all, engaged to be married." He met his daughter's gaze and nodded. "'Tis for the best, Cait."

The door to her father's study clicked shut.

In the thick silence, tension crackled between them and Caitriona fought fury building within her. Rhys studied her meticulously, giving away nothing in the cold sea of his gaze. He loomed over her, scarred and imposing, jaw ticking as he considered her, and her heart picked up pace. It was as if he was looking straight through her skin, into her very soul.

Was he regretting this arrangement?

Her hair had begun to fall from its pins, and curls brushed her temples and neck; her arisaid hung off her shoulder, exposing the expanse of her decolletage; her petticoats had mud on their hems. Midwifery had taken its toll on her; working in the close, cozy quarters of Eilidh's cottage had no doubt put the smell of smoke in her hair and the sign of sweat on her skin.

She was dirty, and tired, and unkempt.

Not at all what a Laird might expect when he sought out a bride.

But his gaze scraped up her body and tangled with her own, and a confusing thrill swept through her.

"Ye ken ye dinnae have much choice in this matter," he said, and she bristled.

She could not deny it.

His next words surprised her. "Neither do I."

"Ye expect me to believe that a man of yer reputation, one of the most powerful Lairds in the highlands, cannae choose his own bride?" Her father would have been appalled at the disdain dripping from her tone. Caitriona could not help herself.

He raised an eyebrow. "Yer father wrote me that ye were well educated, temperate, and prepared to take on the position of Lady of Calhoun Castle. Nae everything is as it's told."

The scathing words shot heat through her, though he did not raise his voice nor move to intimidate her in any way. Swallowing the sting of embarrassment, she tilted her head and clung to the anger with it. "Ye're being forced then?"

Patiently, he explained, "My clan requires a sign of my loyalty to them. Marriage will quell the unrest of those who believe I may leave again."

Caitriona vaguely knew the story. Ten years ago, after the mysterious death of his wife, Rhys Macnammon had gone away to the Continent, reportedly becoming so fierce in war he was unrivaled on the battlefield. His return three years later had been fraught with dissent, and he'd killed his own uncle to take up his lairdship again.

She studied him, taking in the straight lines of his jaw, the slight bump which spoke of a past break in an otherwise aquiline nose, the scar racing through his dark brow to end somewhere around his cheekbone. A fresh cut healed on the skin of his cheek she had not noticed before.

The Laird was not an ugly man. She might have even called him handsome, were it not for his reputation and her fury at this unjust arrangement. But she refused to acknowledge his qualities. Refused to let her mind wander over his broad shoulders, the corded muscle apparent in his forearms where his sleeves were pushed up, the possibility he could lift her like a feather with those big hands.

"And ye're so wanting for choices that ye've no other but me?" she said, scolding her thoughts for where they landed.

The ghost of a smile lifted the corner of his lips, and she blinked. Did the Devil have a sense of humor lurking behind his glowering visage? "Dinnae flatter yerself, I also had the offer of a child of no more than fifteen, a spinster older than my own mother, and a lass of an age who had the unfortunate propensity to faint at the sight of me."

Caitriona tamped down the laugh that threatened to jump from her throat. The thought of some poor lass fainting at Rhys's feet was more humorous than she cared to admit. "So ye thought perhaps ambush would be better." Despite his brief brush of humor, Caitriona could not stop the way her heart dropped into her stomach like a rock.

"Yer father seemed desperate for help," he said, tilting his head and studying her again with those unreadable eyes. "And he spoke of you with pride."

The wrath within her chest cooled a little. Caitriona closed her eyes then, and took a deep breath. Of course her father was proud; he'd raised her to be exactly as she was. Outspoken, educated, determined. Without a son into which these qualities could be funneled, Hamish had taken to giving his daughter much the same liberties a boy would have, outside of formal schooling.

She had spent many days sequestered in his study, reading the books lining his shelves with abandon, voracious to learn and thrilled by her father's encouragement. And after the summer in which she'd fallen in love, and been ruined, he'd pushed her to learn to defend herself. To have a vocation, which could carry her through life…if she never married.

Because, despite the liberties afforded her by her father's modern thinking, neither of her parents ever fully relinquished that particular hope. Marriage was not just for her; it was for them, as well.

She glanced around the room, at the walls which, bereft of her favorite tapestries now, were dusty and empty; the cobwebs high in the corners and edging the frames of her ancestors' portraits; the crack in the hearth of the fireplace. This home, which she loved so much, was falling apart bit by bit. And without money, it would crumble completely.

And though she did not like it, she understood then why her father had chosen to set up the match. What she did not understand, however, was why her father kept it from her. Why she'd been ambushed by the arrangement, as if he did not trust her to accede to his reasoning.

As if called, the door to Hamish's study opened, and her parents came out, hope etched in the lines of their faces. "I hope ye've come to an understanding," her father said, a sad smile on his lips.

She recognized it then. He thought he had no other choice. This was his last attempt to save the home his family had lived in for generations. After his wife could not give him a son, his daughter could not find herself a husband, and he could no longer drum up support should a clan challenge them to war.

Her father was desperate.

So, glancing between him and the man who seemed to be the answer to Hamish Irving's problems, she folded her fury up inside her like a letter crumpled and thrown into a corner, and nodded.

She was bested, for now.

※ ※ ※

Rhys left the next morning with two carriages full of Caitriona's things, and a promise to return in a week's time for the wedding.

The moment his last carriage left the gates, Caitriona whirled to face her father, the rage of a thousands stormy seas roiling in her chest. Though her mother did not have a nurturing bone in her body, Hamish Irving had always wanted a child. Caitriona, he'd always said, was the missing piece of his soul. She was as much a part of him as his very bones.

The betrayal of this match stung more because of it.

"How could ye? Without tellin' me?"

Hamish Irving watched the carriages go, his face stoic. "'Tis how it's done, Cait. 'Tis how it has always been done. I've found ye a good match, and ye'll be thankful for it."

"I'd have been *thankful* to have been consulted upon the matter of my own future," she shot back.

The usual humor with which Hamish conducted himself was gone as he turned his gaze to his daughter. Sadness deepened the creases beneath his eyes. "Yer future is with him now."

"Is there no other way?" Caitriona waved her hand toward the village. "I've babies to deliver. Mothers to tend to. My *life* is here." She could not help the tears pricking the corners of her eyes.

A heavy sigh escaped her father's throat. He seemed much older, suddenly, the worried lines in his forehead deeper and the usually jolly set of his lips absent.

"Come with me, Caitriona." Gently, her father put a hand on her back and guided her inside toward his study.

Grief heavy in her chest, Caitriona obeyed. She wanted to defy him, to rage in his face and shake her fists, but her father had always been the kind of man to inspire quiet respect. She collapsed into the overstuffed armchair opposite his desk and waited. Dust floated through the familiar atmosphere of his study, settling itself onto the spines of his beloved books and into the nooks and crannies of his worn but beautiful desk and chairs.

This study was where Caitriona had spent hours upon hours learning to read, under her father's doting eyes. This is where she had come when her heart had been broken. This was her sanctuary, surrounded by the scent of leather and dust, her father's pen scratching against the paper of his account books. Here, she was safe.

"I ken 'tis not what ye expected, daughter." Her father's gaze was tired, but kind. "But we have never made it a secret that if ye can be married, ye will. The Laird Macnammon is a good man —"

"Good?" Caitriona almost laughed. "Have ye heard nothin' of his reputation? The massacres? The bastard son? Killin' his very own? I think what ye mean is, he's rich as the king and made an offer ye couldnae refuse."

Hamish held up his hand. "Ye cannae believe every rumor ye hear, Cait. I wouldnae hand ye over to a dangerous man, now would I?"

With a snort, Caitriona shot back, "How would I know? Ye didnae even tell me I was betrothed."

Her father stood, and came around his desk to fold Caitriona's stiff body into his arms, cradling her much as he had always done. The familiar scent of cedar filled her nose, and Cairiona closed her eyes.

"I dinnae wish for ye to be unhappy, *mo ghràdh*." Her father's voice wavered as he spoke, the endearment bittersweet now. "But I willnae be here to protect ye forever. And I'd never forgive myself if ye didnae have a future secured before I'm gone."

Swallowing the lump in her throat, Caitriona protested, "I *have* a future. As a midwife."

Her father's chest heaved beneath her head, and he stroked her hair as he had when she was a child. Taking her shoulders, he parted them to look into her eyes. "Ye're meant for greater things than dirtyin' yer hands with common work and ridin' about the country in trews like a wild thing."

To Caitriona, midwifery was not common work, but she held her tongue. She allowed her father to wipe away her tears and kiss her forehead. When he sent her on her way, he was humming the way he always had done when he was pleased.

But she was shattered.

Unfortunate Stature

Caitriona

The day of her wedding came like a bad dream.

Caitriona was standing before the mirror as her mother fussed with the voluminous pleating in the bustle of her gown. Pinned into her wedding garments — a gown in luminous pale blue silk with a wide ruffled neckline and delicate navy and purple floral embroidery on the stomacher — Caitriona could have been a glowing picture of bridal joy.

Instead, she scowled into her reflection, mood dark.

"I always knew ye'd be a beautiful bride," her mother said, oblivious to Caitriona's disposition. Or perhaps she was ignoring her daughter as she reveled in the long-awaited completion of her plans. "But my, Caitie girl, ye look even more lovely than I'd imagined."

It was true. Caitriona's buxom figure was displayed at its best, her waist emphasized by the gathering and pleating at the hips, skirts held out by petticoats and a pannier to exaggerate her curves, her creamy skin glowing against the powder blue silk. The elegant sleeves stopped in a cream ruffle at her elbows, and her usually wild hair had been coaxed into the latest fashion of short curls at her temples and one long spiral draping down her neck. The rest was artfully braided atop her head, wildflowers tucked in here and there to create a crown.

"Ye do look beautiful, Cait," Maeve piped up. In her Sunday best, the woman stood at Caitriona's side, waiting for the call to come downstairs. Maeve would be escorted to the chapel by Rhys as the maid of honor, and Hamish would take his daughter down the aisle.

Sighing, Caitriona fiddled with the lace at her neckline, unable to stand still at the sight of herself. She wanted to tear it all off. She wanted to run off through the halls and foyer into the highlands, never to be seen again. She wanted to rage at her father, her mother, the Laird, all of them with every iota of anger in her chest.

Instead, she said, "Thank you, Maeve."

In an unusual show of nurturing, Moira patted her daughter's arm, then kissed her cheek. "I didnae much want to marry yer father, my love. I ken how ye feel." She squeezed Caitriona's hand. "But ye'll be a grander lady than I ever was. They tell me Calhoun Castle is four times the size of Irving Manor, or more."

Caitriona shook her head. "Do ye really think I care about the size of a castle, mother? I never wanted this. I have no desire to be a grand lady. I just wanted…well. It doesnae matter, does it?" Blinking away the moisture stinging the corners of her eyes, she took a deep breath. "'Tis too late now."

With a tenderness that surprised Caitriona, Moira cupped her daughter's face, tapping away tears with her thumbs. "Do what I did, my darling girl. Busy yourself with the estate. Distract yourself for a while, learn the ways of the village. I'm sure ye'll feel just as needed there as you did here. And with time…well. With time, many women discover happiness and even pleasure with their husbands, ye ken?"

Caitriona nodded, unwilling to consider what her mother meant. The very suggestion of pleasure coupled with the knowledge of whom she was about to marry sent a flush through her entire body.

"Anyway, thank heavens he's tall," Moira said, dropping her hands and fiddling with a curl at Caitriona's temple. "Ye did inherit yer grandmother's unfortunate tendency toward stature."

From the corner chair, Maeve chortled.

Caitriona resisted rolling her eyes at her mother's age-old critique and shot her best friend a look, to which Maeve waggled her dark eyebrows and winked.

From tall child to gangly teen to statuesque woman, it had stuck with Caitriona. She was too tall. Too curvy. Too much. She should be less. It had made her all the more determined to carve out a life for herself, where she could be exactly who she was. Where she could offer her strength *and* her softness to others when they needed it the most.

Hamish came to the door then. "Are ye ready, my girl?" he said. There was a tremble in his voice and his cheeks were damp.

Caitriona's throat closed up, and she took a deep breath. "I think so."

Maeve slipped out, and Moira followed, leaving father and daughter alone for a moment. He held out his arms for her, and she slipped into them, holding tight to her emotions lest she walk down the aisle with raw eyes and a runny nose. She may not have wanted to marry, but she loved her father too much to betray him.

Hamish held her close, tucking her face into his neck for just a moment, and everything else melted away. How she longed to stay safe here in her father's arms. For a few seconds she allowed herself to pretend this day was not happening. She would open her eyes and it would be another quiet day in the village, where she could flit between expecting mothers and new babies, happy and in her element.

But when her father released her, the daydream faded. Somehow, she would always have ended up here: married to a stranger for the betterment of her family and clan, playing the obedient daughter. Every other path was an impossible dream.

Hamish wiped tears from his face. "I'm sorry I couldnae do better for ye, my girl."

Caitriona swallowed through the tightness in her throat, his apology pushing her to the brink of tears again. "Ye did…the best ye could," she said, though she was not sure she meant it.

He shook his head. "I should have told ye. From the start, I should have let ye be part of the decision. But I was so afraid —" He cut off, clearing his throat as shame entered his tone. "I was so afraid ye'd refuse, and then someday when I died ye'd…be uncared for. Alone. And I would have failed ye. And yet, I have failed ye anyway."

Caitriona could not bear it. She threw her arms around her father and squeezed tightly. "I'll be okay, father," she whispered. "I'll be okay." She said it almost as much for herself as for him.

"I wish I could change things, *mo ghràdh*. I wish —" he started, but she hushed him.

"'Tis done now," she said. A solitary tear slid down her cheek. For his sake, she tried to smile. "And ye've gotten me one of the richest Lairds in the highlands. 'Tis nae failure, not if ye ask mother."

A weak laugh came out of him, and he patted her cheek. "More than anythin' else, ye always did ken how tae make the best of things. And I'm so proud of ye."

His words were a balm to Caitrona's wounded heart, and she squeezed his hand, then slid her fingers into the crook of his proffered elbow.

Their journey down the stairs and past the great hall was far too swift. In mere seconds, she and Hamish stood at the end of the procession that would lead them into the chapel, where she would be married. With his back to her stood Laird Macnammon, his broad shoulders clad in a black jacket above his great kilt, which was woven in the dark blues and greens of his clan tartan. His hair was gathered back into a ribbon, and when he turned his face slightly at the sound of their approach, his jaw was tense.

Maeve was on his arm, turning back to meet Caitriona's gaze with a small smile. The piper escorted them all, his happy tune a harsh contrast to the dread growing in Caitriona's belly.

The Devil had come to sweep her away, and she could do naught but follow in his wake.

Walking past the full pews, everything was a blur. As though underwater, her limbs were slow, her senses two steps behind her. Flowers crushed beneath her feet, their sweet aroma wafting up into the rafters. Outside, the rain had begun to pound upon the roof of the chapel, creating a dull roar that matched the noise inside her head.

They were at the front of the church before she was ready. Maeve stood smiling tremulously, and *he* was looking at her, his gaze piercing her very soul. He was resplendent in his wedding garb, dark jacket expertly fitted to his broad shoulders, his great kilt pleated to perfection.

The scar striking through his brow puckered as he scowled at her, and it was not until he took her arm that she realized she had been frozen in the aisle. His fingers heated through her sleeve, setting her skin on fire, and she stumbled up the stairs in the front of the chapel, unable to draw a fortifying breath. The minister smiled down upon them, his voice a drone to her ears.

Her gaze fixed upon the two-handled quaich on the table before them. It was full of amber liquid they would drink after handfasting, which would bind them together, forever. A sip of sharp whisky, a fold of cloth, and they would be wed. Despite the chill of the stone chapel, her palms were slick with sweat.

An elbow knocked into hers, and she startled.

Rhys was glaring down at her. With his hair tied back from his face and his jaw cleanly shaven, he was all sharp angles and dark colors, and simmering with an emotion Caitriona did not know. His jaw twitched. Could he hear the way her heart hammered in her chest? For one breathless moment, she stared into his icy gaze, dazed again by the slide of his palm against her hand. Could he feel the way heat simmered in her skin, and curiosity pinged through her body?

Above them, the minister repeated, "Caitriona Irving, do ye take this man?"

She snapped out of her haze and flushed. "Aye, I do."

"And ye, Rhys Macnammon, do ye take this woman to be yer lawful wife?"

The rumble of his voice answered, "Aye, I do."

With a nod, the minister took their joined hands and bound them in cloth. When neither Rhys nor Caitriona spoke, he urged, "Ye may say yer own vows as ye wish."

Rhys' expression softened as his gaze flicked over her. "I promise to protect ye, all of yer days; in times of famine and times of wealth, whether God brings suffering or fortune, I will always be by your side; I vow to be loyal and true, and let no-one come between us; I offer my sword to protect our family, and my strength to keep ye safe. What's mine is yours, and will be shared in abundance. This I vow until the end of my days."

His voice was a rasp down her spine and she swallowed, her throat running dry. "I..." she started, mind scrambling for the vows she had not planned.

There was a question in his eyes as he waited. Caitriona's belly tightened at the way his focus slid down to her mouth and back up, and she licked her lips to moisten them. Then she said, "I promise to be loyal all of my days; no matter the famine or wealth, whether God brings suffering or fortune, I will always be by your side. I offer my heart to nurture our family, and my hands to keep ye well. What's mine is yours, and will be shared in abundance." Taking a deep breath, she finished, "This I vow until the end of my days."

Rhys held her gaze through the entirety of her vows, the furrow creeping back into place between his eyebrows, his jawline tense. The scar through his brow was emphasized by the clean sweep of his hair, and his shoulders were straight beneath his wedding clothes. The sporran at his waist and blue and green tartan were all the colors he wore. Staring back at him Caitriona really could believe he was every bit the devil they said he was.

The roar of her heart in her ears drowned out anything the minister said after that. Sipping from the quaich, Rhys offered it to her, and the sharp warmth of whiskey heated her to her core. Goosebumps skittered over her flesh when she realized this was the end of the ceremony. He slid a ring over her finger, and she was a spinster no more.

"Ye may kiss yer bride," the minister said.

The Laird hesitated, meeting her own wide eyes with an unreadable expression. Whatever he saw there, he seemed to understand. Neither of them had asked for this.

The graze of his fingertips against her jawline was a beckoning, pulling her closer as he bent forward. The preemptive cheer of their mingled clansmen rose into the rafters of the church, and she flushed. Rhys' gaze darkened. He slid his other hand around her waist, pulling her against him. Through her wedding clothes, he was warm and strong and stony and *terrifying*.

Because when his lips brushed hers, a frisson of desire curled through her, and she gasped into the kiss. She had not asked for the intimacy of knowing he smelled of the outdoors: of the earth after it rained, of pine and musk. But there it was. His fingers tightened reflexively, his big hand curling around her soft jawline as his thumb caressed the curve of her chin as if to say, "You belong to me now."

And then it was over, and she was reeling, and her mother and father were beaming proudly from the pews.

She was Caitriona Irving, Lady of Calhoun Castle, being whisked away into a waiting carriage with only a few moments to say goodbye to her family. There was no celebration to be had afterward; no wedding supper; no confiding in Maeve how terrified she was. No more time could be spared away from his clan, and Laird Macnammon was eager to go home.

Outside, the downpour was so thick Brae was barely visible beyond the manor. She could not even bid farewell to her little highland village as they bustled through the muddy streets and away. It was then the full weight of her situation sank into her stomach like a brick.

She was the wife of the man they called the Devil, and there was no going back now.

THE INNKEEPER'S WIFE

Caitriona

At some point in the journey, Caitriona had fallen asleep against the walls of the carriage. Her new husband ignored her for much of the day, leaving her to stare out the windows at the rain-soaked hills and desperately fight back tears. Rhys was a brooding, silent figure, intimidating despite his wedding attire. There was no newlywed conversation, no informing her of what her new life would be, no attempt at contact. In fact, aside from handing her into the carriage itself, he had not touched her since the ceremony.

The kiss lingered in her memory, the way a curl had loosened itself from the tidy ribbon holding his hair back and caught in the flowers of her crown when he'd pulled away. How his fingers had brushed down her neck for a brief second, so quick she was not sure it had happened. How his warmth had suffused her with anticipation, even after he let her go.

Now, it was well into the night and someone was jostling her out of her hazy, confusing dreams. Something heavy and soft was draped over her, and it smelled of pine and musk.

Caitriona scrubbed at her face with numb fingers and shivered at the bone-deep cold, which had seeped into her as she slept. "Who's there?" Disoriented, she swept her hand over the soft velvet beside her, trying to find a candle. Her fingers crashed into an upholstered wall. Damp misted the entire left side of her, alerting her to the fact she was not in her own bed. The thing draped over her was a length of cloth, woolen and warm.

Rain pounded against the roof and walls of the carriage, filling her ears with a roar. She blinked a few times and squinted at the open door.

Rhys stood just outside in the downpour, hand extended to assist her down. Or at least, she thought it was Rhys; it was so dark she could only see outlines cast upon him from behind, where a large Inn had a singular lamp lit outside to show the way.

"If ye dinnae come out soon, I'll drown," a deep voice said.

His annoyance sparked her into action. All at once the day came slamming back into her consciousness, and she pulled the wool cloth around herself — it was an arisaid, but not her own — and up over her head to descend into the night. Her hand was taken firmly by her new husband, and together they all but ran for the Inn. Despite the short distance and their hurry, Caitriona was soaked through by the time they reached the doors.

Inside, it was quiet and dim, all of the patrons of the Inn having long since gone to bed. A solitary man sat behind a desk in the foyer, dozing in his chair. Feet propped up, his hands were folded over a paunch, and his head lolled precariously to one side. Halting, harsh sounds came from his throat. For a moment, Caitriona thought he was choking. But when they approached, they found he simply snored like an angry bull. It was amusing, considering the man himself was quite diminutive in appearance.

Rhys stepped forward, pulling Caitriona with him as he retained his grip on her hand. Part of her wanted to yank away. To forbid him to touch her. After all, she had not agreed to this union, not really.

She did not want to be here, married to him, traveling in the dead of night and away from everything she knew and loved. But his fingers encompassed her palm and offered a modicum of heat despite the gloves between their skin, and despite herself, she held on.

He cleared his throat. "Excuse me, sir," he said, but his deep tone was drowned out by another bull-like snore from the innkeeper.

He tried again. "Excuse me." Moving closer, he peered over the man. "Rooms have been reserved for us."

When there was still no response, Rhys hesitated. His eyes gauged the room, its low ceilings, the keys on the desk beside the innkeeper's foot, the closed off double doors to what was likely the attached tavern. There were stairs to the left of the desk leading to rooms, and a fireplace to the snoring man's right where coals sent up lazy smoke. The Inn creaked as the storm outside raged on, somehow peaceful despite the cacophony coming from its keeper's throat.

Though the Laird carried himself confidently, his shoulders straight beneath the dark jacket he wore, he seemed befuddled by the sleeping man before them.

Caitriona, cold, damp, and exhausted, did not want to wait any longer. Stepping around Rhys, she picked up the bell Rhys had ignored and rang it as close to the Innkeeper's face as she dared. The noise clanged through the quiet foyer like an alarm and the poor man nearly jumped from his chair, tripping himself over his own feet in his haste to stand.

Behind her, Caitriona could have sworn she heard the faintest chuckle. But when she turned, Rhys was as stoic as ever, jaw ticking and eyes shuttered. He moved to stand beside her as the Innkeeper steadied himself against the desk and looked from one to the other of them, obviously confused.

"Good evening," Rhys said. "I am Laird Macnammon. Three days ago, I paid for two rooms, fires laid, and something to eat, all to be prepared and ready for our arrival today."

Relief settled through Caitriona's tense muscles at his request. Two rooms. She would have her own privacy tonight, to process the day and get a decent night's sleep. No worrying about how the wedding night might go. No fear that he would require more of her than she was willing to give after such a long journey. No embarrassment at her own lack of personal experience with...*pleasure*, as her mother had put it.

She would have thanked him, if she hadn't been so furious about the arrangement of this marriage.

From the stairway there came a clatter, and a woman stumbled down in modest garb, a smudged apron tied around her waist, and her cap askew. She looked over them and turned to the man behind the desk. "Guests, then?" she said, her tone setting the man into action.

"Och aye, of course milord. My apologies," he said, and he flipped open the log book in front of him, running his fingers down the lines. "I see your name here. Ye'll have upstairs rooms..."

The woman edged closer, leaning her plump hip against the desk as she studied the books. "Upstairs *rooms*?"

The innkeeper grunted. "Aye, the suites." He beamed at Rhys. "Only the best for the Laird and his new bride."

Caitriona tried not to flinch at the title. *Bride*. But with her hand still firmly settled within Rhys's warm grasp, and the way he had come ever so slightly closer, brushing her arm with his, she could not deny her position.

"If ye'll tell us which rooms they are, we'll show ourselves up. Meanwhile, send food, and a hot bath if ye have one," Rhys ordered, starting toward the stairs with Caitriona in tow. "My men will bring our luggage."

"Sir!" Behind them, the woman's voice rang out. "The suites...they're —

"Ready as I asked, are they not Sarah?" The innkeeper cut off Sarah's exclamation.

Rhys was still walking, but Caitriona glanced back, and the woman was saying something close to the Innkeeper's ear, too low for them to hear her. Tugging on her new husband's hand, Caitriona stopped him there at the base of the stairs and waited. Pure annoyance rippled over the Innkeeper's face at whatever Sarah had said.

"I told ye, wife, those rooms were to be held!" he chastised her loudly.

The woman's voice wobbled, and she sniffed a little. "Aye, I ken that." She wrung her hands in her apron. "It's just, the Laird is so late in the day, ye ken, and I couldnae just...turn away payin' customers."

"Ye numpty!" The innkeeper burst out. "Ye good-for-nothin, I oughta take ye out back with the strap!"

"I'm sorry, my love, I didnae think they were comin'! And ye ken we need the money, I was only tryin' to make sure the rooms were filled. I didnae ken the Laird had already paid for them, not with ye..." she shot a glance at Rhys and Caitriona, and then lowered her tone. "Not with the money goin' missin' on occasion."

With horror, Caitriona saw the Innkeeper raise his hand, intention clear. Sarah threw up her hands, cowering, and the Innkeeper swung. But before Caitriona could move an inch to defend the woman, Rhys had released her and caught the Innkeeper's arm, forcing him backward and away from Sarah.

"I dinnae take kindly to violence, sir. Especially against women." He held the man's wrist tightly. Towering over the smaller man, Rhys's eyes sparked with barely contained rage. Even in his wedding attire, wet through and clearly exhausted from the day, the Laird was a formidable man. His scarred brow only added to the intimidating cut of his figure, and with his hair wild and falling from its tie he certainly fit the moniker he'd been given.

Immediately, the Innkeeper cowered, lifting his other hand to protect himself though Rhys had yet to threaten a blow. "Forgive me, Laird, I dinnae ken what came over me. I would never…I have never —"

Rhys cut him off. "The bruises on yer wife's chin are from an accident, then? And the marks on her arm?"

Sarah had dark circles beneath her eyes, and though she brought her fingers up to cover her jawline, Caitriona caught a glimpse of purpling on her skin. She had tended to women with violent husbands before. Often, drawing attention to the woman only put them in more danger. Especially when their protectors left.

She met Sarah's gaze and came forward to touch Rhys's arm. "Bruises must be common in this line of work, what with all the cleanin' ye must do to tend the rooms." The words were an out for Sarah, a way for the woman to extricate herself from any blame her husband might put on her later in the form of his fist or his belt.

Sarah nodded. "Aye, milady, 'tis hard work…but I dinnae mind."

Gently, Caitriona gestured toward the stairs. "Are there any rooms left at all?"

Fumbling with the keys attached to her belt, the woman nodded. "Aye, one of the suites is still empty. T' other one is occupied. Please accept my apologies, milord. Milady." She curtseyed deeply. "I didnae ken —"

Caitriona interrupted her. "Please, dinnae worry yerself. I'd be thankful if ye showed me up to the room while my husband checks on our luggage." She took a few steps toward the stairs, then waited for Sarah to precede her.

Halfway up the stairwell, she glanced back. Rhys had the Innkeeper by the front of his shirt, lips moving furiously, tone too low for her to hear. Pure terror crossed over the man's face, and when Rhys let go of him he almost fell in his eagerness to back away, bowing the entire time. He disappeared through the double doorway.

Her new husband looked up and caught her staring. Though shadowed, she could recall the piercing blue of his eyes and did not need to see the color now to recognize the hunger there. A visceral heat flooded her belly, her cheeks growing warm and her knees going soft. Breath shuddering, she held his gaze for one long moment.

But the second he took a step toward her, Caitriona turned and fled up the stairs after the Innkeeper's wife.

THE SEARCH FOR PINS
Rhys

The stables were quiet when Rhys entered, seeking out the handful of men he'd brought with him for the occasion.

Callum was just stabling the last of the horses. Auburn hair flopping over a friendly, rounded face full of freckles, Callum was shorter than Rhys and a little softer around the middle. Years of work with horses showed in his arms and the expert way he handled the restless stallion in the stall.

Murmuring, Callum offered the horse a handful of grain, coaxing him into contentment.

"Thought ye'd be with yer new bride by now," he said by way of greeting.

Rhys glowered at his friend. "I came t' check on the luggage."

With a knowing grin, Callum left the horse and closed the stable door. "That bad, aye?"

"She wanted privacy," Rhys said. "It's been a long day."

He did not mention the incident with the Innkeeper, and how the tight rein he had on himself had loosed the moment he'd seen the man raise a hand toward the woman Sarah. How desire was so hot in his chest he'd been tense all day, trying to keep it out of his mind. How he had watched his new wife go up the stairs, and wanted nothing more than to follow her there and then.

She was not supposed to be tempting. Rhys was not supposed to be tempted.

Callum clucked his tongue and clapped a hand on Rhys's shoulder. "Ye cannae let yer past shroud ye forever, Rhys."

His friend had been there long before Rhys had married the first time, and after Iona's death, Callum had been the one to see Rhys sink into a darkness so black it had nearly been the end of him. After he'd returned from the continent to pick up the pieces of the life he thought he knew, Rhys had vowed no woman would ever hold his heart the way Iona had. She had gutted him.

In one sharp blow, she had shown him love was not for Rhys, and Rhys was not for loving.

"Anyway," Callum said, settling himself on a bale of hay, his plaid wrapped around his shoulders for warmth. "Yer trunks have been sent upstairs already." There was a twinkle in his eye. "I thought ye'd paid for two rooms."

So his men knew, then. With a grunt, Rhys said, "The Innkeeper's a walloper. Beats his wife. Stealin' money when he thinks he can get away wi' it. We paid for two rooms, aye, but he only marked one in his books. When his wife tried to ask about it, he raised a hand."

Callum's jolly expression faded away. "He didnae get far wi' it, I'll wager."

Shaking his head, Rhys began to pace up and down the aisle of the stables. "I stopped him, but there's no tellin' what he'll do behind closed doors."

Brows knit together, Callum nodded. "Aye well, we'll check on the lass before we leave. Maybe give her husband a reason to keep his hands off her. Yer new bride, she saw all of this?"

Rhys shoved a hand through his hair. The way she had stared at him flashed through his mind. Emerald eyes wide, lips parted, her chest heaving as she clutched her skirts in her hands. There had been something curious in her gaze, and something startled, too. To Callum, he simply said, "Aye."

"And now she's…alone?" Leaning his elbows on his knees, Callum watched Rhys with a knowing smirk. "And ye're afraid to go up to her."

Rhys straightened at the jibe. "Haud yer wheesht. 'Tis nae yer business."

Unperturbed by Rhys's command to be quiet, Callum went on, "Ye cannae avoid her, Rhys. She's yer wife now, and ye've duties to attend. We both ken what this arrangement is for."

The reminder irked him. "I cannae just walk into the room and demand an heir, Cal."

"No." His friend shook his head thoughtfully. "But ye'll have to start somewhere. Does the lass ken yet?"

Rhys swore. "We have nae spoken two words together. She slept most of the way here."

Rising from the hay bale, Callum cleared his throat, amusement dimpling his cheeks. "'Tis a lot of excuses for a man who's just taken a bonny new wife."

Glaring at him, Rhys said, "Yer mouth is too big, Callum."

Rhys had arranged this marriage to a stranger to produce an heir, after which he planned to live a separate life from his wife. It was not uncommon in such situations. If others could do it, so would he. Love was not for Rhys. Not then, not now, and not in the future.

But none of his plans had included an ethereal red-haired vixen with fire on her lips, curves that tempted his hands beyond reason, and a world of intrigue in her eyes.

Callum stretched, and clapped Rhys's shoulder once more. "Well, I'm spent." He moved past Rhys toward the quarters reserved for servants and stable hands. "I envy ye, Rhys. I've hay and a room full o' Scotsmen's snores. But ye've got a soft bed, and a pretty new wife to fill it."

Their years-long friendship meant Callum was one of the few who could speak so openly to Rhys and not get his head bitten off. With a grunt, Rhys grasped his friend's forearm in a familiar salute, and bid him goodnight.

He *did* have a wife to attend.

♛ ♛ ♛

It was well past midnight when Rhys entered the room to find his new bride slumped in the chair before the fire, fast asleep.

What the innkeeper had called a "suite" was barely enough space for a four-poster bed layered in dusty quilts and two overstuffed chairs sat before the hearth. There was a separate chamber for washing and dressing, and a nook at the window made up with cushions and pillows to nestle into. A tray of food sat on the small table between the armchairs, barely touched.

Crossing the room, Rhys discovered a bottle of wine on the mantle, and poured himself a glass. It had obviously already been opened. The woman he'd wed barely ten hours ago shifted a little in her chair, and he studied her from his place by the mantle. The flowers she'd worn in her hair for the ceremony were drooping, some already littering the floor, and her thick auburn hair was beginning to fall from its braids. Her curves draped over the chair, begging to be worshipped.

She was luminous.

A far cry from the creature he'd first met in Irving manor, whose apron was smudged with blood and whose cheek had the remains of ash swiped there from a careless hand. She'd been wilder then, so defiant he was taken aback by her boldness. Intrigued by her confidence. Lured in by her self-assuredness.

Gulping down his wine, Rhys swore.

Despite his wish to keep her at arms' length, he wanted her to be happy, and comfortable. The odd crook of Caitriona's neck as she slept would produce a wealth of aches and pains. He could not leave her splayed out on the chair, not when the bed was empty, waiting to be filled. But first, he had to remove a few things.

Shrugging out of his jacket, he laid it aside and set down the now-empty glass on the food tray. From beneath her voluminous skirts, Caitriona's delicate satin wedding shoes poked out. Rhys dropped to one knee, nudging silk and lace up just enough to slide his fingers around her stockinged calf. It filled his hand with a pleasing curve and he swallowed.

Touching her was a mistake.

The innocent grasp of her hand in his through the rain had been different; they had both been cold, wet, and preoccupied. His focus on the Innkeeper and Sarah had distracted him, just enough, from the feel of her fingers between his.

But now?

Now, as he took the heel of her slipper and pulled it off, the catch of her silk stocking against his palm heightened his senses. Brought back the memory of her lips under his, the gasp of surprise he'd absorbed, the brief flash of pleasure in her eyes. Tightening his resolve, he placed her foot on the carpet and repeated the action with her other slipper.

Slow and purposeful so as not to wake her, he slid her leg back to where it had been, and smoothed her skirts down. When he hooked an arm beneath her, her head lolled toward his shoulder, the aroma of lavender scenting her hair. It was more than he wanted to know. Shoving his hand between the chair and her skirts, he firmly settled her legs in his grasp, and straightened.

Caitriona was not a small woman, and the pleasing heft of her settled against him, every lush bit of her pressing against him with promise. It did not help that her head fell back when he moved, exposing the length of her creamy neck and the expanse of her fair decolletage in her wedding gown. It was a creation of pale blue silk and intricate embroidery, set wide on her shoulders to display her ample features to their best advantage.

He did not need to know how she felt in his arms. Not when his mind had already run a thousand wild scenarios about the way her skin might taste. Not when his hands had itched to touch her plush frame despite knowing her for less than two days. What was it about this woman that set his desire aflame in an instant?

Careful not to jostle her, he settled her amongst the worn pillows atop the colorful quilt of the bed, and studied her.

It had been years since he'd had a woman in his bed, but he was aware that there were pins in a gown to keep things in place, and they needed removing before she slept. The last thing he wanted was a bride stabbed in the night by her own wedding clothes. Did he dare try to find them? Or should he wake her, to tend herself?

With every part of his body on high alert, Rhys studied Caitriona's prone form and the gown that was expertly fitted upon its curves.

Her lips parted as she slept, a delicate snore emitting from her throat. Hair wild about her face, a halo of flame and curls, she was brazen even in her sleep. But her nose was faintly red and swollen, and her cheeks bore the still-damp tracks of tears.

A jab of guilt prodded his ribs. She had not asked for this. Nor had he, but he'd more choice than she on what to do in the matter. And despite it all, she had faced situations head on, capable, fiery, graceful, and brave.

Rhys was not looking for love. He had no wish to join their lives in any way but to produce a child, some physical proof of his loyalty to his clan. Perhaps some pleasure could be found between them, if she was not afraid to pursue the shot of desire he'd seen in her eyes when he'd kissed her. It was more than many had, in their situation. But he did not want love.

However, he could not resist the unexpected urge to ensure her comfort in all things. The entire carriage ride here, he'd watched her head loll about as she dozed across from him, and ached to pull her to his side, to curl her under his arm and give her a resting place. In the foyer, urgency to get to a dry room had infused him with impatience, knowing she was wet and cold and miserable.

And now, he watched the slow intake of her breaths in the rise and fall of her bosom, and he could not bear to wake her.

So, he sat on the edge of the bed, and began to search for pins.

Unwelcome Affectations

Caitriona

Caitriona woke to the sun blazing through the room, and sat up in the bed, bleary and disoriented. Her hair tumbled around her, every pin gone, and the stomacher of her dress was no longer attached. In fact, when she looked down at herself, the entire front of her gown had been unlaced and splayed open to reveal her shift and stays.

The Laird was nowhere to be seen.

Sliding her legs over the side of the bed, she scowled at her toes. She had not gone to bed in a half-dressed state. In fact, she had not gone to bed at all. Upon arriving behind Sarah to discover their travel luggage already in the room, Caitriona had decided to wait for her new husband. Her new arisaid was patterned his clan tartan, and it had seemed like an offer. A truce.

Resentment and grief were still thick in her veins, but she could see no use in pretending nothing had happened.

But the comfort of the fire and the haze of wine had triumphed.

Her stomach rumbled. Likely, Rhys was downstairs partaking in whatever food this Inn offered to break fast, and she should join them. She would have to change, though; her wedding gown was impractical for travel. Besides, it was impossible to put back together without its pins, and she did not know where Rhys had put them. A quick scan of the room revealed nothing but her satin slippers, neatly lined up by the hearth.

Standing, she peeled off the jacket of her gown and crossed the room to lay it over the chair by the hearth, smoothing her hands over the embroidery and lace. It was one of the few things she and her mother had done together for the wedding: embroidering blue flowers along the neckline and onto the stomacher. It was simple work, but full of care and love all the same.

Untying her skirts at the waist, she laid them over the jacket, and then removed her stays and petticoats and pannier and deposited it all on the chair. This left her shift, a simple garment with a wide, square neckline, made of comfortable cream linen.

Beside the chairs was her trunk, full of travel garb and enough room to pack up her wedding clothes. Rifling through the neatly-folded items, she pulled out a clean pair of stockings and a simple brown wool skirt alongside a weskit and jacket to wear for the day of travel. Then she folded her wedding gown into the trunk, leaving the stays and petticoats on the chair. She would wear those beneath the rest of her traveling clothes.

But first, she needed to change her stockings, which had been through a wedding, mud, rain, and who knew what else in the day prior. Crossing back to the bed, she sat on the quilt to remove her stockings. One had rolled down over her knee. When she hiked her shift up to expose her thigh, the ribbon which had been around her stocking unfurled completely and fell to the ground.

With a sigh, she picked it up. Her hair fell around her face, loose and curling wildly, and she shoved it out of the way, wondering where *those* pins had gone to. And where had her formidable new husband slept? The side of the bed he should have shared looked untouched. Had he taken the floor? One of the chairs by the hearth?

It was hard to imagine such a big man could find a comfortable way to sleep in such a small chair.

She had the second bit of hosiery halfway up her leg, dressed in only her shift and no stays, when the door opened, and the man in question walked in.

Arms laden with a tray of food, Rhys froze mid-step, eyes dragging over her. A muscle ticked in his jaw. For a moment, they stared at each other, Caitriona caught in the act of half-undress, Rhys's dark lashes flicking from her face to the exposed skin of her thigh above her knee. His eyes lingered there, just for a second. And then, he propelled himself back into motion.

When he kicked the door shut, the spell was broken.

With sure, swift steps, Rhys crossed the room to the overstuffed chairs and set the food down upon the table. His back was to her, but he clenched and unclenched one fist, broad shoulders tight beneath the black leine he wore.

After a long minute of silence, he cleared his throat.

"My apologies, Lady Irving; I assumed ye were still abed." The timbre of his voice sent gooseflesh rippling over her skin.

A flush of warmth crept up Caitriona's neck and her cheeks went hot. She had snapped into action, pulling her stocking up, tying the ribbon around her thigh with swift fingers and folding the top of the hose down over it. "Where are the pins to my stomacher?"

She stood, hesitating. All of her clothes were on the chair beside him. In order to dress herself, and get out of this scandalizing situation, she would have to approach him. Which she did *not* wish to do while covered in naught but the fine linen shift she'd worn beneath her wedding gown.

Rhys lifted his arm to point toward the mantle, not turning around. "It seemed unfit to sleep with those in yer clothing."

"Aye, I'm sure it did," she said, tone infused with scorn. Flustered by the roil of emotions flooding her limbs, she chose anger.

"I didnae compromise ye, if that's what ye're afraid of." There was dark humor in his voice, and she bristled.

"What gives ye the right to remove my clothing? While I *sleep*?"

He faced her then, dark hair pulled away from his face save for one rogue curl that was too short to be tamed with the others. In the morning light, his eyes were the blue of the sea on a cold, clear day. His clothing, however, was stoic as ever. From the black leine to his dark tartan trews and riding boots, he was a veritable stormcloud in the bright room.

"Well," he said, face impassive as he leaned against the nearby armchair. Her clothes were trapped beneath his hand, and he looked down at them. The hint of a smile played around his mouth. "Ye are my wife."

The title pricked at her, a veritable weapon in its own right. "Aye, and I didnae ask for that either, now did I?" She did not *want* to be this man's wife. She did not want to be *anyone's* wife.

Rhys lifted a shoulder in a half-shrug. "Ye're nae the only one."

His indifference infuriated her. Clenching her fists in her skirts, she raged, "Do ye even care? Do ye even care what kind of life ye've disrupted? The future ye've ruined? Ye think ye can simply waltz about the countryside takin' whatever ye please?"

This made him scowl, but he still said nothing.

"Well, ye cannae. Ye cannae just handle me as if I were one of yer horses. Ye may not care what ye've done so long as it benefits ye, but I care. I cared about the people I left behind. I had a *life* back there. People needed me. And now it's all gone, and ye're just standin' there like a…" she sputtered, flustered when he took a slow step forward. "Like a big stram, ye are."

Rhys stalked closer with deliberate movements, not saying a word.

"What are ye doin'?" Caitriona demanded, backing up. But her legs hit the bed, and she could go no further.

"I do care," he said, closing the distance between them. "I care about my clan. I care about their safety."

"Well good then, go take care o' yer clan. They need ye more than I do," she shot at him, warmth suffusing her skin when he stopped just short of touching her, and all she could think of was their wedding day. The brush of his fingers against her neck. His hair tickling her forehead. She *would not* be affected by him.

"Ye are my wife. And as such, ye are part of my clan now." His voice was low, gravelly, rasping over her skin. "So forgive me for considering ye might be stabbed by yer own garments in the night, *wife*. But as part of my clan, 'tis my duty to keep ye safe at all times."

The back of her neck tingled with expectation. Caitriona clenched her fists, feeling exposed in just her shift. She wanted to cross her arms over herself, to cover the indecency of her half-undress. But she stood still. "Wife or no, ye'll not touch me again without permission."

Up close, there were lines weathered into the corners of his eyes, and a second scar ran across his other cheek, lighter than the one in his brow. Gray hair had just begun to touch his temples. At his browbone and across the bridge of his nose where the sun hit were a scatter of freckles.

These small details infused him with a sense of reality, which the rumors and legends had stripped away. He was, all at once, not The Devil of Calhoun, beast of the battlefield abroad.

He was Rhys Macnammon. Laird of a clan for whom his loyalty ran deep, to whom he had given the last decade of his life.

And he was her husband.

Pine and musk invaded her space, with a hint of cold air clinging to the scent, as if he had just been outside. Years of active labor rippled across the width of his shoulders, and in the forearms exposed by his shoved-up leine sleeves. Caitriona could not breathe. When his eyes dropped to her lips, she fought the instinct to worry them between her teeth.

She did not intend to back down, whatever his game was. Those roving sapphire eyes flicked over her shift, pausing at the curve of her hip and the swathe of skin revealed by the wide neckline. For a moment, he leaned closer. So close he could brush a kiss over her lips, and she might not resist.

Then he held up the pile of her clothes between them, pressing them into her hands with an uptick of his brow.

With his face so close to hers the heat of his body warmed her skin, he said, "The carriage leaves in half an hour, and ye'll be on it no matter what ye are — or are not — wearing."

He straightened, contemplating her from head to toe, and then smirked. "I cannae say I would protest if ye wore this, and only this, *wife*. 'Tis fetching."

With that, he turned and left the room.

Caitriona uttered a growl, frustration pushing her to action. Crossing the room to her trunk, she shoved her travel clothes back inside, and rooted around until she found exactly what she was looking for.

The sort of outfit a new bride would never be caught wearing. If her mother had been there to see her, Moira Irving would have had a fit. She pulled on the clothes, plaiting her hair into one long braid, and then looked at herself in the small mirror on the vanity and smiled.

The Laird of Calhoun Castle had set her a challenge, and she intended to meet it head on.

THE LADY OF CALHOUN

Rhys

H is wife was wearing trews.

Ill-dressed for a Lady, smirking like a cat who'd gotten the cream, and striding toward them like she owned the earth itself. As Caitriona approached him, her eyes glinted with satisfaction, and he snapped his jaw closed.

In his travels across England and the Continent, the world at large had deemed highlanders to be savages, illiterate, lacking in polite culture and dress. He'd been labeled as a brute often, which added to his reputation, and when fellow soldiers discovered he could read, it had been a surprise.

They might not follow English society rules at large. Women worked alongside their husbands here, often going barefoot in the warmer weather, and their mode of dress was far more relaxed than an English Lady might be used to. Their relationships were a little less quiet, a little less demure, obedience to one's husband taught, but not often enforced.

But even Rhys, the beast of the highlands, whose people were as uncivilized as they came, was scandalized by the sight of his new wife in her tightly-fitted tartan trews.

Her curving hips swung in the bright, cold sunlight above tall riding boots that outlined her calves, and a white leine with a green weskit and jacket on top. She had draped her green and blue tartan arisaid on like a cloak. It swirled around her shoulders and legs like the deep sea on a warm day, an alluring play of fabric around the shameless display of her figure.

He broke away from his men and met her in the middle of the courtyard. "What are ye *wearin*?" Rhys hissed at her when she was close enough nobody else could hear him.

Caitriona eyed him from beneath her thick auburn lashes. "Ye wished for me to be ready to travel. So I am."

There was a spark of defiance in her gaze.

When Hamish Irving had written of his daughter, he'd painted the picture of a dutiful, willing, and productive daughter, who had been poorly treated in her past, and had a desire to have a family and a home of her own. He had expected, from Hamish's fond musings, a quiet, amenable, solicitous woman. Perhaps a little bit wounded, but eager to move forward with a new life.

His first hint she would not be the timid spinster had come the second she'd turned on him in her parents' foyer, challenging his very presence with an argument. He'd dismissed her reaction as shock, for she had seemed to surrender once the facts were laid out.

His second, on their wedding day. When he'd kissed her, and instead of shying away like a timid maid, she'd leaned into him. Gasped into the caress of his mouth against hers. Set a flame within him so incendiary it sweltered still, like coals ready to blaze to life the second they were fanned.

And now, Rhys let his gaze wander over her hips, the curve of her belly beneath the woolen trousers, and up to the vee at the neckline of the leine. "Aye, I wished ye tae be ready for travel. Nae dressed in so little ye may as well be runnin' naked through the courtyard."

At this, his wife had the decency to flush.

And oh, how lovely it was, the slow creep of pink caressing up her soft neck and into her cheeks. Her freckles winked at him like dark stars in a milky sky, backed by the rose-hued glow of a sunset.

Leaning closer, he said, "And I dinnae care if ye're as bare as the day ye were born, wife, but I cannae say I want my men tae be imagining what else lies beneath that bonny tartan on yer thighs."

She blinked at him, and, though he was sure she tried to stop it, brushed her fingertips over her waist and thigh, before clenching her fist into her arisaid to still her hand. With a flick of her eyes toward his men, all four of whom watched them curiously, she said, "I'm nae less dressed than yer own man there."

A jut of her chin singled out Gillespie Begbie, Angus's oldest son. Besides Callum, Rhys's traveling party was spare — Angus, as always, to aid in protection; Callum to mind the horses and offer his jolly mood to the group; Gillespie, who was learning his father's ways in hopes of being an asset to the clan's safety; and Coinneach Mac Duibh, whose sheer size was enough to intimidate anyone from even *thinking* about a fight.

And, annoyingly, while the rest of his men wore their kilts, Gillespie had opted for trews. Caitriona raised her auburn brow. "And I dinnae ken a single man who's wonderin' after *his*...thighs." She said this last part with the barest hesitation, cheeks still flooded with pink.

Rhys snorted. "Aye and Gillespie isnae a bonny lass with curves so lush they'll haunt a man's dreams and set fire tae all his good intentions, now is he?"

She stared at him, stunned into silence.

He blinked. He had not meant to say the majority of that sentence aloud.

This woman was already setting him off balance, and he did not like it. He did not need a distraction. And by the way she challenged him, his future looked to be full of arguments. Disruptions. She was not the kind of woman to sit back and be meek in the shadows.

He clenched his teeth together, schooling his features back into impassivity.

He did *not* want a wife.

Angus chose that moment to interrupt them. "If ye dinnae plan to bend yer wife over yer knee and give her a good strap for her impudent garb, then we've a long road ahead of us and the day isnae gettin' any younger."

A flash of annoyance ran through him. "Haud yer wheesht, Angus."

The man was too comfortable speaking his mind, and criticizing his new lady to her face was a line Rhys would not allow to be crossed. Even if he was right. He grabbed Caitriona's elbow and led her toward the waiting carriage. "Ye'd best ride in the carriage if ye willnae change."

It took all of his restraint not to cast a glance over her hips again.

She seemed subdued, and he was not sure he liked it. Though he'd known her for less than three days in full, the way her pride had come down a notch bothered him. She pulled at her *airisaid*, covering more of her legs with it. "I'd like to ride for a while."

The request was so quiet, he almost did not hear her. She gestured toward the horses not attached to a carriage. "Surely one of yer men would appreciate a ride inside the carriage to rest?"

Callum overheard her. "Ye can have my horse, milady," he said cheerfully. When she smiled at him, he blushed. "I'm Callum, pleased tae be yer stablemaster. My wife is eager tae meet ye back home."

"Hello, Callum." Her eyes flicked to Rhys, and then wandered over the rest of his men.

One by one, as if compelled by her beauty, they all introduced themselves. Coinneach, he was amused to note, turned red around the ears when she beamed at him. "I'll nae worry about a thing surrounded by the likes of all of ye," she said, and Coinneach looked like he could die a happy man.

Angus was not so easily won. Begrudgingly, he nodded his head at her, and then turned to check his saddle and horse without a sound.

Leaving Caitriona to familiarize herself with Callum's horse, Rhys pulled the man aside and glanced at the Inn, where he caught the Innkeeper's wife Sarah staring at them through a high window.

Callum was annoyingly cheerful. "I can see why ye were so bothered last night," he said with a grin. "She's not quite the spinster ye imagined, eh?"

Rhys scowled at him.

"O' course, no one can compare to my Jenny, ye ken," Callum continued on, ignoring Rhys's glower. "But the new Lady o' Calhoun is a bonny lass." His eyes crinkled at the edges.

"Haud yer wheesht," Rhys snapped. "Did ye do what I asked?" He jutted his chin toward the building.

His friend followed Rhys's gaze. Sarah disappeared from the window. "Aye, I did. But she wouldnae let anyone stay behind for her protection. So we...well, Coinneach...reasoned with the Innkeeper instead."

Shaking his head, Rhys muttered, "I dinnae understand the mind of a woman."

"The Innkeeper's wife is with child." The interjection of a feminine tone made them both whirl.

Caitriona stood there, the sun turning strands of her hair into fire, her expression grim.

Rhys eyed her. "How d' ye ken that?"

She hesitated. "She told me."

He had the impression she was holding something back.

Caitriona waved her hand. "Anyway, drawin' attention tae her now might do more harm than good."

Rhys crossed his arms. "We offered her protection."

Caitriona worried her lip between her teeth. "If ye took her husband out back and showed him a thing or two about respect, what d'ye think he'll do to her for causin' him such trouble when we're gone? He's already stealin' money for drink, and blames her for it."

Rhys bristled. He had not considered this point, and disliked that his new wife was showing him to be a bit of a fool. "He'll think twice about layin' a hand on her again."

"Will he?" Caitriona's voice was without challenge. Instead, she stared at the Inn, something like sorrow in her gaze.

Shoving a hand through his hair with impatience, he said, "'Tis already done. There is naught more we can do." His tone was flat.

Of course he should have realised antagonizing the Innkeeper would only result in a worse future for Sarah. Of course men of his nature never really stopped. But Rhys was so used to having his orders obeyed; so settled in his ways, he had not considered whether the Innkeeper was of the same stock as his clan.

Rhys did not tolerate violence toward women. His father had been something of a violent man toward his mother, and he had seen the effect it had on her. How she kept her eyes low, her hands to herself, her words meek. Lest his father take offense in one of his drunken rages, and punish her for existing around him.

As a boy, he'd always wished someone would stand up to his father, for his mother's sake. Nobody ever had.

It was not until his father had died that his mother had begun to bloom. But by then, her health had suffered, and she passed away not two years later.

Caitriona's voice was soft, regretful. "I dinnae think any of us could have done more. She told me last night she didnae want to leave him. When she came up with the tray of supper. She thinks the good Lord will smite her down if she commits such a sin as steal their child away from her husband. I offered her a place in Calhoun Castle before I left this morning, but she wouldnae come."

Rhys looked at his wife, unsure whether to be angry or impressed he had not thought of offering to take the woman with them.

She mistook his stunned gaze as a question, and took a short breath. "She'd be a good hand in the kitchen, ye ken. That breakfast was exquisite."

"Aye, 'tis a pity," he said finally.

His mind whirled with the insight he now had into an entirely different side of Caitriona. The gentle side, full of compassion and empathy, which he had not yet experienced.

He was not sure he wanted to. For it tugged at a specific place in his chest, a part of him he had buried long ago and did not wish to resurrect. Brusquely, he nodded toward the horses and carriage, and Angus, who approached them with his gray brows drawn together in a scowl.

"'Tis time we go, then," he said.

"Aye," Caitriona agreed, smiling brilliantly at the old man shooing them all toward their horses like a mother hen herding her chicks. "Angus doesnae seem tae like our nattering."

Under his breath, Angus grumbled something about outspoken women, his craggy face disapproving. But when Rhys pinned him with a glare, he only checked the saddle of his own horse. "We need tae get movin', or we'll be caught in the highlands at midnight. Dinnae want tae invite an attack."

The older man had been Rhys's most trusted right hand in battle for years, and took his Laird's safety personally. When Caitriona mounted her mare, Angus grumbled, not bothering to hide his censure.

Rhys only grunted, and mounted his own horse, Sgàil, a great black stallion who was raring at the bit for a run. Muttering a few more choice words under his breath, Angus snapped out a few orders, and the rest of the small procession fell into place. They left the courtyard of the Inn, every one of them eager to get home.

FORSAKING ALL OTHERS

Caitriona

The downpour began halfway through the day, and though Caitriona was happy to ride in the rain, her new husband all but forced her into the carriage to keep dry.

Alone.

By the time they reached Calhoun Castle, the gray skies had emptied themselves and a heavy mist shrouded the stones in mystery. The gates of Calhoun castle passed over them, and she could not help but stare at the massive structure she was to call her new home.

Calhoun Castle was four times as large as Irving Manor. The courtyard was big enough to fit eight carriages side by side, surrounded by a high stone wall upon which a few guards walked, keeping watch. Fog played around the turrets of the multi-storied castle, whose arched windows overlooked an inlet and the stone bridge they had rolled over on their way to the gates. There were three stories looming above, and branching off on all sides were several other structures.

It would take Caitriona a week to familiarize herself with the layout.

When the carriage rolled to a stop, the long, wide steps that led to the grand entry of the castle stretched out before her. Heart a wild hare beating a fast pace in her ribcage, she watched Rhys dismount from the window, his dark curls sticking to his face from the rain, and wondered what life would be like here. Closing her eyes, she pressed a hand to her stomach where a twist of nerves had settled, and took a long, calming breath.

The door to the carriage clicked open, and Rhys offered her his hand. Looming tall, mist swirling around its highest roofs and spires, the castle was much like its Laird: mysterious, dark, hard, and intimidating.

What would her life be like here?

A few eyes snagged on her when she stepped from the carriage into the evening haze. A ripple of embarrassment flushed her cheeks. She was the new Lady of the castle, and here she had shown up to greet them all in trews. Trews thrown on by a rebellious heart and a determination to spite her new husband.

While she was still quite satisfied with the reaction Rhys had given her at her appearance, she wanted to make a good impression in her new home. And Caitriona did not know how kindly the Macnammons would take to a strange new lady who strode into their home in mannish garb without care.

Perhaps, given the rumors that surrounded her husband, a little forgiveness for her unusual garb.

But she did not have much time to ponder this, for a woman was flitting down the grand staircase, her skirts a graceful flutter behind her as she stretched out her arms. "Rhys!"

The Laird Macnammon released Caitriona's hand and caught the woman at the bottom of the stairs with a bear hug, pressing his cheek to her soft brown hair. There was a familiarity in the way his lips curved and his eyes crinkled that stabbed at Caitriona's heart. Clearly, by the way he kept hold of the woman around the waist, they were close.

"Berach sent his men to our lands while ye were gone," the woman said, her voice low. "I fear we may lose Lachlann; he's upstairs. Ye've come just in time." She threw a brief glance Caitriona's way, and if she was shocked by the trews, she showed no sign of it.

The smile faded from Rhys's face. "Callum," he commanded. "Take Lady Irving up to her rooms."

Without acknowledging Caitriona further, Rhys turned and walked up the stairs, his arm protectively slung over the woman's shoulders. They spoke with their heads together, disappearing through the grand carved doors of the castle as if Caitriona did not exist.

A sharp knife twisted in her gut. Who was this woman, whom her new husband followed without so much as an introduction? Were the rumors of his mistress and illegitimate child true? Did he harbor a lover openly in his castle?

"Lady Irving, if ye'd like I'll show ye the way," Callum said. His eyes were worried, but he kept up a jovial chatter as he led her through the doors and into the grandest foyer Caitriona had ever seen.

The high ceiling was punctuated by an arched window at its apex, and several balconies loomed above, where people seemed to scurry to and fro above them. Tapestries hung on the walls depicting legends, and torches were lit everywhere. The ceiling was so high, it was shadowed.

"How...big is clan Macnammon?" Caitriona asked, shocked by the sheer number of people they passed as they traversed the round-ceilinged hallways and up the stairs. There seemed to be no end to people. Whether lounging and sharing a meal, or scurrying about on unknown tasks, or stopping to stare at her and her ill-chosen trews, there did not seem to be one empty room or hallway in the castle.

"Oh, I dinnae ken really. The Macnammons have been around for generations, and the Laird's father was a skilled man in combat and negotiations. Somewhere around five hundred I should think."

Used to Irving manor, where the maids dwindled and her father's relatives were few and far between, she was unused to being amongst so many people in the same building. And even with the bustle about her, the castle seemed vast. As if they could fit every Scot in the Highlands inside, and still have room for more.

There was one Scot Caitriona could think of she wished was *not* in residence at the moment. Roiling with anxious energy, she braced herself. "Callum, the woman with Rhys. Who is she?"

"Och, that'll be Kenna, lady. Ye might have met her earlier, only she thought it'd be better if she stayed behind. With Berach lurkin' around the clan lands, Rhys didnae wish to risk her being attacked." Callum's tone was matter-of-fact.

Caitriona scowled. This did not answer her question at all. "Who is Berach?"

"Rhys's cousin, a right fool. He wants to be the new Laird Macnammon, and he's challenged Rhys many a time. Only this time...well, this time he's threatenin' war. Riling up the clan with talk of instability, a Laird who's so reclusive he has nae legitimate heir, some such bollocks." Callum rubbed his chin.

"And Kenna...is precious enough Berach might hurt her?" She feared the answer, but Caitriona was not one to balk at hard things. If this woman was her husband's mistress, she wanted to know. If he had illegitimate children, which she assumed he did given Callum's wording around the subject, she needed to take it all in stride now.

"Oh aye," he said, opening a thick, well-polished door and showing her into a suite of rooms where the fire blazed merrily. "'Tis nae secret in order to get tae Rhys, one might go through Kenna. Especially after his wife…well, Kenna became important. In Rhys's life."

His words, delivered matter-of-factly and without shame, hit Caitriona like a blow to the chest. She stood in the room, back to him for a moment, mind racing.

"But that isnae a story for me tae tell. If ye need anythin' Aileen will be up shortly with food and a bath and whatever else ye might want." Callum paused, as if waiting for Caitriona to say something.

She took in the rooms, trying to regain her composure. Trying to think.

A colorful quilt covered the large four-poster bed, its tree of life in the center beautifully appliqued in rich greens and blues and browns. Across from it before the hearth, two dark wood chairs welcomed weary souls. Thistles were carved into their backs, and a rising sun rose from the peak, and each had a pillow upon it in the same style as the quilt on the bed, soft and welcoming.

Against the cream walls of the corner, an armoire stood in the corner of the room, and beside it was an open door. Within was a sitting room decorated in heather green, several shelves laden with books beside a comfortable chair, and a fireplace, which was not lit. Another door was to the left of the bed. Caitriona would have to investigate where it led later.

To her surprise, wildflowers dotted the room in beautifully painted vases, brightening the space. Set upon side tables, their colorful purple blooms added cheer to the cozy room. Doing a half-turn to survey her surroundings, she wondered if the closed-off door was attached to her new husband's rooms, as was often the case in such spaces, but she did not ask.

"Thank you, Callum," she said instead, facing the jolly man with a forced smile.

"'Tis nothin', milady. If ye're settled, I'll be off then." Callum bowed a little at the waist. "I havenae seen my wife in days and…well, I'm fond of her, ye ken."

His words only bloomed the hurt in her chest more, but she waved him off. "Go on, then."

"Rest well, lady." The man's grin nearly split his face as he turned to go.

With that, Callum left, and Caitriona could do nothing but collapse into an overstuffed chair, the tightly wound thread of her emotions unspooling with dread.

Tears began to spill down her cheeks, dripping onto the wool of her weskit. Caitriona swiped at the dampness, angry that she was even upset over the known possibility of her husband having a mistress. The rumors about him were rampant. From fathering children in many different clans to murdering one of his own, there was nothing that had not been said about Laird Macnammon.

Until now, Caitriona had ignored most of it. She should not care, not really. It was an arranged marriage, and one she had not wanted. She was here out of loyalty to her clan and her parents, nothing more. It should not sting that he already had a woman here, established and seemingly accepted by the clan. Callum had not so much as batted an eye when mentioning Kenna.

But no woman wished to be spurned so obviously within days of her wedding. Even if it was arranged.

Restless, she pushed out of the chair and wandered the room, trailing curious fingers over the mantle and peering into the armoire. Her own clothes were carefully folded and hung therein, neatly stored as if she had lived there for years. The sitting room led to yet another room, which contained a chamber pot, a wooden table that held a pitcher and matching washbasin, and hooks from which muslin cloths hung to clean herself. A window overlooked other parts of the castle, letting in the dim light of the evening.

The sun would be setting soon.

Wandering back to the main window of her room, she peered through the glass to the small garden below. The clouds had broken, and the low sun turned the sky orange. But the sunset was not what caught her eye; on a bench surrounded by roses, the woman called Kenna sat. Rhys was beside her, his arm protective around her as she stared up at him with wide eyes and trembling lips. Something passed between them, and Rhys put a hand upon her hair tenderly. Then he pulled her close, pressing a kiss to her forehead.

White-hot rage exploded in Caitriona's chest and she stumbled away from the window, hands shaking. There could be no other explanation. Her husband was forsaking his vows in favor of another woman.

Despite showing what she'd thought was obvious interest in her as they had traveled here. The flash of his eyes when she'd walked out in trews. His hand, tightening on her jaw on their wedding day. The kiss.

She shoved these memories out of her mind and clenched her fists. Caitriona was no stranger to rebuilding her life after disaster, continuing on when it seemed impossible. There were plenty of Macnammon clan members, which meant plenty of babies being born. And if they already had one Howdie, well. Two was even better.

It was best to continue doing what she had always done: make choices for herself.

Not for love, not for marriage, and *certainly* not for a man.

RUMORS OF THE DEVIL
Caitriona

Caitriona woke the next morning to the gentle hum of Aileen, who was laying a fire in the hearth. The young maid had introduced herself the night before, finding Caitriona pacing back and forth in her rooms, unable to sit for the anger that forced her limbs into action. Aileen was a gentle soul, and had somehow known exactly what Caitriona had needed: food, a warm bath, and the brushing of her hair, which soothed away her restlessness and put her in a drowsy mood.

Now, she greeted Caitriona with a cheerful, "Good mornin', milady!"

The woman already had Caitriona's clothes laid out for the day, and rose from her place at the fire to assist getting her Lady dressed. With soft brown hair and warm hazel eyes that always held a smile, Aileen felt like a friend.

Changing into a clean shift, Caitriona slipped into her stays, eyeing the outfit the maid had chosen for her. The maroon, yellow, and gray tartan dress consisted of a weskit, short jacket with ruffled cuffs, and a voluminous skirt meant for easy, everyday wear. Embroidery lined the edges of the jacket, intricately done flowers to mimic the lupin that grew in yellow, blue, and pink swathes of summertime in the highlands.

Aileen hummed while she worked, but Caitriona's mind raced. While the maid dressed her, she became keenly aware of the fact her husband had not come to her room last night. No one but herself had slept in her bed, of this she was sure. There was no second impression on the mattress, no garments left behind from another person, and nobody had woken her coming into the room. She would have known if he had appeared, would she not?

It only stood to reason, then, Rhys had spent the night with his lover.

Starting her first day at Calhoun Castle with the knowledge that she was being spurned was not how Caitriona wished to begin her new life. Had her father really been so blind in his assessment of Rhys's character?

Her chest tightened as if compressed by the invisible ropes of the marriage now trapping her here.

Fully dressed, she sat at the vanity in her dressing room so Aileen could put up her hair. The maid seemed quite content as she twisted and primped and pinned. By the time she was done, Caitriona looked far more like the Lady of Calhoun than she had the evening before, her red locks curled artfully and her garments demure.

"Will ye be wantin' breakfast in yer rooms, or will ye go downstairs tae break yer fast, milady?" Aileen folded Caitriona's discarded shift in her hands as she waited for an answer.

Shadows played under Caitriona's eyes, her reflection telling what she tried to ignore. "Is his Lairdship downstairs?"

"Oh aye, he only just went down." She smiled when Caitriona stood and faced her.

"Alone?"

A small furrow appeared in Aileen's brow. "Aye, I think so. Why?"

Worrying the fabric of her skirt between two fingers, Caitriona shook her head. Her husband's mistress was not a subject she wished to discuss with the maid. A sharp longing for Maeve rushed through her. They had confided in each other so much over the years, and she could imagine it clearly.

Maeve sitting in rapt attention, while she paced the floor and recounted the past few days. Her friend bursting with indignation. Offering a solution that was satisfying, if completely unrealistic and often unhelpful.

I ken a good bog where a body willnae be found.

But she would not be thrown aside like some rag, used for a purpose and discarded. Whatever waited below, she would face it head on. Like she always had. Rubbing a hand against her aching heart, she shook her head. "I'll break my fast downstairs. Thank ye, Aileen."

"Will ye need me to show ye the way down?" Aileen gestured toward the door.

The smile on her own lips did not feel like it reached her eyes, but Caitriona hoped the maid knew she was grateful. "No, I'll find my own way."

Leaving Aileen to finish tidying the room, Caitriona fought the urge to clench her skirts in her fists as she navigated the castle. A long, grand hallway led her past portraits of Lairds and families. Several bore a strong resemblance to Rhys, though their garments were markedly older in fashion. The sharp blue eyes and black curls were prominent in his family.

If she had not known better, she might have even said several of the portraits were Rhys himself. Perhaps scarred in different places or not at all, five or six of the men on the walls were only distinguishable from each other by the clothes they wore, or the wives they were with. But the Macnammon men were unmistakable.

Making her way down a long stairway, she followed the sound of raucous laughter and chatting. For a brief moment it felt like home. Friendly talk echoed around the foyer as she entered, coming from the great hall beyond where everyone broke their fast together. It added a layer of hominess to the otherwise vast space.

A large open doorway welcomed her, the aroma of barley cakes and venison pungent in the air. Traversing the foyer, she smiled at a few clan members who greeted her in a friendly manner, and then she was pausing in the doorway of the great hall to assess the room.

Overhead, a haze of smoke lifted into the hammer-beam archways, and bright sunlight filtered in from the far wall's tall windows. It was even more grand than the foyer, with tapestries everywhere, candles lit on tall candelabras, and smooth wood underfoot.

A dais was at the head of the room, and three long tables formed a horseshoe around the remaining walls of the room, benches at the side tables and chairs upon the dais. If she was not mistaken, most of the clan was currently seated and eating.

But when her gaze caught on Rhys, her heart dropped into her stomach, and the tightness in her chest imploded. He was laughing, his eyes crinkling at the corners and his white teeth flashing in the ever-present dark stubble of his beard.

It was the first time she had seen him so openly joyful, and it took her breath away. Dark hair half-pulled away from his face, the single curl over his forehead still refusing to be tamed, his gaze was lit from within.

And it was trained upon Kenna, who sat to his left, beaming at him as if he were her entire world. The woman's hand rested on his forearm as she returned his laughter, her brown hair an artful frame around her delicate face. In the morning light, Kenna was far more beautiful than Caitriona had thought. Eyes a bright, clear blue, she had smooth pale skin and a slim figure expertly dressed in a cornflower gown that accented her complexion.

By comparison, Caitriona was an unwieldy, oversized, flame-headed ogre.

"Lady Macnammon!" Callum greeted her, voice loud enough that Rhys's gaze swung their way.

The laughter faded but the smile remained on his face, and he glanced from her to Kenna and then back again. Leaning close to Kenna's ear, he said something and the woman nodded.

Caitriona had thought she could face this.

But she was not as brave as she had hoped.

Without waiting to see what Rhys did next, she whirled and headed for the grand front doors, fury and grief clashing in her chest in painful waves. All of her determination to rebuild her life here fled with her.

Tears blinded her, and she ran out the door into the bright sun without a firm direction. Nearly tripping down the steps, she fled for the nearest structure across the courtyard.

Inside, the scent of hay and horses greeted her, and Caitriona searched for the mare she had ridden yesterday, thoughts wild. She would leave. She would go back home, demand her father annul the marriage, and accept whatever censure her parents and her clan poured upon her. Anything was better than this. Her own husband was flaunting his mistress in her face while the entire clan watched.

It was too much.

She swiped damp from her cheeks and slowed, the cheerful sound of singing coming from the back of the stables. Interspersed with song, a young boy's voice conversed with the horses.

"Och now Sgàil, dinnae be greedy. Ya right numpty," he said.

Caitriona approached the stall where the voice originated, and peered in.

A boy of no more than ten was pouring feed into Sgàil's trough, singing a ballad. Dark curls brushed his shoulders, and he patted the horse's massive shoulder before turning.

"Oh!" Caitriona blurted, unable to stop herself.

The boy's sharp blue eyes and straight nose were unmistakable beneath his raven curls. It was like a jagged knife stabbed into her already bleeding heart. Unlike Rhys, he had a soft look about him from youth, and freckles spattered across the bridge of his nose and his rounded cheeks. But, like the portraits in the hall, he was irrefutably a Macnammon.

This, then, was the bastard son of the Devil. Did the boy belong to Kenna?

The child seemed about as startled to see her as she was to see him. He recovered quickly, though, and bowed low. "Milady, I didnae hear ye!"

"Forgive me," she said at the same time, and she turned to flee yet again, covering her mouth to keep the sobs from echoing in the stables.

But a massive figure stood in her way and she all but slammed into it, arms flying out to grasp anything that might keep her from dropping to the floor. Heat flooded her as she was pressed firmly against the hard physique of none other than her own husband. Rhys's clear gaze burned into hers. He held her steady against him, large hands wrapped firmly around her biceps.

"Och, Laird, I didnae hear ye either," the boy's voice piped up brightly from behind Caitriona.

"Aodhán, leave." Rhys's command was firm and final.

"Yes, sir," Aodhán answered. The dark-haired boy trotted away and out of the stables, taking up his song again as he went.

Caitriona ripped away from Rhys's grip and jabbed a finger wildly at him. "How *dare* ye?"

Narrowing his eyes, Rhys crossed his forearms over his chest. "How dare I?"

"Ye ken full well what ye're doin', Rhys Macnammon. There are a lot o' things I'm prepared to let pass in a marriage, but this is *not* one of them." Incensed, she clenched her fists to hide the trembling of her fingers.

Far less ashamed than he should be, Rhys leaned against the upright beam of a stall door, long and languid. "What, exactly, am I doin'?"

"We've not even been married three full *days*. Do ye care at all?"

Blinking at her, Rhys raised one eyebrow. "Care about what, Lady Macnammon?"

Was he really so coarse that sitting with his lover at breakfast, in plain view of the entire clan and in front of his own wife was nothing to him? Heart beating against her ribs like a caged bird, she glared at him.

"I didnae believe the rumors at first, but nae more than two days have passed and they're all true." Daring to step closer, to spit the words in his face, she raised her chin. "Every single one. Ye're a black-hearted man, Rhys Macnammon, and I cannae believe my father read your character so poorly."

Pushing away from the stable door, Rhys straightened to his full height. "What rumors d'ye speak of, *wife*?" The last word was a sharp edged knife.

Caitriona would not be intimidated. Waving a hand toward the castle, she raged, "All of it, everythin'. Ye've sown yer seed far and wide, taken what doesnae belong t' ye. Killed yer own. Ravaged every woman in sight."

Rhys stepped forward, his expression dark. "Ye'd best watch yer words, Lady Irving."

The fact that he was threatening her after all he had done sent a white-hot fury through Caitriona. Without another thought, she slapped him full across the face, a sob catching in her throat. Rhys swore, and she raised her hand again.

He caught her wrist before she could repeat the action.

"Our own weddin' night, ye forsake me. For *her*." His fingers were a warm vice around her skin.

"'Our wedding night was in the Inn, if I recall. Ye were asleep before I even came tae our rooms."

She acknowledged his wry correction with a glare. "On my first night *here*. Sitting yer mistress at our breakfast table, ignorin' me the day we arrive for her, and keepin' yer own son with this woman out here in the stables like…like a servant?" The words tumbled out of her, bitter and fervid.

Much to Caitriona's surprise, amusement sparked in Rhys's gaze. His dark brows shot up. "Aodhán?" he said, the corner of his lips turning upward.

"Dinnae try to deny it, Rhys Macnammon. That boy has yer face clear as ye have the face of yer father and grandfather and all the ancestors before ye."

"Och I willnae argue with ye there, Aodhán is a Macnammon. But he doesnae belong to Kenna." Much to her surprise, he began to chuckle. "Kenna! Oh, lass." Loud bursts of laughter filled the air of the stables, and Caitriona scowled.

"I dinnae find any of this funny, *husband*." Despite herself, the flash of mirth dimpling his cheeks sent butterflies aflutter in her stomach.

He shook his head. "Ye listen to far too many rumors, *lasair-chrid-he*."

Flame-heart.

How original, to be yet another man teasing her for her hair and her temper. Ignoring the baited moniker, she yanked her wrist from his loose grip. "I dinnae need to listen to the rumors, not when they've been confirmed by my own eyes."

He studied her for a long moment, dark lashes flicking over her and coming to rest somewhere around her mouth for far longer than she liked. "'Tis a pity yer eyes mistake ye, then. Kenna isnae my mistress." He paused, and the dimple in his cheek deepened. "Kenna is my sister-in-law."

All of the air left Caitriona in a rush. "Yer...what?"

"She was married to my younger brother, Llwyd."

There were few things Caitriona knew about her husband, but his family line was deeply etched in her mind. Her mother had filled her in on his history, and gossip, in the week before their marriage, drilling in the names of Rhys's siblings, parents, and ancestors until her head was full of names that had no faces to match.

Rhys's mother was Welsh, and had given all of her children names from her own side of the family. Rhys was the eldest, followed by Llwyd, and then Gwen the youngest and only girl. Rhys's father had died when Rhys was about twenty, after which he became Laird. A few years later, tragically, Llwyd had died, under mysterious circumstances. He'd left behind a wife and two small children.

The death of his brother was part of the rumors swirling around the Laird now.

A decade ago, they said, he had disappeared with his brother in the dead of winter's sleet and snow. Rhys had returned. Llwyd had not.

No one knew the true story of his death, and it had become part of the Devil of Calhoun's legend.

"Your brother is dead," Caitriona said, feeling hollow.

"Aye. Kenna remarried my cousin, Lachlan Macnammon, whom I trust more than most with the care of the clan when I am gone." His amusement had not yet faded, but he was solemn as he recounted. "The day we arrived, there had been an attack on some of the men collecting rent on Macnammon lands. Lachlan was badly injured. But he'll survive. He woke up this mornin'."

In a few words, everything Caitriona had seen was reframed. Kenna had not been a mistress running to meet her Laird, but a worried wife rushing to her kin for support. Rhys had not neglected her on what would have been their first night at the castle; he had been by his cousin's side, hoping for the best. The scene at the breakfast table had not been flirting and flaunting; it had been sheer relief.

Hot with embarrassment, Caitriona could only utter a quiet, "Oh." If she could melt into the stable floor, she might have done so right then.

AODHÁN

Rhys

The pink flush of Caitriona's cheeks was all-too-distracting as Rhys dispatched her assumptions with the truth.

He could not help but tease her, just a little. "Dinnae worry wife. I have my vices, and my secrets, but a mistress isnae one of them." Leaning closer, he dropped his tone. "I didnae ken ye were so eager for me to come to yer bed. If ye want me that badly, I'll gladly oblige."

"No!" she shot back, the rosy tone of her skin deepening to match the bright color of her hair.

"Well, that isnae very wifely of ye," he said, prodding her with jest.

"I didnae mean —" she started, twisting her hands into her skirts. "'Tis only...I dinnae ken..." The more she attempted to speak, the redder her face became, and the harder she clenched her fists around the fabric of her skirt.

Rhys shook his head to clear his thoughts. He would not let his eyes wander to her elegant fingers desperately grasping fabric; he would not let himself replay the brief touch of her lips under his; he would not remember the scent of lavender that clung to her hair and teased his senses.

No.

He did not *want* to be attracted to this woman. Both of them had been thrust into this situation for practicality's sake. Nothing more could happen. Nothing more *would* happen. Except...

The silence stretching between them was broken by a horse nickering in a stall, and her eyes flicked to the sound. "Whose child is he, then?"

Aodhán.

Her question sufficed to banish any further lusty thoughts from his mind, and he crossed his arms. Reconstructed the wall which, stone by stone, he had built around his past through the years. This is why he had not wanted a wife. This, among many other things.

He did not need someone new, someone who would poke and prod into his past, into areas they did not belong. Someone who felt they had the right to be privy to this part of his life.

This part of his life had been walled off long ago, and he had vowed an oath never to reopen it. For his own sake, for his family's sake, and for the boy. Aodhán lived a happy life here, existing just as he was. He did not need to know how his origins had changed the very foundation of who Rhys was.

Caitriona went on, seeming unaware of his sudden change in mood. "I mean tae say, 'tis obvious he's yers, but does his mother still live?" She was challenging him, her chin tilted in defiance. "Or are those rumors amiss, too?"

"Which rumors have ye heard?" he questioned cooly, denying nothing.

"That ye fathered a son by the scullery maid, born the same time as yer wife died."

Cocking his head, he studied the hope that lit her eyes, that trembled around the edges of her lips and hovered in the rise and fall of her breath. Hope, he knew, that perhaps they were just that — rumors.

And Rhys was not in the practice of dispelling rumors about himself. "The cook," he corrected her.

"What?" Caitriona said, as if the breath had been knocked out of her.

Rhys cleared his throat. "The rumor is that I fathered a son with the cook, Jenny."

For a moment, she sputtered. "Jenny...Callum's wife?"

He nodded, amused by the way her mouth hung open, her flush deepening, indignation heaving in her chest. "Did you?"

Ten years ago, something catastrophic had happened, and his life had shattered. Nobody knew exactly how things had happened, but this worked in his favor. His reputation had grown when he'd left for the continent, and by the time he'd returned he'd decided to lean into the assumptions.

Because at the heart of it all, the truth would rend a hole in more than just his own life. And there were people he loved too dearly to allow the endless night of shame and self-hatred and grief swallow them, as it had him.

Still, perhaps his new wife deserved some iota of the truth. Even if he could not tell her everything. "Jenny and I found each other at a time when both our worlds were shattering." It was as much as he could offer.

"And Aodhán...is her son?" Something like disappointment filtered over her face, and she dropped her eyes to her own hands, which twisted together.

Rhys was silent. This was a conversation he had not expected to have with his new wife so soon. People talked about him, of course. About them. Whispers about the cook of Calhoun Castle, and how she'd borne a child so like Rhys he was unmistakably a Macnammon, were rife. But Rhys had vowed to allow Jenny to expose her own history, in her own time and her own way.

And right now, Aodhán was just a boy. A boy who was happy, free, and loved.

When she looked back up at him, her gaze was guarded. She waited a heartbeat, two, three, and when he offered no answer, she seemed to harden over. Steeling herself against the shock of it all. Taking his silence as confirmation of the rumors. "And Callum...?"

"Callum and Jenny had not yet married when Aodhán was born." Again, it was only half of the truth, but promises made in grief and shame and desperation held him back from dispelling the gossip entirely.

"Well," she said, and the resignation in her tone was almost too much for him to bear. "At least ye didnae compromise a married woman."

Rhys could not help himself. "Oh, but who says I haven't?" he said, smirking. He preferred a fiery Caitriona to a dejected one, he found.

The words had their desired effect. She straightened. Glared at him. Lifted her chin. The freckles across her cheeks stood out beneath her incensed emerald eyes. "My father seemed convinced of your honor, Laird Macnammon, and I dinnae think I have ever seen my father proven so thoroughly wrong."

For some reason, her words stung. Her disappointment, which stormed across her face like clouds over the sea, crashed into him and set him off balance. Once again, he discovered he wished to please her, to make her comfortable and happy.

But deeper than this was a stone wall of resistance so high, he could not fathom bringing it down. Giving in to his baser desires would only cause trouble, for all of them. It was best to leave the wall up. Keep the marriage distant. Do his duty, and no more.

As if he were remarking on the weather, Rhys observed, "Ye've high standards for a woman who's rumored tae be no better than a whore in the stables."

Spinster or no, his wife had come with her own set of rumors. Years ago, it was said that she had given away her maidenhood, and freely. It had been the catalyst to chase away suitors. It had molded her, no doubt, into the woman she was today.

Even so, it was a cruel blow, and he knew it. She flinched against his words, drew in a sharp breath, and adjusted herself to absorb the sting. Something twinged within him, and he shook it off. It was better for both of them that she did not expect much from him.

"At least I am honest about what I have or have not done." Fury was low in her voice.

"So 'tis true then?" Something sparked inside him. Something possessive.

Jealousy.

A low rage simmered at the thought of some other man's hands on his wife. A man who had captured her heart the way he never would. Try as he might, he could not shut it out.

A pleasing pink flushed her cheeks again, but she did not look away from him. "I may have made mistakes in trusting certain men with my heart, but I have...not been bedded."

He leaned a little closer, bracing himself against the stable post beside her, pleased when she took in a sharp breath in response. "Yer innocence is bright as the flames in those cheeks."

"I cannae say the same of ye," she said, not hiding her own frustration.

He liked how head-on she was, despite his reticence to allow her into his life. Into his past. No one had pried the truth of Aodhán's parentage from him, and no one ever would. He had sworn to protect the boy, and he could not break that vow. Not even for his pretty, flame-haired new wife who weaseled her way into his thoughts uninvited.

"Ye're certainly not the meek, fearful spinster I expected, *lasair-chridhe*." He used the name to rile her, to goad her away from asking about his past. And, perhaps, to indulge the irresistible urge to see her flush pink again. "I didnae expect yet another woman coming intae the castle to stir up trouble."

"And ye're not the fearsome, fearless laird I was led to believe ye would be," she returned, brow raised as she looked him over.

He smirked. "Is that all they say about me?"

Caitriona hesitated. "No," she said, shaking her head. "They say ye're heartless. They say ye've killed a man with yer bare hands, and…"

Rhys crossed his arms, body tense. He knew what was coming next. All of his earlier humor faded away as he waited for her to finish the sentence. This, he hated most of all. It was the rumor closest to the truth, and his guilt never left.

Quietly, she finished. "They say the man…he was yer brother. Llwyd."

A sharp anger struck like lightning beneath his skin. Rhys Macnammon, murderer of his own flesh and blood, betrayer of his own family. Even after a decade of fighting to change, he could not throw off the ruthless gossips that spun this half-truth in webs of legend around him. Not after his uncle had challenged him, and lost.

This rumor lived on, and always would.

Closing his eyes, he clenched his teeth together, digging his fingers into his palms in an effort to quell the rage that had risen like a flooding river. When he met her gaze, she recoiled, and a sliver of regret cooled the fire in his veins. But one thing would be crystal clear, if this marriage was to work for the good of anyone.

Llwyd Macnammon's death was off-limits. Nothing could absolve him from his brother's death, no matter how it was told. And the truth might push her so far away, the heir he so desperately needed would never come to pass. Clan peace would be lost. Everything he had worked towards for the last seven years would come to naught.

So he would guard those secrets to his grave.

Gruffly, he said, "I'll be leavin' in the morning. The men who attacked Lachlan are still out there, and it is becoming clear I cannae ignore Berach any longer. I will be back within the week, if I dinnae find where they are."

Caitriona blinked, thrown by the change in subject. "But...we only just got here."

"And my clan needs me."

"So badly ye cannae even stay one day more to settle yer wife into her new home?" There was an edge to her words, but he shrugged them off. She would be better off without him, and the sooner she learned this, the easier it would be. For both of them.

"Kenna and Jenny will help ye settle in," he said.

A flash of emotion rippled across her face. Her nostrils flared, and as he watched she straightened herself in so many subtle movements — pushing back her shoulders, lifting her chin, stepping away from him just slightly. Her eyes became molten, a slow, quiet fury sparking deep within. And she took a slow breath.

Before his eyes she had transformed from a somewhat disheveled maiden to an aloof and regal queen.

"Very well," she said. "Then I wish ye safe travels, *Laird*."

When she walked away, Rhys had the distinct urge to go after her.

But he stayed in the stables, surrounded by the nickering of horses and the scent of hay and animal and dung, hoping he was right.

It was for the best.

THE DUTY OF ARRANGEMENT

Caitriona

Being ignored for an entire week after one's wedding was not an ideal way to begin the position as Lady of Calhoun Castle.

After their argument in the stables, Caitriona had seen very little of Rhys. Embarrassed by her dramatic accusations and blind belief of the rumors, she had kept to her rooms the day after. But shoring up her confidence, she emerged again within a day, and saw neither hide nor hair of Rhys Macnammon. He was busy with clan matters, and when he was not out roaming the countryside, he kept to his library.

Caitriona had never felt so thoroughly unwanted.

Much to her dismay, their fight was becoming castle gossip. She'd heard Aileen whispering about it to a scullery maid, and giggles erupted behind her everywhere she went the day she emerged from hiding. She was the center of everyone's gaze, and it took all of her courage to face the great hall and break her fast with the rest of them.

Her only reprieve came, to her surprise, in the form of Kenna. The woman wasted no time in approaching her.

"Tell me then, Lady Irving, what do ye think of Calhoun Castle?"

Kenna had the kind of eyes that danced like a butterfly through sunlight. Wrapped in the dark blue-and-green tartan arisaid of the

Macnammon clan, she rested her hands beneath her chin, and Caitriona could not help but respond to her smile.

"It's...grand," she said, though the word was inadequate to describe her new surroundings. Calhoun Castle was overwhelming. Inconceivably large. It had so many passageways Caitriona knew she would get lost if she tried to map them all. The high hammer-beam ceilings above them put her into a state of awe.

"Aye, 'tis that!" Kenna said, a dimple deepening in her cheek. "I remember the first time I set foot here, freshly married to my late husband. The archways took my breath away!"

Despite her embarrassment, Caitriona could not help but relax in the presence of kindness that radiated from Kenna like a sunbeam.

"I think it will take a while to get used to the grandness of it all," Caitriona agreed.

Mischief twinkled in Kenna's eyes. "And its Laird? How do ye find him?"

Heat flushed up Caitrona's neck and flamed in her cheeks. Kenna could not have avoided the truth — that she was the source of the Laird and his new lady's first fight.

"He's..." Imposing. Mysterious. Infuriatingly secretive and the bane of her existence. "...efficient."

Kenna bit her lips, clearly suppressing a laugh. "Aye, he gets his way does he not?" Leaning a little closer, Kenna said, "I hope ye dinnae mind me sayin' this, Lady Irving —"

"Cait," Caitriona offered. "Please, call me Cait." She did not quite like the formality of titles and surnames.

Kenna's gaze softened. "Cait." After a moment of consideration, she took a deep breath. "His brother wasnae...a kind man. It wasnae a good marriage for me, and Rhys kent it. I did my best tae hide the things Llwyd did tae me and..." she shook her head. "I may have been in love, but it wasnae...good. And after his death, Rhys was a changed man."

The gossip around her husband niggled at the back of Caitriona's mind. He had not denied the rumors. But he had not answered them, either. "Did he...is it true, what they say about...that death?" There was no delicate way to ask it. Caitriona thought she could be direct, but sitting face-to-face with the widow of the man Rhys was reported to have killed, she could not quite say the words. Not to the gentle, warm, open woman before her.

Kenna's brow furrowed, and she fiddled with the bowl of porridge in front of her, but did not drop her gaze. "I cannae answer ye that," she said, but her tone was open. "But 'tis only because I dinnae ken, myself."

Around them, the hall ebbed and flowed with life. It was still early in the morning, and Caitriona spotted Jenny and Callum breaking their fast together, with Aodhán between them. He laughed at something Callum said, and Jenny shook her head with mock disapproval. And, while Aodhán had clear traits as a Macnammon, she thought she could see a little bit of Jenny in him, too.

The way his expressions moved mirrored his mother's distinctly.

Caitriona did not realize she was staring until Kenna's voice broke through her thoughts.

"Dinnae judge him on his past mistakes." Kenna laid a gentle hand on Caitriona's arm.

Shaking her head, Caitriona half-smiled. "Do ye ken, before I came here I had my own past to reckon with?"

Sheepish, Kenna nodded. "I...might have heard a thing or two. 'Tis impossible nae to hear the gossip of the maids."

Caitriona snorted. "Well. I ken nae everything is as it seems. But I wasnae expecting...well. I dinnae ken what I was expecting. Perhaps all of it. Perhaps something else. It's just I had a life, before this, and...'tis all sudden."

A smile bloomed on her companion's face. "Aye, 'tis that. He didnae even tell us a new lady of the castle was coming until the day before he left."

Caitriona's brows shot up at this information. "But he was writing to my father for weeks!" She'd gotten the impression her father and mother had known for a long time, but then...they'd not told her a thing until he arrived. Perhaps they hadn't been sure until then.

"Ye may have noticed, he isnae very...talkative."

Barking out a laugh, Caitriona nodded. She had only known her new husband for a few days, but it was very clear he held information close to his chest. At every turn, it seemed, a new secret popped up. And at every turn he held onto the answers as if they were precious gems and he a dragon hoarding them.

"Well, anyway," Kenna said, and surveyed the room. When her gaze settled back on Caitriona, she had a small smile on her lips. "I'm glad ye're here, Cait. Rhys has been alone for far too long, and this castle could use a mistress."

Her word choice was inadvertent, and the moment the phrase was out of her mouth, Kenna slapped her hand over her lips. "A lady, I meant! Ye ken, ye're mistress of the castle!"

This only sent Caitriona into a fit of giggles. "Aye, a mistress is just the thing," she said between fits of laughter.

Friendship with the woman she'd thought to be her husband's amour was not what Caitriona had expected, but as they finished up their breakfast, she found she quite liked Kenna Macnammon. Perhaps this, then, was her first true ally in an otherwise unsure place.

THE DEVIL AND THE MIDWIFE

💐 💐 💐

It was no longer a secret: Rhys was avoiding her.

Caitriona had formed a habit now: breaking her fast with Kenna, and sometimes Jenny — who turned out to be another easy friend — in the mornings. Discovering Kenna had children — three daughters — from her previous marriage was a delight. They all favored their mother in temperament, being sweet and flitting about like butterflies, but the striking resemblance between the eldest one and Aodhán was shocking at first.

It seemed the Macnammon genes could not be hidden.

In the afternoons, she formed the habit of taking a stroll around the gardens. Slowly but surely familiarizing herself with the vast rooms and halls of the castles in her spare time. Revealing, little at a time, her knowledge of herbs and healing as the opportunities arose.

On the eighth day since her arrival, she was heading toward the kitchen gardens, ready for her afternoon amongst the greenery. It was a crisp day, and the air did her good. In the gardens everything had begun to bloom, roses reaching their prickly arms toward the sky as a cacophony of red, pink, and yellow petals unfurled in the sun. The space was lush, herbs and flowering bushes settled between the taller roses, all manner of greenery abounding.

Pressing the fragrant leaf of rosemary between her fingers, she spotted several other plants that she could use in midwifery. Pennyroyal for nausea. Vervain for producing milk and treating pain of the abdomen. Yarrow to relieve a woman's pain from bleeding.

A sharp pain sliced through her. That was no longer her life, was it? Midwifery, which she loved, was out of reach now. She was relegated to a life of duty, in a place she was not wanted or needed, to live out her days in regret. All because Rhys Macnammon demanded it.

But she had little time to brood upon this, for a few scullery maids tripped out of the kitchen and caught her attention. Heads together, they were speaking in hushed but animated tones, and giggling. As usual.

"...and then it popped right out, and Liam's been traumatised ever since!" the darker-haired of the two exclaimed. "He's never even *held* a baby let alone delivered one!"

The second maid, a girl of no more than sixteen with wild flaxen curls and shining blue eyes, snorted. "Well, he kent how tae *make* a baby."

They both dissolved into squeals and giggles.

Overtaking them with her long strides, Caitriona interrupted. "Has someone had a child?" she asked, and the matching expressions of surprise, then guilt, then wide-eyed wonder crossing the maids' faces almost made her laugh.

"Yes milady," the darker one curtseyed, and a half-second later, the light-haired one followed suit. Both were clumsy and unpracticed, but Caitriona did not care.

After a moment of awkward silence, the light-haired girl spilled forth a swift and wandering tumble of words. "'Tis only...well, Eileen Dunn, whose father raises goats on the north side o' the village, *she* said that Marcus McMahan said that his cousin Liam McMahan got a girl in the family way — the girl is Mary Macnammon, a distant cousin of his Lairdship, but she's only seventeen, and she ran away from her family — and believe me, her ma was nae too happy about it, nae with everythin' else goin' on in their family — but anyway she and Liam must hae dawdled in the hay and next thin' ye ken they had a baby!"

Caitriona blinked.

There had been far more information in this ramble than she needed, yet, somehow, she had more questions than answers.

The light-haired girl bit her lower lip. The dark-haired maid stared at Caitriona with wide eyes. Both of them wore half-startled expressions of awe.

"And...this baby, who was he delivered by?" Caitriona prodded, unsure whether these girls would stay or bolt. The dark-haired one looked very ready to bolt.

"'Tis a girl!" Encouraged by Caitrion's interest, the light-haired girl went on another wandering ramble. "And tae be sure, nae Liam nor Mary cared what they had, but ye ken Mary's ma was right furious the day she found out Mary got with child, by a fishmonger's son no less, and *in a field* or so I'm told by Eileen who heard it from Sorcha who heard it from...nae, maybe Marcus heard it from Sorcha, and Sorcha heard it from Jessie and — well anyway, Mary was out for a walk and nae supposed tae be seein' Liam at all, but she never did listen tae her ma or da verra well so she was out with Liam and that's when she gave a scream like the devil was chasin' her — that's what Liam said, white as a cloud and shakin' like a leaf — and collapsed right there in the heather."

Caitriona opened her mouth, then closed it, then opened it again. "And...she had the baby in the heather?" Despite being more than she'd asked about, she was beginning to enjoy this girl's wandering way of answering her.

"Och nae!" The girl leaned in, all sense of awe gone as she continued her story. "Because Old Paddy were drivin' his sheep up tae pasture and *he* heard her and ran tae see if she was bein' attacked, and Liam was standin' like a statue starin' at Mary on the ground and he thought she was dead! Liam near had a whippin' by Old Paddy's staff only he started tae cry, and then Mary yelled she was havin' a baby then and there, and Old Paddy made Liam carry her back tae her ma's cottage, only her ma weren't there."

The more she talked, the further from the end she got, and Caitriona bit back a laugh as she tried to follow the girl's story.

"So *then* Old Paddy ran off tae get his wife, but he lives too far, ye ken, and by the time he got back wi' her, Liam was holdin' a wain, and Mary was right near passed out from exhaustion, and that's when her ma got back tae meet her grandchild."

Caitriona frowned a little. "So Paddy's wife is the Howdie, then?"

With a laugh, the light-haired girl shook her head. "Nae, but she has had ten bairns and Paddy kent if anyone could deliver a wain it'd be her. But o'course he was too late, and Liam caught the bairn and said he's never seen anythin' more terrifyin' than a woman bringing life into the world." She bumped her shoulder against the dark-haired maid. "I hear tell she cursed him tae the devil and back for ever gettin' her with child. So now they're gettin' married!"

"Well," Caitriona said. "I wish them well, then."

"I'll tell them ye said as much, milady! Mary will be thrilled. She's been dyin' to have news about..." A sharp elbow was shoved into the girls' side and she squeaked. "Ow! Mor, what was that for?"

Mor rolled her eyes. "She doesnae want tae listen tae the history of half the village, Rhona."

Smiling at the maid called Rhona, Caitriona shook her head. "In fact, I dinnae ken much and I'm eager to learn more." She was about to ask if there was any Howdie in the village at all when both girls' faces grew red and they stared at a point beyond her shoulder, exchanging glances.

"Lady Irving." The deep voice tingled down her spine, and she whirled.

Informally dressed in a loose, dark shirt and tartan trews, the Laird Macnammon was an imposing figure in the afternoon light. The sun glowed about his dark locks, and shadows played under his piercing eyes. Amusement crinkled at the corners of his mouth, but his gaze was unreadable.

A fortress, barred at the gates and refusing entry. The Laird who had met her at her challenges and laughed in the face of her accusations was gone. In his place, a guarded, careful man, who studied her but let nothing slip past his icy countenance.

"Mor, Rhona. Back to your duties," he commanded. Caitriona did not look, but the scuff of the maids' feet was clear behind her, and with a slam the kitchen door shut behind them. She and Rhys were alone.

He did not speak to fill the thick silence between them. Instead, he looked her up and down, eyes unreadable. In the still afternoon, birds twittered in distant fields, and a lamb bleated. The plants around them waved green leaves in the sunlight, basking in its warmth, letting off a faint scent of earth and *green*.

Rhys was out of place, yet right at home. Stony, like the castle walls behind him. Cast like the shadow of a tree upon a lawn, throwing the inescapable gravity of his presence over everything in his path. And Caitriona was unable to look away.

"I believe as lady of the castle, ye'll need to know yer way around."

Caitriona regarded the outstretched palm, his wrist and forearm exposed beneath the bunched-up sleeves of his leine. Veins traced up his arms, sending a peculiar warmth to regions of her body she would rather not acknowledge. "I dinnae need help," she lied.

In truth, she still got turned around on her way from her rooms to the great hall at times, and had been too afraid to traverse the cellars for fear of becoming trapped down there.

But he did not need to know that.

"Aye, ye seem capable of finding what ye want, *lasair-chridhe*." Despite his aloof stance, he let the moniker slip. A muscle in his jaw ticked. "However, 'tis still my duty to introduce my Lady to the castle, and I have been remiss."

Bristling at the emphasis he put on *duty*, she took a step back. "I find my way well enough on my own."

One brow crooked upward. "The clan has questioned yer...*wandering*. I'm told in my absence, ye nearly lost yerself in the cellars."

When he stepped closer, Caitriona's heart began to race. Curse her body and its inexplicable attraction to this man. She wanted to hate him. She wanted to throw this attempt at civility in his face and rage at him for his neglect the past week. She wanted to point out that he had ruined her life, her chances at happiness. And yet...

She *was* finding her own way, little by little. Kenna had become a friend. The maids were getting used to her. There was hope, if the village did not have a midwife as of yet. She lifted her chin, and ignored his hand.

So quickly she almost missed it, his gaze darkened, lashes rising and falling over her. When he met her eyes again, there was raw hunger in his expression. The same hunger she had seen at the Inn: wild, unfettered *desire*. Had he come to enact his full right as a husband?

Aloofness, she could take. Annoyance, she welcomed. Even his shutting her out, while frustrating, was something she could deal with. But his unmasked appreciation of her? The brief, heated, *want* so swift it nearly scorched her?

Caitriona panicked. "I have a matter to discuss with Aileen about my wardrobe. If ye'll excuse me, Laird Macnammon," she blurted, whirling and all but running down the path, which wound away from the castle before making its loop back to the doors.

But his voice stopped her in her tracks. "Caitriona."

It was the first time he had called her by name. Not Lady Irving, or *lasair-chridhe*, or, derisively, *wife*.

Refusing to turn, she was nevertheless rooted in place, every muscle in her body tense.

"Ye cannae avoid me forever," he said.

This incensed her. *She* avoiding *him?* Laughable. Turning, she glared at him. "I wasnae aware ye wished to be in my presence at all, Laird Macnammon. With yer blatant avoidance of me in the week since we have wed, I thought perhaps ye'd be happier to live out yer days in solitude."

His brows furrowed. "Clan business has kept me busy, but 'tis now my duty to ensure ye are cared for. I dinnae intend to neglect yer needs."

"Ye've left me to fend for myself this entire week, Rhys. Ye havenae even come to my rooms, as a husband should. The whole clan is talkin' about it. What do ye ken of my *needs?*"

His reaction was subtle. A slight tug at the corner of his lips. A glint of mischief in his eyes which disappeared as swiftly as it had come. "I would be happy to attend yer rooms and yer bed, if that is what ye need, *lasair-chridhe.*"

Low and gravelly, his voice brought back unbidden memories. His breath tickling the side of her neck. His hard chest pressed against hers. His arms holding her, the corded muscles heavy against her waist.

"No!" Caitriona snapped, but her weakening knees and pink cheeks belied her thoughts. "That isnae what I meant."

"No?" He could not hold back his smile then.

He was a mischievous god, standing there in the sunlight, tanned skin peeking out from the vee of his neckline, a chuckle sounding deep in his chest, dimples forming on his cheeks. Maddening. He was maddening, and infuriating, and...Caitriona did *not* want him.

She pressed a hand unbidden to her cheek, then her neckline, where her arisaid draped over her shoulder and across her chest. His eyes followed the movement of her fingers with interest. Dropping her hand, she clenched her skirts.

"'Tis only...the clan will follow yer lead, and if ye reject me, so do they," she said at last. It is what she feared, anyway. Despite Kenna's kind attention. Despite Jenny's cheerful acceptance of her. She saw the look from other clan members. The judgement. If Rhys treated her as disposable, how would any of them accept her as one of their own?

He took a step closer to her, and held out his palm again. "I admit I didnae plan to change my life simply because a marriage was arranged. But I am aware of the gossip around us now. Let me remedy what I can. Come, I'll show ye around the castle."

Caitriona glanced from his hand to the castle, and despite her frustration, a thrill went through her. He stood there, the wind ruffling his hair, words a sort of peace offering, even as he boarded up his expression yet again, pushing her out.

She did not expect love; she was far past the age of fairytales and arranged marriages rarely turned into love-matches. But she had hoped, someday, to find a union built on friendship. And perhaps this was her opening, no matter how reserved he chose to be.

Pressing her teeth into her lip, she nodded. "Very well," she said, and she took his hand.

The jolt of electricity that shot through her was unexpected. Did he notice her sharp intake of breath? The way her skin was surely beet red as her body flushed with traitorous curiosity?

She nearly tripped as she closed the distance between them, and Rhys let go of her hand to steady her at the waist. It brought her against his chest again, and she grabbed his forearms, instinct taking over. Her fingers grazed the shirtsleeve shoved up to his elbow, and his skin was a flame beneath her palm.

The entire world faded away under the hooded examination of her husband's eyes. His fingers tightened, their warmth soaking through her weskit and stays, and she forgot how to breathe. Once again, he was solid and warm against her, the pine-and-musk scent of him flooding her senses, his lips so close one move would bring them crashing upon hers.

A muscle worked in his jaw.

This close, his scar was a stark white contrast against the olive tone of his skin and the darkness of his brow, puckering through the laugh lines feathering away from his eyes. They were worn into place as if he spent a great deal of time smiling.

Her eyes dropped to his lips, which were full and sensuous and much softer than the rest of him. A small scar nipped at the left side of his lower lip, catching her attention. This man was full of secrets, the scars mere hints at what lay beneath the surface.

Oblivious to her thoughts, he dropped his arms and moved away from her.

"Forgive me, Lady Irving," he said. "This way."

Caitriona's lungs expanded hungrily, taking in the air she had neglected, but Rhys seemed unaffected. Only, he took great care not to touch her again.

A DISAGREEABLE WIFE

Rhys

Rhys woke the next morning buzzing with restless energy.

The day before, he had shown his wife every possible pathway through the castle, introducing her to clan members as they came and went. He should have done it the day they arrived, but Caitriona's fiery nature had burrowed beneath his skin, prodding at the walls he had built and pricking at all his deepest secrets.

His hard-won control was crumbling fast. In her presence, he had all but kissed her before remembering the demand she had made the day after their wedding.

Wife or no, ye'll not touch me again without permission.

God's teeth, he wanted her.

But he would die before he ever took advantage of a woman. Even if that woman had the lush curves of a goddess and a face to rival the sunset. It had been torture to escort her through the castle after holding her in his arms, the image of her softening lips and fluttering lashes a constant companion in his mind.

He had enough to worry about. With the threat of war at his doorstep and the dissent of his clan imminent, he could not be distracted.

Striding through the castle just after dawn, he made his way out to the fields where his men were sparring. It was a routine practice to ensure every man was ready for an attack. The Macnammon clan was powerful and envied by many. With the recent threat of Berach, who planted doubts and sought to undermine Rhys, he knew they could never be too ready.

Three times a week, his men practiced with the broadsword as well as hand-to-hand combat and techniques with a dirk. To the far side of the field, targets were set up for rifle practice. Though he preferred combat with the blade, he had everything modern for his men to do their best in battle.

This morning, however, he was not here to instruct. He was here to fight.

Angus seemed to see it in his face, for he summoned Coinneach, who was one of the largest men and often fought Rhys when he was in his worst moods. Without speaking, Rhys walked to the space reserved for hand-to-hand combat and turned. Coinneach approached him warily, his meaty arms held ready. Regardless of his size, he had yet to best Rhys. Today would likely be no exception.

A few men gathered to watch as they faced off. Despite the energy coursing through him, Rhys walked a lazy circle around the bigger man, waiting. Allowing his thoughts to rile him up. His hand tingled even now with the memory of Caitriona's skin. How she had looked in his arms, fiery and flushed. He wanted to keep her there, capture her lips beneath his, and act out every vivid scene his unconscious painted in his dreams.

Coinneach swung first, and the calculated blow grazed Rhys's cheek even as he moved to avoid the full force of it. He rammed his shoulder into the larger man's stomach and barrelled him backwards, throwing him off balance, expelling the electric energy coursing through his bones. Jumping back before Coinneach could trap him, he swung for the man's face but was blocked. Coinneach moved with an unusual swiftness for his size.

They circled each other for a tense moment, and the clan around them muttered and placed bets on who might win this time.

Rhys was a big man, tall and broad-shouldered, with the honest muscle of hard work rippling down his arms. But he had the grace of one who had always been made aware of his size; trained by years of fitting himself into a world that was too small for him. Coinneach was a bear; the kind of burly strength that had a deceptive layer of softness over hard muscle beneath, and he was half a head taller than his Laird.

Scarred from years of fighting, he knew his way around hand-to-hand combat. The man was always up for a match. Despite his jovial personality, he was a fierce competitor.

A massive fist flew, connecting with Rhys's ribs, and he grunted. Another blow landed, and Coinneach was pushing him across the grass as he retreated from the furious attack. If he was honest, the pain was welcome. Anything to interrupt his thoughts.

"Yer lady got ye soft, eh?" Coinneach grinned, noting Rhys's lack of reciprocation. "I'll thank her later."

Narrowing his eyes, Rhys danced away from another blow, but said nothing. Waiting, allowing the bigger man to exhaust himself little by little.

"Always said it'd be a woman that changed ye," Coinneach jested.

Rhys blocked a fist and rammed a sharp jab into Coinneach's stomach. "I've not changed," he huffed.

"Are ye so sure?" The large man grinned and took a step back to avoid being hit in the face. "Ye've nae come to fight about a woman before."

With a grunt, Rhys swung again and missed.

"Ah but I suppose bein' kept from her rooms is drivin' ye right mad." He pulled no punches. "Any man would go crazy not bein' able to touch that pretty red hair or those bonny curves. She's a tidy woman, that."

It was then that the flames roared to life in Rhys's head. Blood pumping anger through his limbs, his fist connected solidly with Coinneach's cheekbone, and then another plowed into the man's ribs. "Dinnae talk about *my wife*," he spat.

It was all in the name of the fight; no man would otherwise speak so brazenly about Caitriona. But Rhys was unwilling to cease his furious attack. He landed blow after blow until Coinneach was stumbling backwards, swinging blindly and landing a few hits himself.

A wild fist to the brow split his skin and sent blood tumbling into his eye, and he combatted it with a sharp hook to his opponent's stomach.

Coinneach lost his breath but stayed steady. He was a fine match, winding Rhys up even as he was losing. It was just enough to bring him away from his thoughts of his new wife. He pursued, dancing around Coinneach's fists just enough to have the upper hand. Slamming his shoulder into the man's chest, Rhys drove him to tumble over and triumph flooded him.

On the ground, Coinneach lifted his hands, and Rhys let up.

"Ye ken I meant nothin' by it," the man said, jolly despite his loss.

Breathing hard, Rhys wiped the blood from his eye and nodded. The split on his brow stung. "Nae better brawl than yerself, Coinneach."

"Well, Laird, I'm always happy to try bestin' yerself." Coinneach was all smiles.

Around them, the betting losers groaned and handed over coins as they began to disperse. Angus, however, sidled up to Rhys with a knowing look in his eye.

"A bit fierce today, eh Rhys?" He walked beside his Laird, who was now headed back to the castle.

Angus had known Rhys since he was a bairn, and when Rhys's own father was too drunk or too furious to care, Angus had taught Rhys the ways of being a man. In many ways, Angus had been more of a father to Rhys than Archibald Macnammon. As such, he took liberties many would not, when it came to speaking openly with his Laird.

"It's been a while," he said. Angus did not need to know he meant it had been a while since he'd bedded a woman. It had also been a while since he had fought Coinneach.

But Angus saw right through his stony exterior. "Aye, it has." He did not need to say more as he raised a shaggy brow.

Rhys speared him with a glare.

"Coinneach is lucky he's not bleedin' as ye are," Angus tacked on. "Might want to see to that 'afore ye see yer bonny lass."

With a wince, Rhys swiped at his brow again, ignoring the reminder. His wife was, indeed, beautiful. He did not want to think about that. "I'm sure she dosnae care about me."

Angus grunted. The old man still did not approve of Caitriona; ever since she'd strode out of the Inn in trews, he had scowled and grumbled about the lady. "Nae doin' too well on the purpose for this marriage then, are ye?"

Rhys shook his head. "I barely ken the lass, Angus, I cannae pull feelings from a week's worth of marriage."

"Who said anythin' about how ye feel? We both ken that isnae why ye married the lass." Angus did not shy around subjects, and sometimes Rhys wished he would.

Rhys flushed, despite himself. "I've been busy."

Angus snorted. "Busy, aye. But ye havanae been busy in any o' the ways ye need tae be. Ye're nae gettin' any younger, Rhys."

Rhys shook his head. "'Tis nae so simple."

Angus clapped a hand on the younger man's shoulder. "Makin' a wain is the easiest thing in the world, my boy. 'Tis the raisin' them that's hard."

The clan wished for him to have an heir; further proof he would not run off again if things got hard. It had seemed simple at first: arrange a marriage, inform the lady, beget a child, and live separate lives thereafter.

And then Caitriona had faced him, dirt on her cheek and blood on her apron, and the fire in her eyes had awoken something within him. Something primal. Something which had lain dormant for years, and which could, if given the chance, ruin him.

He waved Angus off and strode toward the castle, no better off now than he had been before the fight with Coinneach. In fact, it was possibly worse now, with the thought of what the clan expected of him whirling around in his mind. It was his duty, as a Macnammon, to provide an heir.

He had not known, when he agreed, just how dangerous this would be to his heart. He had not known how his skin would hum with the memory of her brief touches. How his dreams would wake him unfulfilled. How his wife would drive him ever-so-slowly mad, and not even know it.

Anticipation humming across his skin, he strode into the great hall. His wife sat to the right of his place, clad in an emerald green that enhanced her eyes and fiery hair. She was laughing at something Kenna had said, and for a moment he was struck dumb by her beauty.

The sheer radiance of her smile, dazzling everyone in its wake. The softness of her jawline, which begged to be caressed with tenderness. Every lush curve of her, from the strength in her arms to the sway of her hips to the dip in her waist. Caitriona was his opposite in every way, and he longed to gather her in his arms right there in the hall and kiss her senseless.

When their gazes clashed, her lips parted in surprise.

It took all of his strength to rip his eyes from her mouth. The fight had done nothing for him. Every muscle was on high alert.

Taking his place at her side, he began to reach for some bannock, but she stopped him.

"What happened to yer face?" She was agape, a hand pressed to her chest, eyes wide.

He lifted a shoulder and swiped at his brow again, but the blood continued to slide down his skin. "Sparring session."

In an unexpected move, she grabbed his jaw to keep his face still and took a cloth from the table, pressing it to his brow. He stilled. Her fingers held him prisoner, thumb lightly caressing the edge of his lip, her face concerned and only inches away.

"What's this, *lasair-chride*? Concern?" he said, intending to remove her hand from his chin. But she met his gaze and he lost his train of thought.

It had been eleven days since he'd kissed her on their wedding day. Eleven days, and he had since recalled the moment a thousand times. It plagued him now, staring at her. Her eyes contained every colour of a mossy glen, and her dark auburn lashes fluttered like butterflies. A sunset bloomed beneath the fawn-freckled skin of her cheeks, over lips the colour of a rain-damp primrose.

The woman had him thinking in poetry. This was dangerous.

And yet, he could not pull away.

"It must have hurt," she said, fingers warm and oh-so-gentle. A furrow appeared in her brow. "But perhaps ye deserved it." There was a hint of humor in her tone.

Her lavender perfume encompassed his senses and he could not argue. "I did."

Closing his eyes did nothing. She was so close her breath tickled his cheek, and when she was done with her ministrations to his face her hand slid down to rest against his neck, the other one turning his jaw this way and that to inspect for more injury. It was torture.

Reaching up, he grasped her wrist and stilled her movements.

"Ye're still bleedin'," she said, and he peered at her.

Those eyes, so full of curiosity and a little bit of something else. Something he could not quite identify, until her cheeks grew brighter and she glanced from his wrist to his face to his mouth. Her own lip was worried between white teeth until it was pink and swollen as she caught her breath.

And then, she became aware of the eyes upon them, and she pulled away. The loss ripped through him like lightning.

"Thank ye, Cait," he said, glancing at the room, catching the breathless expectation of the women, the knowing grins of the men.

The delighted eyes of Kenna, and beside her, Lachlan's smirk. His cousin was healing well, despite Berach's attacks.

"I'll be fine."

"Aye," she said, eyes stuck to her bowl. Her shoulders straightened, and she began to spoon the porridge into her mouth.

He could have watched the workings of her lips for hours, but with some effort, he turned his attention to the plate before him. A spread of sausage, bannock, honey, and apples had been laid out, alongside porridge and jams — blackberry, blaeberry, and sloe berry.

As always, Jenny was a talented cook. Though the food was simple, it was flavorful and never boring.

Rhys could not focus on any of it today. With every movement of Caitrona's spoon, his mind spun out of control. The entire hall waited to see what would happen next, and he himself did not know. Everyone knew they had fought. The gossip was rife with speculation as to why he had yet to visit his wife's rooms. And now everyone knew he had been sparring with Coinneach, which was a sure tell he was agitated.

He leaned closer to Caitriona and studied her profile. Her lovely nose, freckled and pert; the cheeks, full and flushing prettily. "Tell me, wife, do ye find the castle to yer liking?" His voice was low enough none could hear him but her.

She turned those luminous green eyes on him, one brow raised. "I am surprised ye care what I think, considering I'm just 'another woman come to stir up trouble.'"

Rhys bristled. "Ye're my wife; of course I care what ye think."

"Ye've an odd way of showing ye care," she said, stirring honey into her porridge. "I shall note for the future: abandonment is a sign of affection. Threats forthwith are declarations of love." Her voice was dry.

"Perhaps I am giving ye time to adjust to yer new life before I take what is mine to have," he said, the temptation to rile her too strong to resist. He told himself he only did it to keep her at arms' length, but the truth lurked beneath every jibe. Every time her gaze lit with fire; every time she sank her teeth into that lush lip; every time the flush of frustration spread from her cheeks down her neck into her decolletage...it was captivating.

Caitriona speared him with a glare. "Aye, I am to adjust to my life here, but only within the parameters given, and I shall never ask questions nor attempt to become familiar with those around whom I live. That would never do. Heaven forbid I understand my husband better so I might be a good mistress of his home."

So, she was still angry, then. Glancing around, he muttered, "Watch yer tone, wife." He could verbally spar with her all morning.

But it was the wrong thing to say.

A defiant spark shot through her face, and he fought against the urge to pull her to him then and there and plant a kiss on her mouth. They were, after all, being watched. Amongst the chatter and laughter of the clan and the servants, there were eyes upon them at all times. Coinneach grinned at him, the big man's smirk about as subtle as the sun blazing in the sky. Next to him, Angus glanced up and away, as if his curiosity would not be noticed. Even Jenny was eyeing them with a raised brow.

"If ye expected to marry a meek woman, ye chose horribly. I will nae be silenced, nor sent to my rooms until I am needed." Shoulders straight, she kept her voice even and low, but disdain gleamed sharp and clear in her mossy eyes and clenched teeth.

She was magnificent.

"I didnae expect such a disagreeable wife, no," Rhys prodded. He had not expected a disagreeable wife...but perhaps he needed one.

She scowled at him, unaware of his increasingly libidinous thoughts. "I wouldnae be so disagreeable if ye were nae so...so bull-headed!"

Rhys leaned back in his chair, reveling in the expression of war written across her face like a banner. "I dinnae ken what ye expect, *lasair-chride*."

"Honesty would be nice," she said, and though she tried to hide the tremble of her breath, he heard it.

"Ye want honesty?" He leaned close to her, picking up her hand and running his thumb over the ring signifying their union. Despite her demand, he was losing control of the tight leash he kept on his desire, and he could not help but touch her, just for a moment. She did not resist. "I required a wife to settle a clan war before it began." He was on the verge of telling her he also required an heir, but she spoke before he could go on.

"Do ye not wish...happiness?" she whispered. Her eyes were locked onto their joined hands.

Yes, his heart whispered back. *I want happiness. I want you. I want everything.* He ignored it. "I was happy before. My home was run how I desired, my estate was thriving, my leadership was unquestioned." Until Berach, anyway.

Her auburn lashes fluttered upward. "But ye were alone."

The noise around them seemed to die away, until it was the murmur of the sea swirling around him. Everything faded when he stared into those forest-deep eyes, full of a longing so sharp it burrowed into his very soul. A primal urge to gather her up and meet her soul with his own flooded through him. Thoughts a wisp of cloud in the wind, his gaze dropped to her lips. Her mouth parted, fingers tightening around his own as if to ground herself.

And then the sharp bark of Callum's laugh broke the spell.

Rhys dropped her hand and sat back, surveying the room, searching for an anchor to keep him from being swept away. No one looked at them. It was as if the moment had never happened, except his heart beat loudly in his ears and his body was coiled tight with eagerness. Desperate to regain his own mind, he muttered, "I wed for clan peace, not for dissonance within my own domain."

"Well, it seems ye chose poorly." A thread of hurt wove through her voice and she went back to eating her food.

"It seems I did," he agreed, mood worsening by the second. Every interaction with this woman left him wanting and miserable. He was drawn to her like a moth to flame; aware that in his pursuit of her warmth he would only be singed. But still, he could not resist her light.

And it made him all the more determined to push her away. To do what he had to do, and then distance himself. It was for the best. He could not make the same mistake twice. After all, he had lived a decade knowing very clearly that love was not in the cards for him.

He could not think about the way her chin dropped, just a little, and her eyes now shone with unshed tears. He could not give way to his urge to soothe her ruffled feathers. To ease the wounded air about her, and soften the hard shell she erected around herself. There was a hunt to plan, the gathering of rents to collect, and a clan to appease.

He had no time to consider his wife might be burrowing into his thoughts, and there was nothing he could do to stop it.

A Clan Torn Apart

Rhys

It was the middle of the night when someone shook Rhys awake, and he swung an arm out, disoriented.

"Wake up ye big lump," Angus's voice cut through the hazy state of his mind.

"What is it?" Rhys pulled a hand over his face, visions of Caitrona and her soft hands still lingering at the edges of his consciousness.

Angus tossed a pair of trews at him, and Rhys took them, dressing himself in somewhat of a haze. The older man would not interrupt his sleep without good reason. Dread settled in the pit of Rhys's stomach as Angus gathered his things, though dressing his Laird was not part of Angus's usual routine.

"They've set fire to Euan's barn." The words were grim, and slapped Rhys into full consciousness. "The fire's more than Euan can handle, and if we dinnae make haste it'll take more than just the barn. All of his horses..." Angus trailed off.

"And the men who did it?" He pulled a leine over his torso, grabbed his dirk, and was at the door with Angus trailing behind him in mere seconds. The farm in question was a swift ride from the castle. Perhaps if they made haste, they could track them.

"Rode off toward the north, I'm told."

Berach's men. Rhys had no doubt his cousin had sent his henchmen to wreak a little havoc at the edges of Rhys's land; it was a direct challenge to his authority. Berach Macnammon had never been happy that Rhys had taken up as Laird. Through the years he had threatened, gathered support from other uneasy clan members, and begun a campaign to smear Rhys's name and remove him from his seat as head of the Macnammon clan.

As they shuffled down the dark hall, a familiar feminine voice called out behind them. "What's wrong?"

He turned. Caitriona stood in the shadows, wrapper held tightly at her neck, fire glinting in her hair, like gold-red flames spilling down her back in a glorious display. What he wouldn't do to bury his hands in those tresses. Still and curious in the hallway, she stood tall and plush in her night clothes, and his body responded immediately. But now was not the time to think about his wife.

His wife whom he had yet to touch, other than brief, tortuous brushes of the hand, momentary intimacies that brought nothing but frustration.

"Go back to bed," he said, not moving. Angus stood at his side, glancing between them with knowing eyes. Rhys wanted to wipe that look off his face.

"Can I be of assistance?" She took a few steps closer, and Rhys clenched his hand.

"A man's barn has been lit afire, wife. There is naught ye can do but stay out o' the way." His voice was strained to his own ears, and he winced. If Angus caught that tone, he'd not let it die easily, not without a load of joshing in the morning.

Once again, she moved closer. He could see the outline of her hip beneath her wrapper, and the memory of green in her eyes became reality as she stood in the flickering light from the lamp in Angus's hand. "I have some experience with wounds; if anyone is injured, I can —"

Rhys closed the distance between them, cursing everything in his body for its response to being so close. Lavender teased at his senses, her perfume ever-present in his dreams and now in his waking hours. "If ye wish to help," he said, placing a hand on her shoulder and firmly turning her back toward her room. "Ye will return to yer bed. Ye'll only be in the way."

She stiffened at his words, but obeyed, walking back to her rooms without a backward glance.

Watching her move through the darkness, everything in him wanted to follow her. Angus cleared his throat, and Rhys turned with a glare. "Dinnae start," he warned.

Angus raised a hand. "I said nothin'," he quipped. They continued down the hallway, and he muttered, "But that doesnae mean I didnae see things."

Rhys only answered with a grunt. The night was going to be long.

※ ※ ※

They arrived at Euan's farm to find the raging mass of what was once a barn, and a man nearly inconsolable at the loss of his horses. Rhys helped douse the last of the fire with his men, bringing buckets up from the nearby creek. What else might Berach do in the coming months?

The sun rose slowly over the hills by the time the fire was truly out, and Euan and his family surveyed the remains of their barn with a despair that drove anger deep into Rhys's chest. He approached the younger man and placed a hand on his shoulder. "Come to the castle later; we'll see about replacin' a few horses as well as we can, eh?"

Euan's gaze remained on the coals of his barn. "It was Berach," he said, confirming Rhys's suspicions. "I tried to stop them but he barred us into the house."

Rhys's stomach twisted. What might have happened if Berach had decided to set fire to the house instead? "I ken. I'm sorry." The words seemed inadequate.

"What's he gunna do next, then? Last month it was John's sheep. Month before, Finlay's dogs. Before that, crops stolen, animals disappearing, winter wood sources depleted…bit by bit he's tearin' us apart." Euan finally looked at Rhys. Eyes bloodshot, he had smudges of ash on his cheek and his hair stood up where he'd run his hands through it.

Guilt threaded through Rhys. His cousin had been picking at the edges of his land for some time, but Rhys was reluctant to go to war. If there was another way, he wanted to take it. Marriage was supposed to have calmed the attacks, to show Berach he had no arguments to stand upon, but it seemed his cousin had just upped the stakes.

"Aye," he said, somber. "I'm doin' what I can to —"

But Euan interrupted him. "I'm sorry, milord, ye have our loyalty to the end ye do, but this is…not somethin' a man can take much more of. There's talk in the village, ye ken? People are startin' to notice Berach strikes and ye do…nothin'."

Angus stepped in, eyes warning. "Euan —"

"No," Rhys said, cutting Angus off. "He's right. I havenae done much that can be seen, that is true." Turning back to Euan, he met the man's eyes. "I will do everything in my power to help ye rebuild, Euan."

With a sigh, Euan nodded. "Aye, I ken."

Beside him, Euan's wife spoke up. "But what of the real threat? What if Berach decides to burn someone in their own home?" She was a pretty young thing, with pale curls that framed a freckled face and clear eyes. On her hip, a small child sucked her thumb and watched them all sleepily.

Rhys ran a hand through his hair, taking a moment to look out over the land. The hills were touched with soft dawn light, the sun just beginning to rise over the hills, and soon Euan's sheep would be wandering the grass, happy to graze. Heather spread its hazy leaves in a wild display of lavender, and beyond that the sunny yellow of gorse was a bright contrast. It would have been peaceful, if it weren't for the charred remains of the barn and the many worried faces of his clan mulling about in the early morning light.

"I am nae too eager to start a clan war," Rhys said, meeting Euan's gaze honestly.

"Aye, none of us are," Euan said regretfully. "But we avoid it…at what cost?"

Rhys did not have an answer. And it was all he could think about as they helped Euan corral the animals that had escaped the barn; as they discussed building a temporary enclosure until a barn could be rebuilt; as he mounted his horse and rode away.

The words settled in Rhys's mind like a burr and he could not shake them off.

He was avoiding war, but what would it take from his clan?

An Undeserving Man

Caitriona

Resting her forehead against the cool glass of the alcove window of the hallway above the foyer, Caitriona took in the scene below, but her mind wandered elsewhere.

Angus, whom Caitriona had gathered was one of Rhys's most trusted clan members, sparred playfully with a few of the village boys. They held wooden swords and charged him in turn, tackling his legs and prodding him with their toy weapons until he fell in mock-injury. Upon his defeat, they piled atop him, shouting laughter and cries of victory as they went.

A few chickens clucked in protest, scattering with the noise.

It was the kind of scene she had, once upon a time, imagined she would watch her own children perform. That was a dream long gone. In fact, she did not know if Rhys wanted children, or if she was expected to bear fruit, as it were. He had touted his right as her husband to take her as he wished, and yet...

It had been three days since he had shown her around the castle. After the brief moment in the hallway at midnight, he had not bothered to find her again. All of his time was spent out of doors orchestrating plans for the upcoming hunt, or checking on distant farms to ensure their safety.

Berach, his cousin, continued to plague the edges of Macnammon lands.

Which begged the question: if Rhys had married her to prevent clan dissent, why, then, did she hear grumbles through the halls? Though most of the whispers hushed when she drew near, she had caught enough to know there was something else. Something more than *just* marriage demanded.

But how was she to know what was expected of her if her husband continued to avoid her presence?

Plenty of arranged marriages became convenience only, the respective spouses living their own colorful lives apart after procreation. Rhys himself had said he did not plan to change his life because of this marriage. He already had a son, he had all but admitted outright his and Jenny's affair. Aodhán's Macnammon roots were unmistakable.

Was this it, then? Was her use here over before her life in the castle had even begun? To sit and molder in the halls, useless in the kitchens, not needed to run the already well-oiled machine of housekeeping, a body to fill the seat as needed and look proper?

No.

Caitriona would not have it. She would not be useless, forgotten, or ignored.

Removing herself from the alcove, she started off in search of Rhys. She would face him head on. No more beating around the bush. No more wondering what the clan gossiped about now. No more trying to eavesdrop for any tidbit of clarity or prod Kenna for answers.

The woman was helpful, and willing to chat, but she only knew so much.

Caitriona strode down the hall toward his library. The door was cracked. Nerves fluttered through her belly. What would she say? Their conversations did not have a history of ending well. How did one go about such discussions without imploding, or ending in silence, as they always did?

She could not make demands. She could not ask about his past. She could not allow her own stubbornness to be her downfall yet again.

And, whatever she did, she could not be distracted by the way her heart responded to him. When he had taken her hand at the breakfast table, fiddling with her ring, his thumb sliding over her skin, those little touches had heated her to her core. Dreams of him plagued her; the way his lips had brushed hers on their wedding day; his hungry gaze at the Inn; their brief touches in the garden. His large, warm hands on her waist, holding her to his chest for a brief moment.

His eyes. Glaring, warming, darkening.

Shaking her head, she pushed open the library door to reveal the warm interior of his study. He was not there.

Bookshelves filled the walls, precious tomes tucked into every nook and cranny, comfortable chairs set before a roaring fireplace, a large mahogany desk centered at the back wall. This was where he hid himself away.

There were hints of him scattered about the room. A jacket tossed on the chair; a half-empty mug of ale on the desk; a half-full plate littering the side table. It was as if he had just left, or was about to return.

Above the fireplace, his family portrait hung. The resemblance between himself and his siblings was strong.

Trailing her fingertips over the books on his desk, she gazed curiously up at the portrait. His father was a large man with broad shoulders and bright eyes, his ruddy face stern, a tartan bonnet perched at a jaunty tilt upon his head. Sharp eyes stared back at Caitriona, older than his son's but just as intense. Beside him, Rhys's mother was elegant, with a tumble of blond hair and a warm green gaze. The brother, Llwyd, looked so much like Rhys Caitriona might have assumed they were twins. The tilt of his lips was full of mischief.

Their sister, the youngest, was a bonny child with light curls like her mother and bright eyes like her father and brothers. She clung to her mother's skirts, and half-hid her face.

And then, there was Rhys. No more than fifteen in the portrait, still soft around the edges. Looking just like Aodhán, down to the small dimple teasing his cheek and the merry mischief in his gaze.

They looked happy together, loving. Rhys's father had his arm around his wife, and the children leaned against their parents with an ease the artist had captured well. But according to Moira Irving, Rhys's family was shattered. After their father's death and then Llwyd's demise, their mother had wasted away and eventually passed on. Gwen had disappeared several years ago, some said to devote her life to Christ, others surmised she'd run off and gotten married in France.

Rhys was the only sibling left.

The only descendants of Diarmad Macnammon were Kenna's children, all girls.

A peculiar thought occurred to her then. This marriage was to unite his clan and quell the dissonance rising because of his tenuous position as a family man. From what she had gathered, many of his clan felt a man without a family was a man without reason to stay. And Rhys had already abandoned them once before, after the death of his brother.

For three years, he'd roamed the continent, fighting in wars, working out his grief. Coming back a changed man. A man to whom they still gave their loyalty, but with limits. They wanted him to have a tether, something he would never leave behind.

Did that mean—

"Did ye require something, *lasair-chride?*" Rhys's deep voice startled her from behind.

She whirled.

He stood beside his desk, his dark curls ever escaping from the tie binding them back, and she took a sharp breath, cheeks flushing against her will. His unexpected arrival coupled with the realization there might be more expected of their marriage had butterflies clamoring in her stomach.

She clenched her skirts and took a calming breath. He was just a man. A man who had wed her for clan peace, and seemed to discard her thereafter. She should be angry with him. Furious, in fact. He had ripped away her future. And yet...

Rhys began to shuck his cloak in the dark, warm space, tossing it over the armchair and shoving his sleeves up. A habit of his, it seemed. The deliciously bronzed muscle of his forearms caught her attention, and her palms tingled with the sensation of those dark hairs against her skin. Was she really so weak to be distracted by *arms*?

Blinking, she raised her gaze to his. He was...admiring her? His eyes dropped down her figure, lingering at her hips, taking a slow trail up her waist to the hand pressed against her decolletage.

"What is it you need?" he asked, his voice husky and warm, and her knees wobbled. Traitors.

"My parents never allowed themselves to go to bed angry with each other," she blurted.

It was not what she had meant to say. It was not the firm inquisition she had meant to put forth, to clear the air between them and set things straight once and for all. It was honesty. It was an offer to get to know her better.

It was, if she was frank with herself, longing.

Her parents had many faults and fought often, but beneath the constant prattling of her mother and the patient endurance of her father, they were dear friends.

Rhys raised one dark brow, a flutter of bemusement crossing his face. "Never?"

She shook her head, swallowing against the sudden dryness of her throat. "My mother realized early in their marriage that if it was to work, they couldnae allow things to come between them. They couldnae simmer with unspoken grudges through the nights. She said...to leave unspoken bitterness was to invite the devil into one's room."

He laughed, a sudden, deep bark of a sound. "And ye, have ye come to invite the Devil into yer room?"

Heat rushed up her neck and flamed in her cheeks, but the tightness in her chest had loosened. In its place was warmth, liquid and pleasurable. "Do ye see yerself as the devil?"

Crossing his arms, he settled into a languid position against the desk, long legs stretched before him. "The name precedes me often," he said with a nod.

The Devil of Calhoun. Womanizer. Beast of the Battlefield. Killer of his own blood.

Comparing the moniker to the man before her, whose eyes glittered with storms and who bore the scars of his past like a badge, she did not doubt he had once been fierce. He could take anything he wanted by brute force, and probably had.

But then there was Rhys Macnammon, the Laird who threatened an Innkeeper for abusing his wife. The man whose first thought seemed to always be for the safety of his clan; who spent the majority of his time doing physical labor alongside his people, even though he did not have to. And Rhys Macnammon did not quite match the things said about him.

Most of the last two weeks, he had spent his time ensuring his lands and his people were safe.

Tilting her head, she studied him. "I dinnae think ye're the devil at all."

"No?" Rhys narrowed his eyes when she stepped closer.

"I think ye're hiding."

"What is it ye think I hide?"

It was a risk, prodding beneath the surface once again, and she shrugged. "I dinnae ken. Ye've done nothing but avoid me in person, in touch, in words. Would a devilish man do that with a woman who belonged to him?"

Rhys made a low sound, and her heart skipped a beat.

"The truth is, I need to know what my place is here. What use am I to you? I cannae live a life forgotten, pushed to the corner, useless. No more cryptic words and half-hidden meanings. I cannae live my life wondering what I am to *do*."

Catching her breath, she watched his fingers tap against his arm, afraid to see refusal in his eyes yet again. He was breathtaking, infuriating, and confusing, and she did not know what to do with herself in his presence. Up until now, fighting had been the easiest response. But she could not live a life fighting the man to whom she was wed.

Gathering her courage, she met his gaze again. It was dark, his eyes unreadable, his jaw tense. "If ye wish to live separate lives, never speaking except when necessary, then say so. I cannae live a life where I am not sure whether ye wish to touch me or reject my companionship entirely. I —"

He shifted to stand, his presence filling the room and closing in on her where she stood. The heat from his body warmed her when he stopped no more than a step away. "I've made it clear I didnae wish for a wife," he said.

There it was. Her pride stung. "I ken as much, but —" she started.

He reached out as if to touch her, but stopped himself, and crossed his arms instead. "I wanted solitude. But the clan made their demands. Take a wife, or give up my position as Laird. Prove my loyalty to the Macnammon line, or give up every investment I've made in this land and these people. Give up the life I love."

"But what of me? What did ye intend to do with the wife ye did not want?"

"I had not considered...that she might be unhappy with the arrangement." He seemed transfixed on her mouth, his voice so low it was almost a whisper.

Fighting every part of her that wanted to melt under his gaze, she returned, "No woman wishes to be an afterthought."

"I have money, power, land. Plenty of manors and cottages she could live in, if she wished, for the rest of her days. She is free to create her own life. To make her own friends. To live as freely as she wishes." The sadness in his words surprised her.

She shook her head, skin tingling with anticipation. Aching to be touched by the hand he'd taken back. "She does not wish for land, or houses, or money."

Rhys's gaze was liquid sky, bright and warm and endless. "What does she want, then?" His eyes held her captive, and she could not breathe. Could not move. Could not think.

"Companionship."

Electricity crackled between them, an irresistible pull closing the gap between their bodies. She tilted her chin upward, lips softening, heartbeat pounding like the hooves of a doe, aching and needing and hoping.

But he did not slide his arms around her waist. Not right away. Dragging his eyes from her mouth, he rasped, "You said once that I wasnae tae touch ye without yer permission. Does this still stand?"

Caitriona shook her head. She was not sure she had the wits to do more.

It was almost a relief when his palm slid to the back of her neck, his other hand hot and firm against her back, and he molded her body to him. They fitted together as if they had been made for each other. Her soft curves melted against the hard, long planes of him, and she could have sworn she was floating.

Floating away, held down by the delicious weight of his warmth around her, his fingers in her hair, his lips brushing butterfly-soft against hers. Tasting. Testing. Growing hungry for more. Both palms framed her face, and he drew his thumb over her bottom lip, studying her as if she were a precious gift.

Caitriona was no longer sure whether she held herself up or whether it was his arms anchoring her to him that kept her from melting into a puddle on the floor.

But he hesitated. Resting his forehead against hers, he shook his head. "What if I cannae give it to ye? This companionship ye desire?"

Dazed, she clung to the linen of his shirt and tried to regain her bearings. "Why?"

He dropped his arms to her waist and held her against him, big and warm and infinitely appealing, his curls brushing her temples, his touch weakening every joint in her body. "There is untold danger in the hands of a beautiful woman."

His gravelly tone warmed her from the tips of her ears to the ends of her toes and everywhere in between. But his gaze was closed off. There was something more there. Something he was trying to keep from her.

Caitriona dared to press her palms against his cheeks, forcing him to look at her. "Why won't you let me in?" she said, aching.

Something beautiful and fragile was forming between them, waiting to be strengthened and set free. If he would allow it.

His voice was a growl. "I cannae love again."

Caitriona ached. "Because of Iona?"

His late wife was integral to the rumors that surrounded him. With a death as mysterious as his brother's, Iona Macnammon's name was whispered, like a ghost one dared not to name lest it come back from the grave. It was common knowledge that Rhys's first marriage had lasted only a few years. She had disappeared after childbirth. The babe had gone with her. Neither had returned alive.

He had gone so still she was sure he could hear the pounding of her heartbeat. "Is she the reason ye willnae love again?

Rhys straightened abruptly and let her go, leaving her bereft of his heat. In just a few steps he was across the room, and the space around her grew cold, despite the fire blazing in the hearth. The sensation of his hand against her skin lingered as a slow bloom of hurt grew in her chest.

When he turned and faced her, his ever-impassive mask was up again, as if nothing had happened. "I dinnae want to speak of her."

But Caitriona had been let in, and she would not let him push her out again. "I know she died. But there's more to it, isn't there?"

Straightening away from his desk, he passed her to pick up his cloak and slung it over his arm. "I see now why ye were a spinster," he said. "No man wanted to be shackled with the woman who would never leave well enough alone."

The sting was deep. Lifting her chin, Caitriona glared at him, fresh tears shimmering despite herself. "Perhaps no man has ever been truthful enough to admit he made mistakes, too," she shot back.

Rhys closed the distance between them, glowering. "I've a right to my own secrets."

Standing tall in the onslaught of his presence, she cursed the tear sliding down her cheek. "Dinnae ye care?"

"Care?" Confusion flickered over his face.

"Dinnae ye care that every rumor surrounding ye slaughters yer name, and in turn those who are associated with ye? Dinnae ye care they will gossip about me? About the fact that ye've barely touched me in nearly two weeks?" The wounds were deep and overflowing, and Caitriona could not stop her words. Did not want to stop them. "I cannae live alone, Rhys Macnammon, and if my own husband refuses my presence I *will* take a lover. I willnae be forced to live alone by a man simply because he is too weak to face his own past."

This sparked a flame deep in his eyes. Tension rippled across his jaw, his throat working as he swallowed. "No wife of mine will take a lover."

His voice was the heart of a raging storm, deceptively calm, infinitely dangerous.

"Oh, dinnae worry, *husband*, I shall ensure my lover is discreet." The sarcasm dripped from her tongue. "I willnae cause *more* rumors to ruin yer illustrious name."

Sweeping toward the door on a wave of anger fueled by embarrassment, anguish, and broken dreams, she paused with her fingers on the handle and looked back.

Surrounded as he was by tomes and shadows, he looked formidable indeed. Around him, the firelight flickered off the walls, sending shadows playing across the room despite the brightness of the day outside. He was watching her with a riotous glare, hair a tumble of black curls over his forehead, mouth set in a thin line.

Caitriona would not be cowed. "I willnae be a sacrifice made by the decisions of men who have nothing to lose."

Something softened his gaze, just for a moment. "I have everything to lose."

She laughed, but it was jaded. "Losing the position of a man in power is nothing compared to losing freedom itself. Freedom that a woman has to fight for, only to have it ripped away yet again at the whims of men."

"Ye are free to live how ye like. Ye are free to live elsewhere. But I willnae be cuckolded. It is my right as yer husband to ask that ye honor this simple request." He stood, tried to come closer, but she swung open the door.

"If the man I was forced to marry cannae even honor his wedding vows, I am no longer bound to my own," she said, and she strode down the hallway, praying he did not follow.

Of course, Caitriona did not intend to take a lover, but she would never admit this to a stubborn, arrogant, bullheaded man. He would never understand the price she had paid for her freedom. The rejection, the pain, the constant disappointment of her parents.

All because a man had tried to have his way with her against her will, and failed.

But the blame did not fall on the man. It never would have. It had fallen squarely on her shoulders, and her future was ripped away. It had taken Caitriona years to rebuild, to find herself, to find her purpose. To pursue true freedom, which asked no man for permission.

And then, when she had finally liberated herself to do what she wanted to do, to delve into a life unhindered by the rules of society, she'd been trapped once again. Trapped by a marriage she had not asked for. Trapped by the fact that her only perceived worth as a woman was to run a home and be a pawn in the politics of the land. Trapped by the loyalty her clan did not return.

Trapped, infuriatingly, by the ever-tempting thought that perhaps there might be more to Rhys. To them. To the butterfly-soft touch of his lips and the heady warmth of his hands.

Right then, she hated herself for being swayed once again by the hope blooming softly in the gentle caresses of an undeserving man.

THE HEART'S CALL
Caitriona

The next morning, Rhys was gone.

Caitriona had awoken reluctant to face her new husband, and came down to break her fast expecting...well, she did not know what. The softening of his anger in the library haunted her. The way he had not stopped her, though she declared she would take a lover. It was contradictory given the tender way he had held her. The rose-petal touch of his lips.

Cheeks pink with memory, she arrived in the great hall with a dash of trepidation, only to find his seat empty at the table.

He had gone with his men to collect the rents and hunt. They would be gone for a week. Kenna witnessed the flutter of disappointment crossing Caitriona's face, and gathered her hand up with the tenderness of a sister.

"Dinna fash, Cait, he'll be back before ye ken."

Caitriona straightened her shoulders and shook her head. "'Tis of no concern to me whether he comes back or nae."

Kenna's brows shot up, and she let out a surprised laugh. "I see," she said, bemused.

Ripping a bannock in half, Caitriona spread cheese on top, the soft, slightly tangy crowdie adding a creaminess to the bread, and then drizzled honey on her first bite. The bannock was warm and dense, and she sighed in enjoyment. There were blaeberries on the table this morning, and fresh milk, and pats of butter to enjoy in porridge or on their bannock.

The great hall was considerably less noisy, as about fifty men had gone with Rhys, and the women and children left behind were far less rowdy than their male counterparts. Little squeals of laughter rose up into the hammerbeam ceiling, and the fires were lit. Everything was warm, welcoming, homey.

Caitriona caught sight of a woman so great with child she waddled, and bit the inside of her cheek. Lady of Calhoun be damned. Had she forgotten who she was? Caitriona Irving did not let a man dictate her life, or mold her future. Why should she allow it now?

"Tell me, Kenna…is there a village Howdie?"

Swiveling her attention away from her children, Kenna tilted her head. "Nae since Old Mary passed on, why?"

Taking another bite of bannock, this one with cheese, honey, and a blaeberry, Caitriona chewed thoughtfully. "'Tis only…back in Brae, before the Laird came along, I was the village Howdie."

"You?" Kenna sat back, her eyes widening. She surveyed Caitriona again, as if seeing her friend in a new light, and then the corner of her lips tipped up. "Rhys didnae say anythin' about his new bride bein' a midwife."

Caitriona shrugged her shoulders and grinned. "He doesnae ken. I would have told him, but my mother…well, she was afraid I'd be tried for a witch, or branded a hussy. Although I dinnae ken what all that worrying did for her, I was already gossipped about for the latter."

Kenna bit her lower lip to hide a smile. "Aye, I ken a little of yer past. Ye and the Laird have that in common; too much gossip on idle lips I'll wager."

Caitriona nodded. "Anyway, after the unfortunate moment in which my future...changed...I decided I had nothing better tae do than take up midwifery. I read about it in one of my da's books. And after our own Howdie began to teach me, I fell in love with the work. Bringing a wain into the world is...miraculous. And those mothers! Their strength, their fragility, their entire being giving life. 'Tis a wonder." To her own surprise, Caitriona felt tears pricking at the corners of her eyes. She swiped one away.

Kenna had a fond look in her eyes. She glanced at her own children, who had left the tables and now chased each other at the edges of the room. "Children truly are remarkable. I cannae say I enjoyed birth, though. And carryin' a bairn? Och, the aches and pains in those last months are torture."

Caitriona did not know what it was like to be with child, and the all-too-familiar ache bloomed in her chest again. "I miss the work," she said, pensive. "Perhaps while Rhys is gone, ye can help me...make it known? I cannae see any use sitting here in this castle useless, when I am already a perfectly knowledgeable Howdie and obviously —" She tilted her chin toward the pregnant woman — "There is a need for one here."

Kenna chewed on her lip again. "Aye, I can. Only..."

Caitriona waited. When Kenna did not continue, she prompted, "Only..?"

"Ye might want tae talk it over with Rhys first," Kenna said after a moment. "There are things in his past that might...well. He might like tae have a say in the matter, is all."

Caitriona narrowed her eyes. "I dinnae plan to let any man dictate my time, nor my future," she said. Memories of another man controlling her life, taking away her choices, and drawing a path she could not escape shored up her determination.

Kenna frowned. "But ye're a married woman now, surely ye'll want yer husband —"

Caitriona stopped her with a hand on her arm. "Aye, I'm a married woman. And my husband has barely spoken to me these past two weeks. He has no use for me. If I'm to live here, I cannae sit idle."

Something amused shone in Kenna's eyes, and she conceded. "Verra well then, I'll help ye."

※ ※ ※

After breaking her fast, Caitriona wound through the castle halls toward the gates, fully intending to enjoy the freedom of Rhys's absence. It was time to ascertain whether her midwifery could be of use here. Kenna had agreed to spread word around the castle for her, and now it was time to visit the village and get to know her people.

The day was clear and crisp, with no sign of the usual springtime clouds that dominated Scotland's weather. She drew in a deep breath of the fresh, cool air and smiled as she passed a few children. They regarded her with open curiosity; she was taller than most women, and something of a novelty to most of them.

She'd been told, by a very amused Jenny, the children of the clan thought it a wonder the Laird hadn't scared her away yet. While Rhys was not cruel, he was large, dark, and silent, and inspired a fearful respect in the younger ones. And with the stories told of his time in battle at bedtime, or around the fire, they'd taken to viewing him as some sort of half-man, half-beast, as if he was out of a fairytale.

With a basket on her arm, ready for whatever she might forage while she was out, Caitriona strode toward the gates, fully intending to enjoy her freedom.

The young lad standing guard at the gates looked a little afraid of her.

"Good mornin', Iomhar," she said, smiling at him. "I think a wander down to the village is in order." She was eager to go beyond the walls, used to being the master of her own plans.

Not quite meeting her eyes, Iomhar stepped a little in her way and said, "Good mornin', Lady Irving. I...I cannae let ye pass."

With a scowl, she propped a hand on her hip and stood at her full height. "Do ye care to explain why?"

Stuttering a little, he answered, "His...er...his Lairdship said ye're nae to leave the castle grounds alone until he returns."

Crossing her arms, Caitriona raised an eyebrow at him. "Well. He didnae tell me any such thing." Irritation flared. Only yesterday the same man had told her she was allowed to live freely, doing whatever she wanted, living wherever she pleased.

Perhaps threatening to take a lover had affected him more than she'd realised.

The guard shifted from one foot to the other, gaze downcast, cheeks growing redder by the second. "I...er. He did say if ye wanted tae go to the village, ye could take someone with ye."

This boy was not the problem, though. Taking pity on his nerves, she quelled her irritation and smiled. "I'll not place ye in danger of disobeying yer Laird. Perhaps ye'd find me an escort?"

Red tinged the tips of Iomhar's ears, and he scrambled to do her bidding. "Aye, milady, right away. Thank ye."

Caitriona watched him go, and tried not to be petulant.

After her disastrous yet anticlimactic love affair with Niall, she had been free to do as she pleased. No one would have her. Her suitors had fallen away, gossip ruining her reputation quite thoroughly. What little dignity she had left, Caitriona squelched with her antics. Ladies did not ride bareback in trews. Ladies did not roll around in the field besting men in hand-to-hand combat. Ladies did not run about in the muck, hunting like barbarians.

Moira Irving had given up on her daughter's restoration into everyone's good graces after a while.

And Caitriona had liked it that way. Becoming a spinster and taking her life into her own hands had been the best thing in her life. Midwifery fulfilled her soul in a way no paltry love affair ever had. She had been able to traipse about on her own, whenever she had wanted to, at any time of day. Safe on her father's lands, untouchable thanks to spiteful gossip.

She was so used to her freedom, being commanded to stay by an absent husband felt like a challenge.

The guard returned with Jenny, who had a basket upon her arm and a smile in her eyes. "I'm glad I've caught ye," she said. "I've a few errands to run in the village."

The young watchman finally met Caitriona's eyes, and she gave him a brilliant smile. Already a bit pink, he flushed all the way to his hairline. Tipping his bonnet at Caitriona and Jenny as they passed, he let out a nervous breath. "Are ye sure —"

"Iomhar, we're more than capable of walkin' to the village ourselves," Jenny said. "But if ye're that concerned, ye can come too."

He shook his head and stepped back. "Nae, missus, we're short handed as it is till the Laird returns. I only...well, ye will bring her back?"

Caitriona almost rolled her eyes. "I'll bring *myself* back. And Jenny, too." It was a little jab, a subtle reminder that she was the lady of the house and a grown woman able to mind herself. Whether or not her husband thought of her as capable was yet to be seen, but she would not give him any reason to doubt her now.

For a few moments, the two women strolled in companionable silence. Wildflowers brushed against the tips of Caitriona's fingers, and in the distance, white spots dotted the field where a flock of sheep lingered. Closer, a fold of cows meandered through the grass, their shaggy coats ruffled by the breeze. They looked up at her and Jenny, rumbling greetings deep in their throats.

Caitriona smiled at the broad faces and dark eyes of the cows, and then glanced at her companion. "Thank ye for coming with me."

Jenny shrugged. "Och, 'tis nothin'. I needed to stretch my legs, and I've business in the village anyway."

"I just wanted...out," Caitriona admitted.

"Aye, I ken how it feels," Jenny responded. "Truth be told, I've been trapped in the kitchens for far too long. It does a body good to be out in the sun."

The women were silent for a moment, but it was comfortable. As if she and Jenny had known each other for years. Somehow, the cook put her at ease almost right away. With her plump, pink cheeks and the youthful twinkle in her eye, she had an ease about her. She looked younger than Caitriona's twenty-seven.

How long had she and Callum been married? How long had Jenny been at the castle? How had Aodhán come to be? Of course, Caitriona could not ask these things; she did not know Jenny well enough. But she ached for answers.

"I hope I dinnae speak out o' turn, milady, but...his Lairdship is doing the best he can." Jenny's voice was quiet, apologetic. "He isnae used to having a woman at his side. Especially nae one like yerself."

Caitriona almost laughed. Here she had been telling herself not to ask intrusive questions, and Jenny came out with that. "A woman like myself? How d'ye mean?"

Jenny's cheeks pinkened. "Ye're...more outspoken than he expected." There was a smile on her lips. "I ken he wanted a spinster; if I may say so, I dinnae think he expected a woman with a mind of her own. It's been ten years since his wife died, ye ken, and he was young and...well, the man was a right idiot then. Maybe he still is now."

Caitriona did laugh then. "Aye, I'll not disagree with ye there." Pausing, her eyes wandered over the hills, the village tucked into them, the cows grazing on highland grasses. "Was she...Iona, what was she like?"

Jenny adjusted her basket on her arm. "Oh, young. Reserved, like. I cannae really say. I was...well. I had my own trials to face then." A shadow crossed the woman's face, there and gone again before Caitriona could say a thing. "Anyway, I was just a scullery maid then, nae the cook yet."

She was directing the conversation away from Rhys's late wife. Caitriona let her. "Well I'm glad ye're the cook now; I dinnae think I've had better meals. Nae even at home."

Home. Irving Manor was not home any longer. A pang of sadness pricked at her heart.

Jenny did not seem to notice. Waving her off, the woman clicked her tongue and shook her head. "'Tis nothing special, milady."

"Cait," Caitriona said. The title felt far too formal. "Call me Cait."

The other woman flushed with pleasure. "Cait," she said. "It suits ye."

Another silence settled over them. They were nearly at the village now, and the thatched roofs shone gold in the sunlight. Life bustled around them, children chasing after each other with delighted squeals, dogs barking, friendly faces everywhere.

"Kenna tells me there isnae a Howdie in the village," Caitriona said, and Jenny looked her over with curiosity.

"Not at the moment, do ye…need one?" A spark of delight was in her eye.

Caitriona shook her head. "Och, no. I dinnae…we haven't…I'm sure ye've heard the gossip around the halls. It's true."

Jenny clucked her tongue as they walked toward the market. "An idiot, he is," she muttered.

The pungent smell of fish filled the air. It was the season for fishing, and the fishmongers had set up a small market, where their catches were on display. Everyone looked forward to these occasional market days; not only to expand their diet beyond the simple fare of rye breads, root vegetables, milk or cheese, and whatever berries were in season — but also because the Chapmen had come to town.

Traveling merchants, they offered goods such as jewelry, ribbons, cloth, household goods, books, and even medicine, and their arrival was looked forward to in every remote village of the highlands. Not only did they bring goods which were hard to acquire, they brought with them all the news of the world.

Caitriona did not have a chance to expand upon her desire to become Howdie, for Jenny was already chatting with one of the Chapmen, a jolly fellow who displayed a range of wares from trinkets to candlesticks to questionable tinctures. She haggled with him over kitchen wares with expert authority.

Everyone was out on this fine day, browsing wares and trading tidbits of gossip. Children darted about, chattering, nibbling upon sugar plums and basking in the sun. Happy to trail behind the cook and soak in the friendliness of the village, Caitriona followed Jenny around the market displays. Everyone seemed eager to meet the new mistress of Calhoun Castle.

It healed a little of the loneliness which had settled in her soul.

They had just finished arguing down the price of imported flour, which would be delivered to Calhoun Castle within a fortnight, when a heavily pregnant woman crossed Caitriona's path. Two small children trailed after her.

A strained smile crossed the young woman's face, and she went to curtsey but gasped, placing a hand on her belly. Caitriona reached out but the woman waved her off. "Thank ye, milady, but ye dinnae need to worry about me."

"Sorcha!" Jenny said, coming up beside Caitriona. "Ye've not had the child yet?"

Weariness was etched in the youthful face of the mother, her clear blue eyes red-rimmed and her lips pressed thin. "It's close, I can feel the tightening."

"Aye, I remember that feeling well." A moment of sadness passed through the cook's eyes, but it was gone as quickly as it had come. Jenny only had Aodhán. Had there been others?

"I suspect this bairn will arrive within the week if the signs are true." Sorcha shifted from side to side, hooking a hand beneath her belly to relieve some of the pressure.

Jenny watched Sorcha's children run around them in circles, smiling. "Send word to the castle the moment he comes, aye?"

Sorcha nodded. "I may send for ye when it's time, Blair isnae too keen to deliver the baby."

Caitriona's heart skipped a beat, and before she could think she blurted, "I could do it." After all, Kenna had confirmed there was no village Howdie.

Both women turned to her, surprise evident in their expressions.

Rushing on, Caitriona explained, "I was the village Howdie, before...everything. Back in Brae. I havenae obtained a license from the church yet, but our own midwife passed on over a year ago and it was just me after that."

Sorcha laughed, then winced and pressed a hand into her back. "Well, of all the things..." Despite her obvious discomfort, she was smiling. Jenny was bemused, but pleased.

"Forgive me if it's too much, but if ye dinnae mind...?" Caitriona twisted her fingers into her skirts, afraid she was intruding or saying too much. "His Lairdship doesnae seem to...I have nae much to do, ye ken, and I planned to be a midwife for the rest of my years. It's...it's what I love."

Gaze kind, Sorcha took Caitriona's free hand in her own. "I would be honored, milady," she said, grinning.

Caitriona let out a relieved breath. "Thank you. I cannae tell ye what this means to me."

"That's settled, then!" Jenny piped up. "I'm done here, milady — Cait," she corrected herself, the use of Caitriona's name seeming foreign on her tongue. "And his Lairdship has me workin' my fingers to the bone in the larders to prepare for his return, so if ye're ready...?"

Caitriona's stomach dropped at the mention of Rhys. What would he say to her inserting herself as the village Howdie? "Aye, I suppose so. I'll be needin' to visit Sorcha more, but...all in good time."

Leaving instructions to fetch her when the time came, she and Jenny walked back toward the castle. Rhys's return loomed heavy in Caitriona's mind, dread forming a pit in her middle. Would he protest? Would he, as her mother had, inform her her place was in the castle as a lady and not in some dim smoky hut delivering babies like a common wretch? Moira Irving had not liked to get her hands dirty.

But Caitriona shook it off. This was her chance to follow the calling of her heart.

She could not worry about what her new husband might think now.

TROUBLE IN THE HIGHLANDS

Rhys

Rhys did not know if he could take on any more goats.

Raising his eyebrows at Callum, who sat tallying the rents as the farmers and tenants brought their due one by one, he willed the man to refuse yet another bleating beast to add to their already prolific following of livestock. So far, aside from the three cows, twelve goats, and the unfortunate amount of fowl they'd accepted, they also had wagons full of anything but coin.

A fine weave of tartan in great lengths. Several bags of rye flour, and several more of oats. Many, many ribbons and other bits of precious fabrics. One or two finely made dirks. A finely made chair. One farmer had even tried to offer his young son to work the stables at Calhoun. Rhys had refused the trade on principle, but offered a position when the boy was older, if he should want it.

And now, they were being given another goat.

Callum took the poor beast and tied it to the back of the wagon with the rest, and waved the man on.

"'Twill be a noisy trip back home," Angus grumbled, glaring at the ducks, chickens, and three roosters making a racket in the back of the wagon. Behind them, the goats bleated, and a few sheep rumbled in confusion.

"Livestock will sustain us through any season," Rhys said, practicality always winning out when it came to the rents. Animals produced food. Food kept them alive. Besides, his own stock of coin was not small, and if he could relieve the stress of some of his tenants by accepting live trade in lieu of money, he would.

Whatever benefitted the entire clan suited him just fine. These people would need their precious coin to pay for household goods when the Chapmen came around; who was he to impede their survival?

So long as they were not offering him the last of their livestock, that was.

A few had tried. Rhys had turned them away. Told them to pay him next season. Had Callum tuck a coin or two subtly into the hands of those who looked the most weary. The widow, whose husband had been killed by a boar and for whom chickens and her dry goods were the only way her children survived. The lad who could have been no more than fourteen, bearing the burden of his younger siblings on his back, refusing to accept too much help even though both his parents had died.

To Rhys, a clan was not successful if the least of them were suffering.

And even though he had been fully in charge for seven years, the remnants of his father's greedy hand and his uncle's neglect rippled through the clan still. It would take years to right the wrongs of the previous Lairds, but he was trying.

"If that's it, we'll move on," he said to Callum, who was noting the last of the offerings in the books.

They were at the northernmost edges of Macnammon lands now, where the terrain was rougher and the clusters of cottages were fewer and further between. Mist clung to the highlands like a ghost, its cold fingers brushing against his cheeks and stealing warmth from his fingers. Though it was close to summer solstice, it felt like early spring still up here in the furthest reaches of the highlands.

Rhys was mounting his horse when she approached him. A young girl, still round-faced and pink-cheeked like a child, but her eyes spoke of things she was too young to know. The arisaid wrapped around her like a cloak was worn to holes in some places, and she met his gaze almost defiantly.

As if someone had told her to leave him alone, and she was here anyway. "Milord, there's talk ye've taken a wife, to appease your clan. Is this the only step ye'll take to protect us from Berach?"

She could not have been more than ten, but she spoke with the calm and clarity of someone twice her age.

Rhys studied her. At the periphery of his vision, Angus was clicking his tongue and grumbling, as usual. "Aye, I have taken a wife. But if more is required, I will do it."

The girl's wide gray eyes shone with tears, though she did not let them fall. "Then ye'll go after my sister."

"Yer father already spoke with me about this, young lass," Angus blustered. "'Tis nothin' we can do."

Rhys ignored his man. "Where is she?" he asked the girl.

She pointed toward the hills behind them, and Rhys saw the subtle signs of her fear then. Her finger shaking. Her lip trembling. Her breath releasing in a shaky gasp. "His men took her there. Tae the abandoned cottage just beyond the hill."

"And why did nobody tell me before?" Irritation settled in his chest as he turned to Angus, who was shaking his head.

"It has been weeks, Rhys," Angus said, arms crossed. "She's likely dead, or close to it. There's no telling if she'll even be there still."

"I heard her cry," the girl said, and her voice broke. "I heard her scream upon the night, only three days ago. She's still alive!"

Rhys turned his attention back to the young girl and scowled. "Why did none of your own go after her?"

Her chin lifted and she speared him with a scathing gaze. "Who among us is fit tae fight men such as Berach has? My brother went after her, and he didnae return." She gestured to the few clan members still milling about behind her, and Rhys looked at them. Really looked.

Farmers, exhausted from their work. Young boys, inexperienced in battle. Women holding their families together. And elders.

They were not warriors. They were not fighters. They were just trying to survive.

"We will go look for her," he said with finality.

Angus grumbled.

"Leave the wagons here, tie up the livestock. We'll be back by sundown. Take yer weapons, but do nae attack unless I say so." His orders were obeyed with a swift precision he had trained into his men over the years. But before they turned toward the hills, he looked at the girl again.

"What is your name?"

Tears slid down her cheeks now, but her gaze had not softened. Arms crossed, jaw steely, she had more fortitude than most of his warriors. "Morven, milord. And my sister's name is Lilleas."

He nodded. "How old is she?"

Morven swiped a hand across her cheeks. "Fourteen, sir."

"We'll bring her back, Morven," he said. "But ye must be prepared for nae more than a body to return."

It was a harsh thing to say, but the girl deserved to hear the truth. Her sister was likely dead by now, or had been moved with Berach's men to a new place, to be passed around and played with as they traveled. It sickened him to think of what might have happened to the girl. But he would not leave without trying.

※ ※ ※

It took half a day to reach the empty cottages.

They sat nestled against rocky outcroppings, golden thatched roofs dull and unkempt, no smoke rising from the centers to indicate anyone was there. The mist was heavier here, shrouding everything in a white cast that limited their vision and chilled them to the bone. The gray stone rose up around them, craggy and sharp, topped with highland grasses and heather.

There was very little color up here.

Dismounting, Rhys approached the first cottage and shoved at the door. It was stuck tight, the wood swollen in its frame. He grit his teeth and put his shoulder against it, heaving. After a few moments, it finally groaned and gave way, opening to a dark, smoky interior where no life was present.

The firepit in the center of the room had not been used in years; cobwebs clung to the rafters, and the sudden flap of wings confirmed a bird or two had made their nests in the roof. It smelled of mold and rotting hay. He exited the cottage, gratified to see his men pushing their way into the others.

There were seven in total, and one by one they inspected inside and looked around outside for any signs of Lilleas or Berach's men. Rhys was scowling at the telltale signs of hoofprints at the edge of the fifth cottage when Angus called for him.

The man stood in the door to the last hut, face grim. "She's here," Angus said as Rhys approached. "But 'tis nae pretty."

Rhys started to push in the door when Angus stopped him. "And ye may want to go slow. Quiet."

Nodding, Rhys made his way into the cottage, where the only light came from the open door and a small fire in the center. The flames were so low, the smoke dissipated before it reached the ceiling. A motionless lump was half-curled around the warmth. The chairs around her were scattered, some furniture knocked over. A half-eaten bannock lay beside her on the floor.

Anger fissured through Rhys, and he tamped it down. "Lilleas, I've come tae bring ye back tae yer family," he said, stepping quietly toward her. Not wishing to alarm her with his largeness, he pulled one of the chairs over, and sat for a moment.

The girl's hair was a matted mess, hanging limpid and filthy over her neck. She had no arisaid, and her stays hung loose over her shift, the laces tracing a path over the floor. A blanket was over her legs, gray and dirty.

"I cannae go home," she said, voice so quiet he could barely hear her.

"Aye, ye can," Rhys answered. "Ye are safe, now."

Even in the dim light, it was not hard to see the bruises. Rings of purple around her neck. Raw, chafing wounds on her wrists. Harsh marks on her arms, clearly left by rough hands. Rhys did not close his eyes against the violence so clearly written on her body; he did not deserve to escape what his hesitation had done.

His hesitation to call out his cousin, to go to war with Berach and end it once and for all. As he surveyed the girl before him, who was just burgeoning upon blossoming womanhood, but still so young, fury boiled within his chest. And shame. Shame he'd been ignoring the clear calls to war for the sake of his own comfort.

"I'm going tae pick ye up, now," he said, giving her time to absorb his words before he stood.

When he closed the distance between them and bent down, she flinched. Her fingers twitched, as if she was about to throw her hands up and protect herself. But she was too weak to do much more than take hold of Rhys's jacket and bury her face in his arm.

"Please," she whispered. "Please don't take me back. Just let me die here."

Up close, her lips were chapped and a trail of tears had made a clean line on her dirty cheeks. Her hair might have been blonde, were it not for the dirt caked into the matted curls, and he could see a resemblance to her sister Morven in the shape of her jawline and nose.

She was so young. Too young.

"Yer family has been looking for ye," he said, leaving the filthy blanket behind as he took her out of the cottage. Angus took one look at them and jerked a blanket off the back of his horse, where his pack had been rolled up neatly.

"Oh, no," she said on a sob. "Morven cannae ken what I've done."

Rhys frowned. "Ye've done nothing wrong, child."

"But I have," she wailed. "I let them. I let them do anythin', just so long as they didnae go back for her. I couldnae let them take Morven too. I shouldnae have wandered off, father told me to stay close. I shouldnae have gone looking for early blaeberries. I shouldnae have—"

"Ye did nothing wrong," Rhys cut her off. "Ye are not to blame." Fury was burning a hole in his chest, and though he was gentle with the girl as he handed her to Callum so he could mount his horse and take her again, he was ready to snap someone's neck.

Angus had mounted his own horse already, and approached them. "Well," he said wearily.

"If ye ever refuse tae help a child like this again, I will kill ye myself," Rhys snapped at him.

Angus had the decency to look ashamed. "They said she'd been gone for nigh on three weeks, I didnae think —"

"No, ye didnae think, did ye. Ye didnae think about how any child Berach threatens is a threat to us all. Ye didnae think about the fact 'tis the women who keep the clans alive, nae the men. Ye did nae think that tae ignore this is tae give Berach the permission tae do as he pleases." Scrubbing a hand over his face, he tucked the girl safely into the blanket around her, and anchored her on the saddle in front of him. "I am nae my father, nor my uncle."

Angus would not meet Rhys's gaze.

"Do not make this mistake again, Angus." Rhys worked hard to quell the simmering anger in his belly. "We will offer to take her and her family to Calhoun; she may need medicine and doctoring they cannae give her here."

When he urged his horse forward and out of the hills, his men followed without question.

THE ROAD TO DANGER
Caitriona

By the end of each day of Rhys's absence, Caitriona was further ensconced in her place at the castle. Spending her time somewhere between mild housekeeping duties Jenny brought her, embroidering with Kenna, visiting Sorcha and other women who were with child, or gathering herbs from the gardens to begin her library of infusions, balms, and tinctures.

At her request, Aileen and Jenny had taken it upon themselves to transform one of the lower rooms of the castle, lugging out dusty tapestries and unused furniture to clear the space. It became a waiting room of sorts, where her patients could come to her with their needs. While she was willing to wander the countryside visiting cottages, most preferred to come to her.

On one side of the room, behind a wooden partition, a comfortable chaise lounge was settled, its surface covered in blankets and pillows. Here she could examine the women as they came, ensuring their babies were well and their bodies suffered no ill during their pregnancies. On the other side of the privacy screen was a comfortable rug and a box of wooden toys and dolls with handmade dresses. Most of the women had children, and those children needed to be distracted.

On the other side of the room, close to a window, was her desk. Here, she was able to keep records, write lists of needs, and organize her things. Herbs hung from the low beams of the room, a shelf full of jars and tools filled the wall, and, finally, a small bed was behind a second partition. Just in case someone needed rest. Or, perhaps, a mother delivered her baby at the castle.

With a plethora of soft furnishings, comfortable chairs, and plush rugs set all around the room, it was a cozy space. It was *her* space.

When she was otherwise occupied, she was in the stables. Back home at Irving Manor, the stables had been her favorite space. With Moira's lack of motherly instinct, much of her childhood had been spent between the kitchens, the stables, and the fields. She was comfortable amongst the proud animals, the scent of hay and manure full of memories.

And, despite her decision to leave some things alone, Caitriona could not quite stifle her curiosity about the boy who frequented the stalls, a softer, more cheerful child-version of her husband. Jenny was fast becoming her friend, and it was natural to see Aodhán popping in and out, his smile always wide when he saw her.

Besides, there was a pregnant cat who had settled herself in one of the stalls, and Caitriona had plans to bring a kitten or two into the castle.

Aodhán was happy to introduce her to the animals. He had Callum's gift for the gab, regaling her with tales of the horses. Whom they liked most, what they begged for, and why they were named. Each had a name describing their manes or personalities, much to Caitriona's delight.

Eurwen was as fair and white as her name denoted; Sgàil her counterpart as black as night. Aifric was called such for her pleasing and friendly demeanor; Cathal, meaning battle, was a stallion with a somewhat challenging attitude. And so it went down the line until each horse was as familiar to her as if she had named them herself.

Eight days passed, then ten, then nearly two weeks. Most of the clan folded her into their everyday lives without preamble, and she learned tidbits here and there. Rhys had been married to Iona for two years, until her death. Tragically, his brother had died shortly thereafter, and the gossip had begun to stir. Though Rhys already had a reputation from his time abroad, the Battle of Sheriffmuir had piled more legend onto his history.

Leading his men into war in support of the Jacobites had hardened the Laird. Rhys had returned a fiercer man, his brow scarred and the darkness he'd held at bay shrouding him with rumors that nobody could untangle. Berach, meanwhile, had found his opportunity to cause dissent within the clan. When Rhys withdrew into himself after Sheriffmuir, the man had touted his own position, and Rhys's unstable actions in battle — his support of the Jacobites a sore spot in the Macnammon clan.

Several of the clan families left in support of Berach Macnammon, while others wavered on the edge of decision, making demands. Caitriona was not supposed to hear some of these stories. The ones of clan indecision. The moment it became apparent that she was listening, voices grew hushed. The subject changed. She was pushed out again.

Jenny, however, was quite open with her. The cook and her husband had been married for eight years, and experienced many miscarriages. Aodhán was their only living child. Jenny watched the boy as if he were the most precious thing in her world, and Caitriona supposed he was. Whether his parents were blood or not, there was no question about it: Aodhán was theirs in every sense.

Yet, despite the comfortable habits forming in her days, Caitriona was restless. So much was said behind closed doors, and she had her own suspicions on what the Laird was not telling her about their union. When he returned, she was determined to question him once more.

On the seventeenth day of Rhys's absence, Caitriona jumped at the opportunity to visit a pregnancy outside the village. Suffocated by the routine, the rain that had made its way into the highlands and not stopped, and the whispers that swirled when she grew near, she was eager to expand her wandering.

But Jenny and Kenna were busy, and the men who had been left behind grumbled from their warm spots by the fire, ale in hand and stories half-told.

Caitriona was not so sure she minded. For the last two weeks, she'd been tailed by someone at every turn; accompanied by Jenny, Kenna, Iomhar, or one of the others who had been informed she could not leave alone. And while she had gotten to know the clan well and did not mind company, she was becoming desperate to be alone.

Telling Kenna she was retiring to her rooms, she slipped away through a side hall and out to the stables.

The rain pattered lightly, chasing most of the guards into their alcoves. As Caitriona crossed the courtyard and slipped into the warm, dark, quiet of the stables, she prepared to be stopped. Eurwen whickered in recognition, nosing her shoulder and nudging her waist, demanding an apple or a carrot.

Caitriona had come empty-handed. "Sorry, girl, I've nothin' for ye today. Come on," she said, leading the horse out of her stable and glancing around.

The pregnant cat wove around her feet, purring and trilling little meows. No one was there but her. She decided not to bother with a saddle; she was familiar with riding bareback, and it would be but a short ride anyway. Someone was sure to catch her leaving. The quicker she left, the better chance she had of getting out unnoticed.

At the gates, she was met with resistance. Iohmar was on duty again, and eyed her with caution. "No escort, milady?"

Caitriona pulled her hood over her head and shook her head. "Surely I can visit Sorcha in the village without botherin' anyone. I ken my way well enough."

Iohmar shook his head. "The Laird's orders were —"

"I ken that, Iohmar. But surely one trip willnae do any harm. I'll be back before ye ken."

Eurwen tossed her mane, impatient to run, and Iohmar sighed. "If ye wait here, I'll fetch someone to go with ye."

With a smile, Caitriona settled her hands patiently on Eurwen's neck. "Go on, then."

As soon as the man was out of sight, she hopped off Eurwen and led the horse to the man-height door beside the massive gates. It took several minutes for the gate itself to rise up. The door, however, was *just* large enough to permit Caitriona and Eurwen to walk through single-file.

On the other side, she swung herself back onto the horse and grinned. "Go on, girl," she urged, pointing them in the direction of the village. The wind against her cheeks felt delicious and free. In a few moments, she was far enough from the castle that nobody could have caught up with her.

It had been weeks since she had been in charge of herself and fully alone. Between the clan's careful watch of her and her newfound busyness as the village Howdie, Caitriona had few moments in which to just be herself. Not the Lady of Calhoun Castle. Not the midwife inundated with more pregnancies and new wains to monitor than she had expected. Not Rhys's unwilling bride.

Just, Cait.

It felt wonderful.

Very few people were out in the mist, and she rode through the village unchallenged. Passing Sorcha and Blair's cottage, a niggle of guilt ate at her heart, but she shrugged it off. She would be back at the castle in an hour or two. The remorse of deception was a small price to pay for this brief taste of freedom.

She did not slow until she had made her way further into the rolling highlands of Macnammon lands, where the only eyes upon her were those of the cows huddled under whatever shelter they could find. Shaggy faces stared at her from beneath trees, beside rock faces, or at hedgerows and stone walls.

They did not mind the damp, and neither did she.

Breathing deep in the fresh air, she closed her eyes. Whether or not she was on Macnammon land any more, she did not care. She just wanted to wander. Though she had only been married less than a month, it felt like ages since she had rambled about the highlands, lost in her thoughts.

Rhys would be angry if he found out she'd run off, and she wondered how he would punish her. If he would rage at her, or if his disappointment would be silent. Would he fault those who were supposed to be with her at all times? Would Iohmar bear the brunt of his anger?

The icy blue eyes of her husband glared into her memories, but so did the feather-light touch of his lips. The heavy warmth of his arms. The attraction she could no longer deny. She wanted to know what he hid from the world; she wanted to return his anger strike for strike; she wanted to yell and fight for her way in his world.

The desire to know him, as a wife knew a husband, ran sharp and deep within her.

A flush rose in her cheeks. Rhys was a man of mystery, and she wanted to unravel him. Part of her was angry at him. For pushing her away. For refusing the confide, though they barely knew each other. For acting as though their marriage meant nothing.

The other part of her was drawn to the idea of more, and she was afraid her attraction to him would become irresistible. And if he did not let down his walls, she would be lost. Trapped in a place she did not want to leave, yet did not want to stay. With feelings that were not returned.

She took a deep breath and opened her eyes. Dwelling on these emotions was useless until he returned.

The rain had become a downpour, soaking through her cloak and hair, and Caitriona guided Eurwen to turn around. She had hoped for a longer ride, but she was cold and the rain did not look like it would let up. She'd at least had enough time to sort through the restlessness in her bones, and she had come further than she'd realized.

And she was not alone.

Startled by the appearance of a man twenty feet away on a large brown stallion, she urged Eurwen to trot, trying not to show her nerves. How long had he been staring at her? How long had she been unaware of the company, lost in her own thoughts beneath the clouds?

When she glanced back, the man followed, a small distance away but closing. He flashed her a smile and she was unsettled by the glint of his teeth. The grin did not reach his eyes. He looked more like a dog baring its fangs in warning than a man offering a reassuring gesture.

Fear settled into the pit of her belly.

Perhaps he is going home, she told herself. *Perhaps, like me, he is merely out for a ride through the rain.*

But the more she urged Eurwen on, the closer he came. The rain obscured all sound of his horse, and she could not stop her backward glances. His gaze was fixed upon her through the deluge. Tightening her knees around Eurwen, she nudged her again. The quicker she could get home, the quicker she would be warm, dry, and safe.

It was hard to breathe in the onslaught of the storm, panic wrapping itself around her throat and squeezing its greedy fingers. The man was no more than five feet behind her now, and the leer on his face was telling. Bulky beneath the cloak he wore, the man had a thick nose and a pudgy jaw obscured partially by a reddish beard.

He leered at her, and Caitriona knew she would be unable to fight him off if he caught her. But some part of her still argued that perhaps he was traveling the same road as she by chance.

As if he read her hesitation, he called out, "What's the new mistress of Calhoun doin' in a downpour like this? Are ye lost?" A glint of malice was in his eye.

Without answer, Caitriona dug her heels into Eurwen and urged the mare, "Go!"

The rain did not let up, but the pounding of hooves behind her was loud now. Caitriona's heart beat in time, threatening to explode from her chest as she clung to Eurwen. Rain slapped against her skin, and her sopping wet dress clung to her legs.

Home. She wanted home. She wanted Calhoun castle with its nooks and crannies tucked away around vast spaces, with the clan who opened up their days to her despite her husband's distance, with the cozy stables and the pregnant cat and her newfound study filled with herbs.

Had anyone realized where she had gone yet? Did Jenny worry after her? Was Iohmar sending someone after her?

The rain was too heavy to see the village, and Caitriona was lost in a haze of gray panic. Glancing back, her chest clenched. A large hand reached out for her arm. As if everything had slowed down, she stared at the fingers curling around her bicep, and then a deadweight pulled her from Eurwen's back and slammed her into the ground. Her head hit something hard as she landed.

Caitriona saw stars. A black haze washed over her vision, pain lancing through her head, her shoulders slapping against the mud. The rain pounded against her face, and all she could do was fight for breath. Gasping. Sputtering. Forcing her lungs to expand.

The large man had landed beside her with a grunt, but he was not moving. Dazed, Caitriona scrambled to her feet and whirled. He had let go of her when they fell. Ignoring the throbbing in her head, she hiked up her skirts and ran.

But she did not get far. A heavy figure tackled her to the ground, the man having recovered enough to lunge after her. The weight of him pinned her down, his hand groping her waist, her hips, her chest. His breath was hot against her neck, and her skin crawled.

"Ye *are* the new lady of Calhoun Castle, aye?" His voice was a low rasp in her ear as he scrabbled about her person, his fingers inching into her pockets and pulling out their contents. A kerchief. A few coins. A pretty rock she had picked up earlier that week and never placed anywhere.

Ignoring his question, she wriggled as much as she could to get an arm out from under his grip. It was useless. He yanked her up to her feet as he rose and repeated the question. "Answer me, wench! I ken the stories. I've heard of the Laird's new bride, a stable whore with red hair and curves meant for one thing."

Fury arced through her. "I am nothing of the sort, and ye will unhand me immediately."

The order was weak, given the wobbling of her chin with cold, but she stood tall and tried not to let her teeth chatter. She was the same height as her assailant, and it gave her courage. He might be large, but she was not afraid. Silently, she thanked her father for his support anytime she had asked for training to defend herself. To fight like his men fought.

The man leered, his hand snaking over her neck, yanking her arisaid free. "I've heard ye'll spread yer legs for any lad that asks."

Marriage or not, her reputation had somehow found her all the way out here. The rumors that held only a grain of truth could never be shaken. It was then that she began to understand why Rhys did not want to talk about his past. Anger simmered through her veins.

Taking a full breath, she focused her eyes on Eurwen where the mare had stopped a few feet away, and she jerked against the man's hold on her wrists. One of his large hands held both of her arms while the other was clumsy against her front.

Letting the air out through her nose, she squared her jaw and did the only thing she could: she dropped her head forward and then threw it hard into the face of her captor. Pain radiated from the contact point up into her forehead and her vision blurred for a moment. But it worked.

With a startled curse, the man let go of her to clutch at his face.

"Ye broke my nose, ye—"

Caitriona was running before he could finish his sentence. Reaching Eurwen was swift, but mounting her with mud caking her shoes and water weighing her skirts down was not an easy task. Desperation flowed through her veins, for her pursuer shouted obscenities at her from behind.

Barely latched onto her horse, Caitriona commanded, "Home!"

To her infinite relief, the mare did just that. With her mistress clinging to her mane, Eurwen galloped toward Calhoun Castle, and Caitriona did not look back to see if her attacker followed.

Every muscle in her body was tense as they passed the fields, splattered mud through the village, and traversed the stone-paved road up to the castle. Had he followed her? She was loath to check. A headache throbbed up her neck and temples, the chill of her hair and dress making it impossible to keep the shudders from wracking her body.

Whether the man followed or not no longer mattered; she was pounding toward Calhoun castle and the gates were open, and then she was safe.

Eurwen slowed as she brought them home, and Caitriona dared to look behind them. Relief combed its calming hands through her when no-one was there. The man, whomever he was, had not dared to come this far.

But then a deep, familiar voice cut through the air, and trepidation struck her anew. "What in the bowels of hell are ye doing?"

Caitriona turned and met eyes as cold as the rain itself. Rhys had returned. And, if possible, he looked angrier than she had ever seen him.

SECRETS BROUGHT TO LIGHT
Rhys

Guilt was written all over his wife's face as she sat atop her horse in the driving rain, cheek purpling, shuddering with cold.

Rhys wanted to gather her into his arms and shield her from the downpour. He also wanted to rage at her for putting herself in whatever danger she'd just run from — and it was obvious she had been running. Sitting there clinging to Eurwen's mane with her lips going blue, Caitriona's eyes had flashed with genuine fear when she'd come through the gates.

But she straightened her shoulders now and met his gaze primly. "I...went for a ride," she said, her answer shaking with her body.

His men were making quick work of stabling their horses and dispersing the rents, lugging venison and wild boar to the butcher block from their hunting efforts. In the end, they had brought home five cows, seventeen goats, and so many different kinds of fowl he did not want to count. They had also brought the injured girl, Lilleas, her sister Morven, and a few extra chickens from their father.

The latter had stayed behind, wishing them a better life. He was an old man, and did not look like he would live much longer. Shame had been etched into every crevice of his brow when Rhys had returned to the village with his daughter, who had sobbed into her father's arms so brokenly even Angus shed a few tears.

When her tales had been told, her tears dried and the filth washed from her by the caring hands of the women in her village, she had told Rhys resolutely she would like to come with him. And her sister. There was not much for them in the dying little huddle of cottages now. And, he suspected, she was afraid.

The girls would be settled into the castle for now.

The bustle of the courtyard was dying down, though, and the moment Caitriona had burst onto the scene, his attention had narrowed to her. Nothing else existed but his wife, shivering atop Eurwen, trying so very hard to keep her chin from wobbling.

Reaching out a hand, he ran his palm over Eurwen, checking the mare for injuries. "Were ye alone?"

Caitriona sank her teeth into her lip, and nodded. It was a small movement, a peek behind the brave front she put on, and he scowled. The blasted woman. If this was more of Berach's doing, he would leave tonight. Put an end to the man's life once and for all. First Graham Macnammon's daughter. Then Lilleas. If Berach's men had harmed Caitriona...

No man touched his woman and lived to tell the tale.

"I told Jenny ye were nae to leave without —" he started, but Caitriona cut him off.

"I prefer to be informed of yer whereabouts and requests in person," she said. Her tone was lofty.

Rhys stood at her knee and peered up at her, frustration coiling through him. "I didnae think ye'd take kindly to my barging in before dawn to inform ye of my whereabouts. Especially given our...situation."

What had happened to her? There was a welt on her cheek, and the freckled skin below her eye was beginning to bruise. Her mass of wet hair was a tangle of curls and grass, and her dress was muddy all over. The simmering anger which had remained with him throughout the rest of his travels began to grow.

But impulsive attacks would do nothing. He would have to come up with a plan.

"Regardless," she said, shoulders regal despite the rain and her thoroughly-soaked appearance. "I dinnae want to be ordered about by the lad at the gates."

"Ordered about?" He barked a laugh, but it was bitter around the edges. He should have taken more precautions. He should have left Callum or Angus behind to protect her. Any manner of thing could have happened, and he had not done enough to keep her safe. "None of my clan would ever order ye about. I, however, have no qualms ordering ye to get down from that poor horse so we can all escape the rain for a warm fire and a good meal."

He stood back, allowing her space to dismount.

Caitriona hesitated, studying him with wary eyes. The woman looked exhausted. He would have hauled her off the horse himself, except he did not think it would help matters much. They had parted on uncertain terms. Her, furious at his cold treatment and many secrets. Him, wanting her more than was safe for his sanity.

When she slid from the horse, he told himself not to touch her.

But then her legs buckled beneath her.

In less time than it took her to protest, he was gathering her into his chest, half-supporting her weight, studying her carefully. Needing to get them out of this blasted rain.

Panic lanced through him. There was blood on her skin, trailing down her neck from somewhere beneath her hair. "Ye're bleeding," he said, voice coming out harsher than he had intended.

Dazed, Caitriona put a hand up to the back of her head and brought her fingers away. Rain mingled with the blood on her fingertips. "Oh," she whispered.

There was no patience left in Rhys's veins. Tucking his arm beneath her legs, he swung her up and into his arms, alarmed by the chill emanating from her body where it pressed against him. He was barking orders as he strode toward the castle, snapping demands at everyone on his way through the foyer.

All of the fight had gone out of her when he had taken control. Any other time, he might have reveled in the feel of her, the valleys and hills of her tempting his hands to action. But right now, her cheek drifted toward his shoulder and her eyes began to unfocus, and the fiery determination he was just getting used to was gone.

Fear settled into his gut. Old memories surfaced, of another woman settled cold and blue-tinged in his arms, and he shook them away. That was then. This was now. Now, he held a chilly but very much breathing Caitriona, and he would not lose her.

Clutching her to his chest, he could not traverse the halls fast enough, taking the steps two at a time. Her skirts dragged against his legs, sodden and weighted, and she pressed her face into the crook of his neck, seeking warmth. She smelled of rain and earth and something faint and herbaceous. Her lashes fluttered against his skin.

They reached her rooms while several maids brought a large tub in and set it to one side of the fireplace. Thankfully, a fire had been laid. Rhys deposited Caitriona on one of the overstuffed chairs and knelt before her.

She was more conscious than he had expected, her eyes following his movements with a sort of dazed alertness. But her entire body shuddered, hands trembling as she clenched her skirts, breath wavering. Without hesitation, he pulled her shoes off. She jumped. Sitting forward, she hid her stockinged feet beneath her skirts with a gasp.

"We have to get these wet clothes off, ye'll be sick." He did not wait for her answer, but tugged her from the chair and gestured to her stays.

Caitriona touched the bare skin at her decolletage and he was glad to see a pink flush make its way up her neck. "Ye're just as wet as I!" she protested, but it was weak.

They both knew it. He was damp about the collar and his hair dripped, but beneath his woolen greatcoat he was dry. She was dripping puddles upon the floor, unable to stop the shaking that overtook her.

He ignored her words and began to unlace the ribbons of her shift, trying not to touch her more than was necessary. Right now, he needed to get her warm. He needed the color to come back into her cheeks and her lips. He did *not* need to be distracted by the way her skin freckled lightly around her collarbones.

"I can do it myself," she said, shooing his hands away.

Rhys stepped back and removed his coat as he watched her, spreading it over one of the chairs to dry. She fumbled with the laces, her fingers clumsy and, no doubt, too cold to function properly. But he waited.

Because, to his relief, her lips were no longer blue. The blood was concerning, but she had regained her ability to glare at him, even as she struggled with her clothes.

With a huff, she dropped her arms, one hand resting on the chair to support herself. Her shoulders sagged and she swayed a little.

"M-mmy hands are too cold," she said, stumbling over her words just enough to worry him.

He set to work, undoing the stays and sliding them from her damp arms. The fabric of her chemise was wet as well, and clung to her. Saying nothing, he made quick work of her garments, untying her skirt, removing the petticoat and pockets, and tossing her pannier to the side. All that remained were her chemise and stockings.

Maids worked around them, picking up the wet things and setting out a clean shift, putting extra blankets on the bed, and bringing food.

Clearing his throat, Rhys stopped. It was the first time this woman had *not* looked him directly in the eye. "Sit," he said.

Her lips parted, gooseflesh rolling over her skin, and she sat without argument.

Rhys lowered himself to one knee, put a hand lightly around her calf, and waited for her to meet his gaze. Behind him, the door opened and maids began to bring in buckets of steaming water. "Ye're wet to the bone, and ye're bleedin'," he said.

Caitriona let out her breath in a long shudder, and stared at his shoulder.

"Caitriona," he prompted her. "*Lasair-chride.*"

The muscles of her throat worked, and the blood on her skin stood stark against the pale expanse. A desire to wrap her up in his arms and never let go overtook him, so strong that it shocked him. This woman had come into his life like the blazing sun: so bright she was impossible to ignore. The ice around his heart had begun to melt the moment she had lifted a defiant chin to challenge him.

His thumb brushed the ties around her stockings, which hung by her knees. "We need to get ye into that tub. May I...?" Rhys tried to clear his throat, tried to keep his eyes above her neck. But his breath stuck somewhere around his collarbone, and his gaze...

The skin just above where the lace of her chemise ended grew pink. He wanted to graze his fingertips over the freckles there. He wanted to feel the heartbeat pounding in her neck. He wanted to kiss her again.

"I can manage," she said, the flush racing up her skin to her cheeks as he watched.

Rhys gave her space. Rising, he sat in the chair opposite her and settled his chin on a palm. "What happened?"

"I went for a ride and Eurwen spooked." She untied her stockings and rolled the first one off with deliberation, still avoiding his direct gaze.

"D'ye make it a habit of riding bareback?" The intimacy of their current situation was not lost on him, but he tried not to allow his baser thoughts to influence his eyes. She was injured, cold, and shaken. Now was not the time.

Caitriona nodded, working off her second stocking. Not looking at him. Staring above his head, in fact. "I rode bareback often. I prefer it to sidesaddle."

The maids had finished filling the tub, and left with curious stares at their Laird and Lady. A large fur had been laid before the base of the tub, soap and towels laid out alongside clean clothes for both of them.

"I see," Rhys said, suspicious of her avoidance. "And ye were quite adept?"

"Aye, I was — am." She dropped the second stocking on the floor, cheeks bright and eyes averted.

She had fallen off her horse while galloping bareback, but professed to be accomplished. "So adept that I watched ye burst through the gates half-atop Eurwen in the pounding rain, and even that could not unseat ye. And yet...ye fell when she startled?"

Fidgeting with the thin fabric of her chemise, she met his gaze, jaw set, eyes defensive. "Aye, I did. What of it?"

She could have been killed. Rhys shot out of his chair and paced the room, fighting for control. This precocious, defiant, bright-as-the-sun woman had been attacked, and she would not admit it. She would not ask for help, would not accept his strength. It chafed at him. Crossing his arms, he let out a long breath and settled his gaze upon her.

"What happened?" He tried to gentle his tone. She did not trust him. And why should she? From the moment they had met, she had been subjected to what he wanted. What he demanded. What he set forth as law. Not once had he tried to offer what *she* wanted.

"Like I said, I fell." A shudder ran through her, and she curled her arms around herself, as if protecting herself from whomever had left the infuriating bruise on her arm.

His mind flashed back to finding Lilleas in the dark cottage, bruises scattered over her body. Bruises on her arms which mirrored the one on Caitriona's skin. Beneath the instant anger, a helpless fear was banding around his lungs. He needed to make sure his wife was okay.

His wife. The words settled deeply, gripping him with the realization he could not control how he felt around her. *For* her. He was beginning to care more than was wise, and there was nothing he could do to stop himself.

Closing the distance between them, he knelt and cupped her cheek. Trying to be gentle. Trying to instill a sense of trust, which he had been neglecting. "If someone hurt ye, I need to know." Unable to stop himself, he smoothed over her jawline with his thumb. "'Tis my job to protect ye, and if I have failed to do that so soon into our marriage I —" He stopped, throat tightening and stealing away his ability to finish the sentence.

Caitriona seemed to sense his panic, for she leaned into his palm, just a little. "I am okay now, Rhys."

Her small movement, relaxing into his touch, calmed him. "Secrets will do ye no good," he said. But the chill of her skin soaked through his distraction. "Ye're cold as ice. Ye must get into the bath immediately."

When she stood, it was on unstable feet, and he reached out to her instinctively, then paused. "Can I help ye?"

His hands hovered between them, aching to touch her. Decency kept him from moving, though she was wet and miserable and cold, waiting for her response. And it was a small thing, but she nodded, and there was a crack in the dam of emotions welling up inside him.

When he took her by the arm, sliding his hand around her waist to steady her, time stood still upon the gasp bursting from her lips. "What is it? What's wrong?"

She stared up at him with those luminous eyes, curls stuck to her soft skin and round jawline, and shook her head. "Nothing, it's just…"

The moment her knees gave out, he burst into action. Without a thought, he swung her up into his arms, and alarm swept through him. Eyes fluttering closed, she raised delicate fingers to the blood on her neck, the blood seeping into her hair and darkening her scalp behind her ear.

"God help ye," he said, and then shouted for Aileen. For anyone. Footsteps scuffled outside their door and one of the scullery maids stumbled in, gaze darting about with curiosity. "Fetch Fianna."

The castle healer should have been his first thought. Berating himself for his lack of foresight, he lowered Caitriona into the bath, not caring when his sleeves dunked into the water. With a gentle hand, he pushed her hair away from the wound and scowled at it. There was a lump there, oozing and no doubt very sore.

"I must have hit my head when I...fell off Eurwen," she said. She did not stop him when he took a cloth and began to wipe her skin, washing away dirt and blood and grass. Her hair was growing heavy in the water, and he folded a sort of pillow out of a linen cloth to lay on the back of the tub, urging her to lean back onto it.

Pouring water over her long locks filled the silence in the room, interrupted only by the popping of the fire. Caitriona had her eyes closed, and if not for the way she worried her lip between her teeth, he might have thought she was asleep.

"I am sorry," he said, working the grime from her hair as gently as he could.

She peered at him. "Why?"

"I am sorry that ye dinnae trust me enough to tell me what happened." It chafed at him, knowing someone had attacked her, knowing she was afraid to say who, or why. "I have nae been a good husband, and I dinnae blame ye for being angry with me."

When her lips parted, he shook his head, moving from her now-clean hair to her arms. "Dinnae speak of it more now," he hushed her. "Tomorrow, we will...discuss things."

The fabric of her chemise floated in the water, concealing most of her body. But her arms, with their gentle strength beneath soft flesh, and the dimples at the elbows, lay bare and streaked with mud on the edge of the tub.

"I am sorry, too," she said, her voice soft. Rhys met her gaze, and desperation flowed through him. "I didnae mean to cause anyone trouble, I just —" Her eyelids fluttered closed and she leaned her head back again. "I dinnae have a good history with...men."

The words left her in a quiet hush, and he realized she had lost consciousness.

Fianna entered then and set to work. After a few moments of hovering, Rhys was shooed away as more maids entered carrying cloths and herbs and all manner of things he did not recognize. Caitriona stirred as they circled her, tending her with gentleness and care.

She was in good hands.

Rhys left, his stomach growling with a reminder that he had yet to rest himself. But he could not put the conversation with his wife out of his mind.

There was more to speak on than just her attack. There were reasons why Berach would be wanting to get to her; reasons why this marriage was endangered even though it had only just begun. He had been holding back from her, hoping to solve the problem of his cousin's dissent without starting a clan war.

But it was clear this plan was not working. Not just because they'd attacked his wife; but because they'd attacked the edges of the clan. Lilias. Ewan's barn. Alasdair's sheep. All of it pointing toward the inevitability of a war he did not want.

And despite his marriage to this woman, there were still people amongst his own who grumbled. He'd only done half the job; only fulfilled half the promise. Could he then demand they go to war for him, when he had not even done what they'd asked of him?

He would have to tell his wife of the other condition to their marriage. The heir the clan demanded from him, a successor for the Macnammon line. It was not something he had broached with Caitriona, and regret filled him. He should have been honest with her from the beginning.

He could only hope that she would listen, and not hate him for it.

A Thread of Hope
Caitriona

The distinct and penetrating sound of a snore brought Caitriona to consciousness, alongside an unfamiliar weight settled over her hand. Rubbing her temples gingerly, she glanced toward the source of the noise.

One of the large chairs had been dragged from the fireplace to beside the bed, and the broad frame of her husband occupied it, legs stretched out before him as he slept. His arm was flung out across the small gap between the bed and the chair, and his fingers wrapped around her own. The sight warmed her.

She had never seen him so unguarded and unaware. His dark curls were untidy around his face, framing an unshaven jaw and inky lashes hiding the intensity of his eyes. Something had changed last night. A nervous, eager tightness spread through her belly remembering his gentle ministrations. His apology. His respect.

Caitriona stared at their hands entwined on the edge of the bed, unsure of herself for the first time. These past few weeks, she had been so determined to cling to her anger. To fight the unwelcome change of an arranged marriage, despite the loyalty to her parents and clan that had her wed in the first place. She wanted to be angry that he had stolen away her freedom. Her future. Her life.

But then the clan had enveloped her. Welcomed her as not just their Lady, but also as their Howdie. Twined their way into her heart with their joys and sorrows, their eagerness to please her, their warmth and familiarity. She realised over the last few weeks that she had come to love this place and these people.

And Rhys had admitted himself he, too, had given up a life he was accustomed to. Perhaps she should have a little more grace. After all, the man had lost a wife and child, and was now forced to change his life yet again for a marriage he had not anticipated. From the sound of it, Rhys was happy as a bachelor.

They were not so different.

With slow, deliberate movements, she shifted in bed, trying to scoot upward and backward toward the headboard. The movement made her stomach lurch and a lancing pain shot through her head. She bit her lip and groaned.

Before she could even register his wakefulness, Rhys was looming over her, his movements almost too quick for her eyes to track. In fact, now that she was upright everything seemed too much for her eyes. The sunlight streaming through the windows, the concerned actions of her husband, the feel of her own eyelids scraping against the grit of sleep. Everything sent a sharp pain through her head.

"How do ye feel?" Rhys's deep voice was still raspy from sleep.

Caitriona ignored the urge to brush his hair from his forehead and instead leaned against the pillows he adjusted behind her. "Like I've drunk too much ale and been in a brawl. Which might have been more fun than…falling from a wet horse."

The furrow in her husband's brow sent a flush of embarrassment through her. What if he didn't believe her? The man who had attacked her had known the rumors around her. And, if she was honest with herself, she was ashamed. Ashamed she could not protect herself.

Ashamed she had been caught unaware, ashamed she needed protecting.

She, who had worked so hard to be self-sufficient, who tried to ensure she did not have to ask for help, who gave up the idea of marriage and partnership and love...needed someone.

Needed *him*.

"I'd...like to sit by the fire," she said. Throwing back the blankets, she scooted to the edge of the bed and settled her feet into the soft fur on the floor. She was in a clean shift. Arms bare. Toes naked against the floor. She had no memory of changing.

Rhys swung her up into his arms without hesitation, as if she weighed nothing, and she gasped. It was a singular pleasure to be hefted into this man's arms, more so because Caitriona was used to being of a certain size. Most men would have struggled under her weight, and though she loved her body and all its curves, she could not deny feeling like too much some days.

Cradling her to his chest, he walked toward the fireplace. "To the chair with ye," he rasped.

So he felt it too. The heat that raged through her at every point of contact. The burning desire which had been set free in his study two weeks ago, and could not be contained. She had thought his absence might dampen these feelings, but it seemed they had only grown more intense.

Settling her into the armchair, Rhys laid a blanket over her lap and dragged the other chair close. He was, as always, dressed in dark trews and a black leine, and with his hair down he looked quite wild. When his gaze dragged over her, anger simmered there.

With one large finger, he traced the unmistakable shape of a hand that bruised her pale bicep, the imprint telling all. "Ye are no longer allowed to leave the castle."

"Not at all?" It was Caitriona's nature to bristle at an order. Though she understood, if she could not leave, she could not check on Sorcha, nor Mary, nor any of the other women relying on her to deliver their babies.

Rhys turned her face so the wound on her head was visible to him. "What happened?" Again, he demanded answers she was afraid to give.

She chewed on her lip. If she told him, would he yank away the purpose she had found here? The thread of hope that had begun to grow within her? With a little shake of her head, she stared at her fingers.

A fraught silence fell between them. Rhys traced the line of her jaw, the scrape on her neck. His hand fell to hers, and he picked it up, drawing over each of her fingers before tucking her palm against his.

"We brought two girls back with us," he said suddenly. "Lilleas and Morven. They are from a village up north, the furthest from Calhoun, tucked away in the hills. Not many go up there, and they keep to themselves. They are farmers, mostly, nae fit for fighting."

Caitriona looked up at him. His gaze was distant, sad.

Clearing his throat, he continued. "We were about tae leave after collecting the rents when Morven stopped us. She's a wee lass, nae much older than Aodhán. Her sister, Lilleas, had been taken by Berach's men. Taken and...God only knows what they did tae her."

Caitriona had never seen such a desolate grief in a man's eyes. Raw fury mixed with horror, and though no tears dampened his gaze, Rhys's sorrow was clear and sharp. An ache bloomed in her chest as she listened.

"Angus turned Morven away, before she came tae me. It had been so long, and her father hadnae been able to go after Lilleas, and he was sure she'd be dead." He clenched his teeth, jaw flexing, swallowing hard. "We found her in an abandoned cottage in the hills, filthy, bruised, and begging us nae to take her back. Tae let her die there."

Caitriona did not want to breathe, her heart squeezing so tight it might shatter.

He scrubbed his face with his free hand, and took a deep breath. "She is only fourteen." It was then a single tear traced from the corner of his eye. "Only fourteen, Caitriona. She could be my child."

Caitriona's vision blurred, her own tears flowing now. But beneath the sorrow was fury. Fury at the men who had attacked and abused a child; fury at herself for not fighting back harder; fury at those who should have protected her, and didn't.

He reached over and wiped the tears from her cheeks. "I cannae tolerate lies that directly hinder yer own safety," he said then. "I willnae let anyone else be harmed due to my own neglect. And if I cannae trust ye to tell me when things happen, then I cannae let ye leave."

She nodded then, knowing now her secret-keeping was only doing them both harm. "I was pulled from Eurwen," she admitted. "While I was out riding for a bit of fresh air, I came upon a man. He followed me and I ran, and he…knocked me off the horse."

Though his touch on her skin was gentle, Rhy's jaw turned to steel and his gaze was hard. "Who was he?"

Caitriona shook her head. "I dinnae ken. I've nae seen him before." She could not meet her husband's eyes any longer. This entire situation reminded her too much of Niall. The way he'd taken advantage of her, and left her to ruin. How everyone had believed him, charming and good-natured as he was. How those she once called friends had cut her off in favor of Niall's story.

"He followed ye to the village," Rhys said. It was not a question.

"I didnae see…whether he did or not," she said, digging her nails into her palm.

"Aye, but Callum did," Rhys told her.

Caitriona met his unreadable gaze and fought the urge to shrink away. He had known the entire time. At no point had her half-truths been believable. He knew, and he had another account confirming the truth. A flush of mortification rushed into her cheeks. How could she have been so foolish?

"Did he...recognize him?"

Rhys shook his head. "Nae, he was too far away to identify."

Relief flooded her, but then Rhys continued, "There are nae many expectations I have of this marriage, *lasair-chride,* but honesty is one of them. I will not allow ye to leave if ye cannae be forthright with me. Secrets cannae be kept between us. "

A laugh escaped her, and with some of the fondness she realised was growing in her heart, she replied, "Aye well then, get confessing Rhys Macnammon, ye're the one who keeps his past in a shroud."

Rhys raised an eyebrow. Amusement was in his gaze, but still he protested, "My past is...private."

This chafed at her. What did he think she would do, if she knew the truth of the rumors that surrounded him? Caitriona rubbed her forehead, a headache beginning to form. "Private? As ye said, secrets will do us no good. I was just attacked by a man who not only kent who I was, but also where I lived and that I was married to ye and..." She stopped when Rhys grunted.

"He knew ye?"

"Aye, he called me by name. I swear I didnae ken the man, but he knew me. And he knew ye."

Anger flared out from her husband's gaze. "Why did ye not tell me immediately?"

Frustration welled up within her. How could he go from sharing raw, deep emotions in one moment to being blockheaded and obtuse in the next? "Why should I? We've spent less than a week together, despite nearly a month that has passed since our wedding. Ye barely speak to me. Ye dinnae share my rooms as most husbands would, ye havenae acknowledged me beyond what seems to be duty, until now. I didnae even ken if ye'd care I was hurt. I didnae ken if ye'd even take my side in the matter."

"Why would I not?" He studied her, impassive now.

"Ye told me yerself ye didnae want to be married. Ye didnae want a wife. Ye didnae plan to honor this marriage as anything but a formality. Why should I trust ye, if ye will not do the same and tell me...*anything* of yer past?"

To her utter confusion, he took her hand and muttered, "Ye dinnae ken anythin' about me."

"Of course not!" she burst out. "Ye refuse to talk to me. Ye left to gather rents and hunt without even a warning and left me behind. Wondering about the rumors. Wondering what my place is here. Wondering about...the boy. If I should be jealous, whether there are other women..."

"There are no other women." He was quick to cut her off. Threading his fingers through hers. Sending waves of heat up her arm at the contact, heat that chased away her frustration.

Which, of course, was irritating in itself. How was she to get any answers when the man was staring at her as though he wanted to devour her?

"What do you want with me?" she said. It was not what she had meant to ask, but the question tumbled out anyway. One languid look from him was enough to send every argument flying from her mind.

He leaned into her space, his knees brushing hers through the blanket, and his thumb grazed the circle of her ring idly. "My cousin, Berach, has stirred up some doubt in the clan. They didnae like that I never remarried. Never had a family of my own. That I wanted to keep to myself. The Macnammons prize their bloodline, and...as Laird, I am expected to...continue that line."

Her suspicions had been correct. "Ye need an heir."

When she said it, he swayed closer still, as if pulled by an invisible string. "Aye," he said.

Caitriona was not quite processing. It was as if there was a lag between the deep growl of his words and the questions she had in return. "But ye dinnae want to — with me..."

"Caitriona," he said patiently, slowly. "There has never been a moment I didnae want ye." If a storm could be housed within a man's gaze, then all of the sea was raging in Rhys's eyes.

The words blazed through her. Swirled in her mind. Toyed with her heart. Dizzy with his nearness, she could only cling to the anchor that was his hand around hers, and whisper, "Then why push me away?"

"I cannae suffer such loss again," he said, quiet, his words nearly lost in the raging of her heart in her ears.

"Ye willnae lose me," she said, leaning into the hand he placed on her cheek. The way he caressed her, fingers claiming her skin, tracing her freckles, had her ready to give him everything.

Thumb tracing the edge of her lips, he studied every inch of her face, and her skin flamed beneath his palm. Her entire body was on fire. Was this what a marriage could bring? This intense need to be with him, to wrap herself into his arms and never let go? The dizzy thrill of it all pushed her off balance and she swayed.

He scowled and leaned away from her. Then touched her forehead with the back of his hand. Turned her face one way, then the next. When he touched the side of her head, blood came away on his fingertips and he made a disapproving sound.

"Ye need rest, wife," he said, and gentled his tone. "Ye're hot as a flame, and I'm worrit about the wound on yer head. I'll send Fianna up with a tonic."

When he stood, his gaze flitting from the unmade bed to the clothes on the floor to her face, she was swirling with questions he had not answered. Did he, or did he not, intend to create an heir with her? The thought sent a flush through her. The last three weeks of wondering had come to a head, and she was not sure where they stood now.

But he offered no answers as he strode to the door, bowed in her direction, and said "Get some rest."

He left the room, and she stared at the closed door, more confused than ever.

Action Rewards the Bold

Caitriona

Rhys had not returned to her rooms, and the next morning, feeling far better and strengthened by broth and the care of Fianna and Jenny, Caitriona decided to take things into her own hands. If her husband was afraid that she would not be protected alone, she would show him what she could do.

But first, she needed to check on Sorcha. And perhaps she would seek out the girls Rhys had spoken of — Lilleas and Morven — to ensure they were settled comfortably. To see if they might need her for anything.

Pacing toward the trunk at the foot of her bed, Caitriona pulled out her trews and leine, smiling. Rhys had stared at her plenty the last time she'd worn the garments. A gleeful part of her wanted to spark that same reaction again, though she donned the outfit for practical purposes. Plaiting her hair and tying it off with a ribbon, she inspected her face in the vanity mirror.

Bruises on her right cheek were purple and blue, and the wound on the back of her head was hidden in her hair. Her complexion was paler than normal, but the color in her cheeks was high.

Despite the attack, she was feeling energized. A full day in bed and a good night's sleep had done wonders.

Pulling on her boots, she exited the room and headed for the kitchens. Aileen was coming up the hallway toward her. "Good morning, Aileen. Where is his Lairdship?"

Aileen grinned at her. "He's in the back field. The men are having a bit of archery and combat today, milady." Nodding her chin at Caitriona's legs, Aileen said, "It looks like ye're about to join them."

Caitriona smiled back. "I've business to attend in the village but then...who knows?"

She continued on, raring to expend some of the energy filling her limbs. After a quick bite to eat, checking on Lilleas and Morven, and her visit to Sorcha, she would join her husband in the fields. Rhys likely expected she would be lying abed for a week, but she could not be still. *Would* not be still.

Caitriona had never been one to stay down when she was kicked.

Besides, sore though she was, she was not an invalid. She passed into the kitchens and found Jenny, who offered her porridge and honey. Kenna was there as well, and two young girls sat at the kitchen tables, one golden-haired and wan, the other gray-eyed and vivacious. These, then, were the girls Rhys had brought back with him from the hills.

"Lilleas, Morven," Jenny said by way of introduction. "This is Lady Caitriona Irving of Calhoun Castle."

Both of them hopped off their stools and dropped into curtseys and "Miladys," but Caitriona waved them off. The younger one, Morven, studied her with great fascination, taking in the tartan trews, bright red hair, and sheer height of her with a wide gaze.

Lilleas, on the other hand, barely met her eyes. Her cheeks were hollowed, and she had the look of someone who was struggling to find hope. Kenna sat beside her, and her gaze was worried when she met Caitriona's eyes. Lilleas and Morven were about the same age as Kenna's daughters.

"Dinnae fash with formal greeting, please. Ye are welcome as our kin here." Caitriona crossed to the table and took the proffered bowl of porridge from Jenny. "How do ye find Calhoun?"

Morven grinned. "Och, 'tis grand! Did ye ken there are *fifteen* highland ponies in the stables? Of course ye did, ye're the lady of the house. Fifteen! And they've all got names! 'Tis a wonder, we never had a pony at all."

Caitriona smiled and leaned a little closer to the girl. "Aye, I did ken that. And I ken all of their names, too."

"Oh, 'tis lovely," Morven breathed. "My father said we was goin' tae get a pony for my tenth birthday, but then me ma died, and…well." A tinge of sadness crossed her face.

"I am very sorry for yer loss, Morven," Caitriona said softly. "It must be very hard."

The girl's lip trembled, but she did not cry. "She wasnae well, ma'am. Nae for a long time. We all kent she was gonna die."

A sob wrenched out of Lilleas, and Caitriona began to stand but Kenna reached for her first. Wrapping an arm around her shoulder, the woman soothed, "there now," and pulled the girl's head to rest on her bosom.

For a moment, a solemn silence filled the room, save for the crackling of the fire and the bubbling of stew. Morven scrubbed a tear away from her cheek, and went to her sister, cuddling up to her other side so she was surrounded by arms and comfort. Lilleas, wracked with grief, buried her face into Kenna's chest, as if she wanted to disappear altogether.

None of them had dry eyes by the time Lilleas straightened, cheeks pink, face damp, but looking a little better.

Jenny, ever brusque and practical, set a mug of steaming tea before both girls, and nodded. "This will help set ye tae rights," she said softly. Her own eyes were gleaming with tears.

Caitriona wiped her eyes and put a hand on Lilleas' back. "His Lairdship told me a little of what happened tae ye, Lilleas. I ken I am a stranger to ye, but if ye should need anything at all, I ken a bit of what it's like. Tae be…" she couldn't say the words aloud, for her throat closed up.

This girl was so young, still. Just a child, really. Barely of an age to have begun her monthly courses, still soft with the features of youth. She should not know what it was like. But she also should not be alone.

"I ken what it feels like, after such an event. Tae some extent." She took the girl's hand in hers, gratified to see the slight opening in Lilleas's expression. Meeting her gaze head on, she said fiercely, "It was nae yer fault, do ye hear me? It was never yer fault, nae matter what ye did. Nae matter what ye said."

Lilleas sniffled, and nodded. "Aye, *he* said that too."

Caitriona looked around at Jenny and Kenna, both of whom shook their heads a little. "He?" she asked Lilleas.

"His Lairdship."

Warmth suffused Caitriona's heart at the thought of her big, dark, fierce husband reassuring this girl. Ensuring she knew she was not to blame. "Well, he's right. 'Tis nae yer fault, and if ye have any…concerns, come see me. I ken how tae help with…" She glanced at Morven, who was listening with rapt attention, and sighed. "There are herbs ye can take, should ye…need them."

A sliver of hope lit in Lilleas' eyes then. "There are?"

Caitriona nodded. "Aye, and I ken what they are. If ye but ask, I'll make ye a tea. Ye dinnae have tae worry here. Now," she said, smiling at Morven and meeting Kenna's eyes. "Have ye met Kenna's girls yet? I think ye might make grand friends."

At that, Kenna rose, too, and smiled. "Aye, 'tis time for ye tae meet! They've been biding their time, letting ye get settled in. Come now, I'll show ye the way."

Caitriona mouthed a silent "thank you" as Kenna led the girls out. They were in good hands.

Taking a deep breath, she sat back at the table and resumed eating her breakfast.

"Jenny, do ye need anything from the village?" she asked, hoping the cook would want to walk with her. After the attack on her person, and hearing Lilleas's story, she would no longer risk going out alone.

Jenny shrugged. "I could use the fresh air at least, why?"

Finishing off her porridge, she stood. "I promised Sorcha I would attend her this morning."

"Does…his Lairdship know?" Jenny was ever responsible "Callum said ye're nae to leave the grounds…"

With a sigh, Caitriona shook her head. "He said I cannae go alone, so here I am. Askin' ye to come with me. I'll tell him, I promise. Just…after we return."

When the other woman gave her a doubtful look, Caitriona took her hand.

"Please, Jenny. I dinnae mean to cause any more secrets between myself and the Laird; as soon as we've returned, I'll seek him out. But ye ken, he's…very stubborn. And Sorcha is near her time. I need to attend to her."

After a long pause, the cook wiped her hands on her apron and agreed. "Och, well, I've been meanin' to visit Deirdre. She's got a fine hand at embroidery and I need help on my new stomacher."

Elated, Caitriona led the way out the kitchen door and to the stables.

"Hello, milady!" Aodhán greeted, ever cheerful. His jolly grin reminded Caitriona of Callum, though the boy looked nothing like the man. "Ye'll be wanting yer favorite mare again, aye?"

Caitriona nodded, glancing between Aodhán and Jenny, trying to see the similarities. And there were some. A certain expression around the eyes. A similar hairline. Perhaps even his tone of voice.

He brought her a saddled Eurwen, and handed her an apple as well. The cheeky mare was quickly becoming used to treats every time she was ridden, and Caitriona was a pushover. The sweet animal could have whatever she wanted, so far as her mistress was concerned.

Hefting herself up, she swung her leg over the horse and wondered if she would get any looks today for the way she rode. It was improper of her to be riding astride, but then so was everything else she was doing. Wearing trews and a man's shirt, sneaking away from the castle once again, performing midwifery despite her position.

If Angus saw her, he might have a fit of apoplexy.

Aodhán saddled a horse for his mother and bid them both farewell as they rode out.

The journey to the village was quick, and Jenny left her at Sorcha and Blair's with a promise to return in a half-hour's time. Small voices yelled inside as Caitriona knocked, and then Sorcha herself opened the door. She was still in her shift and wrapper.

"Milady, 'tis wonderful to see ye up and about!" She pulled her wrapper closed around herself. "Forgive my appearance, I find it harder and harder to attire myself when I need not leave the cottage."

"Please dinnae trouble yerself, Sorcha. After all," Caitriona said, gesturing to her legs. "I'm wearing trews. I've only a short time and wanted to be quick."

Sorcha laughed. "We make quite a pair, do we not? Come in! The child is surely moving; I am quite sure he or she has dropped downward since I saw ye last."

The woman's gait was labored and she waddled with the newfound pressure in her abdomen. But her belly was oddly shaped, not as rounded as it had been, and worry trickled through Caitriona. "I'd like to feel for the child's head."

Guiding the woman to the bed, she glanced at Sorcha's girls. They were playing by the fire with dolls made of rags, and did not pay attention to the women other than a few shy glances. As their mother lowered herself to the bed, Caitriona could see the baby was pushing heavily to one side, making her belly appear lopsided.

She helped Sorcha lay back, and settled her hands on the thin fabric of the chemise over her lower belly. A frown worked its way between her brows. The bairn's head was not where it should be, as she suspected. The baby was breech.

"Sorcha…I need to turn the babe. 'Tis not positioned how it should be and if ye were to labor like this…" She shook her head. "It might be painful."

The baby kicked her hands as she prodded Sorcha's belly, wondering if it was too late to try. She had assisted the midwife of Brae once or twice in turning a bairn, but had never done the deed alone.

Sorcha's brow furrowed with worry. "What must I do?"

With firm and careful hands, Caitriona felt for the child's head and body. "I need ye to take deep breaths, and do everything ye can not to tense yer belly."

To her relief, the bairn seemed to have some room to move yet within the womb. Using her palms, she locked eyes with Sorcha, and nodded. Pushing one way, she felt the resistance of Sorcha's womb as another false contraction rippled, and Sorcha took a deep breath, calming herself.

When her belly grew soft again, Caitriona pressed against the baby and guided it downward, humming a mindless song. By Sorcha's wide eyes and the teeth sunk into her lip, Caitriona knew it was painful. But in less than a minute, the bairn had turned again, and Caitriona sat back with relief.

"I believe 'tis done," she said, helping the woman up into a sitting position. "Ye'll want to bind yer belly until yer water breaks. It will help the bairn stay where she — or he — is positioned."

She helped Sorcha wrap a long, sturdy piece of cotton linen around her belly in a way that was firm but not too restrictive. "Thank ye," Sorcha said, slowly rising from the bed. "It will be soon, I think."

Caitriona watched as the other woman began to breathe slowly, focused and still until the next bout of tension passed. "These are false throws, aye?"

Often in the days or even months before the baby was born, the mother had many false starts, doing nothing but adding more discomfort to the entirety of the pregnancy. For a new mother, it could be a disappointing tease. For experienced women, it was simply another symptom to contend with.

"Aye," Sorcha agreed, easing into a chair. "It happens more and more these days."

The young woman had a glow about her which sent a tinge of jealousy through Caitriona's heart. This, someday, might be her. But would she be as beloved by her husband as Blair loved Sorcha?

The knowledge that her husband desired an heir to achieve clan peace sent a peculiar warmth through her limbs.

With a few instructions to send Blair the moment her labor started in earnest, Caitriona let herself out of the cottage.

At the same time, she saw Jenny walking down the path toward her, and a dark presence to her right loomed. Heart racing, she whirled, only to realize it was one of the castle guards she had seen many times before. He leaned against the cottage, casual, and it was obvious he had been waiting for her.

Did Rhys have his men following her now?

Caitriona greeted the guard with a smile. "I suppose Rhys knows I'm here, then?"

The man shook his head. "I'm assigned to protect ye, milady, but I didnae tell him ye'd left the castle. He'll be training the men, with no head for known' his wife is missing. Again."

"I'll tell him," Caitriona burst out. "Dinnae say anythin'. I'll explain everything to him as soon as I can."

The guard stood straight as Jenny came alongside them. "I cannae control what he does and doesnae ken, Lady. But I'll nae say a thing."

Relief spread through her. She wanted Rhys to hear it from her own lips. The desire she had to be a midwife was far too personal and precious for his anger to eclipse her reasons. They mounted their horses and the guard fell behind them in an easy gait.

※ ※ ※

Back at the castle, Caitriona left Eurwen in Aodhán's capable hands as she enacted her plan to break down Rhys's walls.

Beyond the stables, the clanging of swords and whirring thwap of arrows drew her. It was a bonny day, the clouds offering a cool breeze with the sun peeking out every now and then. Someone had taken a scythe to the grass to clear the way for combat, and the sweet smell lingered in the air.

Rhys was not hard to spot, for he was a head taller than the rest of the men and stood to the side, critiquing form and aim as he watched. No one seemed to be aware of her approach. A shadow of doubt passed through her. Was this the right decision? Would this break the barriers between them, or serve to raise them higher?

After his protective proclamation yesterday, she was eager to prove she *could* protect herself. If he would allow her to do so.

It was then she realized he was staring at her. The questioning in his gaze gave her courage, and she lifted her chin. Now was not the time to give in to fear. Now was the time to act.

Grabbing a short sword, she strode toward Rhys and ignored the stares of the men as they became aware of her presence and the way she was dressed.

Comments and quiet chuckles followed her. Rhys glared at his men, but they were unaffected. When she reached him, he grabbed her arm and pulled her away from the lawn.

"What are ye doing out of yer bed?" Rhys hissed. "Dressed like this?"

Caitriona gripped her short sword tighter and kept her shoulders straight. "I can protect myself."

Rhys narrowed his eyes, dropping his gaze over her figure. "No, you cannae —" he began, but she cut him off.

"I am not as helpless as ye may think." She nearly crackled with energy.

"Nevertheless, I dinnae want to endanger ye, not here or anywhere else." Rhys scowled down at her.

"I am not the meek and quiet wife ye hoped I would be," she said. "Or did ye hope to fill me with child and keep me locked away forever?"

The jibe was half teasing, half full of a challenge. When Rhys closed the distance between them, still a head taller than her despite her height, she felt her knees weaken. And it was not from fear. "This isnae a conversation to have in front of my men," he said, voice low and scraping down her spine.

"Aye, but here we are." She blew out her breath and tried again. "While I shouldnae have lied to ye about the attack, at least I've been truthful about everything else."

He laughed. The bark of amusement rang over the field and several men glanced their way. "Have ye now? So then, what about yer running away to the village again this mornin', after I asked ye to stay in the castle?"

A leaden weight settled into her stomach. How had he known? "I brought Jenny with me," she said, not backing down.

Rhys stood in the sunlight, a halo of light around his black hair, his blue eyes gleaming with irritation, his forearms tensed for a fight.

She could not bring herself to apologize. Not when he had kept so much from her. But she could prove herself, as someone who could protect themselves against danger. Ignoring the fluttering in her stomach, she hefted up the sword. "That willnae happen again. I promise ye, Rhys, I can protect myself. Let me prove myself to ye."

Eyes raking over her body, he shrugged. "Suit yerself." He waved one of his men over, a younger lad who could not have been older than fifteen, and jutted his chin at her. "Yer lady wishes to fight," he said to the boy. "Ye're not to hurt her." There was a dark warning in his words.

The young man nodded and faced her. Caitriona smiled. She would best this boy with ease, as she had done many times in her own fields, with her own sparring partners. Even with her knee still aching and her arms feeling bruised, she had confidence she would overthrow the younger man's advances. She raised an eyebrow at Rhys in a silent challenge, and then looked again at the boy.

"Verra well," she said, and readied herself for a fight.

Today, she would show her husband who he had really married.

ENEMY AT THE GATES

Rhys

She had bested three of his men in less than ten minutes' time, and Rhys did not know whether to be embarrassed for his men, or proud of his wife.

Whatever he had expected of his new wife upon arranging this marriage, it was not her. The woman smirked at him, her long braid swinging down her back, her full hips indecently exposed in those well-fitted trews. She could not be hidden away, no.

This woman deserved to be seen.

He had been aware of the rumors surrounding her. It was one of the reasons he had pursued the arrangement; surely a spinster nearing her thirties with no prospects and a ruined reputation would jump at the chance to be Lady of one of the most powerful castles in the highlands.

But she was so much more. The moment she had walked through the chapel doors, looking radiant and unlike any of his expectations of a meek, mousy, unassuming wife, Rhys knew his plans were all for naught. Standing beside her at the altar, offering her vows of love and care, he'd been unable to stop admiring her. There was a glow about her drawing him like a moth to a flame.

But his past loomed like a dark monster and he could not fall for a beautiful woman again. It was easier to incite her wrath and keep her at arms' length than to open up the memories plaguing him. If he fell in love with this woman, he would be unable to keep away from the reminders of what he had done.

The events leading up to his dark and troubled past had begun much the same as this. A wedding, a beautiful woman, and falling in love.

Caitriona flipped her opponent onto his back and held her sword to his neck. Yet another triumph. His men were now cheering her on, having gone from disbelief to admiration to intentionally volunteering to fight her in an attempt to see which of them could best her.

She was an impressive woman. With her height and curves, one would not expect her agility and strength.

When she lifted her gaze to his, a spark of desire ran through him. He wanted to drag her from the cacophony of men around her and kiss her senseless. He wanted to see if the roundness of her belly was as soft as it looked. He wanted...

She was raising her sword to point it at him. "What about you, my lord? Will ye test my skills?"

Rhys laughed, charmed by her confidence. "It would be an unfair fight, *lasair-chride*." He used the term to ruffle her feathers, but part of him had grown fond of the moniker. She was, in all ways, a woman with fire in her heart. "Ye're injured and have fought four men before me."

"Ach, ye're afraid I'll best ye too?" she baited him, and the words brought a round of riotous jeers around them.

Glancing at his men, who all watched with eager anticipation, he shrugged. "I warned ye."

Caitriona held her sword ready, but Rhys did not pick up a weapon. He walked toward her, knowing from having studied the way she fought he could best her in a few moves. Surprise rippled across her face when he nodded. The calculations ran through her eyes; she took in his empty hands, his relaxed stance, and his guarded gaze, and she tilted her head.

And she dropped her sword.

Rhys was about to protest that she keep the weapon when she took him by surprise with a whirling kick to the knee. It pushed him back just enough to tip him off balance, and she did not relent. While he scrambled to steady his feet, she lunged toward him and drove her shoulder into his chest. The cheers going up around them seemed to fuel her determination to knock him down.

His men yelled her name in encouragement when she attempted to knock his foot from beneath him with her own. It spurred him into action. He had yet to make any move but conceding to her attack, but if he did not act she would take him down.

Bracing his leg against her attempts, he grabbed the arm she'd thrown out in a wayward punch and twisted her around till she was forced to put her back to him or have her limb broken. He did not wish to harm her, but she attacked with such fury he could only think of defense. She elbowed his gut with her other arm, and he was about to grab both shoulders and pin her to the ground when she linked her ankle around his leg and threw him off balance.

It surprised him, and his grip slipped. Caitriona jerked away, whirling to face him again, her green eyes sparkling. Despite himself, he caught his breath. She was beautiful. The fight blazing in her eyes, her curvaceous figure clad in tight trews, the vee of her leine dipping dangerously low. If it weren't for the fifty pairs of eyes on them, he might have taken her here on the grass. But he had to win this fight, for his own reputation.

She lifted her chin with familiar defiance, and he grinned. Up until now, he had been playing with her, but he no longer wanted to tease. Lunging forward, he used the most unfair move he had: the weight of his body against hers. In a moment she was pinned beneath him. He could feel every curve and roll of her wriggling against him as she attempted to escape the crush of him atop her. Supporting himself with his arms, Rhys met her eyes with satisfaction as a blush heightened in her cheeks. She felt it too.

Dipping his head until his lips were a breath from hers, he said, "Relent."

The tilt of her chin brought her mouth even closer to him. "Ye're a dirty fighter, and a cheat."

"Aye, well. My pride was on the line." He settled his eyes on her lips, wishing they were alone. Wishing he could steal her breath away with kisses and warm her body with his own. But his men watched and cheered at his victory, and the wound on her head seemed to be bleeding again.

Did the woman have a death wish?

Rising, he pulled her up with him and waved his men off. "I think we are done here," he told them. He kept a firm grip on Caitriona's hand and headed back to the castle.

It was time they broke through whatever this stage of defiance and arguments was, and settled on a civil middle ground. He could not go on sparring her, verbally or physically. Not with the vicarious way she seemed to throw herself into everything she wanted. At this rate, she would break a limb.

But his path toward privacy of a closed door was interrupted when Aodhán ran to his side and announced they had four of Berach Macnammon's men held captive in the stables. Swearing under his breath, Rhys changed his direction, still pulling Caitriona in his wake. It crossed his mind she could not have chosen a worse moment to discard her lady's attire in favor of this outfit that hugged every curve of her body, but no matter. Of all his worries, Caitriona's current dress was the least troubling.

Berach's men coming this close to the castle and threatening his wife's safety was the first.

THE WRONG WIFE
Caitriona

Caitriona followed Rhys with a growing sense of embarrassment over her appearance. Striding behind him in form-fitting trews, she was disheveled head to toe, with grass stains marring the white leine she wore, her hair coming undone from its plait, and dirt smudges all over her person.

And now, they were going to confront their enemies, while she looked like a bedraggled woman whose sense of propriety was too far gone to be respectable.

Walking through the courtyard of the castle toward the stables, she resisted glancing at her husband. Something primal ran through her veins after the fight. The weight of him lingered in her mind; the feel of his arms pressed against her shoulders; the way he had made sure to keep the bulk of his body from crushing her; the intimate flutter of his heartbeat in the curve of his neck.

She swallowed. Could he hear the pounding of her heart against her ribs?

The stables were not as quiet as usual; a great deal of noise was being made as men argued back and forth with members of Rhys's clan. It did not take long to locate the prisoners, tied with their arms above their heads in ropes that looped around a beam and held them almost dangling. Their toes only just brushed the ground enough to find purchase, but not quite enough to be stable.

Several of Rhys's clansmen stood guard with rifles held casually over their arms, as Angus paced, eyes steely and arms crossed.

Two of the men were young, looking barely old enough to hold a dirk, much less join a clan war. One was older, with gray streaking his dark locks, and a stony gaze which gave away very little. And one was bald.

With a black eye, a very recently-broken nose, and an unmistakable beefy form.

Caitriona's breath caught in her throat, and she gripped Rhys's hand with desperation. Should she tell him? Rhys was already walking up to the oldest of the four, looking him up and down, demanding answers.

"Tell me ye're here tae make a peace offering, or I'll have my men shoot ye in the head," Rhys said, his grip on Caitriona's hand the anchor which kept her from capsizing at the unexpected sight of her attacker.

He met her gaze and smirked. She could not breathe. Could not think. Could not speak.

"We came tae greet yer *Lady*," the older man said, a sneer on his lips.

Rhys dropped her hand and stepped to the side, blocking Caitriona from the man's view, and she closed her eyes. Her heart raced and her stomach twisted; she thought she might be sick there on the stable floors.

"Ye have nothing tae say to her," Rhys said.

There was a peculiar rushing in her ears, and it was not until Angus put a hand on her arm she realised she was breathing a bit too rapidly. Her head was light.

"Awright, lass?" Angus said, his voice low enough only she could hear him. Despite his seeming disapproval of her, and continued gruff treatment, he was softening. Little by little. Occasionally, she caught him smiling at her jokes, when he thought she could not see him. Now, his stern face was kind.

She clenched her fists. Blowing air through her lips, she nodded. "I'm fine."

Perhaps if she said so, it would be true. With concentrated effort, she drew breaths in through her nose, slowing the rhythm of air until her head was no longer rushing and her senses came back to her. Settling her gaze on Rhys's back, she reminded herself she was not alone. She was among men who wished to protect her.

Her attacker, who still leered at her, was tied to a beam and could do nothing.

Angus, beside her, was scowling between her and the bald man. But he said nothing more.

"Berach does nae wish to accept a peace treatise. If ye dinnae give up yer position as laird, he will take it by force," the older man was saying to Rhys.

"How does he intend to do this?" Rhys said idly, his tone calm. As if discussing the weather. "He has less than half the men, no resources, and ye've been on the run for years. What, exactly, does he think he can do?"

The older man's gaze flicked to Caitriona then, around Rhys's shoulder. "Well, ye might take care to keep that wife of yers within yer sight."

A snarl emitted from her husband, so animalistic even she was a little afraid. When he spoke, his tone sent chills through her. "I dinnae take threats upon my family lightly, Murdoch. Ye'll keep my wife's name out o' yer mouth."

"Tis nae threat, 'tis only advice," Murdoch laughed, despite his situation, and Caitriona found her bearings again. She was *not* going to be intimidated by these men.

Straightening her shoulders, she let anger take over, sending a steely resolve up her spine and anchoring her feet to the ground. They could not touch her. She stepped out from behind Rhys, and took his hand.

The man who had attacked her stared. Studied her face and body. As if searching for a weakness. She lifted her chin, challenging him to say something. To dare expose himself as her attacker, to the beast of a man beside her, whose dark gaze was already full of warning.

"Angus, take them to the cells," Rhys said, raking his gaze over each man with a cold fury. "We'll question them one by one. If any of them touched Lilleas…" He stopped for a moment, cleared his throat. Went on. "Seventy lashes."

Seventy was almost enough to kill a man. Caitriona glared at her attacker, wondering what Rhys would do if he knew this was the man who had harmed her. Wondering if she should say as much. She might have wanted to take out her fury on him just then, but she brought life *into* this world. Could she condemn him?

But as Rhys's men shoved Berach's lackeys past them, her attacker damned his own fate. "Ye're lucky ye've got yer husband tae hide behind today, lass," he sneered as he passed her.

Beside her, Rhys stiffened.

Caitriona met the man's gaze and narrowed her eyes. So be it. "Aye, perhaps I am. But ye failed even *without* his Lairdship by my side," she shot back.

The words had barely left her mouth when Rhys grabbed the front of the man's shirt and shoved him against a stall door so hard his head bounced off the wood and he let out a surprised grunt.

"What did ye say, Seumas?" Rhys demanded, only inches from the man's face.

Seumas' eyes widened, but he did not cower. "Yer wife is lucky ye're with her today. She wasnae so protected when I found her —"

Without allowing the man to finish, Rhys whipped him around and all but threw him out the stable doors. The man stumbled, and the clansmen around them parted, no one stopping Rhys as he grabbed the back of Seumas' shirt, keeping him upright, but forcing him forward. Out into the clear day. Onto the stones of the courtyard.

"Angus!" Rhys barked. "Cut his arms loose."

A flutter of confusion marked the Seumas' face. Angus did as he was told. Free now, unbound and facing Rhys as the Macnammon clansmen casually made a circle around them, Seumas' eyes darted around for escape. He was a big man, broad and muscular, but Rhys was taller. And Rhys was furious.

Caitriona stood in the circle of clansmen, unable to look away from her husband. A dark beast in the sunlight, his hair falling around his face, his gaze fiery, the scars upon his brow marking the violence he'd been through. No doubt, signs of violence he had returned. He stood in the middle of the circle, dangerous as the eye of a storm.

"I willnae beat a helpless man," he said, voice a low rumble of thunder. "But ye're nae helpless now, are ye?"

Seumas clenched his fists and brought them halfway up his body, readying himself into a fighting pose.

"Ye like tae attack unprotected women, aye?" Rhys had not moved. Did not flinch when Seumas threw a wild fist toward him. It barreled straight for Rhys's midsection, but in one smooth move Rhys's hand came up and grabbed Seumas' wrist, twisting it away and throwing the man sideways.

Seumas stumbled to his knees, but hopped up again and faced Rhys with clumsy moves. As if he were afraid Rhys might attack while his back was turned.

Rhys took one step closer. "Ye think I'll nae attack ye, just because I havenae been drawn into a clan war? That I'm nae gonna protect the women of the clan, because Berach has been allowing ye tae do unspeakable things, and ye think I've turned a blind eye?"

Seumas threw another punch, this time at Rhys's face. With a tilt of his head, Rhys dodged the fist. There was a beat of silence, when Seumas realised he'd missed again, and the fear lodging itself in his eyes was almost pitiable.

Almost.

In a blur of motion, Rhys' fist met with Seumas' jaw, but Seumas did not fly back. Instead, he was spun around, his neck locked beneath Rhys's vice-like arm, and Rhys was snarling into his ear. "Ye may nae live tae regret touching my wife."

Seumas purpled under Rhys's grip, and when he was let go he gasped for air, whirling around only to be met with another fist to the cheek. This one split his skin, and blood poured forth. Seumas threw his punches wildly, connecting once or twice with Rhys's body, but Rhys did not concede.

Like a battering ram, he landed blow after blow upon Seumas' face and body, until the man's eye was swollen, his cheek a mess of blood and bruising, his breath coming in harsh wheezes. He was relentless, his rage so dark Caitriona had no problem imagining him on the battlefield. Vanquishing his enemies.

He was an unstoppable force of anger. It rippled through every part of him. Dressed in his black liene, his teeth bared and his hair wild about his face, towering over most men by a head, he was a terrifying sight to behold.

Seumas backed away, holding his hands up in front of his face, and a strangled laugh escaped him. "I dinnae regret it," he said, spitting out blood. "I dinnae regret touching yer wife. That lush body —"

Rhys's hand shot out and latched onto Seumas' throat. He said nothing, but towered over the man, muscles rippling as he squeezed.

Seumas' mouth fell open as he gasped for breath. "Berach told me tae take her." There was a sort of glee in his eyes, even as they bulged from his head. "He wanted...tae see...if ye —" But he did not finish.

Rhys smashed his fist into the man's lips. "Ye dinnae deserve tae lick the ground she walks upon, and ye dared tae touch her with yer filthy hands."

Finally, the man broke. "...mercy." Seumas rasped.

The sharp snap of a palm against skin rang through the now-silent courtyard. Seumas' other cheek began to bleed. "The Lord may have mercy on yer soul, but I am the Devil. And I am nae so forgiving."

Everyone was watching, waiting with bated breath. No one dared to step in and temper the furious Laird. Caitriona glanced around, and realised none of these men looked like they *wanted* to stop Rhys. They all seemed gratified by his reaction.

When Rhys let go of the man's throat, he dropped to the ground. Rhys stood above him, almost unrecognizable in his wrath, and Caitriona pressed a hand to her throat. The Beast of the Battlefield was before her, and she could not breathe.

A thick moment of silence passed, filled only with the sound of Seumas' labored gasps as he lay there, afraid to move, every muscle tense, waiting for his judgement.

"Stand up," Rhys grit out through his teeth.

Seumas flinched. Looked around the circle. Struggled to get his hands beneath him, swaying for a moment on his knees, before he hauled his large body into a standing position. Only for Rhys to grab the front of his shirt and pummel him again. And again. And again.

Seumas sagged.

Rhys did not stop.

Caitriona's stomach turned. "Rhys," she said. Quiet. A little afraid. Almost tempted to let him kill the man for what he'd done to her, and what Berach's men had done to Lilleas.

Seumas was unconscious now, his face mottled and almost unrecognizable. He was only upright because Rhys's hand fisted into his shirt, holding him in place. Another slap rang through the courtyard. Caitriona flinched.

"Rhys!" she said, louder this time.

Fist midair, Rhys looked at her. The rage in his face was so visceral she nearly took a step back.

"That's enough," she said.

Blood splattered across his cheek, and more dripped from his knuckles. It was not just Seumas' blood on his hands; his own skin was split from the beating. "He doesnae deserve —"

Caitriona stepped closer and put a hand on his cheek, silencing him. "No, he doesnae deserve yer mercy," she said. "Men like him will never deserve to be given mercy for what they have done." Taking a deep breath, she looked at the sagging, unconscious figure hanging from her husband's fist. "But if we dinnae deal with him in a trial for justice, and he dies by the brute force of our hands, we are nae better than Berach."

Rhys blinked.

Looked around them at the faces of the clan he trusted. The men who watched with judgement of their own. Whose anger was as apparent on their faces as Rhys's. Then his eyes returned to her.

The rage did not subside, but his grip on Seumas loosened, and the man fell with a thud to the courtyard.

Without breaking his gaze on her, Rhys ordered, "Angus, clean him up and take him to the cells. We will decide what tae do with all of the prisoners later. They are nae to be left alone; a guard will be posted outside the cell doors at all times."

Behind her, Angus replied, "Aye, Rhys."

Seumas was hauled up from the courtyard and dragged away, leaving a bloody trail behind him.

"Come," Rhys said, and she put her hand into his without question.

He did not release her as he guided them through the courtyard to the castle doors. It was almost time for the noon meal, and the halls bustled with life. Maids cast curious glances at Rhys's bloody face as he took her through the hallways and into the quiet of his library. The room was still and dim, a sanctuary away from the bustle of the day.

As soon as they entered, he let go of her to pace to the long window, which faced the road up to the castle. His hands were fists at his sides, muscles in his arms tense. His rage was palpable from across the room.

He would have killed Seumas if she had not stopped him. Of this she was certain. And Caitriona could not quite say she disapproved, but she did need to know what kind of man she was married to. This man, who expected her to produce him an heir.

Who wanted her to mother his children.

She needed answers.

"Did ye kill yer brother?"

Rhys did not face her. His shoulders heaved, and he snapped, "I am responsible for his death."

His voice was terse, unwelcoming. But she did not back down. If he wanted her to give him everything — her life, her body, her womb

— he had to offer something of himself in return. He had just beaten a man nearly to death for touching her. And while this fact sent an undeniable thrill through her, she was beginning to see more and more why his clan demanded surety from him.

This man did not seem settled.

"What happened?" she prodded.

There was a long silence before he spoke.

"It doesnae matter any more." He turned and his gaze simmered, cutting straight to her soul. Blood still spattered over his cheek, and her breath caught in her throat. Warmth curled through her, unexpected and electric.

The violence, written all over him in blood, all for her.

No.

She could not give in to this man. She was not attracted to this…this glowering. The Devil of Calhoun, who embodied his moniker so fiercely in that moment. He was nothing like the gentle, loving partner she'd dreamed of once upon a time.

He was a beast.

And yet…

Caitriona shook off her wayward thoughts. "If it matters tae me, yer wife, then yes. I think it concerns ye tae tell me."

"Why?" He took one step toward her, and her cheeks warmed. "Why must ye ken what happened a decade ago, in a different life, tae the man I was then?"

She watched him close the distance between them. Smoothed her palms over her hips to keep from crossing her arms over her chest. Heat curled within her when his eyes followed the movement.

"I cannae live a life of not knowing," she said. "Not knowing what kind of man shares my bed. What kind of man will…father my children." She was sure her entire body was aflame as she uttered the words. "If ye wanted a silent wife, ye chose wrong."

When his eyes darkened, it was not rage. "Aye, I did."

She swallowed. Waited. Wondered which of her questions he was answering.

"Llwyd died by my hands." The statement was dark, dangerous. But as soon as he said it, some of the resentment lifted from his gaze, and he took a deep breath. "Some of the story isnae mine tae tell, and ye'll have to ask Jenny to ken it all. But Llwyd was...much like our father. A manipulative, greedy man, whose hunger couldnae be slaked by the having. Nothing was ever enough for him. Nae his own wife. Nae his own children. Nae his own purpose."

Caitriona was rooted in place, captured in rapt silence by this widening of the door into Rhys's past.

"He...stole something precious to me. Something irreplaceable. And I killed him for it." He studied her, still a man of mystery despite giving her these answers.

"What did he take?" Caitriona pushed, unable to stop herself from asking. She needed to know.

Only a foot away from her now, he looked her up and down. Taking in her trews, her billowing leine, her unbound hair. Gazing at her as if she were a precious jewel. Rare. Worth every blow he'd given to Seumas.

Then, without fanfare, he said, "My wife."

IONA

Rhys

The gravestone of his late wife was newer than the rest. Roses grew in wild bunches around it, framing the rounded top with abandon, their bright colors a stark contrast against the grey stone. In thick letters not yet covered with moss, it read:

>HERE LIETH THE BODY OF IONA MACNAMMON
>SPOWSE TO RHYS MACNAMMON
>WHO DEPARTED THIS LIFE THE 19TH OF MAY
>AND YEAR 1710
>AGED 24 YEARS

Caitriona stared at the headstone, her bright red hair a halo around her face, her eyes calculating. Rhys knew she would have questions. A lot of them. She always did, and he was beginning to value her openness. Her need to *know* him, in ways no one had ever demanded before.

Around them, the graveyard was lush with spring growth, roses clambering over the stone walls and archways, moss covering headstones, bees flitting from flower to flower.

It was the kind of quiet that instilled calm; not really silent, but *alive.* Birds trilled to each other, and Highland cows mooed to their young. Someone laughed in a courtyard, the sound nearer, but subdued. Clegs buzzed past here and there, and the glint of their yellowed wings caught the sunlight. And, moving through the leaves, trembling in the eaves of the castle, the breeze whispered.

Rhys was at home here. He'd visited often over the years; the death of his father, his mother, his brother, and his wife all marking an era of his life in which loss was a constant companion.

He had shied away from Caitriona's questions, because of this. Knowing he must revisit painful and sometimes damning memories. Knowing what he needed from her, afraid she might deny him the heir the clan demanded if she knew the truth. His past was not heroic, nor could he be absolved of his brother's blood. He'd been afraid. More deeply than he had wanted to admit, Rhys had been afraid of losing her.

Because, just as deeply, he was falling in love with her.

The revelation had rocked through him the moment she'd put her hand on his arm. Stopped him from killing Seumas. Claimed his violence as hers, and said, in not so many words, she was a part of his clan. *If he dies by the brute force of our hands, we are nae better than Berach.*

A simple statement, but one that spoke volumes. She was committing herself to his clan with those words. He owed her this truth.

"Iona did not die in childbirth," he offered.

She blinked up at him, the revelation clearly unexpected. For a moment, she studied his face, then the headstone, then the surrounding graves. She would, he knew, be looking for the gravestone of his child — the child Iona had given birth to, right before she'd died.

Before she could ask more, he continued. "The match was good for both of our families; Iona's father was aging past the point of being able to care for his family, and our clan wanted to strengthen their borders. So, the Craigs joined their land with ours, on the promise that I would provide Iona with security after her father died."

She stood in the sunlight, the breeze blowing her bright curls across her cheek, and he wanted to reach out and brush them away. But he would not allow himself to touch her again. Not until she knew.

Not until *he* knew.

He wanted her to stay.

He rubbed a palm over his face. "We married very quickly; agreement was made, the wedding was held, and she was mine. I was…desperately in love with her. And she with me. Or so I thought."

For a moment, they stood quiet, the rustling of the willow overhead a calming presence as the buzzing of the bees in the roses hummed around them.

"But then she endured several losses. Pregnancies that didnae hold. The midwife was…uncaring. Said Iona's miscarriages were a sign from God, and that perhaps she needed to confess her sins to heal her barren womb. It was cruel. And it shattered her." He trailed off, a dark cloud washing over him as his eyes settled on the stones. Somewhere deep inside him, anger still rose on Iona's behalf. Despite what she had done to him.

"Sometimes I think it was the midwife who caused Iona to lose so many. But after four long years…we had success. She became pregnant, and carried it till the time came for the child to be delivered."

He clenched his fist, overcome with sudden, sharp emotion. He had loved Iona. The thought of having a family with her, of growing old with her, had been very real. They'd been young, she'd been beautiful. Vivid. And, eventually, tragic.

But the feelings he'd had for Iona paled in comparison to how he felt looking at Caitriona. The fierce protectiveness. The harsh fear when she had ridden into the courtyard battered and bruised and bleeding. The primal *need* for her to be okay.

The instant, all-encompassing, irresistible urge to be with her. Night and day, she was the flame to which he was drawn. The light he could not ignore.

"What happened?" Her voice was soft. Tears edged her gaze, not falling, but shimmering with unashamed honesty.

"She left with Llwyd." The admission was less painful now than its discovery ten years ago. But it still stung. The anger. The fear. The loss.

"Oh, Rhys." She reached out to touch his arm.

He took a deep, calming breath, and lowered his eyes to the connection between them. Her skin against his. Her fingers wrapped around his forearm. Peace spread through him.

"Shortly after she gave birth to our...child. When I found them, Iona was barely alive. The midwife hadnae delivered her afterbirth properly; she was bleedin' too much and didnae ken till it was too late. She died in my arms. The child — a boy — was..." He cut off, throat closing in with a grief so deep it haunted him still.

The tiny baby, skin blue with cold. Wrapped in nothing but a linen cloth. Clinging to his mother's breast, voice a hoarse wail against the frozen Scottish winter wind. "He didnae live much longer than his mother."

Caitriona pressed her hand to her mouth, eyes shimmering with tears. He found his own cheeks were wet, and he did not care. If she was to know him, to *truly* know him, she needed to hear all of it. To see *all of it*. His brutality. His anger. His sorrow.

"I found Llwyd in the middle of the snow, carrying firewood back to the cottage. He swore he was trying to care for them." This was the part he did not want to say. The reaction he did not want to see. He closed his eyes, and forced it out past the emotion clogging his throat. "I couldnae stop. Didnae hold back. He was cold, and slow, and I was…so angry. It wasnae a fair fight, and wouldnae have been fair even if it hadnae been winter. Even if he hadnae been half-frozen. I've always been the bigger one, the stronger one. I knew I was killing him, and I didnae stop."

When he opened his eyes, Caitriona was motionless. Tears still welled in her eyes, but she had dropped her hand, and she was staring at him with an emotion he could not read.

"I left him in the snow, still breathing but too battered to stand. I left him, and I took my dead wife and my child, and I buried them here, and I never looked back." He wanted her to know the full truth of it. He had killed his brother. Perhaps not by taking his last breath with his own hands, but by leaving him to die in the snow, beaten and bloody and unable to save himself.

She deserved to make her own decision on whether she would have children with a man who killed his own.

When she touched his cheek, it was a wonder to him. "I understand," she breathed. There was no disgust in her gaze. No judgement. No pity.

Her fingers brushed over the scars on his cheeks, the still-present blood he'd not yet wiped away from Seumas' beating. She touched his lips, her skin so feather-light, so gentle. Her luminous eyes, the deep green of a forest on a summer day, rapt upon him.

And there was grief there, too. But not for herself. For him.

Rhys reached up and stroked the pad of his thumb over the wetness of her cheeks almost reverently. He did not deserve those tears. "Ye must not cry for me, *lasair-chride*. It was a long time ago."

"I offer my heart to nurture our family, and my hands to keep ye well. This I vow to the end of my days," she said, repeating the vows she'd made on their wedding day. "And I cannae verra well fulfill those vows if I am impervious to yer pain."

Turning his face into her palm, he pressed his lips to her skin. This woman was a gift he did not deserve. "I owe ye an apology," he said against her hand.

Vines trailed overhead, their leafy tendrils swaying in the breeze. The sun was warm on his hair, and life was all around them. In the flowers that bloomed against the stone wall. In the far off mooing of the highland cows in the field. In the laughter of children playing games in the courtyard.

Caitriona hummed with some amusement. "I never thought I'd hear ye say those words!"

A smile tugged at the corner of his lips. "Ye are every bit as troublesome as a wild mare, did ye ken that?"

Her brows shot up, and she laughed. The sound was intoxicating. "That isnae an apology."

"Nae," he agreed with a smirk. "But 'tis the truth."

The crinkles around her eyes as she smiled drew him in. Picking up a strand of her hair from her cheek, he let it slide through his fingers.

"I should have explained my needs before ye were ever forced into this arrangement. And for that I am sorry."

To his surprise, she blinked away tears. Dropped her chin, staring at their entwined fingers for a moment, before looking back up at him. Her gaze was soft, damp. "Thank you."

Taking a note from her, he said, "I vow to be loyal and true, and let no-one come between us." Smiling wryly, he added, "Nae even when 'tis my own numpty self. Perhaps especially then."

He began to walk backwards, pulling her with him. "Lady Irving, it seems we have some unfinished *clan business* to attend."

Caitriona raised an eyebrow, bemused. "Clan business?" She allowed him to lead her to the archway of the graveyard, where vines tangled above them and the stones were mossy with age.

He nodded, stopping beneath the greenery, pulling her closer. "Aye. The Clan demands an heir, 'tis up to me — and you — to provide one. I'd say that's *very* unfinished business."

Her eyes dropped to his lips, flitted to the dimple forming in his cheek, rose up to his gaze. The blush rushing up her neck and over her cheeks was tempting. Inching her backward until the solid stone of the archway hit her shoulder blades, he dipped his head.

"I accept," she said, and her voice was breathy.

Amused, he answered, "Do ye?"

For once in her life, Caitriona did not have a snappy answer. "I dinnae ken. What is it I'm accepting?"

He made a low sound, and brought the escaping curl of her hair up to his lips. "Have ye nae listened at all?" he teased.

"I never listen," she said.

A truer statement had never been made.

Rhys was so close a breath would bring them together. "I willnae take ye if ye dinnae wish it. If ye dinnae wish to live with a man who took the life of his own kin. I'll go to the parish and annul the marriage. I'll provide for ye to go wherever ye please, if ye want it."

He leaned infinitesimally closer, curled her hair around his finger, and waited. A long-dead hope budded within him, and with it, a terrifying sense of possession. This woman could command him with a whisper, and he would obey.

If he lost her...

Caitriona's eyes flitted over him, and she chewed on her lower lip. "No more talk of livin' separate lives?"

He nodded, once.

She let out a slow breath. "I ken this isnae what ye wanted; as ye ken 'tis nae what I wanted, either, this marriage. But I have begun to love yer clan. *Our* clan. And while I am nae so naive as to expect a love match, at the very least...I ask for companionship. "

Rhys cupped her face in both his hands, tracing his thumbs over her soft, pink cheeks, gratified as they grew rosier beneath his gaze. He would give her anything. She was maddening, independent, a force of nature. She could demand the moon, and he would be compelled to hand it to her in a silver quaich.

With reverence, he took one small step back, and took her hand, bowing over it. Giving her the choice she'd not been given before. "Caitriona Macnammon, it is my greatest honor to offer myself as yer humble companion as long as we both shall live."

She pulled her lip between her teeth to stop a grin, and he winked at her. "I accept," she said. The simple words sent a thrill through him.

Languid and slow, he backed her against the archway and kissed her, drinking her in like a fine wine. This was not the butterfly-soft caress of their first kiss; nor was it the needy, erratic fury of the second time.

It was purposeful. Ripe with promise and a newfound trust. She melted into him, fingers finding purchase in the collar of his leine, and her lush figure under his hands was malleable. A ripe feast to be discovered, admired, cherished.

"*Buinidh tu dhòmhsa, lasair mo chridhe.*" Lips still touching hers, he put the promise of a lifetime into every word. *You are mine, flame of my heart.* "Let's go inside."

Hidden Confessions
Caitriona

For the second time that week, Caitriona woke to the distinct rumble of a snore. There were new sensations nudging at her awareness, too. The weight of the arm thrown over her belly. The tickle of breath rushing over her neck. The chafe of a day-old beard nuzzling into her skin.

Doing her best not to shift too much, Caitriona stretched in the soft morning light, and turned to peer at Rhys. There was an intimacy in seeing him asleep. The way his lashes lay against his cheeks, brushing against the laugh lines indelibly worn into his skin. Hair tousled and strewn across his forehead in a way that made him look almost boyish, despite being nearly forty years of age.

Longing pooled through her, settling into her breast with a surprising ache. She wanted this to last. But she had been wooed and broken before, and the ease with which he relaxed against her felt fragile. Tentative. Fear mingled with awe; after all, she'd never suspected Niall of his treachery.

And yet, he had betrayed her anyway.

Tenderly, she rested her lips against his forehead and took a deep breath, memorizing the minute details of the morning. His fingers twitched against her hip, and he muttered something unintelligible.

Caitriona pulled back, unsure if he was awake. Though his lids remained closed, the word came out again. *Iona.*

A sharp pang slashed through her. Of course his unconscious mind would dredge up his past lover. The woman with whom he had been in love with all those years ago. It should not have surprised her.

But still, after hoping their marriage might become something better than two strangers sharing a castle, it felt like some kind of betrayal to be bedded while he dreamt of another woman. Even if that woman was long gone. Even though that woman had been unfaithful to him.

Shaking her head, Caitriona closed her eyes. It was a foolish thing to be hurt by. She could not expect him to forget about his wife, no matter how long it had been. No matter what had happened between them. Especially not when this marriage had been arranged for convenience and nothing else. When she had prodded and poked and needled him at every turn.

When she was...well, herself. A woman with a tarnished reputation who chose to spend her time wearing mens' clothing, whose ability to keep house was limited, and who had pursued an occupation that her husband knew nothing about.

Guilt trickled through her.

At some point, she would have to tell him about her midwifery. But would he tolerate her occupation, when a midwife shared the blame in Iona's demise? She would be tending the births of many bairns, seeing many pregnant women in her study. The topic of pregnancy would take much of her time. How would he feel, being so close to it all?

His words rang through her head. *It shattered her.*

Rhys's arm tightened around her, and Caitriona's gaze flicked back to his face. A darkly pleased sound purred in the back of his throat. She flushed. They had shared a bed, yet she felt strange and unsure when his eyes met hers.

He pressed a kiss to her shoulder and raised up onto one elbow, fingers trailing a line up her arm, circling the freckles on her shoulder. Electricity followed in the wake of his touch, the intent in his gaze sending waves of warmth crashing through her.

His words from the gardens played through her mind. *Buinidh tu dhòmhsa, lasair mo chridhe.*

You belong to me, flame of my heart.

All of her senses focused on the path he traced over her collarbone, up her neck, and to her jaw, where he brushed a thumb over her lips.

When he lowered his head, a sudden panic swirled through her. "Ye called out for Iona."

Rhys did not move away. "Did I?"

If she nodded, her lips would meet his. "Do ye dream of her?"

Amusement brought out the dimple in his cheek, and when he pressed a kiss to her lips he was smiling. "Does it trouble ye that I would?"

A hundred questions and a thousand emotions ran through her in quick succession. It felt ridiculous wanting to answer yes. "It shouldn't."

"But it does," he said. With his words was an unspoken invitation to continue with her thoughts, and he leaned on his hand, waiting. The fingers caressing her jaw had not moved away.

Not since the days of sitting with Niall under the willows and foolishly spilling every emotion to him had she let herself be vulnerable with a man. When he had left her to deal with ruin in the wake of his actions, she had closed herself off. She might say what was on her mind, and act on impulse, but Caitriona no longer shared her most tender emotions.

When Niall had taken advantage of her, she had let him. She had let him do things with her a decent woman would never do, and behind her back he had defamed her, letting the rumors grow until she could not recover her reputation. Not when she had willingly gone unchaperoned, to places where women only went with men when they planned to give up more than a kiss or two. Despite her innocence, her own actions and Niall's deceitful boasting had trapped her in a web of her own making.

Only her mother believed her, but the damage was too great for Moira Irving to reign in.

Now, she feared opening up would shatter the fragile trust growing between herself and Rhys. In so many ways they were strangers to each other still. She did not want to give up the chance for more just yet.

"I dinnae ken what she was like," she said, avoiding the guilt over her secret occupation in the village. "I ken it was a long time ago, but every woman wonders...how she compares. When there were...other s."

Rhys touched her cheek, which grew warm with embarrassment, and then brushed his fingers through her auburn curls. "Ye dinnae compare in the least."

A sharpness hit her heart. "Oh."

But then he continued. "One cannae compare a sunset to the blithe warmth of the summer sun. A wide moor to the heather-covered hills of the highlands. *Lasair mo chride,* ye are as different from Iona as a river to a tree." He tugged on her hair and nuzzled against her jawline. "Ye're more trouble, too."

Pleased by his poetic words and his teasing, she laughed. "I do my best."

"Anythin' else ye'd like to know?" He seemed distracted by the tendrils of her hair that splayed out on the pillow. He could not stop running his fingers through her curls.

"What was she like?"

For a moment, he was quiet. He studied her, and she could not help but touch his face, his scars, wondering. When he spoke, his voice was far away. "She was quiet. Strong, but subdued."

A sense of inadequacy wriggled into her chest. She tried to push it away with humor. "I never quite learned that lesson."

Rhys smiled, but she could tell his mind was still in the past. "Iona learned it too well, I think. I couldnae tell what she was thinkin' half the time we were married. When she…lost our bairns, she retreated even more. And I was too young and glaikit tae ken what to do."

"I'm sure ye did what ye could," Caitriona responded. She could not imagine Rhys being young, nor idiotic as he had just called himself.

Shaking his head, he went back to stroking her hair. "I dinnae think I could ever have been what she wanted."

The admission was raw, and Caitriona gazed up at him, dazzled by the softness that had not been there before. The open way he met her eyes, nothing hidden between them. "She must have been glaikit and blind nae to want ye."

She said it before she knew what was going to come out. Rhys raised an eyebrow, teasing. "Ye never stop sayin' exactly what yer thinkin', do ye?"

"I'm sorry," she said, blushing. He must find her ridiculous.

"For what?" he said. "Iona wasnae in love with me. I didnae ken who she loved until the end. I'd much rather ken ye're outright mad at me than never be privy to what yer thinkin' at all."

Her cheeks grew hotter, and she bit her lip. "I never was one for keepin' my opinions to myself."

"That much I have learned," he said, the laughter in his voice almost insulting.

She needed to tell him about her midwifery. Yet, the way he smiled at her, the edges of his eyes crinkling, the dimples in his cheeks deepening, she could not. It was the most candid he had been with her, and she did not want to shatter this newfound intimacy.

He pressed his lips to her shoulder, trailing his mouth up her neck, and Caitriona melted into the feeling. Guilt still fluttered through her, but the small, insistent way he nipped her jawline had her thoughts in a whirl and she threaded her fingers through his hair with a sigh.

This bond was more fulfilling than she could have imagined. The way he stared at her as though she were the most beautiful thing he had ever seen, eyes glittering like the surface of the deep sea. The way he claimed her, surrounding her in his embrace, until he was all she could see. All she could feel. All she could need.

The confessions about her midwifery could wait.

FORTUNE AND SUFFERING

Rhys

Though he was loath to admit such a thing, Rhys was afraid.

He and Caitriona had decided to break their fast outdoors in the fields, where the warmth of the sun shone overhead and the air was fresh. Settled on a blanket, they'd brought a basket of food from the kitchens and he could not rip his gaze from his wife as she laid out the food between them.

This woman was an all-consuming flame he could not resist, no matter how hard he tried. And he had tried. From the day he had first seen her, dirt-smudged and defiant in her father's foyer, to watching her walk down the aisle on their wedding day, glowing with a radiance that shone in her auburn hair and flamed from her eyes, he had done nothing but try to resist her power.

And he could not.

His first wife had shattered him in a way no man wanted to admit. Angry and full of regret, he'd shuttered himself away from every possibility of being vulnerable again after her death. Though his physical wounds had healed over time, the scarring in his heart still ached from time to time, like a bone that had not knit together properly after a bad break.

Iona's death had broken him, as the circumstances around her and his brother's illicit tryst and subsequent demise had become secrets he had to keep. He had to protect his family. Rumors grew, and he allowed them to take over the narrative. To paint him as the villain, as the womanizer, the deceiver, the Devil. Because he would not allow Iona's betrayal to ruin more lives. Not when it had already shattered his own.

But in the wake of all that happened, he had closed off his hurt so well even he did not understand the lasting impact of his wounds.

Perhaps he never would have understood, had Caitriona not come into his life. Even before she began to poke and prod in her brazen way, she had had an effect on him. He had worked hard to ignore her. To convince himself this marriage was for the continuation of his family line, nothing else.

He had not wanted to know the exact softness of her auburn hair, the way it brushed against his skin and smelled of lavender. He had not wanted his hands to ache with the memory of her curves, the softness of her belly, the warmth of her skin.

Their union had been solely to gain an heir and facilitate clan peace. And yet...

She refused to be kept at arms' length. Persistent and curious, she was a flame lighting up every possible desire within him, and try as he might he could no longer ignore how much he wanted her. Since the day he'd first seen her, he'd been plagued by a need that was impossible to resist. And it scared him.

On their wedding day, he'd been half-drunk and rigid with his own stubbornness. He had not wanted to look at her, nor touch her, for fear the dam would break and his actions would lead to more than his heart could handle. She'd walked through the doors of the chapel, more radiant than he could have imagined, and awareness of her had slammed through him like a waterfall. Gown fitted to perfection over her lush curves, her hair shining and full of flowers, her luminous eyes burning through his icy demeanor on contact.

It was then he had known without a shadow of a doubt: he would never be able to resist Caitriona Irving-Macnammon.

And in his fear, he had pushed her away. The woman who held his heart could break him, and he did not want to go through that again.

But Caitriona was not Iona, and he was faced with two options: to avoid the wounds he had locked in a box somewhere deep within for years, or to trust her. To trust that she would not shred his life to pieces the way Iona had. To tell her the full story, or as much of it as he could, without breaking Jenny's trust too.

"Rhys?" Caitriona said, and he realized then he had been staring at her in silence as they ate, absentminded about what he put in his mouth.

Rubbing his face, he tried to bring himself back to the present day, away from the musings about his past. Taking her hand, he kissed her palm. "I thought perhaps we could use some time to familiarize ourselves with each other."

A blush warmed her skin. "Was last night nae familiar enough?"

He dragged his gaze over her body, the reminder of the way they'd spent their night tangled in each others' arms a pleasant one. "Familiar with the body, aye," he said and was pleased to see her turn pinker. "But I confess, I cannae very well ask ye to be the mother of my child without some familiarity of the mind as well."

Caitriona's lips parted to take in some cheese, and he wanted to kiss her. But he was not here to repeat last night's actions.

Yet.

"I was glaikit to assume I could obtain an heir without needin' a relationship with his mother. And for that I apologize," he said.

A small furrow appeared between her brows. "Would it be disappointing if we had a girl?"

"Why would it be? I had a sister, after all, and several nieces whom I love dearly." The thought of several wee lassies with wild auburn hair and mischievous green eyes flashed through his mind and he smiled.

But the fear persisted. In a different form now. Fear that she, too, would experience the losses Iona had. Fear that she might also suffer the death that his first wife had; a death brought on by the careless actions of a midwife. A woman who had treated her so poorly she retreated further and further into herself with every loss.

As if she had read his mind, Caitriona spoke. "Do ye fear I'll lose my bairns, like Iona did?"

"Aye," he said, the old wounds rising. He reached out and cupped her cheek, unable to stop himself from touching her.

Caitriona leaned into his palm. "I willnae leave ye like she did."

The statement was full of gentleness. Sitting beside him, her hair loose and spilling around her shoulders, the deep green of her dress emphasizing her milky skin and forest-colored eyes, she was all he wanted.

"Rhys, I..."

He pulled her to him and smothered whatever she had been about to say with a kiss. Her fingers curled into his leine, anchoring him there, and he reveled in her softness against him. The way she fitted so perfectly into his arms, and into his life. The way her curves filled his hands, even as her words filled his silence.

He could not wait to spend years discovering everything about her, and the revelation seared through him with desperation. Desperation not to lose her, as he had Iona. Desperation to keep her safe from

Berach and his constant barrage of vile actions. Desperation to ensure that she wanted him as much as he wanted her.

When he pulled away, her eyes were soft, lashes fluttering as she bit her lip and studied him. Her hand had come to rest upon his cheek, and she fingered the scar there gently. "I cannae imagine ye as a boy. Were ye as serious as ye are now?"

She settled herself against his chest, leaning into him with a familiarity that was new and thrilling, and he draped his arm around her waist. When she lifted a blaeberry as if to offer it to him, he went to take it, only for her to pop it into her mouth with an impish smile.

"I was the mischief maker, if ye must know," he said.

Caitriona lifted another berry, this time straight to his mouth, blushing all the while. "Were ye? That seems...impossible."

"Does it, now?" he drawled, reveling in the pink tinge of her skin. It pleased him. He wanted to make her glow in all the ways he had seen last night. When she was happy, impassioned, she grew warm and full of light.

"Ye're always so..." With a small shake of her head, she did not finish the sentence.

"So...what?" he prompted, fingers drawing a languid trail over her waist. He was surprised to find he cared what she thought of him a great deal.

"It seems that...perhaps ye havenae kent someone ye can truly trust yerself with in a long time," she said, her tone careful. She ate another berry.

The woman was perceptive. Since Iona's death, Rhys had not let anyone in. Receding far into himself, he'd allowed rumors to inform his family and they had believed lies for far too long. So long, it felt impossible to right the wrongs said about him.

And then, with his mother, father, and brother dead, when his sister Gwen had run away and left behind a note she was devoting her life to Christ in a nunnery, he'd been the only one left.

Nobody remained to whom he could confess the truth.

Until Caitriona.

"Ye have a way about ye that makes a person feel seen. Truly seen," he said.

Caitriona watched him, waiting. Her eyes perceptive, gentle. Full of something he was not able to identify. Something soft, something sad. Something that dug deep into his heart and terrified him with its intensity.

"Llwyd wasnae the only man Iona desired," he said, before the years of mistrust could build another wall. "I dinnae ken for how long her attentions wandered to other men. I had given her all of myself, but she...didnae want it, I suppose."

Caitriona's hand met his, her soft fingers threading their way between his larger ones, comforting. There was no pity in her gaze, but there was pain. "I'm sorry," she said.

It was a simple thing, but her words spread a balm over the deep ache in his soul like nothing ever had. "Does it trouble ye, when I speak of her?"

"It only troubles me that it brings ye pain. That her actions marred the trust ye might have given me, if she hadnae...done what she did. But I understand now, why —" She cut herself off, sucking her lower lip inward, tempting him to tease it back out with a kiss.

"What is it ye understand?"

"I understand why even in the midst of passion, ye gave me yer body but the deepest part of ye remained hidden."

There was desire in her gaze, desire flaming from the tips of her fingers as they touched his jawline and her caress flooded through him.

He captured her jaw in his hand, tilting her head back to meet her lips with his own. She melted against him, and he broke away from her lips to brush kisses down the lovely expanse of her exposed neck.

When she made a small sound, it was all he could do not to act right then. To take advantage of the blanket and their partial seclusion, and revisit last night. But he had not come here to make love to his wife; he had come here to know her in more than just the biblical sense.

Quelling his desires, he laid her down on the quilt, moved the basket and foodstuffs, and stretched out beside her. Weaving their fingers together, he propped himself up on one elbow to watch her as she lay with her hair spread about her head like a sunset.

The smile she gave him was radiant.

"Over the years, I learned that showing my true feelings invited questions I didnae want to answer. So I kept to myself." With a shake of his head, he smiled. "But I didnae account for a woman like ye to come along, and hiding away doesnae work so well in a marriage, does it?"

The curve of her jaw softened when she laughed, full and beautiful. "I've upset all yer carefully laid plans, eh?"

"Aye, ye have." And he was better for it.

"Are ye...are ye disappointed?" There was something fragile in her tone, and her gaze drifted away from his face to the sky above them.

"Why would I be?"

"Ye wanted someone very different from myself, I'll wager."

"I am beginning to find that what I thought I wanted was not what I needed," he said, memorizing the way she chewed at her lip when she was unsure of herself.

She would not look at him. "Ye didnae want me."

How could she say this now, when he'd spent the entire night worshiping her in every way possible? Did she not realize her hold over him? "Caitriona, I didnae want *anyone*."

The depth of her gaze grew shuttered, and he gently turned her chin until she would meet his eyes again.

"I spent ten years alone, betrayed by the woman I thought was my greatest love, widowed and bitter. I didnae want to marry again, aye, because I didnae *want* a marriage spent separately. A marriage of emptiness, meaningless, forced upon me by a clan who doesnae trust me." He sighed, feeling as though his explanation was doing more damage than good. "I didnae want marriage, because I didnae want to be hurt again. I didnae want to burden anyone with my past, the rumors, the things I'd hidden so deep I didnae ken if they would ever be unburied."

"It must have been a heavy burden, to hold those secrets alone," she said, and the fragility had softened into understanding. As if she could read his mind. Her thumb stroked along the side of his finger. It was an absentminded movement, but his focus pulled to their hands and the electric feel of her skin against his.

"Do ye nae have secrets?" he asked.

Caitriona shrugged. "I keep very little to myself. Anythin' ye ask of me, I shall tell ye."

It was an invitation, and he took it. Anything to avoid his own past. "Well, then, are the rumors true about yerself?"

He was teasing, but she sighed. "I havenae...well, *hadnae* slept with a man, if that's what yer askin'."

"What did happen?" Curiosity got the better of him. He'd only heard whispers about her from the usual places. Gossips in town who made it their business to find out what they could about his wife.

Some of his clan members, who knew the neighboring clans and their history.

He'd not given his wife's past much thought until now.

She stared up at the sky. "Niall was traveling when I met him. I was nineteen, and had been out in the fields avoiding my mother's strict instructions to practice needlework by doing the very thing she hated — riding in trews."

Rhys snorted at the thought of a young Caitriona sneaking away in trews to spite her mother. "I like them," he said.

She smiled, but did not look at him. "He said a few pretty words, and...well. I was young, unmarried, barely courted, unspoken for. Most of my friends were already married and havin' bairns, while I was planning how to next sneak into my father's hunting party. It was...nice. To have a man interested in me, for once."

How could any man resist her? Rhys was baffled by the revelation that she had not had multiple suitors. His wife was irresistible in every way.

With a deep sigh, she relaxed and the memories began to play over her expression. Her nose wrinkled a little, and he wanted to kiss it. "He stayed in the village all summer long. Drinking with the men, writing poems and singing songs to entertain, and thoroughly enticing me with promises of what could be. Everyone saw us together, and I was not always careful to ensure we were amongst company. And one night...well, he hinted he might want to ask me something special. He did not say it outright, but I gained the impression that he'd spoken to my father."

A quiet fell, and he noted the tinge of pink in her cheeks. He wanted to wash the embarrassment away, to assure her she had nothing to be ashamed of. But he let her continue.

"So I let him lure me away, to the glen that was well known. A spot I later found out is where men and women went when they didnae want to be discovered. But I didnae ken that then. I was too naive. He took me there, and he spun more pretty words, and he promised we would marry as soon as he could come back for me, but that he had to leave to find his fortune. And when he kissed me, I thought it was the most wonderful thing I'd experienced. But then he...didnae...wouldnae stop."

Her tone was low, aching, and even before she put it into words, Rhys knew what she was going to say. Anger flared within him, but he stayed still. Had she ever spoken to anyone of this moment who had believed her? With the rumors that still floated about, he suspected not. People did not let scandal die, and those wounded the hardest were often the ones hurt most by the whispers.

"He didnae get further than ripping my skirt, and tearing off my stomacher. When I got back to the village, there was already talk. One look at me was enough. Niall had already begun to spread the tale by the time I made it back to my mother. And when I told her the truth...it was too late."

Regret laced her tone, and anger, too. "I had inflicted a wound on his neck, but he covered it with his collar and no one would believe I tried to fight him off. I swore after that I would learn to protect myself, so it could never happen again. A lot of good that did me."

She was referring to Berach's man attacking her. Rhys shook his head. "Ye did what ye could."

"I never should have let him get to me. I was so *stupid*. I ruined my own chances, my family's reputation, and my father's name. All because a man said some pretty words and I thought I was in love."

Taking her face in his hand, Rhys made her look at him. There were no tears in her eyes, but the pain was plain as day. The anger.

Not only had Niall attacked her, but everyone around her had let her down in their disbelief of her innocence. Rhys knew what it felt like, to have those closest to you place blame when what you needed most was understanding.

Reigning back the rage he felt toward Niall on her behalf, he said, "It wasnae yer fault."

Surprise flashed over her features. "I let it happen. I was so trusting. I never once stopped to listen to the advice of my best friend, my mother, when they told me to be careful — I let myself get carried away in the romance of it all, and —"

"Ye may be responsible for yer own actions, but so he is responsible for his." He cut her off. "Ye didnae ask him to do what he did. In fact, ye fought against it. Ye are not to blame for what this man did to ye."

Her eyes grew misty, and she let out a heavy breath. "No one has ever said that to me before."

The way she looked at him, with her breath catching in her words and her eyes wide as the years of hurt rolled off her chest, filled him with a deep sense of protectiveness. Cupping her cheeks with his hands, he brushed his lips against her forehead. "Forgive me," he said.

Caitriona's fingers came up to cover his. "Ye've done nothing wrong," she answered sweetly.

"Aye, I have," he replied. "I've been a glaikit fool, speakin' hastily of what I'd heard, knowin' nothin' of yer true past. I used the rumors I kent about ye to stop ye asking questions I didnae wish tae answer."

A wry smile graced her lips. "My da used to say 'twould take the devil himself tae stop me askin' questions. And then he married me off tae you."

A laugh escaped his chest then. "Have I stopped yer questions, woman? I think not."

Mischief rose in her expression. "Even the Devil of Calhoun is no match for an Irving woman's tongue."

"But ye're the Lady of Calhoun now," he reminded her. "I've a few tricks up my sleeves yet, dinnae ye forget it."

The mirth bubbling in her eyes was irresistible. Brushing her lips with his own, he reveled in the arch of her body against him, her response immediate and wanting. She was *his* woman. *Lasair mo chride.* The flame of his heart. If this was to be their relationship, he relished the thought of the days to come.

Breaking away just enough to look into her eyes, he took in the flush of her cheeks, the soft readiness of her lips. A smile played about the corners of her mouth and he wanted to worship every inch of her. Every curve of her body, sumptuous and full beneath his hands; every dimple in her skin and the roll of her belly when she sat; he could not get the thought of her out of his mind. His wife.

She was sweet-smelling clover warmed in the summer sun. She was a sunset flooding his world with its painted glory at the end of the day. She was the balm of a summer rain soothing his tired soul. She was *his*.

"What is it?" she asked hazily, a glow about her face.

Grabbing her waist, he rolled so she was atop him, and grinned. Her hair fell around them, a bright curtain of shimmering curls, and as the strands of it tickled his skin he pulled her down and said against her supple lips, "'Tis a good day."

The sudden shout of her name startled both of them and Caitriona scrambled off of him, straightening her skirts and flushing beet red as she stood. Rhys rose with her, tempted to send whomever it was straight back the way they had come. But he settled for feeling the weight of her against his side as a young man from the village appeared, face red from running.

"Milady!" he gasped, not giving Rhys a second glance. "Sorcha's screamin' somethin' awful, the wain is on its way, and I'm afraid —" he cut off with a sob.

Caitriona glanced at Rhys, and a flutter of guilt crossed her expression. But she burst into action before he could respond. "I'm coming," she said.

Rhys knew Blair well, and had been aware that his wife was expecting another wee bairn. But what did Caitriona have to do with it?

She did not quite meet his eyes. "Rhys, I'll need a horse and clean cloths and supplies brought from the castle. Jenny will ken what I need."

Dazed, Rhys merely nodded, picked up the basket, and followed his wife back to Calhoun Castle. She was already instructing Blair to go back to his wife and wait for them there. By the time they'd reached the castle walls she was running, and so was Rhys. Several questions flew through his mind while he did her bidding, but he kept them to himself. Why she was being called upon to help deliver a baby, he did not know. But he knew the urgency of such situations, and would not bar her from doing whatever she could to help.

At his bidding, Jenny was bringing supplies, and Caitriona disappeared into one of the rooms off the foyer. He barely had time to comprehend what lay inside the room as he followed her, for she was a whirlwind of activity. Herbal scents surrounded him. To one side, a wooden screen gave privacy to a chaise longue; to the other side was a wall filled with vials and bottled herbs and dark jars of which he did not know the contents. Dried flowers and plants hung everywhere.

This room had been unused the last time he'd set foot inside, and now it appeared to be a fully functioning den full of potions. Was his wife a witch? A healer? He scowled at the cozy hearth, puzzling it out in his mind. Surely she would have told him if she was a midwife.

After all he had confided about Iona's death, surely she would not keep this from him.

But when she met his gaze, regret flashed through her eyes and he knew. "Will ye help me?"

Rhys stared at her, the silence around them heavy with anticipation. A sharp twinge pulled at his heart. She had not felt safe enough to confide this in him. She did not trust him yet. But he pushed it aside. "Aye, I will help ye."

They could discuss this hidden information later. When he had full time to sort through his feelings on the matter, and she was not mid-action.

Her shoulders loosened and she took a deep breath. "I'll need someone to keep Blair calm and…possibly aid me in turning the wain in its mother's womb. Can ye…do this?"

Memories of Iona laboring painfully through hours of childbirth bombarded him. The listlessness that had hit her after every bairn she'd lost. Her despair when yet another pregnancy did not take.

The midwife's harsh words.

He took a deep breath and held out his hand to his wife. "Tell me what ye need me to do, and I'll do it."

What happened in the next few hours would be essential to the life of Sorcha and her child. And he would do everything in his power to help, regardless of how he felt. His wife had hidden an important part of her life from him — something he now suspected she'd been hiding from the very first — and he needed time to adjust. To evaluate.

Following her to the stables, he mounted his own horse and rode with her to the village where she swiftly dismounted and entered the hut without announcing herself. Within the cottage, Sorcha labored on the bed as Blair held her head and hands, looking as though he might faint with every contraction running through her body. Two small children sat in the corner with their grandmother, and another woman was wringing a cloth to be placed on Sorcha's forehead.

Anticipation was heavy in the air. With a serene calm, Caitriona greeted them, and Rhys followed her lead. Despite the time of day, the hut was dim and stuffy. Rhys met his wife's eyes, and an unspoken question passed between them: was he ready? They faced life and death together.

Surprise ran through him. He trusted her, and he was prepared to face whatever she threw his way. Clearing his throat, he nodded, and the vows from their wedding day ran through his head.

In times of suffering, and times of fortune, and all that lay between.

A Reckoning
Caitriona

In the dim quarters of the cottage, Caitriona moved with confidence, hands steady and words calm. No-one could see the trembling in her chest and the whirling of her thoughts.

Sorcha wailed from the bed, and her sister Ailsa worked quietly putting water to boil over the fire as Rhys shooed the children and grandmother outside and away from the noise. Everyone moved about the small space in a hush, whispering to each other as the moans of the laboring woman filled the air.

Rhys seemed to know what she needed done before she asked anything of him. He had uncovered the one window in the hut, cracking the door open to allow the air into the stifled room. While she made Sorcha comfortable on the bed and set everything up for delivery, he settled her things beside the bed, ensuring she had a place to rest should she need it.

He filled the space with the confidence Caitriona needed in that moment. Not once had he questioned this venture, nor demanded she tell him why she was working as a midwife without his knowledge. He simply followed her, as though he'd been doing this for years. It soothed the regret filling her chest.

Iona's passing in childbirth weighed heavy on her mind as she spared a glance toward Rhys. Though his face was calm, his fingers jittered by his side. Perhaps she had been selfish to ask him to come with her. She should have asked Jenny or Kenna to assist; it was thoughtless of her to put him through this.

But it was done.

Pulling him aside, she found comfort in the way he followed without protest. She was not unconscious of the way he threaded his fingers through hers momentarily, his large hand warm and steadying around hers. "I need ye to help me turn the child. It is breech and she'll bleed to death if it doesnae come now." She kept her tone low, but her breath trembled. "Can ye do it?"

Rhys glanced at the laboring woman, taking in her pained expression, and then back at Caitriona. Like her, his aura was quiet, but his eyes told a different story. "Aye," he answered, squeezing her hand before releasing it.

They crossed to the bedside. "Sorcha, I have to turn the bairn within ye again. He didnae stay the first turning." She took Sorcha's hand and placed it carefully into Ailsa's. "Yer sister will be here with ye, and Rhys as well. It will hurt as before, but ye *must* do exactly as I say or ye both will die." She did not mince her words. They all knew what was at stake.

Breath short, Sorcha nodded. "Please, Cait. Anythin' for the wain." Another bout of pain rippled through her and she closed her eyes, inhaling slowly, focused on staying calm through the throws of labor.

"Let me know when it has passed." Caitriona placed a reassuring hand on the woman's shoulder. Turning to Sorcha's sister, she instructed Ailsa to prepare everything they would need for the baby's arrival. It would be harder this time. Sorcha's throws were coming fast, and Caitriona would have to work between them.

Rhys came to her side. "What do I need to do?"

His jaw was tense, and he pushed his sleeves up with restless energy. In the tight space, he filled her vision, broad-shouldered and towering above them all. Though she had seen glimpses of it in the past few days, she still wondered: could this man become the gentle force she needed?

Taking a deep breath, she gestured to Sorcha. "She still has time. When this pain has eased, I will try to push the bairn's head down. He's but a wee way sideways; luck is on our side. It will be painful for her, and I need her to be as relaxed as she can be given the circumstances. I need ye to be her support. Ailsa must help me with the delivery."

Anticipating their needs, Sorcha's sister had already begun warming blankets and boiling cloths. Rhys pulled a stool over to the side of the bed. As if by magic, everything about him softened. He settled beside Sorcha and took her hand.

"I want ye to tell me about yer bairns. I didnae hear their names, bonny wee wains they are," he said gently, voice quiet.

It was exactly what Caitriona needed him to do. Distract, give her something to focus on. He must have been remembering Iona, for as he spoke to Sorcha his forehead creased with worry. Haltingly, the woman told Rhys about her children. Fiona and Flora, they were called, and they wanted a brother so badly.

As she spoke, Caitriona applied oil to her hands and moved them around Sorcha's belly, applying hard pressure as she worked to turn the child between the throws of her labor. Sorcha's voice faltered, but she kept her eyes on Rhys.

It seemed as though hours passed as Caitriona massaged Sorcha's belly, feeling the baby's head and body to turn it downward. Before her marriage, she had done this but once, and under the strict guidance of the village Howdie before her. It was only a lucky few who were able to turn a bairn in the mother's belly during labor. Those with larger bellies seemed to fare better, and though Sorcha was small, Caitriona had already turned the child once. She was determined to do it again.

Sorcha cried out at the pressure, and time seemed to stop. The babe was nearly turned but they faced the hardest part now; Sorcha would need to relax in order for the child to fully settle into place. "'Tis nearly done, Sorcha; I ken 'tis hard, but ye must try to breathe. Dinnae be afraid; this bairn will be hale and hearty."

She met Rhys's eyes. He was watching her with an intensity that burned through her skin, the weight of his gaze so tangible she could feel it settle into her bones. Slow and steady, he began to sing a lullaby, filling the room with a deep baritone so full of emotion Caitriona's eyes blurred with tears.

She blinked them away. Beneath her hands, the babe kicked and squirmed in its mother's belly. Sorcha's muscles began to relax as Rhys's voice soothed away her fears, and Caitriona applied gentle pressure to the bairn within, feeling the child turn in her hands. In a matter of moments, it was done.

"Sorcha, can ye sit up?" The child would settle into a birthing position much better if she was upright.

Wordlessly, Sorcha nodded. Rhys was right there to support her weight as she heaved herself upright, and much to Caitriona's satisfaction a splatter of liquid gushed onto the floor at the change in position. Sorcha let out a low moan and reached out for her sister.

"Good, Sorcha. Very good." When Ailsa settled by her sister's side, Caitriona said, "She will need support through these pains. Her time is close."

While Sorcha labored on the edge of the bed, Caitriona and Rhys created a clean space for the child to be born. A beautifully knit blanket hung by the fire, warming, and she gathered cloths with which to clean up the afterbirth. Spreading a blanket on the bed to catch the fluids that would come out when the child was born, she snuck a glance at Rhys.

If he recognized this quilt as one pilfered from his own castle, he showed no sign of it. His eyes were locked on the laboring woman, his brow furrowed, the moment of stillness revealing a tic in his jaw, and restless hands at his sides. Caitriona reached out and touched his arm.

"Blair and his children will need to eat, and perhaps rest," she said.

Rhys nodded, and his face was unreadable when he looked at her. "I'll speak with him."

Outside, the light was fading fast. Had it really been so long? Time seemed irrelevant as they readied for the coming of the child. Caitriona had no time to consider what might have been going on in her husband's mind, for Sorcha let out a wail and she snapped to attention.

"The babe is coming!" Sorcha gasped.

Caitriona's instinct took over, and she began to breathe slowly and loudly, to help regulate the laboring woman as well as herself. Speaking nonsense in soothing tones, she focused on Sorcha, who half-squatted, half-bent over the bed. Nothing mattered but the laboring mother.

Squatting beside the woman, Caitriona felt for a head and was pleased by what she found. Sorcha was wailing loudly, her voice shaky and panicked. "I cannae — I cannae stop!" Her entire body rippled with the urge to push.

"Aye, 'tis good, Sorcha. Hold yer breath, and bear down. 'Tis what yer body wants." These words had been repeated by the midwife with whom Caitriona had trained, many, many times. To wail was to lose strength, and they did not know how long this phase would take. With growing confidence, she instructed Ailsa to sit in front of Sorcha and support her.

THE DEVIL AND THE MIDWIFE 253

Instinctually, Sorcha widened her stance, and Caitriona took a deep breath. It was going to be okay.

In what felt like a lifetime and barely minutes all at once, Sorcha threw all of her might into pushing and a pale, wrinkly bairn was born into Caitriona's waiting hands. Working swiftly, Caitriona and Ailsa helped Sorcha to lay back on the bed while the child was placed on her chest. The babe had a fuzzy covering of red hair just like its father, and as soon as Sorcha pulled her new baby onto her chest, a loud cry filled the room.

Relief rippled through Caitriona, and Ailsa laughed.

Settling the fire-warmed blanket over mother and child, Caitriona gently checked fingers and toes and other features. "Oh, what a beautiful wee one!"

Sorcha peered at her baby and adoration flooded her face. "Is it a boy?" she asked, hope strong in her voice.

Caitriona nodded. "Aye, a boy. Strong and hearty, too!" As she spoke, the baby's crackling cry filled the room, and they all cooed at him.

The placenta would follow soon, so Caitriona set about tying off the cord. When it stopped pulsing, she cut it free as close to the bairn as she could, and told Sorcha to let her body push out the afterbirth. She would need to check none of it had broken off within the womb.

Ailsa seemed quite fascinated as she checked over the organ, and she showed the younger woman the marvel that was the tree of life on this thing which had kept the bairn alive in its mother's womb for nine months. Cleaning up the area and disposing of the afterbirth, she watched Sorcha urge her newborn son to nurse.

"What will ye call him?" Caitriona asked, warmed by the sight of mother and child.

Sorcha rubbed a soft hand over the fuzzy head, and smiled. "Ruadh. Ruadh, my little red-haired boy."

Rhys appeared in the doorway, and the worried lines in his forehead disappeared the moment his gaze lit upon Sorcha. "Blair and the wee ones are anxious to see the bairn; shall I let them in?"

With a dreamy smile, Sorcha nodded.

Blair rushed in the second Rhys called out the door, his daughters piling in after him like giddy lambs. They crowded around the bed, coos and squeals abounding at the sight of their little red-haired boy.

Caitriona glanced around her. Ailsa had been productive while she checked on Sorcha's afterbirth, and most of the cottage was clean again. There was nothing left to do, really, save to ensure Sorcha did not bleed too much, and check her again in the morning.

Giving Ailsa strict instructions to send for her immediately should anything seem amiss, she paused a moment to admire the scene. Sorcha was surrounded in a glow of happiness, with Blair at her side and Flora's and Fiona's blonde curls wild as they snuggled up to her side to see the now-nursing Ruadh. In the dim light of the cottage, soft voices mingling with the crackling of the fire, it seemed nothing could be more perfect.

A peculiar ache spread through Caitriona's chest and she pressed a hand to her stomach to assuage the sensation.

What was it? This trickle of intense yearning, clenching around her heart and setting her stomach aflutter? She met Rhys's gaze across the cottage and saw a mirror of her own emotions in his eyes. There it was. Longing, deep and pure. Not a raging desire, but something more delicate, breakable, like an errant flower in false spring, blooming in the face of the snows yet to come.

With a flush, she realised. It was hope.

For too long, Caitriona had given up all her dreams of becoming a mother. Of having a family of her own, a wain at her breast, of wild-haired children clamoring in her arms. Her deepest desire had been ripped away from her long ago, and it had taken years to accept. Now, in the face of a new marriage, the demands of the clan, and the newfound trust between herself and Rhys, children were no longer a lost hope.

They were a necessary part of a future she had only just begun to accept.

Rhys held out his hand, and she slid her palm into his, and they emerged into the dusky last light of the day. Exhaustion was heavy in her limbs as they walked, riddling her muscles and back with aches she had not noticed before. Her husband's hand was rough and calloused around hers, and she leaned into his strength, needing a good sleep and time to sort out what she was feeling.

"Thank ye," she said, her heart welling. He had known exactly what to do for her in that room. "I dinnae ken what I would have done if ye had not been there."

His eyes tripped over her face and dress, pausing on the apron and the basket in her hand. "When I first saw ye, ye had much the same mess on ye as now."

Caitriona's cheeks grew warm. Their first meeting seemed distant now. She had been so upset, so determined to stay within the bounds of the life she had created for herself. "Aye, I remember," she said.

"I didnae ken ye were a midwife."

The statement was simple, open, without censure.

Caitriona worried her lip with her teeth. "I should have told ye. I meant to, but with the attack and everything else I didnae have the time. And after ye told me about Iona, and the midwife who...mishandled her, I — well, I didnae ken how ye might react."

"As I said, *lasair-chride*, it was a long time ago." Despite his reassurance, his brow furrowed and he was not looking at her.

Caitriona's fears began to rise again. What if this drew them apart, when they had only just begun to forge trust? "I know. But keepin' the truth from anyone is not in my nature. I was with Sorcha yesterday in the village. I'm sorry I didnae tell ye."

He shook his head. "Dinna fash, *lasair-chride*." Looping his arm around her waist, he pulled her close as they walked, the faintest crinkle of a smile at the corners of his eyes. "But if the parish found out ye were practicin' without a license, they might put ye on trial for witchcraft."

Caitriona snorted, relieved that he was not upset. "'T'would only be fitting that the Devil of Calhoun had a witch for a wife."

The rumble of a laugh sounded deep in his chest. "Aye well, 't'would not be the first rumor I've dealt with."

The castle loomed into view, lit from behind by the rising moon. Caitriona slowed her walk. "Do ye really not care?"

Rhys shrugged one shoulder. "I care about yer safety, and ask that ye not visit anyone without me or one of my men at your side."

"But it's...not proper for the Lady of the castle to pursue an occupation," she said, her mother's voice nagging inside her head. *A Lady does not wander about covered in blood and wearing trews.*

Rhys chuckled. "I didnae think propriety could stop ye."

The moon lit his dark hair with silver, and peace overwhelmed her. It had never crossed her mind that her husband might *not* try to stop her doing what she'd always wanted to do. Sure, he had told her she could live her life however she desired, but that was before she'd known Iona died by a midwife's careless actions. Before their future expectations had changed.

"Propriety couldnae stop me," she said, halting in her tracks. Realizing as the words formed on her lips, they were true. "But you could. Midwifery isnae for the faint of heart; there will be sleepless nights, and days gone, and I cannae promise that I willnae carry burdens with me. As ye well know, not every woman and child...survives."

Rhys touched her cheek with gentle fingers. "Do what makes ye happy, wife. I will be by yer side."

The words put a lightness in her soul that had not been there in a long time. "Then perhaps I'll apply to the parish for a license."

Pulling her to him, Rhys brushed his lips over hers. "It can be arranged. Later. Now, I think ye need a decent supper and a thorough bath."

Caitriona tried to hold herself away, but he kept her firmly in his grasp. "There's blood on my dress!" she gasped when he nipped beneath her ear.

"Aye, there is. Better go up to our rooms and take it off." He backed her toward the castle, and she let out a half-laugh, half-startled-cry when she tripped backwards.

Lit by the moonlight alone, they were still very visible to the castle guards, and she was mortified when someone called out.

"Do ye need help, lady?"

"Haud yer wheesht, Iohmar, 'tis yer laird with her," Rhys answered, humor in his tone.

Iohmar peered down at them and retorted, "Aye, I ken, that's why I asked her."

"I'm fine, thank ye Iohmar," Caitriona replied, laughing. Her stomach growled. "Just a bit hungry is all."

Rhys took her hand and they passed through the gates. "Why don't ye go up to our rooms, I'll tell Jenny to prepare us a meal," he said as they entered the castle. "I'll send up a bath as well."

Bed was a heavenly thought, and Caitriona set off without argument. The halls still bustled with activity; after supper, things were being put back into their place, cleaned, a few rounds of ale being shared before bed. The candles had been lit and lent a warmth to the otherwise dark hallways. It was the sort of atmosphere Caitriona loved best. That time when everything slowed down, when people were happy to be done with their work, when the castle was content.

She was halfway to her rooms when whispers of her name reached her ears, accompanied by a giggle. Slowing her walk, she paused.

"I've heard she bed ten men before marrying the Laird," one voice said with a snort.

The other replied, "Aye, and the only way her family could get rid of her was to marry her off to him. Poor man, shackled with a loose woman he doesnae even love."

There was a gathering of sighs and giggles, and then — "I'd like to show him what real love is like."

A laugh. "Maisie, ye've been infatuated with his Lairdship since ye were naught but twelve."

"Have ye not eyes, ye numpty?" Maisie retorted.

"Oh aye, I have," the second maid simpered. "His Lairdship may be fifteen years older than meself, but he's got nae a flaw on him. E'en me ma has sweet eyes for the Laird. Though she'd gie me a whippin' for saying as such."

"I saw the Lady o' the house fightin' him t' other day," Maisie said. "In trews she was! He didnae look too happy."

"Aye, 'tis nae becomin' of a lady to fight, and lookin' like she does? No wonder the marriage bed was empty so long." Censure was in her tone. "O' course, she could do to wear proper clothes and she wouldnae be half bad. But och, the fightin' like a lad in the field!"

"I'd like to fight him," said Maisie, giggling. "Into his bed."

Both of them burst into furious snickers. "And finally feel those arms, och what a pleasure."

A flush of embarrassment flooded Caitriona from her cheeks to her toes. The frank discussion of luring her husband into bedding them was one thing, but the censure about her appearance struck a deeply buried hurt within her. For a moment, she considered slinking away to find another path to her rooms, but then she straightened her shoulders.

She was Caitriona Irving, the Lady of Calhoun Castle, not some trollop hiding in the shadows.

Shaking out her hair and swiping a hand over her dirty skirt, she lifted her chin and swept around the corner. Moira Irving had drilled the elegance of a commanding and regal walk into her daughter, and now was the time to use it.

Two girls of no more than seventeen huddled together in the corridor, hands over their mouths as they stared at her. Shame was obvious in their gasps and bright pink cheeks.

The shorter one dropped a curtsey and nearly fell over in her haste. "Milady!"

The taller one, whose dark hair was slipping from her braids, followed suit. She would not meet Caitriona's eyes. "Lady Macnammon, we — didn't hear you."

"Perhaps it's time for ye to both be abed," Caitriona said. "And not gossipping in the halls about yer Laird."

They both had the decency to blush and drop their gazes. "Yes, milady!" they said quickly, and all but ran past her.

Reminding herself how ridiculous she had been at their age, Caitriona made her way up to her rooms and let herself in. The room had been tidied up, and the bed was made. A fire blazed in the hearth, warm and welcoming, and the first round of hot water had already been poured into the large tub sitting before the flames. She had no time to step away from the door before more women bustled in. They curtseyed in acknowledgement and went about pouring their buckets into the tub.

But Caitriona caught their gazes flitting over her bloodied dress, her wild hair, and her dirty hands. She was not blind to the way they exchanged glances between themselves as they left.

"Shall I stay to help ye undress, milady?" one of the women asked. It was the mother of one of the girls in the hall, that much Caitriona knew.

"Nay, thank ye." Caitriona smiled at her. "I can do very well by myself."

The woman hesitated. "I...I heard ye delivered a bairn today?"

Caitriona began to undo her stays. "Aye, a boy."

A smile lit the woman's face, and her round cheeks were merry. "A blessing," she said. After a few seconds of indecision, she blurted, "My oldest, ye see, she be expectin' and...well our last midwife wasnae so gentle, ye ken?" She stared at the floor rather than meet Caitriona's eyes, as if embarrassed to be asking for help.

Before Caitriona could answer, Rhys walked in. He looked every bit as tired as she felt. "Effie," he said, nodding to the woman.

Effie curtseyed and backed away without a word, intending to leave.

"Effie?" Caitriona called out when the woman had reached the door. She waited until Effie met her gaze to say, "I'll speak with ye tomorrow about yer daughter."

Relief settled into the woman's features. "Thank ye, milady."

Rhys's eyes darted between Caitriona and Effie's back with some bemusement. "What's this, then?"

Pulling her stomacher loose, Caitriona set about untying her stays. "Her eldest daughter is with child." Despite her exhaustion, a smile crept onto her lips.

"Ah," Rhys said, stripping off his jacket and undoing the buttons on his woolen vest. The plaid garment dropped to the floor and he untied his leine, pulling it over his head. Shadows played with the planes of muscle across his abdomen, and several scars bit into his chest, evidence of the battles he had fought and won. Unable to look away, she watched the slide of muscle in his biceps as he divested his boots and tossed them aside.

Everything about Rhys was powerful. Commanding.

His dark head lifted then, and when he caught her staring he grinned, his scarred eyebrow rising. "Do ye like what ye see?" He faced her, a dimple appearing in his cheek.

"Ye're incorrigible," she responded, flushing. Turning to the bath, she let her stays and petticoats drop.

Despite the clear admiration in his eyes, the way he'd nuzzled her neck earlier, the gossip about her appearance rang through her mind. Was she...enough? Caitriona had been teased about her height and her size many times throughout her life. She was as tall as the boys, too tall. And until womanhood had shaped her into something more proportionate, she'd been ungainly. Clumsy. Her curves had been rolls in the wrong places.

With the curse of red hair and a plethora of freckles, she'd been through everything to lighten the blemishes, to make her complexion smooth. Makeup was a must, when visitors came. In her courting years, her mother had piled complexion-cream on her, painting her with cosmetics to hide the unsightly freckles covering her face, neck, and shoulders.

Until one day, Caitriona had simply said, enough. If a man did not want her with her undesirably bright red hair and far too many freckles, she did not want him, either.

But the insecurities stayed with her. And right then, she felt too tall. Too blemished. Too much.

Without looking behind her to see Rhys's reaction, she slipped from her chemise and into the tub. The evidence of midwifery was on her hand and under her nails. No wonder the girls in the hallway had seemed so horrified; she must have been a sight to behold, bloodied and stern.

While she washed the day away from her skin, Rhys pulled a chair over to the tub and sat. Dressed in naught but his plaid and stockings, he picked up a brush and began to run it through her hair, loosening the knots away and massaging her scalp. The gentle ministrations lulled her into a drowsy state, weighed down as she was by the exhaustion only found in a hard day of work.

"Did it bother ye, to be around a woman in labor?" she asked, having wondered the entire evening whether memories of his wife plagued him.

Rhys hummed low. "I didnae find the memories as troublesome as expected. But those cries are...not easily forgotten."

The rhythmic brushing paused for a moment when she asked, "And when I labor as she did...how will ye feel?"

"I've not had time to consider," he answered, deep in thought. Almost instinctively, he began to braid her hair. A part of her heart melted at his care. "Do ye fear birth?"

It was something Caitriona had never considered, because the prospect of children had been taken away so long ago. "I...dinnae ken. I never thought I'd be any closer to birth than as a midwife."

"Do ye *want* to be a mother?" The question was unexpected.

Nobody had ever asked her this before. It was always assumed. *Someday, you will marry. Someday, you will have wains of your own. Someday, you will grow up to be the Lady of the House, you will manage your family, you will be the matriarch.* Moira Irving had trained her for this, or at least...tried to. It had been a fact of her life until Niall stole away her future with one simple act. These things had been predestined, chosen for her based on her sex alone.

She turned to look at him, careful to keep her now-braided hair out of the water. "I...think I do."

He was relaxed, watching her in the warm light of the fire, softer and far less intimidating than he had been on their wedding day. Was it a trick of the firelight, or was it the knowledge that he would hold a laboring woman's hand and sing her a lullaby to ease her way? He was not the glowering Devil everyone painted him to be, but a being full of humor and pain and desire and memories haunting him in ways very few cared to understand.

"Does it not scare ye?" he asked, when she said no more. "The pain? The possibility that ye might die?"

Caitriona shook her head. Somehow, she knew this question was more about his own past than her current worries. "Nae, it doesnae scare me. Many a woman my age has borne children and lived long lives after. There is risk, but...I know more than most."

"Hmm," he said, eyes shifting to the fire.

"Does it scare you?" she returned the question.

His gaze shuttered as she rose from the tub. Though she desperately wished to cover herself from his languid gaze, Caitriona did not rush to hide behind the towel. She dried herself thoroughly, attempting to appear unbothered, but blushing head to toe. They had shared intimacies she'd never dreamed of sharing with anyone, and yet she felt odd casually taking on the full role of a wife. Pulling a chemise over her head, she rubbed her arms.

The gooseflesh on her arms was not from a chill.

Rhys rose and pulled a blanket from the bed. When she held out her hands for it, he shook his head. Wrapping it around himself, he sat in the chair again and motioned for her to come to him. Her face was heated when she settled into his arms. He closed the blanket around both of them.

"I dinnae want to face that loss again," he said, adjusting so her head was nearly level with his. He was a good deal taller than her, but sitting as she was in his lap removed much of the space. With a small smile, he touched her cheek. "So take care not tae die, aye?"

She leaned into his palm and returned his smile through a yawn, content in the warmth and the ease of the moment. "I'll do my best. I happen tae know a very good midwife."

Mischief wrinkled the edges of his eyes. "I heard she's a witch, and she scandalizes the maids by wearing trews."

Caitriona giggled sleepily and settled her head on his shoulder. "Och, I think I half scared them to death tonight, covered in blood as I was. 'Tis a good thing I wasnae also in trews today."

Rhys' fingers made circles on her thigh, slow and pleasantly rough against her skin. "I think they're a fine garment on ye. Ye should wear them more."

"Hmmm," was all she could manage to say. Despite the tingles that followed in the wake of his touch, her eyelids would not stay open, and she sank further into his lap, yawning again.

He kissed the top of her head and stood, taking her to the bed. A deep humming lullaby filled the room, accompanied by the crackling of the fire and the small sounds of Rhys readying himself for sleep. His voice was soothing, filling her with contentment and an emotion she set aside to identify later.

By the time he'd undressed to slide in beside her, she was already half-asleep. He settled his arm over her side, pulling her back against him firmly, and she sank into his solid warmth with a hum.

"Go to sleep, *lasair mo chride,*" he said. And, as she drifted away into the welcome darkness of a dreamless sleep, she thought she heard him say, "*Dia a dhìon, a ghràidh m'anama.*"

God protect her, love of my soul.

THE PARISH LICENSE
Caitriona

Caitriona woke as the sun rose. Rhys still snored away beside her, arm thrown recklessly over her waist as was becoming familiar, and she smiled. For all of his attentiveness during the day, Rhys was dead to the world when he slept. Pressing her face a little closer to his neck, she breathed in the warm scent of him.

There were many things to do: Sorcha to check on, a new pregnancy to tend to, Lilleas and Morven to check on, herbs to gather, a store of midwifery supplies to replenish, a parish license to obtain.

But the weight of her husband's arm around her and the boyish softness to his face in the morning light were distractions. She traced the dark lashes against his cheek and studied the lines forming at the edges of his eyes. Lines she knew had begun to indelibly mark his face with the mischief he often displayed. She had never expected she would find companionship like this. With a sigh, she slid from under his arm, taking care not to wake him.

She was halfway dressed when his deep voice accused, "Where are ye sneakin' off to?"

Caitriona turned, still tying up her stays, and smiled at him. There was certainly no self-consciousness in him. He lay with his arms behind his head, chest fully exposed, not a lick of decency in his gaze.

"Sorcha will require attention; I must ensure that her ah...her bleeding is normal, and the bairn is able to nurse."

"Can ye not attend her later?" The wickedness in his grin was unmistakable. "I've need for some attentions as well."

She bit her lip, trying not to laugh. It was certainly a tempting proposal, but she knew giving in could lead to hours lost from the day, and she wanted to attend Sorcha before luncheon. With a shake of her head, she crossed over to his bedside, almost fully dressed. All she needed was her *arisaid*. Bending over, she pressed a kiss to his lips. His hand was heavy on her neck, possessive and warm. Never had she felt so wanted.

"I must break my fast before I leave, and gather some herbs to aid in her healing. That alone will take an hour, and I would like to visit her by midmorning." She touched her now-tousled hair, clicking her tongue as she redid the braids.

Rhys was incorrigible. Sitting up, he wrapped his hands around her waist and pulled her into his lap, pressing her back against his chest as she tried to tuck her arisaid around her shoulders and neck.

Artful fingers plucked the fabric away, and he let out a contented hum as he nipped his way up the base of her neck. "Do ye need me to accompany ye?"

How she wished she could stay here, wiling away the hours in his arms, beneath his lips, succumbing to the desire in her veins. His day-old beard scraped against her skin, sending tingles of pleasure down her spine.

But she had a bairn to check on, and a new mother to care for. She wiggled out of Rhys's embrace and snatched her *arisaid* from the bed where he'd thrown it. "I'll be back before luncheon; dinnae fash. 'Tis a quick trip. "

Rhys grabbed his leine, gaze full of misgiving. "Have ye no sense of danger, hen?"

She shrugged. "I'll take Iohmar with me."

Worry creased his forehead, and he pulled his shirt on. "I dinnae ken if the lad will be enough, Caitriona. Ye ken what Berach's men can do. I dinnae want to risk yer bein' attacked again."

It was on the tip of her tongue to remind him she had bested several of his men, but the furrow between his brows stopped her. A very real fear was buried deep in his gaze. She sobered. Remembering the way he'd immediately beaten Seumas to a pulp. Knowing, now, a great deal of that rage was fear. "I'll take someone else with me, if ye think 'twould be better."

Slowly, he nodded, as if calculating the possibilities. "When will ye be wantin' to apply at the parish for a license?"

Caitriona frowned, thrown off by his change in subject. "I ah...as soon as I can?"

"Go then," he said. "I'll come to ye in an hour's time, and we'll go to the parish together. They cannae verra well refuse the Laird of the castle now, can they." His lips tipped up at the corner, and he winked at her.

Caitriona's chest welled with an emotion so sudden and wild it ached. He had just offered her his power, after everything she had hidden from him. "You would help me in this?"

"'Tis my duty to make my wife content, is it not?"

The ache in her chest exploded, flooding her with warmth and tears that blurred her vision. She blinked them away. "Thank you."

With a tisk of his tongue, he studied her with bemusement. "Ach hen, 'tis only a license."

She shook her head. "It is...so much more." It was freedom. Autonomy. Trust.

Words failing her, she took his face and planted a sound kiss on his mouth, needing him to feel the things she could not say. Without hesitation, he embraced her, running his hands through her freshly-neatened hair and over her straightened clothes until she was breathless.

When she broke away, her arisaid was, somehow, missing again. Rhys had one hand behind his back and a smirk on his lips.

"I'll need my arisaid back," she said, a lump still lodged in her throat. She would *not* cry about this.

"Ach," he clicked his tongue in disappointment. "Ye look better without it."

Still, he offered her the garment. She tucked it back into place and straightened her hair. When she looked up at him, a touch of worry creased his brow.

"Take care, wife," was all he said.

She smiled. "I will."

※ ※ ※

In the castle gardens, Caitriona gathered lavender and mint, which were calming, as well as meadowsweet for any pains Sorcha might have. The morning was clear and mild, the sky hazy and a cool breeze ruffling over her hair. She could have spent her entire day here in the thriving garden, where everything was green and fragrant. But, basket in hand, she started down the road toward the village, Iomhar trailing behind her.

It was a short walk, and she savored it. Flowers bowed their heads in languid form, bluebells nodding as she passed and thistles puffing out with purple blooms. Though standoffish with their prickles and thorns, they were a valued plant and she made a mental note to stop and dig some up on her way back. The root was edible, and the leaves and flowers were useful for treating disease of the liver.

Sorcha's home was on the edge of the village closest to the castle. Smoke bloomed from the chimney above a golden thatched roof, and Ruadh's lusty newborn cry reached her ears even from this distance. She smiled. The baby's wails were loud and indignant, a good sign.

Iomhar settled himself against the wall of the cottage to wait, and she smiled at him.

When she knocked on the door, Blair answered. An air of pride hung around the faint smile on his lips and the twinkle in his eyes. "Mistress Irving, come in." He stepped aside for her to enter.

"Good day, Blair. I hear your son already, he'll be a strong one aye?" She surveyed the simple yet efficient cottage.

Sorcha sat on the edge of their bed, holding Ruadh to her breast with an exasperated, loving roll of her eyes. "'Tis right there, ya wee wild one," she said in a low voice. Snuffles and grunts answered her, and the baby finally found his latch.

The glow of new motherhood lit Sorcha's gaze as she stared at her son. She was all softness, vulnerable in the careful way she moved to sit back on the bed, in the relieved huff of breath when Ruadh latched, in the wince of pain as her milk let down. These first few days were so beautiful.

Settling on the edge of the bed, she studied Sorcha and the baby. "How is yer bleedin'?"

Sorcha lifted one shoulder as Blair pulled his daughters away to play before the fire. "'Tis the same as the others have been, milady."

With a smile, Caitriona corrected her. "Call me Cait, please. I'm nae yer lady here, I'm yer midwife."

The other woman relaxed a little, and glanced at Blair. "I dinnae want tae worry him," she said, voice soft enough it would not carry to her husband or children. "Only...the after-pains seem far worse. 'Tis hard to ignore them this time; when they come, I can scarce walk across the room."

Caitriona nodded. "But yer bleeding isnae worse?"

"Nae worse than my others. Only the pain." She dropped her eyes to Ruadh. "Especially when he's nursin'."

"I'll need to feel your womb, but likely 'tis normal. Some women experience worse pains as they age, and later children come." She placed a hand on Sorcha's arm to reassure her. "We must attend yer bleeding, but if it hasnae worsened I believe it is simply the way of yer body. Ye might apply meadowsweet if it becomes too painful. Or willow bark. I'll leave ye with both."

"Thank ye...Cait." There was a shy smile on Sorcha's face.

"If yer bleeding worsens, I will come. Ye need but summon me."

The rest of the visit went swift, Caitriona allowing her ritual habits to take over as she checked Sorcha's womb to ensure it contracted properly, made a poultice and a blend of tea for the mother to partake for pain, and asked questions about Ruadh's feeding. She had a balm for soreness in her basket, and pressed it into Sorcha's hand.

"Sheep tallow and lavender. 'Tis safe for the babe, and seems to soothe well until ye adjust to the feedings again." Ruadh was sound asleep against his mother's breast by the time she was ready to check him. "May I?"

Sorcha handed up her child, cooing when he let out a loud cry at the transfer. "Ach, he's a loud one, this boy."

Caitriona laughed. "'Tis good to hear his cries. He's hearty and strong!"

The baby's colour was pink and healthy, his hair but a fuzz of orange against soft skin, his eyes squinting at her as if to say, "Ye're nae my mother!" Swift and practiced, she inspected his fingers and toes and the short bit of umbilical cord still attached, then re-wrapped him and cradled him for a moment. "What a lovely boy ye are, Ruadh. Ye'll be up and runnin' after yer sisters in nae time, eh?"

Settled into the crook of her arm, Ruadh began to calm. Wonder overtook her. How perfect every tiny lash was; how bright his eyes; how soft his plump cheeks. One arm poked from his swaddle, covered in the light reddish fuzz that seemed to be all over his body. In a few weeks it would be gone.

The ache in her chest grew again as she stroked his little arm softly and then tucked it back into his swaddle. "He's perfect," she said, almost whispering. Why did she want to cry, for the second time that day?

A sudden knock on the door startled her out of her reverie, and she turned. Rhys ducked inside, bringing with him a rush of cool air and the scent of rain. When his gaze found her, she grew warm. His eyes dropped to the bairn in her arms, and she barely heard his congratulations to Blair and Sorcha as he closed in on her.

His hand slid to the small of her back as he joined her, and she was all too aware of his warmth beside her. With surprising gentleness considering his size, he cradled the baby's head, admiring the new bairn. Ruadh stared sleepily up at the both of them.

"I'm nearly done," she said, voice low.

"Take all the time ye need," Rhys responded. "I sent Iohmar back tae the castle. I'll wait for ye."

When she looked up at him she was surprised at the softness in his gaze. Caitriona had never considered whether Rhys might *like* children. They must have one, for the sake of clan peace, but *want?*

Until now, it had not crossed her mind.

Louder, he said, "A blessing be upon ye and yer son." He pressed a kiss to the fuzzy, tiny forehead, and it sent butterflies swirling through Caitriona's midsection.

It was never a question of wanting children, she knew. She'd always wished for a family.

But now, she realised, it was more. She wanted *his* children. She wanted a family *with Rhys*.

Dazed by the revelation, she handed Ruadh back to a beaming Sorcha, patted Blair on the arm, and bid them farewell. "I am but a walk away; I will happily come if ye need *anything* at all."

"We are honored by yer care, Milady," Blair said as they went through the door.

She smiled at him. "I am honored by your trust in me."

The day was vibrant despite the rain that had begun. Beneath the gray clouds, the thistles and bluebells made a colorful array in the fields, and the earth seemed to breathe in a sigh. Raindrops trickled down her skin, but Caitriona was not chilled.

Rhys had taken her basket and looped his other arm around her waist. A flurry of emotions ran through her. His touch, coupled with her realization that she did indeed wish to build a family with him, was intoxicating. And terrifying.

This new future spreading out before her was an echo of her past hopes, which had grown dim and forgotten over the years. She had made peace with her spinsterhood, convinced herself she did not want bairns of her own, a family to raise. She loved being a midwife, and children could complicate things. The long, sleepless nights were impossible with a child at her breast or tugging at her skirts.

And she had only just found her freedom.

"Oh!" she said, remembering then Rhys had come to help her with the parish license. They were almost to Calhoun Castle's gates now. "The license! We must go to the church to obtain —"

Her abrupt change in direction was stopped by the arm around her waist that did not move. "Och wife, ye've no need."

A sharp disappointment spread through her. Was he rescinding his offer of help? Would he prevent her from being a midwife after all? She looked up at him and was met with a wink and a raised brow. He let go of her.

From somewhere in the confines of his shirt, he pulled out a simple page and handed it to her. "'Tis already done."

Caitriona's mouth fell open. She snatched the paper from him and read the flowery writing, which granted Caitriona permission to perform midwifery, *without* the use of magic, forced payment, or untoward concealment of the birth from the church.

The ache in her chest grew. "Ye did this for me? In so short a time?"

"Aye," he said, cheek dimpling.

"But how?" Caitriona had assumed the process would be long and tedious, and had dreaded going to present her skills as proof that she deserved a midwifery license. The parish in Brae had refused her several times, despite her position as the daughter of the Laird. Or, perhaps, because of it.

Rhys shrugged a damp shoulder. His black leine clung to him like a second skin in places as the rain became a downpour, and his dark curls fell around his face with abandon. With the devilish tweak of his lips and the mischief sparkling in his eyes, he almost looked otherworldly. Like a dark fairy prince, come to trade her soul for her deepest desire.

When he took her hand and drew her near again, she knew she could never refuse him, no matter how much peril her soul was in.

"Ach well, the priest couldnae verra well deny the Laird whose generous donations keep his beloved church afloat."

Caitriona narrowed her eyes at him. "Ye didnae threaten him, did ye?"

The priest was a kind man, serving his flock on weekdays just as often as he preached to them on Sundays. She could only imagine the scene: the diminutive, somewhat paunchy, kindhearted priest cowed before her hulking, tall, devilish husband.

All for her.

Rhys's smile did nothing to convince her. "Of course not!"

When she raised a brow, he waved his hand.

"Ach, well. Perhaps a little. But he was more than happy to oblige me."

No one had ever been so kind to her. Not only had he supported her desire, he'd gone out of his way to ensure she was licensed and no one would stop her from doing what she loved. It was so opposite of everything she had come to expect, she could have cried. Perhaps she was crying.

The rain made it hard to tell.

"I dinnae...I dinnae ken how to thank ye," she said, wiping at her face and hiding the parish license beneath her apron to protect it from the damp.

"I can think of several ways," he replied, voice full of meaning. At her laugh, he pulled her flush against him and planted a kiss on her lips. It startled her, but she leaned closer and thrilled at his affection. They were standing by Calhoun castle's gates and anyone might walk up on them.

Having only ever been kissed in secret, by a man who later betrayed her, it was a new kind of validation to be claimed so brazenly. So uncaring of who saw them. Caitriona leaned into her husband, the idea of a family growing like a weed in her mind.

Maybe she could make it work, somehow. Maybe she *could* have it all.

Rhys made a deep sound in the back of his throat when he pulled away, breathless.

"Does it nae bother ye that yer wife holds an occupation," she asked, teasing. "I'll be more useful than ye."

He did not relinquish his hold around her waist. "The castle has run without a lady of the house for nearly ten years, *lasair chride*. 'Tis true the marriage was arranged and I expected my wife to take her rightful place as Lady of Calhoun...but in truth, being tied down by expectation has never appealed to me. And I wouldnae thrust that upon you, either."

"But surely people will talk?" Rumors had ruined her life, and her old fears reared their head.

"Let them," he said. Running his hand up her back to her neck, he squeezed gently. "Nothing will benefit the many people under my lairdship more than a marriage in which *both* parties are content."

She ran her hand over his arm, marveling at the muscle tensing beneath her soft touch. "Then, milord," she said, blushing but bold. "What is it that will make *ye* content?"

He dipped his head and claimed her mouth again, then growled when his name was called. "I'm afraid we cannae satisfy my contentment just yet."

Caitriona broke away and glanced toward the castle. One of Rhys's men, whose name she had not yet learned, was walking toward them. She made to move out of her husband's arms, but he would have none of it. His arm roped around her waist again, and he held her firm against him.

"What is it, Craig?" he addressed his man.

"Milord, Duncan has arrived and waits to meet ye and yer wife."

"Inform him we'll be up shortly," he said. To Caitriona, he explained, "Duncan is an old friend. He and I have known each other since we were lads; he comes every so often to bring news of what happens beyond my reach. He's just back from France, I believe."

They approached the castle at a sedate pace. Secure within Rhys's grasp, she pondered how much her life could change in such a short time.

Barely four weeks ago she'd been newly wed and furious about it. She'd refused to bear Rhys's child, clan be damned, and cursed his name.

Now? She relished her role as his wife. Their future together. *Whatever* it might bring.

When they entered the castle, there was a bustle of activity in preparation for their guest. Rhys strode with confidence, past the maids who watched them with alert eyes, and Caitriona trailed behind. Some of the maids still eyed her with censure, but she paid them no mind. Let them gossip. She could handle it, she was learning.

She had always been a confident woman, but having the support of her husband had bloomed something different within her. This, she realised, was the permission to let go of caring quite so much what anyone else thought. With Rhys at her side, they could take on anything.

In a few short turns, they entered the great hall, where Craig chatted with a man Caitriona could not see. But his voice sent a shock through her.

It couldn't be.

This voice from her past, from the worst of her memories. It was a coincidence. Someone who sounded eerily similar. It had to be.

Heart beating against her chest like a bird trapped in its cage, she came closer to the man and Craig, and Rhys's body blocked her view for a moment. "Duncan! 'Tis good to see ye again." He turned to Caitriona, pulling her to his side again. "May I introduce to ye my wife, Caitriona Irving, Lady of Calhoun Castle? Caitriona, this is Duncan. One of my oldest friends."

Shock rippled through her, and she went through the motions of an introduction with her blood roaring in her ears. It took all of her reserve not to send the man packing, throw him out the door and down the stairs of the castle.

Standing before her, the picture of friendliness and joviality, not an ounce of recognition on his face, was Niall MacBrighde. The man who had all but ruined her life.

An Old Friend

Rhys

There was something wrong with his wife. Rhys may have been well on his way to being properly sloshed, but even he could see it.

And it was not just the peculiar way in which she greeted their guest. Duncan had bowed and simpered over her hand, and for a moment Rhys saw a flash of something odd in her eyes. But the expression was schooled away before he could assess it. With a nod and a smile, she'd stepped away from Duncan and put a healthy amount of space between them.

In the moment, he'd appreciated her reserve. Duncan was a little *too* charming at times, flirting even with married women. It had never bothered Rhys before, but when the attention was thrown recklessly at his own wife, he bristled. If the man was not more careful, Rhys would have no qualms putting a fist in his face.

So Caitriona's cool behavior had not alerted him at first.

She had excused herself shortly after, begging exhaustion, and he had waved her off. He and Duncan had a lot to catch up on. As unexpected as the arrival was, Rhys was eager to speak with his friend and hear of his adventures. He had noticed his wife's absence for the rest of the day, but she'd gotten little sleep over the past few nights.

It had not seemed too odd to him when she'd sent word she was resting.

But then, she had stayed tucked away. Sent her excuses for dinnertime. Stayed in her rooms at night. *Her rooms.* Not his.

And now, at supper the next evening, the first time he had seen Caitriona since Duncan's arrival, he could not stop glancing at her. Duncan, also deep in his cups, regaled adventure after adventure on his left, but Caitriona, on his right, was...worrying. She'd put the same spoonful of porridge to her lips five times now, without taking a bite.

A furrow was between her brows, and he wanted to soothe it away with kisses.

He settled for resting his hand upon her knee beneath the table.

She looked at him and the furrow softened. A small smile appeared on her lips, and it was a balm to his soul. No one could see his hand, nor her knee, nor the way he nudged fabric up, up, up and away until he found the softness of her thigh beneath his palm, and squeezed.

A gasp escaped her, and she grabbed his hand, bringing it away from her leg, and up to the arm of her chair. He grinned. Her cheeks were flushed, her eyes alight. Much better than the brooding.

Leaning toward him, she said low in his ear, "A bit much to drink, Rhys?"

"'Tis only a bit of ale," he said. God's teeth, she smelled like heaven. Without shame, he brought her hand to his lips and pressed a lingering kiss to her fingers.

Public affection was often frowned upon, but he did not care. In fact, he was pleased to do anything he could to banish the gossip amongst the younger maids. Many of them still whispered about Caitriona in the halls.

Speculation over whether his wife was too tall, too buxom, too freckled, too enterprising, too challenging. Too *much*.

It was baseless chatter. Rhys liked Caitriona just as she was. And he took this opportunity to remind anyone watching.

Caitriona was radiant this evening. Skin a pale cream beneath her constellation of freckles, her hair braided and coiled around her head in shining auburn plaits, she sat proud and tall and *his*. The rising of her breast quickened under his gaze, and her neck flushed. He was staring.

Proper behavior demanded subtlety, but he did not want to be subtle. Could a man not admire his own wife with open appreciation? His eyes dropped to her luscious, petal-pink mouth.

Caitriona burrowed her teeth into her lower lip and he leaned closer.

A rough pat on his shoulder reminded him Duncan still sat on the other side of him, and was booming hearty laughter to the room.

"Ye've married a pretty lass, Rhys, I'll give ye that," Duncan slurred, grinning from ear to ear. The man was a fool. Rhys wanted to wipe the doaty smile right off his friend's face. "Tell me, how did ye come to ken yer wife, then? Rumor has it, she's a past as wicked as yers." The words were crass, and everyone knew it.

How had Rhys never stopped the man before? Over the years, he'd heard many uncouth words come from his friend's mouth in reference to women. It bothered him, yes. But he had shrugged it off. It was just Duncan's way. Shock everyone, then follow up with a laugh and a jest and a charming grin to make everyone forget his rudeness.

Beside him, Caitriona stiffened.

Friend or not, he'd overstepped. "Ye'd be wise nae to listen to rumors, Duncan," Rhys warned, sipping at his ale.

He'd be wise not to insult Rhys's wife.

Duncan's expression lost its shine and he tipped his chin down in a half-apology. "Pardon my tongue, Lady Irving. It's been a while since I've sat amongst refined company." To his credit, he seemed sincere.

Caitriona met his eyes and raised an eyebrow. "Do ye often degrade the finer sex in front of their faces, or do ye save that for *unrefined* company only?"

The man blinked, and Rhys wanted to roar with laughter. His worries melted away as the fire rose in her eyes. Perhaps he did not need to defend her. After all, she had more than proven to him she could defend herself, hadn't she?

"Och, 'twas a jest, milady. I only meant Rhys never leaves the castle and I'm...er...surprised to see he's taken a wife. Which he would have had to leave his lands to meet, ye ken? I thought...er..." He sputtered to a stop for a moment and then shook his head. "Rhys would have had to *hear* of ye, through —"

"A reputation so great it spread across clans?"

Though his head buzzed with the warm comfort of a good ale, even Rhys could hear the warning in her tone.

But Duncan did not know her, and he nodded with relief. And idiocy. "Aye, exactly."

"And to which rumors do ye refer, Mr. MacBrighdes?"

Duncan's gaze fluttered from Rhys to Caitriona to the rest of the hall, where plenty of eyes were locked on their exchange. Caitriona had not lowered her voice, and it was clear by the expression on Craig, Kenna, Jenny, and Callum's faces: their conversation was far from private.

"Only that...er...well, ye...were a spinster?" His answer was lame.

Caitriona hummed low in her throat, and Rhys grinned. She was blazing with fury, but so still and calm a man might think he was safe. Duncan was *not* safe. "Of all the rumors that have followed me through my life, Mr. MacBrighde, that is the most boring of them all. Surely you could have come up with a better one. Perhaps the time I rode bareback after a runaway mare in nothing but my leine and some pilfered trews? That one lingered for quite a while. The sight of my hair unbound and wild about me was the talk of town."

Duncan looked cornered, a man about to be destroyed. And Rhys would let her. The man deserved to be taken down a notch; he'd done it many times over the years. Perhaps not enough. And Caitriona was *magnificent.*

"Or perhaps the time I dressed as a young man and joined my father's hunting party to spear a wild boar? After all, 'twas only after my blade pierced the animal that they discovered me." Aside to Rhys, she said, "I had an unfortunate encounter with the boar's tusks, ye ken, and I was bleedin' so badly I had to give up my disguise. The scar is still...well. Somewhere. Ye can discover that later."

Rhys' gaze dropped to her hip, and the memory of a divot there distracted him. She'd never told him about the boar. He'd never noticed the scar. Well. That was just one more thing to discover about this delightful, beautiful, absolutely incandescent woman.

Amused, he watched Duncan's expression change from bemusement to disbelief to dread. The man had poked a bear, and now he faced its claws. *Her* claws.

"Or maybe," Caitriona said, the challenge in her voice palpable now. Her calm was unbroken, but her tone was a knife's edge, ready to destroy. "Maybe 'twas the rumor that spread the widest, eh? The one about how I'm just a whore in the stables, and any man can have me?"

Rhys winced. The tables closest to them were silent, everyone gawking at Caitriona's bold words. And yet, he could not help but be proud of her. Taking her past like a bull by the horns, wrangling it into submission in front of the entire hall. She really was a marvel.

"That one is the most devious, ye ken, because the man who started it tried tae take what is mine from me, and when he couldnae have it, he destroyed me. With every brand of vitriol and lies he could."

Duncan had turned white, the smile gone from his face. "Er...I hadnae...heard that one," he said weakly.

"Nae? Well. 'Tis nae true. He never had me, and if I ever see him again, I cannae promise I'll nae slit his throat." The words were shocking, but Rhys was more taken with how direct they were.

As if she spoke face-to-face with the man in her past, who had ruined her for so many years. Impossible, though. Duncan did not know the Irving clan, and every man here was too well known to Rhys. No man in his clan would harm a woman under his watch, and if he found out they had, he'd cut their hands off himself.

Duncan cleared his throat and sipped his ale. "Well Rhys, ye certainly picked a fiery one." His attempt to lighten the mood was weak.

Caitriona settled back into her chair, regal as a queen and calm as the eye of the storm.

Rhys took pity on his friend. "I didnae hear the rumors till after we were betrothed, but I paid them little mind." He went back to squeezing Caitriona's knee under the table. The room had begun to waver, just a little. "And as soon as I saw her, I kent I'd have no other woman."

The colour had begun to return to Duncan's face. "Ye've always been an unconventional man, my friend, but I didnae think ye'd marry by arrangement again. Or at all."

Rhys laughed. "Ten years alone was long enough. I was in need of a wife." He did not include the clan's dissent, nor his need of an heir.

"Hamish Irving has been an ally of the Macnammon clan for years, and I found his letter of recommendation...*interesting*."

Duncan studied him. "Seems ye found the daughter interesting as well."

Rhys glanced at Caitriona, whose expression had become curious. "Aye, I did that."

When his wife smiled at him, he could not look away. "I am a lucky man," he said.

Caitriona warmed under his gaze, and put her hand atop his with a smile.

"Och, perhaps we can arrange tae find *me* a wife, eh?" Duncan interrupted.

Raising an eyebrow, Rhys turned to his friend. The man was winking at Caitriona, as if she had not just knocked him down a few pegs for his earlier rudeness. A rush of something possessive tightened around his chest. "Ye're too ugly for any woman so pretty as my wife," he said to his friend in jest.

They both knew Duncan had always been more lucky with women. "Aye, The Lady of the House is a beauty far beyond me, that much is true." He flashed a grin at Caitriona. Recovering from verbal set-downs was Duncan's specialty, and always had been.

If he was more sober, Rhys might have noticed how Caitriona's return smile did not reach her eyes. He might have seen the way it dropped from her lips the moment Duncan turned away. And he might have wondered why.

But he was too enraptured by his wife, and too possessive of her to let Duncan out-charm him. "I think you'll find, if ye stay for long enough, she is a remarkable woman in more ways than one."

"It will be my pleasure to discover," Duncan said, the flirtation back in his tone.

The man had no shame.

But Caitriona's eyes remained on Rhys as she stood. "I believe all ye'll discover is that I am a very *tired* woman. Excuse me, gentlemen. I must retire early."

"Of course," Duncan said, and rose. At least he had some semblance of manners left. "'Twas a pleasure to finally meet ye. I look forward to deepening our acquaintance."

Caitriona nodded, and bid them goodnight.

As she left, Rhys was blindsided by an intense desire to follow her. To tell her *interesting* was far too small a word for everything she was. Rhys himself did not deserve to breathe the air she expelled.

She was far more than just a pretty woman.

The depths of her soul ran deeper than the sea, her strength like a storm upon the waves. She never wavered from her path, brave and impetuous and impulsive, so hardy she could weather a thousand icy winters, but so soft she deserved to thrive in a world of spring. He would trust her with anything — his very life, if it ever came to that.

It was alarming how fond he was becoming of his wife. Despite his best intentions, she had worked her way into the empty shell of his heart, and was filling it with *all of her*.

And Rhys was terrified.

A HUSBAND'S DUTY
Caitriona

Caitriona paced the room, unable to rest.

Anger surged through her limbs. Niall — or rather, Duncan — was unchanged. Arrogant and swaggering, mindless of the damage he might cause. Thinking only of himself.

He was just as she had remembered. Mousy brown hair tousled artfully to appear nonchalant. Dark eyes, more wrinkled around the edges now, but still leering at times. A grin to cover all his wrongs with humor.

'Twas a jest, milady. He'd said variations before. When she confronted him, demanded he cease his rumor mongering. *'Twas a jest, lassie. Dinnae take it tae heart.*

A cold fear lodged in her heart.

Rhys had done very little to mitigate the actions of his friend. Though he had seemed entertained by her thinly veiled fury, most of his interactions with Duncan were amused. Did he condone the man's crass manner? What if these past few weeks had been a farce to gain her trust, and he changed? What if she could not give him an heir and he cast her aside like Duncan had?

It was a troubling shadow on her husband's character to be associated with the likes of Duncan Niall MacBrighde. She had felt so safe, up until now. So sure of a bright future, a new beginning. A man she could trust.

And now?

She shuddered violently, memories plaguing her mind, her body, and her soul. Nothing could erase the horror, the moment Duncan's attention had turned from exciting to terrifying. The shame. The anger. Oh, the anger. It never left. It had nowhere to go and burned low and hot like coals which, given fuel, flamed to life again.

Men could not be trusted.

Not even, it seemed, her own husband.

In the dim light of the room, she struggled to breathe. It was usually a comfort to enter the space, with its tapestries warding away the cold, the fire blazing away, the chairs offering sanctuary at the end of the day.

But today, the air was stale. The fire was too hot. Her skin crawled and her limbs itched and the silence stretched on and on.

It would be hours before Rhys returned from supper. Hours of regaling the past with his *old friend*. Hours of being in the presence of the man who had ruined her. Hours of listening to Duncan brag about exploits which were inflated for his own ego.

Had Duncan bragged of his conquest of her, once upon a time? Had he mentioned her name to Rhys, all those years ago when he'd ruined her reputation? When he'd visited Rhys later, had he told the story to make himself the hero? The jilted lover? Licking his wounds and seeking pity like a wolf faking its own injuries to reel in its prey?

If Rhys had known it was him, she could never trust him again.

Pain sliced through her heart like the edge of a sword. She could not bear to lose again. Everything she held dear was here. Her midwifery. Her future. Her security.

Rhys.

A heavy sob escaped her, and she covered her mouth. The sound was loud, even to her own ears. She could not stay here in these rooms where the reminders of everything she'd come to love lay. A kilt slung over the armchair with abandon; a bouquet of wildflowers from Rhys nestled in a vase; her slippers by the bedside. Their bed, made neatly, her robe on one side and his on the other.

The memory of his hands, so gentle. His eyes, softening at the sight of her. His laughter, filling her stomach with butterflies.

She swallowed, hard.

She loved him.

She loved him, and she could not trust him. She loved him, and he'd only married her for an heir. She loved him, and his oldest friend was her worst enemy. She loved him, and she did not know if he valued her enough to choose her over his past.

Caitriona threw open the door and fled.

※ ※ ※

The night air was damp and calm. Roses burst forth in a glory of petals and thorns beneath the moonlight, creating a thicket of wildness even within the cultivated flower beds. Here amongst the herbs and flowers, she could ground herself. Dig her fingers deep in the dirt. This, she could trust.

These herbs would not betray her.

She'd grabbed a basket on her way back through the castle, careful to avoid the common rooms and slipping out through the kitchen. Everyone was still at supper. So she sought out the areas of her life she could control. Herbs. Balms. Tinctures. Midwifery.

A lantern burned brightly beside her, showing the moon-garden herbs with their soft leaves and silvery colors. Lavender, lamb's ear, wooly thyme, burdock. Thriving, giving off their herbal scents and calming her mind. She found comfort in the quiet work.

Though not many herbs should be gathered at night, nobody would look for her here, and she could regain control of her emotions.

Or so she thought.

Rising, she wiped her hands on her skirts and picked up the basket and lantern, intending to return to her midwifery suite to hang them for drying. But when she turned, she rammed straight into a tall, solid figure, who grunted and gripped her arms with large hands. Rhys.

She knew before she looked up; the scent of him filled her with an ache. Her heart would shred to pieces if he sided with Duncan.

"Ye wernae in our rooms," he said, words slurring together.

He was drunk. Caitriona yanked herself away from him and lifted her chin. "Perhaps I wanted tae be alone."

He raised an eyebrow. "Disappointing, for I didn't."

"Go back to Duncan, then." She trembled, and hoped he could not see.

Rhys snorted. "He's an amiable friend, Caitriona, but I dinnae think I wish to sleep with him."

If she had been in a better mood — if this was not about Duncan — she might have laughed. Her husband, swaying a little, was already chuckling at himself.

"Come to bed," he said, holding out a hand.

Fear lanced through her. Pushed him out of her already-bleeding heart. "Are ye always this obtuse? I. Dinnae. Want to."

A furrow appeared between his brows. "Why?"

Rain started to fall, a mist at first, and then a downpour. Rhys did not move. Hand held out, dark hair damp and curling, he stood like a statue, waiting. His jaw chiseled, his scar puckering as his brows drew together, his eyes glittering. The effects of the ale seemed to fade away.

He was so beautiful. So dark. So dangerous.

"Why are ye pushing me away, *lasair-chride?*" he said, so quiet she barely heard him over the rain.

She let out a shuddering breath. Why was she pushing him away? Because Duncan's appearance had reminded her of the inevitable pattern every beloved person in her life followed. Support her dreams, use her to their advantage, and then leave her to pick up the aftermath.

Duncan had done it, filling her head with pretty thoughts and taking his fill of her, then ruining her reputation for any other man. Her parents had followed suit, allowing her to build a life for herself until it was no longer convenient for them, and then selling her to the highest bidder.

And Rhys would do it, too. Whether or not he realised it then, someday, he would have his heir, and he would no longer need her. He supported her now, because as he'd said himself, it was his duty to make sure she was content. Until she gave him the heir he desired, it was in his best interest to ensure she lived a life that made her want to stay.

But when she bore him a son, he would have what he needed.

What would become of her then?

Shoring up the walls of her heart, she straightened. "It is an arranged marriage, Rhys. What do ye think? Ye married me to acquire an heir, nothing more."

Rhys blinked. The shock rocked him backward a little. "...acquire...?"

"Perhaps I dinnae wish to be treated like a plaything, an object to be traded and used and discarded when my purpose is fulfilled." The words were sharp. Her breath shuddered through the air.

She needed him to deny it. She needed him to reassure her that he was on her side. She needed him to want *her*. To choose *her*. Not his past, his future, his success, his clan. Her.

But he dropped his hand. "Do ye really think that little of me?" Anger threaded itself into his tone. "After everything I've done for ye? Ye think I do all of this because...I want an heir?"

"Ye said it yerself," she retorted, anger and fear mangled and messy in her breast. "'Tis yer duty to fulfill the clan's demands."

"Duty!" he exploded. His laugh barked through the night. "Aye, 'twas only duty. Duty that pried the secrets from my soul. Duty that drove me to procure yer license like a madman. Duty that has me standin' in the pouring rain arguin' with ye like the glaikit fool I am."

She wanted to ask about Duncan, to see if he knew. But she could not bear it if he did. "I didnae ask ye to get me the license. I didnae ask ye to —"

"No." He cut her off. "No, ye didnae ask. Of course ye didnae ask. Ye dinnae need me, do ye? Ye dinnae *want* to need me."

"No! I dinnae!" She was yelling now, the bloom of panic sending its thorns through her chest. "I didnae want to be taken from my home. I didnae want any o' this. I didnae want to leave my patients; my best friend; her babies. My parents! I was *happy there*."

As she grew wilder, he grew quieter. "And ye arenae happy here."

Caitriona heaved a breath. "I...I'm..." A sob choked her. She *had* been radiant. So happy she could float. *Too* happy. And she had too much to lose. She shook her head, wanting to put it into words, but faltering. "I dinnae ken."

He took a step back. The rain had soaked his leine, and it clung to him in the darkness, the shadows of his body stark in the rain and the lantern's glow. "I see," he said.

Caitriona took a sharp breath, and all the fight left her. They stared at each other, rivulets of rain trickling down his face, her eyelashes damp, her body cold. She wanted him to fight, but he studied her with a gaze almost too clear.

"I'll be in our rooms, if ye should choose to return," he said. "But I willnae force ye to stay."

When he turned and walked away, a chill settled into her chest, deep around her heart. She should have stopped him. She should have run after him and begged his forgiveness. She should have gone with him to their rooms, curled into his chest, and reveled in his warmth.

But she watched him go, knowing all the while her heart went with him, an empty shell in its place.

※ ※ ※

All was quiet in the halls when Caitriona returned to their rooms.

It would do her no good to stay locked away in her own suite, mouldering in regret. Rhys was not her enemy; it was not he who had betrayed her. Anxiety fluttered in her stomach, but she let herself into the room and set about getting undressed.

A large bulk in the bed belied Rhys's presence burrowed beneath the quilts. With swift fingers, she undid her bodice before the fire, and peeled off layer after damp layer. Untangling her wet hair from its braids, she combed her fingers through and plaited it again. She was shivering by the time she slipped under the covers.

Rhys's warmth was tempting. But she stayed close to the edge.

She did not want him to hear her cry. Wounded and desperate, she pressed a fist to her lips and sobbed silently. Tears dripped from her cheeks and pooled beneath her cheek, dampening the pillow.

Caitriona had thought love would feel like butterflies, light and tripping, giddy with its bloom. But this love, it pierced through her, so heavy its weight pressed the air from her lungs with need.

The box holding in her biggest fears had cracked open, and she could not seem to shut it.

Curling harder into a ball on the edge of the bed, she pushed her face into the pillow, unable to stop from shaking. The night stretched out before her, dismal and dark. Despite her husband's large form in the bed beside her, Caitriona was alone.

Or so she thought.

Rhys shifted, the weight of him sinking the bed as he wrapped a strong arm around her and pulled her into him. Warmth surrounded her.

"Dinna fash, *lasair-chride*," he said, voice rasping. "Dinna fash."

With gentle hands, he wiped away her tears and tucked her into his chest. His lips pressed into her neck once, twice, three times. But he did no more. He simply held her, until her heart stopped racing and her hands stopped trembling, and she was drowsy in the safety of his embrace.

If she had this, she could endure. Rhys was her future. She would tolerate Duncan's presence, and she would leave the past in the past. It could stay buried and never be unearthed again. As long as she could get through Duncan's visit, however long that may be.

She tried to shift, to turn over and face her husband, to apologize for her rash words, but his arms were too heavy. A leg was flopped over hers, as if to keep her from leaving him. "Rhys?" she whispered, wanting to clear up this mess before morning.

But a guttural snore answered her.
Laughter bubbled up in her chest.
She could apologize in the morning. For now, it was time to sleep.

Neeps and Currans
Rhys

Rhys woke up before dawn.

Rain rushed against the windows, the winds relentless as the storm raged, and he sighed. He wanted nothing more than to stay in his bed, his wife nuzzled in his arms and sound asleep. Their quarrel last night had confirmed what his addlepated brain had picked up on earlier: something was wrong.

Sure, their marriage had begun with a singular goal in mind: to birth an heir and salvage the Macnammon line. It was not a flattering proposal, to tell a woman she was only useful for the bairns she could produce. But surely she understood he saw her as more now.

When she had come to bed, he had been relieved. He'd assumed she would go to her own rooms again after their fight, and he would be awake all night in misery. But she'd come to his room, settled into the bed, and begun to cry...and his heart had cracked a little.

She needed him. Even if she did not trust him, she needed him.

Now, he had to find out why she was throwing walls up around herself. What had changed in those precious few hours? What had he done? Was it Duncan? Did the man wound her more than he had thought?

His pride in watching her brazenly throw all of the rumors in Duncan's face had been so great, he had not stopped to consider she might be hurt by Duncan's behavior. Staring at Caitriona, he traced the lines of her face with a feather-light touch, wishing he could wake her. Knowing she needed to sleep.

He brushed his lips across hers, careful not to disturb her, and slipped out of bed. Today, he had to make his rounds about the village, to ensure flooding had not washed out fences, roofs were well-thatched, and nobody on his lands suffered from the ill weather. His father had been less involved, preferring to send men out to do these things for him, but Rhys enjoyed the work.

He wanted to be grounded as the Laird, and that meant toiling alongside his clan, doing the dirty work. He was only as good as his clan; if they were suffering, he was not doing his job.

Duncan came with him, and he was glad for it. The man never ran out of a tale to tell, and whether they were all true, nobody could really say. But Rhys enjoyed it nonetheless. It kept his mind off his troubles with his wife, and the misery of the wet, rainy day.

As they rode toward the first farm on their way, his friend surprised him. "I should apologize for my rudeness toward yer wife last night, Rhys. 'Twas the drink makin' me forget my manners."

Rhys studied Duncan's face. The man was open, his eyes sincere. "Ye never did behave yerself in front of a beautiful woman," Rhys said, and shook his head. But a smile was on his lips.

"Aye, 'tis my solitary flaw." Duncan grinned.

It was easy to forgive his friend for the blunder, faced with their years of friendship and his jolly nature. "Keep yer muckle gab to yerself, and I willnae knock yer head off yer shoulders," he said, amused.

But his amusement was short lived as they came upon an entire flock of sheep slaughtered in a north field. Duncan sobered. The hillside was dotted with at least twenty fluffy white bodies, red splotches staining their wool. Anger shot through Rhys. This was a clear message, and he did not have to guess who had performed such cruelty.

Berach Macnammon was becoming bolder by the day. This was far closer than his last target.

As he slid from his horse, the owner of the sheep and the field approached them. Raibeart was older than Rhys, and had been a shepherd on these lands since Rhys's father was Laird. The man's shoulders slumped as he surveyed the remains of his flock.

"Raibeart," Rhys said, coming close and clasping the man's forearm in greeting.

"'Twere Berach's men, I'm sure o' it. Saw a pair o' blaigeards leavin' the area a few hours ago ridin' hard." Reibeart shoved a hand through his white hair. "Yon o'er north hill."

Rhys clenched his jaw. "We'll help clean up this mess. I am sorry, Reibeart."

"Ach well, I kent it be comin'. Yer clan needs ye, Laird. Young Berach is gettin' right bold wi' his mischief." He glanced around. "There's me sons." Over the ridge, three hulking men came, hauling carts behind them.

Between Rhys, Duncan, and Reibeart's sons, the slaughtered sheep were soon piled into the carts to be taken to the village butcher. The young ones would be used for meat; the older ones, for their wool and whatever scraps could be salvaged. Rhys made a mental note to send Reibeart payment for the flock.

It was, after all, his fault that his cousin still ran unchecked through the clan, wreaking havoc any way he could. When he got back to Calhoun, he would set about talking to Angus and making plans.

Plans he dreaded.

Plans for war.

THE DEVIL AND THE MIDWIFE

Leaving Reibeart's land, they continued on. Duncan had his hood pulled high, but even the rain and the unpleasant scene they'd just dealt with did not seem to dampen his jovial attitude. Over the next few hours, they checked nearly twenty homes between the village and the farms. A few fences needed mending, one of which had been sawed through in an obvious act of destruction, and one tenant's roof had a nasty leak.

Sheep went astray in fields as they tried to get around overflowing creeks and flooded marshes, and Rhys and Duncan dutifully helped to corral them. And then, they harvested the turnips and carrots from a garden when they found Fenella Macleary frantically pulling them out of the waterlogged earth, her children working alongside her, soaked and shivering.

If the plot of food got too flooded, the roots would rot in the earth, and the Maclearys would have no vegetables in their pantry. Sending Fenella and her bairns indoors, Rhys and Duncan had spent the better part of an hour pulling up the neeps and currans, fingers going numb in the muck,

Wet, muddy, and exhausted, they were ready to return to Macnammon castle. The prospect of a warm fire and a hot meal lifted their spirits. And, in Rhys's case, the thought of his wife waiting for his return put a lilt in his step.

"So, ye've got yerself a wife, eh?" Duncan eyed him with a far more thoughtful expression than his usual numpty grin. They had nattered away at many things as the day went on, but the conversation had revolved around Duncan's last five years, and Caitriona had not been mentioned.

Rhys nodded, warm with the thought of her. "Aye."

"And how does married life suit ye? Ye were quite settled as a bachelor last time I saw ye." His tone was amused. "And it bein' an arranged marriage, I'm surprised ye seem so...fond."

Rhys shrugged. "I didnae expect the arrangement to amount to much, given it was a negotiation over land and heirs, but Caitriona is...remarkable."

It was an understatement at best. Their marriage showed promise. Perhaps, with time, it would flourish into a love like his grandparents; strong enough to weather any storms.

His granda and nana had been married young, and their years permeated with enough sadness for three lifetimes, but their bond had never broken. Annag Macnammon had survived her beloved husband by only three days. Once Eòghann had breathed his last at the grand age of seventy-two, Annag had deflated and lost all will to live alone.

Rhys had never expected he might find a connection so close, after his first disastrous marriage. But with Caitriona, he had a spark of hope. When they arrived back, he would find her, gather her up in his arms, and smooth over whatever this whole disagreement had been. Nothing was worth fighting with her for; he wanted to fight *for* her.

"Ye seem thoroughly taken with her, my friend." Duncan studied him. "One hopes she feels the same." Almost under his breath, he added, "A man can never tell."

There was something odd about his tone. Rhys watched Duncan swiftly school away a bitter expression beneath a laugh, but the smile did not reach his eyes. Trouble in his own life? Rhys was not one to pry, so he nodded, and waited.

It did not take long for his friend to raise his voice above the wind. "Women. Ye can never be too sure what they're feelin'."

To the contrary, Caitriona was forever voicing her thoughts and opinions. Prying into his life. Laying her emotions out for all to see. "Never hurts to ask," he replied.

"To be sure, but how are ye t' ken whether they be lyin', or just not tellin' the whole of their thoughts?" Annoyance plagued Duncan's words.

Rhys shook his head. "Surround yerself with people ye can trust, and the rest will sort itself out."

Duncan scoffed. "'Tis nae so easy as that."

"Nae, 'tis not easy. But in time, ye learn."

He knew Duncan's frustration well; he had lived through it with Iona. Always wondering what she wanted. Always suspecting she was unhappy. Never knowing for sure, until after she had died and left him with a mess to untangle. In the years since her passing, he had learned to guard himself with everyone, only letting a select few into his inner circle.

Duncan was one. Caitriona another. Jenny and Callum, he trusted with his life. Kenna knew most of his history, as did Lachlan, her husband. Most of his men, too, were those who would never betray him, and he did not doubt them for a second.

Up ahead, Calhoun Castle loomed from the ground like a hulking beast, towering and shrouded in mist. The rain had begun to let up, slowing from a torrent to a drizzle, and behind the castle the highlands rolled upward. Ever green and lush, they provided a backdrop for the stone walls, defying heaven itself to provide more beauty.

Stony craigs jutted from the hilltops in a stark contrast of gray. Heather offered its gentle purple hues to the scene, and highland cows dotted the way.

The view never failed to take his breath away. This was where his soul belonged, here in the highlands, with the woman he loved.

Had he not been on a horse eager to get home, he might have been struck still in shock. But Sgàil, knowing a warm stall and fresh hay awaited him, picked up his hooves to hurry the way back. Rhys stared at the castle and revisited the revelation.

He was in love with Caitriona.

He should have recognized it last night at supper. The way pride swelled in his chest when she showed her strength. The overwhelming desire to curl her up in his arms and protect her from all ills. The desperate need to be with her at all times. His enjoyment of her bordered upon obsession.

He wanted to watch her work, her face lighting up as she spoke of her passions. He wanted to give her everything, even if it meant she was independent of him. Even if it meant she did not *need* him. He wanted her to thrive. To know she was his equal in everything.

She *was* his everything. And he was afraid she would leave him. Like Iona had.

He needed to tell her.

When they entered the castle courtyard, Aodhán was there to take their horses. Soaked through and exhausted, Rhys and Duncan headed for the steps, wanting hearth and food and sleep.

But one of Rhys's men intercepted them on the stairs. "Milord," he said, catching Rhys's attention.

Angus was a steady, reliable sort of man, whose main job was to ascertain if Rhys had enemies, and what their plans might be. Though short, the man was brawny, red-bearded, with a stoic glare at the best of times. One would have to be desperate to cross him.

"Aye Angus, lookin' a bit crabbit today, eh?" Rhys grinned at the man's ever-grumpy expression.

Angus' scowl deepened. "Berach was seen on the northern property, nae too far from the village." Eyes flicking to Duncan and then back to Rhys, he grunted. "He's got five men wi' himself, nae tellin' where their camp may be."

Rhys sobered. "Reibeart reported the same this mornin'; his flock is gone. Slaughtered. Did ye see weapons?"

Angus shook his head. "Nae tellin. A few dirks and a dag or two. I wouldnae be surprised if they were lookin' tae start a skirmish."

Rhys scrubbed his face with his palm and nodded. It was normal to carry a knife or pistol in the highlands; nearly every man did when traveling over the land. But his cousin's men could not be trusted. Angus' sighting confirmed, for him, these were the same men who had slain Reibeart's sheep.

"I wouldnae travel alone if I were you," Angus said.

"Aye, thank ye Angus." He clapped a hand on the man's shoulder. "My cousin seeks trouble, and he'll find it plenty. I think…'tis time. Tae bring the war he wants to his doorstep. But right now, I need to find my wife. She needs to know he is close."

More importantly, Rhys needed to know if the scoundrels who had attacked the girl Lilleas were with Berach Macnammon's posse. If they were, they faced certain death.

Lilleas and Morven had settled into Calhoun with ease, inserting themselves as kitchen maids without question. Both of the girls had a strong desire to work, to be useful. He suspected they wished to make themselves valuable so as not to be dismissed.

And while Morven seemed to thrive here, her once too-wise demeanor melting away to reveal a child still hidden beneath, Lilleas was reserved. She performed her work efficiently, quietly. Did not make friends. Spent her free time huddled by the fire, or secreted away in alcoves, keeping to herself.

Rhys had come upon her the day after they'd arrived, sobbing in deep, quiet, wracking sobs as she hid away in the corners of the castle.

A sickening suspicion had risen then, but he did not ask. He meant to have Caitriona check on the girl, to ascertain if what he suspected was true. But there had not been a moment yet, and he still worried about her in the back of his mind.

The memories made Rhys's blood boil. He would destroy whomever had touched the child. Though her bruises were fading, and her matted hair, which had been shorn to cut out the matting, was now a shining blonde, there was still much to resolve. And he needed his wife's help.

Eager to find Caitriona, he strode into the main hall and shook off his wool cloak, Duncan not far behind. The room was bustling with activity, fires high and candles lit as maids prepared the tables for supper. At their appearance, a young girl came and took their wet cloaks, hanging them over a chair by the blazing hearth.

Nodding his thanks, Rhys made his way to his rooms for dry clothes, and to find his wife. "I'll see ye at the supper table, my friend. Should ye need anythin', the maids will bring ye whatever ye ask."

Duncan's gaze caught on a passing woman, who returned his flirtatious smile. "I'm sure they will."

They parted ways, and Rhys passed through the halls with eagerness. At this time of day, Caitriona would be getting ready for supper. Or so he hoped. Like an impatient schoolboy, he all but ran up the last flight of stairs and smiled when he heard movement within their rooms.

Throwing the door open, he stepped in...to a startled Aileen, tending the fire.

"My apologies, milord!" she squeaked, standing and wiping her hands on her apron. "Milady is nae yet returned, and I wanted to make sure the room was warm for both of your returns."

"Nae yet returned?" Rhys tugged his jacket off and tossed it over a chair. "From where?"

"I dinnae ken, truth be told." The maid gathered an armful of dirty laundry and started for the door. "But earlier she was in the laundry, speakin' with Effie."

"Thank ye, Aileen," Rhys said, dismissing her. When he had changed from his damp leine and kilt into a dry shirt and tartan trews in blues and greens, he set off to find Caitriona. His garments were informal, but he did not care. He wanted to tell Caitriona everything he had realised, and it did not matter what he wore.

But the laundry was empty and dim, all of the chores there done for the day, and no sign of his wife was to be seen. Impatient, he moved through the halls into the kitchen, which bustled with life.

Jenny ordered the kitchen maids around as they prepared supper, and Effie assisted with tableware and dishes. Kenna sat bent over the table, tallying something in the books. For a few years now, she'd taken on the role of housekeeper, and he was eternally grateful.

"Have any of ye seen Caitriona?" Rhys asked as they all looked up at him.

The cook shook her head. "Not since late this mornin'. She took Iohmar and went off to check on Sorcha and the bairn. She came back to stock her apothecary, but since then I havenae seen hide nor hair of her."

Behind her, Effie piped up, "And then she was to check on my Beitris."

Kenna tapped her chin with her pen. "I wouldnae be surprised if news has spread of her midwifery; she may well be in the village somewhere. 'Tis the season for this sort of thing."

"Mary the Butcher's wife has taken to bed recently. Cannae keep her meals down; nae even mashed neeps and tea." Effie squinted toward the ceiling, thinking. "And then there's Florie, Reibart's daughter by marriage; aye that's an interesting one, quick marriage, eh? And Dorathea — ye ken her sheep, they've the best wool this side o' the Loch, and —"

Rhys waved his hand at her. "I'll follow the trail, then."

"Shall I send Callum to help ye?" Jenny offered.

"I'll go out to Beitris and Alan's. Have Callum and Duncan search the village," he said. Drawing closer to Jenny, and low enough the other women could not hear him, he said, "I've been meanin' tae speak with ye."

Jenny put her hands on her hips and met his gaze. She was far shorter than him, a plump woman with pink, round cheeks and a youthful face. Callum adored her to distraction, and Rhys had always respected her no-nonsense way of thinking. "Aye, what is it?"

He chewed on his cheek. What he was about to say was delicate. Private. "Caitriona has questions. About Aodhán."

Jenny's gaze softened. "Go on," she said.

"She knows about Llwyd. Iona. All of it. Everything except...Ao dhán." He watched as Jenny's memories played out in her eyes. The fear. Grief. Uncertainty.

Her brow furrowed. "Well, 'tis easier, now that she knows about Llwyd and his...proclivities."

Rhys scrubbed his face. This discussion came up rarely, but it brought back unpleasant memories for both of them. "If ye'd like tae tell her yerself, I'll leave ye to it."

Jenny mulled it over. Glanced around, wiped her hands on her apron. And then shook her head. "She's yer wife, Rhys. And sure Aodhán isnae yer child, and 'twas nae yer fault...but I willnae stand in the way of her knowin', whether it come from you or me. If ye wish her tae ken ye and I didnae...well."

"I do," he said, simply. Knowing it would cost Jenny some pain to retell her story, as it always did.

She nodded again. "Best go find her, then."

Putting a hand on her shoulder, Rhys gave her a small smile. "Thank ye, Jenny."

A tightness remained in his chest as he made his way out of the kitchen. With the threat of Berach's men coming closer and closer, there was no telling what they might do next.

And Beitris lived to the north.

He did not wait to see his commands enacted; in a few moments, he was atop a reluctant and complaining Sgàil, riding through the rain toward the foothills of the highlands. He refused to entertain the fears roiling low in his belly. Caitriona may well have been kept by a long visit. There was nothing the Scots loved more than a hot cuppa and a chance to sit and blether.

He would not allow room for the worst of his fears. Not until he had confirmed she was somewhere other than Beitris' or the village.

Sgàil's long legs made short work of the road between the castle and the farm, but it was still close to dark when they arrived. Sheep bleated from the barn behind a small cottage nestled into the stone around it as if it had always been there. Smoke rose into the mist, hazy and gray against the mossy rocks, and the thatched roof glistened in the mist.

At least the rain had stopped.

A dog rose from where it lay beside the door and huffed at Rhys when he dismounted. He held out his hand, and the hound sniffed it in an uninterested sort of way, then lay back down and watched him with bored eyes.

A merry voice answered Rhys's knock, and the door opened to Beitris Dunbarr's smiling face. Much like her mother, Beitris had round, rosy cheeks and a grin that crinkled her nose. Their home was cozy, the walls hung with small family tapestries to keep out the cold, and the floors worn in from years of little feet pattering around.

Before their marriage, Alan had lived here with his mother, who had since passed on.

"Milord!" Beitris gasped, standing aside and waving him in out of the weather. "'Twas blowin' a hoolie outwith, is something wrong?"

Caitriona was not there. The cottage was filled with the crackling of logs, bubbling of soup over the fire, and the pleasant scent of herbs filling the air. But his wife was nowhere to be seen. "I came for Caitriona; she hasnae been back to the castle. D'ye ken where she might have been off to?"

Beitris shook her head, red curls bobbing. "I ken she meant to visit Mary, the butcher's wife, but that was hours ago."

Behind him, the wind followed Alan into the house. "Och, milord! Didnae expect ye —" he stopped, seeing Beitris roll her eyes at him.

Rhys nodded at the man in greeting and backed toward the door. "Alan. I'm in search of my wife."

"Ah," Alan said, hanging his cloak and kissing his wife on the cheek. "She was in the village at the butcher's. I dinnae ken where she went after that."

Beitris patted her husband fondly on the chest. "Aye, I've told him that already."

"I willnae drip on yer floors longer, then," Rhys said, and turned to the door.

"Is somethin' else wrong?" Alan asked, sensing the urgency in Rhys's tone.

Running a hand through his hair as he tried not to let his thoughts spiral, Rhys grunted. "Berach Macnammon is camped to the north, and he's killed Reibart's flock. Dinnae travel at night, if ye can help it.

Lock yer doors. And for the love of St. Andrew, dinnae wander about alone."

He left, mounting Sgàil and pointing him in the direction of the village. He was running on borrowed time now; the sun would be setting soon, and it was hard to see the way beneath the cloudy evening sky.

Curse his glorious, capable, stubborn wife and her independence. She was alone out there somewhere. It was all he could do not to let his mind travel down the road of "what if."

Swallowing hard against the knot in his throat, he urged his horse forward and hoped that Callum and Duncan were having more luck than he.

An Agreement
Caitriona

By the time Caitriona left the last home in her new rounds of visits, the sky was growing dark. It was easy to pass the day doing what she loved. Whether it be riding out in the fields, or digging her fingers into the garden dirt, or wandering about as the village Howdie, Caitriona never noticed the passage of the day until it had gone.

And if she kept busy, she did not have to think about Rhys. Their argument. Her regret. His tenderness when she'd come to bed.

Her fear of becoming useless to him, once her purpose was fulfilled.

After checking on Sorcha one last time, Caitriona had traveled up to see Beitris, the laundress's daughter, then Mary the butcher's wife, then Florie, whose friend Dorthea was in for a visit as well. Iohmar had grumbled a little the more women they visited, and after a while she had sent him back to the castle. She was rarely alone through the day, and was confident she could do well enough by herself.

Though he put up a protest, Iohmar clearly did not wish to spend the rest of his day slogging through mud and soaking up the highland rains, so he went.

Word had spread around the village that the new mistress of Calhoun was also the new Howdie of the village, and if it weren't for her book of records, Caitriona might not have been able to keep track of who was whom, and whose babies were due when.

She'd been popping from cottage to cottage, checking bellies and squeezing round baby cheeks, and advising the health of new mothers for hours. And she did not have to stop to eat, either. Each new cottage brought another offer of tea, where shortbread was plenty and gossip was grand.

Now it was evening, and she had one last stop to make.

This cottage was an outlier to the north of the village, a ten minute walk from the rest, and smoke rising from the opening in its roof promised a warm fire to dry her toes, which were sodden through despite her boots. An eerie feeling crept over her the closer she got to this cottage, which gave her pause.

As if she was being watched.

Oighrig Kennaird opened the door for her, a bubbly and forthcoming woman who did not stop chatting from the moment Caitriona walked in. She shooed two wild-haired children to the corner, and they settled on the ground to build a wee house of sticks, which they populated with straw-made dolls in dresses made of fabric scraps.

A mug of indeterminate hot liquid was pressed into her hands — Caitriona's fifth of the day — and she was barraged with the woman's excited chatting as she went about her routine.

Caitriona did not mind it.

"Ye're too kind, Lady Macnammon; I didnae think his Lairdship would ever marry again!" Oighrig was round and pink, her dark hair a halo around blushing cheeks, big blue eyes fluttering and expressive with every word out of her mouth. "Lord love him, the Laird needed a wife."

Caitriona held back her laughter and gestured for the woman to lie back so she could check her belly. It was already growing round; perhaps the woman was further along than she thought.

"Nae that he was incapable, ye ken, 'tis just he must have been so lonely in the castle alone. Well, he wasnae alone; every man and woman in the clan would fight to the death alongside him, aye? Er, not every man; I suppose Berach is a rotter; the fella has never been content with the Lairds, he wants that power for hisself but he's a right impetuous numpty."

Oighrig did not even pause for breath. "And then o' course the death of his last wife, a sorry situation. I dinnae rightly ken what happened, but ye ken what they say. 'Tisnae the Laird's fault his wife couldnae keep herself to her own bed, aye?"

Caitriona bit her lip, amusement bubbling up in her chest. If she ever needed information, she knew where to come. "I'm sure it was hard for him," she agreed.

The woman continued her chatter, not seeming to notice whether Caitriona answered or not. Wind raged on outside the cottage, but within they were comfortable.

Oighrig's cottage was much like its owner: a pot bubbling merrily over the dancing fire in the middle of the room, a well-loved patchwork quilt spread over the bed to one side, and wildflower bouquets spilling unchecked from every pot, cup, and vase the woman had.

The floor was dirt, as was common in the highland cottages, but beneath the bed was a colorful scrap rug, made from bits of fabric tied together and braided until it reached a size to be wound round and round and sewn in place.

At the far end of the long, rectangular cottage was a lower area with a makeshift fence, where the animals stayed. It was common enough to see family cows cozy in the other end of the home, as most could not afford a separate outbuilding for their livestock. Oighrig's highland coo was currently staring at them, lazily chewing its cud.

Smoke clung to the rafters, adding its earthy aroma to the scent of animal, dried grass, and whatever was in the vegetable stew over the fire.

"He's a fair Laird, and too good a man to be alone," Oighrig was saying. "Perhaps 'tis good that Berach set a bit o' doubt in the clan's mind. Oh, I'm nae sayin' the *doubt* is good, but here ye are! And I'm sure when ye have a child o' yer own, especially if 'tis an heir, all this talk of Berach takin' over the lairdship will go away."

A blush stole up Caitriona's neck at the mention of a potential future child. "I certainly hope so," she murmured, finishing her examination and packing her kit.

"Ach, my apologies milady, I shouldnae open me muckle gab but I cannae help it. Greer, bless him, says the Lord kent he needed a natterin' wife tae make up for his lack o' gab. He's a quiet one, aye, but I dinnae need a man o' many words."

Caitriona smiled. "I can see that," she said without malice. "If ye need me, ye ken where to find me, whether it be for midwifery or a bit of gab."

Oighrigh adjusted her clothes and escorted Caitriona to the door. It was dark outside. "Do ye want Greer to take ye back to the castle? 'Tis late and I dinnae think ye should be alone, there's no tellin' who lies await."

"I'll be fine," Caitriona said, and bid the woman goodnight. A lantern was pressed into her hand as she left. She called back her thanks.

It was no longer raining, but the mist was heavy in the hills and there was no moon to light the way. Holding her light up, she tucked her cloak around herself to stave off the cold. Basket hooked over her arm, she picked up her pace, longing for home.

The quarrel with Rhys had been plaguing her thoughts between every visit. Would he be angry with her when she returned? He'd soothed away her tears last night, but he'd also been half-drunk and drowsy. This morning, he had not even woken her up before he left, to say goodbye. To reassure her.

Shivering, she wished for the reassurance of a hound by her side. Her father had two large dogs, who often shadowed her when she went on her walks, and she missed them. It would have been a comfort to have a warm, living being beside her in the dark, eerie quiet.

As it was, every sound was an enemy. The stand of trees whispered sinister things in the breeze, and even the slightest snap of a twig in the darkness made her startle. Her own footsteps were loud on the pathway. Why had she sent Iohmar back to the castle?

There was no use peering into the dark mists surrounding her and wondering what was in them; it heightened the panic building deep in her gut. She did not want a repeat of the last time she'd been out alone.

Resisting the urge to check the path behind her, she stared straight ahead and went over the visits she had made today. There were twelve expectant mothers in total — some due in the summertime months, some quite early still and expecting a winter child — and four newly-born bairns beside.

Her future here was bright, as the clan folded her into itself as one of their own, and she was so afraid it would be ripped away.

So afraid the man she loved would one day tire of her.

The village should have been getting close by now, and as she peered through the darkness, a small glow appeared, floating above the ground toward her. Caitriona was not a suspicious sort, but at the moment, she wondered if the faeries were out. Perhaps she'd be swapped out for a different version of herself.

The version Rhys thought he was going to marry. Quiet, unobtrusive, pliable. Willing to perform her duty and then fade into the background. Would he miss her, then? The real her? The one who had fought him from the very beginning; who forged her own path despite her circumstances; who allowed her heart to be displayed on her sleeve without shame?

Would he miss the version of her prying into his past, ignoring every protest and order, blazing her way into his life whether he liked it or not?

But her musings on faerie creatures was short lived, for the orb grew closer and revealed a new problem: Duncan, lantern swinging from the end of his arm, looking every bit as surprised to see her as she was him. Upon a highland pony, which meant even if she wanted to run, she could not.

Schooling her features to hide her alarm, she came to a stop in the middle of the path, his pony stretching out a curious nose to snuffle her for treats. "Hello, Grizel," she said. She knew all of the horses by name now, thanks to Aodhán, and Grizel was a lovely little thing who begged for apples.

"Rhys is worried sick, sent me and Callum out to find ye," Duncan said, not dismounting. His expression was jovial as always, and even in the dark he appeared unassuming and mischievous. Like a dog who, though obedient to its owner, might prove dangerous to a stranger without provocation.

Caitriona would have preferred the faeries. At least one *knew* they were up to no good. With Duncan, she could not tell. Circumventing the pony, she continued to walk, eager to return home and be away from Duncan's side as soon as possible.

"I was visiting a new patient," she said by way of explanation. "Oighrig is a bit further away than I expected."

He followed her on Grizel. "Aye well, 'tis good I found ye. Walking alone at a time like this doesnae seem like such a good idea," he said.

Aye, Caitriona thought. *I've run into the likes of ye.* Out loud, she said, "I've nae been alone until now. But if needed, I can protect myself just fine." As a warning, should he remember her and decide to make advances, she patted her pocket, where a dirk was hidden.

The vague shape of the village came into view as the moon emerged from behind the clouds. Though there were no windows in these cottages to show the light within, there were still clues of life there. Smoke rose from the roof openings, filling the air with its pungent scent, and a dog grumbled as they passed. A baby's cries rose up, and then a mother's voice singing a lullaby.

Calhoun castle was close, and Caitriona was eager to find Rhys and distance herself from Duncan.

"Well. Anyway, I'm glad to see ye're doing well." His voice slowed her down, and she looked at him. Duncan's expression did not give away his meaning.

Did he mean here and now, because she'd been missing upon Rhys's return? Or did he mean since he'd seen her last, and ruined her life and prospects almost irreparably? She did not have to wonder for long.

His voice was quiet. "I regret the way I...we...left things. All those years ago."

A sharp, intense rage set the coals in Caitrona's belly on fire. "Ye *ruined* me. Ye destroyed my future. Dinnae dare place any o' that blame on me, Niall." Addressing him by the name he'd given her seven years ago reminded her all the more why she wanted to get home. She picked up her pace.

"Come now, Caitie girl. 'Twas only a kiss!" He nudged Grizel faster to keep up with her. "I was a bit drunk, and young and glaikit, aye, but I didnae mean anythin' by it."

Caitriona whirled. Grizel halted. Duncan lurched forward and nearly fell off. "Do. Not. Call me. Caitie." Every word lashed from her like a whip, snapping in the air between them. "We are nae friends. I dinnae care to revive *anything* with ye. I dinnae wish to relive those memories. I dinnae wish to hear yer apology. I only tolerate your presence because you are Rhys's friend and this is the single thing ye have in yer favor. That perhaps, *perhaps*, my husband's judgement is worth something and ye've changed."

Duncan held up his free hand. "'Twas a mistake, I ken that now."

Whether he referred to spreading rumors that destroyed her life, or calling her Caitie, Caitriona did not care to find out. She turned and marched forward again, done with the conversation.

Almost.

They were within sight of Calhoun castle, its windows glowing in the darkness, when she stopped him again. "If ye breathe a word of who ye are to Rhys, I will end ye in yer sleep."

Duncan coughed. "He doesnae ken?"

"He kens about my past. About a man who lured me to a lover's grove and spread rumors to ruin my life when I wouldnae give him what he wanted. He kens about the villain ye were then. But he doesnae ken it was *you*." She glowered at him. "And he's enough on his mind to sort out without findin' out his oldest friend is his wife's worst memory, so ye will. Not. tell him."

Duncan dismounted and held out his hand. Caitriona glared at it with suspicion.

"A truce," he said. When she made no move to take his proffered hand, he sighed. "For Rhys's sake. I willnae tell him who I am to ye.

But ye must return the favor. Stop actin' like I'm here to ruin yer life again."

Caitriona did not trust him.

When she still did not take his hand, he sighed. "I was a young, addlepated fool with an inflated ego, who'd just been rejected by the most beautiful woman he'd ever met. I didnae mean so much harm by it, but I am sorry for what it caused. I was wrong for what I did to ye."

"Aye," Caitriona said, for once agreeing with him. "Ye were."

"So. Truce? I willnae breathe a word of it to Rhys; ye'll accept my apology and we'll move forward as friends." Duncan was contrite, almost believable. Features a play of shadow and warmth from the lantern's glow, he edged a little closer and tilted his head. "Ye have nothin' to worry about."

She had everything to worry about. She took his hand and shook it, and wondered if she was making a mistake. "We begin again, then."

JENNY'S SECRET
Caitriona

They entered the castle to Rhys and Callum still shaking the damp from their hair and knocking the mud from their boots. Worry creased lines into Rhys's temples, and he was saying something low and angry to his friend.

Duncan, beside her, spoke up. "Found her." He put his hand on her lower back, as if to guide her forward, and she wanted to slap it away.

But she didn't. They had agreed, after all, to move forward as friends. She allowed Duncan to escort her closer, and gave him a curt nod when he retreated.

Rhys's gaze snapped to hers, and it was furious. The eyes raking over her were hot as coals. Had he been anyone else, she might have recoiled at how fast he moved toward her, tall and dark and full of anger. He grabbed her arms in his big hands and inspected her, looking for injuries. When he found none, he released her and shoved a hand through his wild hair.

"What in the devil's name were ye thinkin' traipsin' about the countryside without anyone t' ken where ye went?" he snapped. "Ye could have been dead!"

Caitriona bristled. "I had Iohmar with me for most of the day, and everyone in the village kent where I was, ya big numpty. I didnae make it a secret."

Duncan and Callum wisely faded away, leaving the hall empty as their Laird and Lady faced each other.

"Ye should have told *me*." He did not relent. "I've told ye before nae to wander."

Caitriona threw up her hands. "How could I tell ye? *Ye* were off traipsin' around who kens where! I woke up to an empty bed!"

"Aye well I expected my wife to stay put! 'Tis nae weather for a jaunt!" He loomed over her, water dripping from his hair onto his dirty leine.

Shaking her basket at him, Caitriona shook her head. "I wasnae *out for a jaunt*. I was with. My. Patients. Perfectly safe. From the looks of ye, ye were in the weather more than I was!"

Mud was splattered over his cheek, and the shoved-up sleeves of his leine revealed dirty forearms. "Why can ye nae listen to what I say, woman?! I dinnae care if ye walk all the way to France, but dinnae go alone!"

She let out a grunt of frustration. "Aye, perhaps I shouldnae have sent Iohmar home ahead of myself, but the lad was shiverin' in the cold and I didnae plan tae leave the village. If I am to be a midwife, this will be my life, Rhys. I cannae always wait for someone to come with me."

He growled. "Perhaps I shouldnae have obtained that license."

The words cut through her. Crushed her soul. "Ye cannae expect me to sit useless in this castle, holed up in a room with naught but idle hands. 'Tis nae what I was meant to do." All plans to make amends flew out of her.

"If ye cannae obey my orders, ye cannae leave the castle. Do ye ken what might happen?"

He towered over her, and she shoved a finger into his chest. "Aye! I do ken what might happen! I might go right back to my own clan, because at least there I wasnae controlled by a glaikit bully-rag!"

"That isnae how it is here, and ye ken it very well." He glowered at her. "Do what ye will. Just dinnae go alone."

"I can find my way just fine! And I have a dirk. Ye ken how I can fight!" She put her basket down, too frustrated to stand there in the hall still fully enrobed in the muddy cloak and boots she wore. "Oighrig and Greer's cottage is the furthest, and 'tis only a quarter of an hour north o' the village."

At this, Rhys stilled, watching her peel off her layers with steel in his eyes. "Devil take ye, woman," he said, so quiet she could barely hear him over the crackling fire. "Berach and his men were spotted north o' the village today. We dinnae ken yet where they are camped, but they killed twenty-five of Reibeart's sheep. Spread them over the hills in the north like a bloody warning."

Caitriona's stomach dropped. She had been out there, in the dark, where Berach's men were roaming the hills. The man who'd attacked her on the road could have done it again. And she was too stubborn to listen, despite her own husband trying to warn her.

She pressed a hand to her belly, which knotted with worry. "I'm sorry." She *had* been stupid.

Rhys's anger seemed to melt away. "Caitriona, I ken…I ken this isnae the life ye wanted. But I am nae tryin' to rein ye in." He cupped her face in his hands, warm and rough. "I'm trying to protect ye."

She nodded against his palms. "I know." Her voice came out in a whisper. Of course she knew. He'd nearly beaten a man to death for bruising her. She *knew* how he felt.

The mud streaked across his cheek was down his neck, crusted on his leine, even scattered in his hair. He was filthy. Caitriona did not think she'd ever seen a more beautiful man. He sighed.

"Since ye've arrived, Berach's attacks have only grown. I fear he's doubled his efforts because of our marriage. Because he didnae expect me to follow through with finding a wife, and now he's afraid he'll lose." He rubbed her cheek with his thumb, studying her face as if he might never see her again. "But now, he kens how much I have to lose."

Caitriona's fight left her body. What could she say? She had been so ready to defend herself, to argue she didn't need to be coddled and held back like a child, but she'd been so wrong. Berach might use her as a tool to kill Rhys, and she had not considered this before.

"I'm sorry," she said again. "I'm a fool."

He dropped his forehead to hers. "Aye well. So am I."

He pressed a gentle kiss to her lips, and when she threw her arms around his neck, he pulled her against him. She melted into his warmth, tension leaving her in a flood. Fool she was, through and through, for no matter how much they fought she knew she could never leave him.

"So then," he said against her lips. "A bath, and then ye can tell me all about yer day, aye?"

He pulled her with him, and she followed without question.

※ ※ ※

Later, they lay in bed content, Rhys's face pressed into her neck, her entire body luxuriating in the warmth and drowsiness of bed and Rhys and darkness. She traced a lazy line from his shoulder to the muscles of his bicep and back again, delighted by the weight of his arm over her belly. She wanted this to last forever.

"Jenny and I had a chat today," he said suddenly, breaking through her hazy thoughts.

She tilted her cheek toward him. "Did ye?"

Nodding against her skin, he kissed her neck and then pushed up onto one arm, resting his head against his hand. "Aye. She gave me permission tae tell ye about Aodhán."

The words brought her to full alert. The boy in the stables, who worked so merrily and looked so like her husband, and been a niggling curiosity in the back of her mind for weeks now. But, knowing his parentage involved Jenny, she had not pursued the knowledge. Part of her was scared, even now, to know the truth.

Rhys taking another man's life, she could handle.

Rhys taking a woman to his bed who was not her, and having a child from that union? Perhaps. Perhaps not.

Even if she did like the woman. Even if she had no doubt there was no attachment between them now. Even if she did think the boy was sweet.

But she waited, and said nothing.

After a moment of studying her face, Rhys went on. "Aodhán was born six months after Iona died, a few months before I left for the continent. Jenny was unmarried then; Callum did nae even ken Jenny existed, then, nor did she know him. She was a scullery maid in the kitchens, and her mother was the cook."

Caitriona held her breath, mind whizzing with curiosity. The months did not quite add up; surely Rhys had not been unfaithful to his beloved wife. It seemed very unlike him, despite the rumors. What she knew now was at odds with that possibility.

"I've said it before, but my brother was never content simply having what belonged tae him. He had tae be taking. Always. And if he couldnae have what he wanted, he lashed out. He and Iona had been...keeping their secret for almost a year by then, and I'm told they had a disagreement. She threw him out, while I was away on clan business, and he retaliated.

"He'd noticed Jenny, a pretty young maid with a bonny figure, and he knew Iona was familiar with her as well. So he...took her."

He went silent. In the dim light thrown from the fire, she could see his throat working, and his brow was furrowed. Some relief had begun to ease the tense muscles she hadn't realized she'd been clenching, and she resettled herself. Drew her fingers along Rhys's cheek.

"'Twas nae...she did nae..." He struggled to say the words. "She didnae want him to."

"I understand," Caitriona said, heart aching for the woman.

"Of course, Iona was jealous, and so she...took him back. Their affair ended...as it ended. But by that time, Jenny kent she was with child. Despite explaining the situation tae her mother, the woman didnae react... very kindly. She threw Jenny out o' the castle, called her a hoor, threatened to disown her and the bairn.

"I overheard it all. So...I dismissed the cook. Replaced her with Jenny, who was more than capable of running the kitchens. And asked her what she wished tae do with the child, with her story. She already knew Llwyd was dead, had a secure position in my kitchens." He sighed and turned his face to kiss her palm.

"If ye ken Jenny well, ye'll see she's as soft-hearted as they come, and she always has been thoughtful. She kent Llwyd's wife, Kenna, had only just given birth tae a bairn nae three months before his death, around the time he...well, ye ken. And she didnae wish tae break the woman's heart further with tales of her husband's continued perfidy.

So she asked me tae leave it be. Tae see what the child might look like when he was born, and then she'd decide.

"And as ye ken, Aodhán came out looking every bit a Macnammon. Just like my brother. And just like me." There was a tight smile on his lips. "As I'd promoted her tae cook, a single woman with child, ye can imagine the gossip that began. Everyone assumed the bairn was mine."

Caitriona nodded. "Aye, well. 'Twould be hard to dispute he's a Macnammon. Did it nae bother Jenny? Tae be seen as yer mistress?"

Rhys shrugged one shoulder. "Aye, it did. But it also offered her some protection. Ye see, nae man alive would dare tae speak ill of the Laird's mistress, nor his by-blows. And since she was thinkin' of Kenna, too, and how Kenna might feel knowin' her husband betrayed her with more than just one woman and…had a son by another woman, well. We let it be. She was protected and her skills as cook were great enough that even when I left for the continent, none of the clan held her any ill will."

Caitriona traced his throat with one finger. "So he's yer nephew," she said softly, smiling.

"Aye. And while I was away, Jenny met Callum, and Callum was smitten. Has been ever since then. He's taken Aodhán into his heart as his own son." He captured her hand in his, and brought it up to his lips, kissing her fingers one by one. "Of course, Callum kens the truth, but outside of him and myself, nae other creature in this world knows."

"Except now me," she corrected him.

"Aye, and now ye. Aodhán will be told someday, when he's older, but Jenny doesnae wish tae break the lad's heart just yet. Truth be told, 'tis a benefit for Aodhán, as well, tae be thought of as the Laird's son."

Caitriona pulled his face toward her, brushed her lips against his, and hummed. "Well, I'm glad he's part of this family, however it did come about. Thank ye for tellin' me."

He nipped at her lip. "No more secrets, aye?"

She nodded, but as he moved to wrap her in his arms, guilt trickled into her chest. He'd just given her the answer to the last mystery about himself, and she still had not told him about Duncan.

Warmth suffused her from head to toe when he pressed kisses over her neck, her shoulders, her collarbones, his hands tracing up and down her form. Claiming her as his own.

"Rhys?" she said, her voice breathy under his expert touch.

He grumbled, pulling away from the particularly sensitive spot just below her ear. "More questions already?"

She hesitated. He'd given up so much of himself for others. Offering Jenny his reputation and his protection, even when he did not have to. Giving up his own comfortable freedom to reassure his clan. And even with his loyalty, so many had betrayed him. His uncle. His cousin. His own brother. His wife.

He'd lost everything.

Perhaps she could endure Duncan's presence, see if he was a changed man from all those years ago, before she said anything to Rhys. After all, he did not deserve yet another friend to be ripped from him. She could live with Duncan's presence, so long as it was kept distant.

For Rhys's sake.

Curling her hands into his hair, she shook her head. "Nevermind," she whispered.

Humming his approval, Rhys dragged his lips over her neck and then covered her mouth with his.

Everything else could wait.

A FOOL IN LOVE

Rhys

Morning brought the news of a scuffle in the night, to the north of the village yet again.

A few of Berach's men had attempted to set fire to a barn, but were stopped this time by the men standing watch. One of their enemies was captured and held now in the stables; the other had been killed.

Rhys took the news at the door, and then turned to Caitriona, who rose from the bed in a disarray of wild auburn hair and sleepy eyes. How he longed to return to his bed, bury his face in her hair, and wile the day away in her arms.

But if he did not quell this feud with Berach, the goddess in his room would never be safe to wander as she wished. Rhys had to admit, he did not mind the fire in her, which brought a new argument every few days. It was this very fire which had captured not only his heart, but the heart of his village.

His clan had begun to defer to her rather than him with their problems. Their ailments and arguments were dissipated with effortless grace, firm kindness, and hidden amusement by his Lady. The trust they had in her was almost insulting. It had taken him years to garner the respect of his people in such a way.

He stripped off his nightshirt.

"Must you go?" Caitriona said, handing him his leine even as she protested.

"Aye, " he answered. "This man knows where my cousin has camped. I'll get the answer out of him. And then I...have tae go after him. I have tae stop this."

Pulling the garment over his head, he wrapped his arms around her, marveling in the lush softness of her. The curve of her belly, the plumpness of her hips, the strength of her arms. How beautiful she was, standing there in her nightgown, the morning light catching the bright tones in her hair, like flame around her creamy skin.

"Was anyone hurt, of our own?" She tilted her head as he nuzzled the soft skin below her ear.

"I dinnae ken," he said. "But I'll find out soon enough."

He was reluctant to release her. Burying his hands in her hair, he pulled her into a long kiss. The scent of her, like lavender and honey, enveloped his senses, teasing and tempting him to forget the day and just stay. She clung to his arms, fingers digging into his biceps, and made a sound of disappointment when he broke away that nearly broke his resolve.

"I can come with ye," she said, picking up her chemise and stays, tying petticoats around her waist as she dressed. Her long fingers were deft and capable, and he was entranced by their movement as she put on a bodice and pinned it in place.

Arisaid tucked securely around her neckline, she began to braid her hair into a crown around her face. He wanted to undo all of her work, to watch the wild locks fall around her face, see the flush of her skin beneath his touch...

He shook his head. "I willnae be long. Ye'll be safer here. Until I ken where Berach is, I dinnae want ye wanderin' about."

The corner of her mouth tipped up. "Orderin' me about again, eh? Ye ken what happens when ye do that."

He stepped forward and caught her lips with his again. Hands full of her braids and pins, she could do nothing but lean against him and let him have his way with her. She tasted of chamomile and berries, and she was more precious to him than his own life.

"Ye have work tae do here, still," he said. "Ye ken Morven and Lilleas?"

Caitriona nodded. "Aye, I've spoken with them a few times now. Morven is a bonny child."

And she was. The girl blossomed under the care of the clan, and everyone was fast becoming fond of her. She was a songbird in their halls, her high voice enthralling and her golden curls like the back of a bird's wing.

But Lilleas..."Her sister, Lilleas...might need ye." He tamped down the anger and said as evenly as possible, "I think she could be...in the family way."

Instant fury lit within Caitriona's eyes. "I was hoping 'twould nae be this. She's just a child."

"Aye, I ken." He rested his forehead against hers for a moment. Wanting to forget the horror of finding Lilleas bruised and battered and filthy on the cottage floor. Wanting to forget the low, desperate plea to let her die.

"Ye'd better catch the men who did this tae her," Caitriona said fiercely, her anger vivid.

"I will," he replied. Admiring the set of her jaw. The determination of her gaze. "Be safe, my woman," he said, and he released her.

Caitriona grabbed his hand, pressed it to her lips. "And you, husband."

He wanted to spill his heart to her then, to tell her what she meant to him. But it would have to wait. He had a prisoner to interrogate, and she was far too tempting.

He left before his heart could convince him to stay.

⚜ ⚜ ⚜

Callum waited for him at the stable doors.

"What damage was done?" Rhys asked, walking alongside the man as they entered the building. "Any injuries? Did anyone of our own die?"

"Brian took a blow, and Greer was burned. The others are fine. And the barn is still intact." Callum stopped him before they reached the last stall in the stable, where the prisoner was being held. "Rhys, he's only a boy. I dinnae ken what sort o' ragtag bunch Berach has gathered, but...he's young."

"And the man who died?" Rhys nodded at Duncan, who stood guard.

Callum shook his head. "No more than twenty."

Duncan clicked his tongue. "This mewling 'as done nothin' but beg to be let go."

Opening the door of the stall, Rhys was greeted by a lad of no more than sixteen scrabbling to his feet, the evidence of tears plain on his face. With ruddy cheeks and the barest sprouts of a beard, the boy had red-rimmed eyes and a stubborn set to his chin.

He glared at Rhys, but the effect was rather of a puffed-up-kitten, as he was a full head and a half shorter than the Laird.

"Who are ye to Berach, then?" Rhys knew his clan well, and this boy was not one of them. It did not surprise him Berach would have to rally up support outside of the Macnammon clan.

The boy's eyes flicked to Duncan, and a flash of terror washed over his expression. It was hidden before Rhys could acknowledge it. "I dinnae hae t' tell ye nothin', " the boy said, spitting at Rhys's feet.

"No, ye dinnae have to tell me," Rhys said, leaning against the doorpost, relaxing his stance but still on full alert. "But ye'll want to. Eventually. What's yer name?"

"All I need to tell ye is a message from Berach," the boy answered.

Rhys studied him, noting the stiffening of his chin, the unsure hunch to his shoulders, the spots cropping up on his cheeks. "All right, what does Berach want?"

"He says ye better keep watch over that pretty wife o' yers. Wants tae ken how Greer's wife is doin'; seems yer own wife was there for a long time yesterday."

Instant rage shot through Rhys and he grabbed the youth's shirt, dragging him up until they were nose to nose. Toes barely scraping the floor and arms flailing for purchase, Berach's lackey squeaked his surprise.

"Where is he?" Rhys ground out. "Where is the coward, and why does he send me nae but scrawny bucks who can barely hold their own?"

Despite his precarious position, the boy had the audacity to grin at Rhys. "He's too smart for ya! Been watchin ye and yer wife dawdle about for some time now. Won't be long now till she goes to deliver a bairn and doesnae return."

Not looking behind, he ordered, "Duncan, go to my wife. Make sure she doesnae go anywhere alone. And I mean *anywhere*."

A hand clapped his back. "Aye, I will." Duncan said. "Dinnae be too hard on the lad, Rhys. He's barely weaned."

There was humor in his tone, and their prisoner shot a glare behind Rhys before he was dropped unceremoniously to the ground. He did not catch himself in time, and tumbled into the hay like a broken doll.

"As for you," Rhys said, backing out of the stall and glancing at Callum, who stood ready. "Remove his shirt, give him a few lashes. See if he's more willing to tell us where Berach is after that."

Lashing could be utilized in many ways; some dealt a cruel hand, striking to draw blood. But Rhys did not condone senseless beating. The lashing came at the hand of the one he trusted most to be fair — Callum — with a leather strap which held no barbs. It would sting, but it did not cut the skin.

Watching as the boy was stripped and his arms tied up, Rhys shook his head. Already, the boy whimpered. If this was Berach's army, Rhys had little to fear.

Callum caught his eye, and Rhys held up five fingers. Five lashes, dealt fair, and the boy would be properly humiliated but none the worse for wear. Other than a sore back and the shame of his current situation.

To his surprise, the boy did not cry out as he was dealt his punishment. Though his chin trembled and his arms shook, he was silent. When they freed him, he pulled his shirt back on, for the first time displaying real fear. Rhys towered over him again.

"I'll let ye go on one condition. Ye get yerself back to yer master with this message," Rhys said, glowering at the boy, who now trembled with fear. "Any man who touches my wife *dies*."

Standing aside, he motioned to the guards at the gate to let the boy go, and without a backward glance the lad took off like a whipped pup. If he'd had a tail, it would surely be between his legs.

Aside, to Craig, Rhys said, "Have him followed. See which direction he goes."

He knew Berach lay somewhere in the north, but how far and where, he was not sure. There were plenty of hills and caves to hide in thither, and scouring them could take days. Once he knew which path the boy took, he could be far more certain of his cousin's whereabouts.

And then, he could plan a proper attack.

Striding into the castle to find Caitriona, Rhys stopped at the great hall first. He had not yet broken his fast, and it was past time for food now. Kenna handed him a bannock and some fresh berries when he sat. Lachlan was fully healed now, and sat beside his wife.

"What became of the prisoner?" he asked. The man had been aching to rejoin his clansmen and fight, but Kenna was forcing him to stay with her for the time being. For her own peace of mind.

"A bit of lashing from Callum, and off he goes to lead us to Berach. He doesnae ken that, of course. I've had him followed."

"Callum hates doing the lashing," Kenna piped up. She and Lachlan had lived at Calhoun for five years now, and were as integral as Jenny and Callum now.

Rhys shrugged. "I ken that, but this makes him the most fair. 'Tis not a job for a cruel man."

Lachlan scowled. "And do Berach's men deserve fairness, Rhys?" He was far more combative, ready to fight at any challenge. Protective of his clan, and his wife.

Rhys chewed his bannock slowly, eyes drifting over his clan. The children playing around the edges of the room. The happy chatter filling the air. "Aye, they do."

His cousin shifted, ready to argue, but Rhys did not let him.

"Every man deserves the chance to change, Lachie. Some may nae take it, but some have nae even been given the benefit of a new life.

Many of Berach's men are young. Too young to see their faults, too eager to forge a life of their own. He preys on that. Promises them grandeur, gallantry, pricks at their pride. They've never had someone tell them they were worthy before."

Lachlan hummed, but did not argue. Though he tried to hide it, Rhys could see he understood.

"I dinnae wish to end lives so young. So malleable. So yes, we will deal with them fairly, and offer them a different way. If they dinnae choose it, so be it. But at least we will have tried."

A comfortable silence settled between them as he finished his bannock, broken occasionally by the scrape of a wooden spoon against a bowl, and the crackling of the fire. Rhys didn't know what he would do if it weren't for those who helped run his castle.

Casually, as if discussing the weather, Kenna piped up, "So, when can we expect yer own wains tae arrive?"

Rhys nearly choked on his apple. "What?"

Kenna's eyes sparkled with mischief. "Ye clearly love the woman, Rhys."

Lachlan let out a loud laugh. "Kenna's been knitting a wee baby blanket in the evenings, and 'tis nae for us."

He raised an eyebrow. "Kenna, do ye ken somethin' I dinnae ken?"

She rolled her eyes. "Ya big numpty. I'll nae be tellin' ye if yer own wife is with child, but I ken she wants it as much as ye do."

"How do ye ken such things?" Were they so obvious the entire castle knew?

"Och Rhys, anyone can see ye makin' eyes at each other a hundred falls away." Grinning, she popped a few berries into her mouth.

He did not want to acknowledge the blush rising up his neck. What was he, a green lad mooning over a pretty girl? Clearing his throat, he straightened. "Well. Perhaps I need tae have a talk with my wife, then."

Kenna nodded. "She's gone to deliver Dorathea's bairn. Ye might have a hard time settling her down long enough to *have* one of her own."

Disappointment flooded him. He would be of little use to her right now, in a cramped cottage with a laboring woman. While she had put him to work at Sorcha's birth, he knew what he had to say could wait. He could wait. He had waited ten years for this. A few more hours would not hurt it.

"Please tell me she took someone with her," he said.

"Aye, Duncan is with her. She wanted to wait for ye, but Dorathea's been laborin' all night as it were, so she couldnae spare another moment." Kenna paused a moment, and then with the slowness of one choosing careful words, added, "She didnae seem pleased to see him."

Rhys blinked at her. "What do ye mean?"

Kenna shook her head. "I cannae put my finger on it, but I dinnae think yer wife likes Duncan much."

Rhys could not deny it. While they had not interacted more than a handful of times, he had the impression she found Duncan's sense of humor distasteful. But she said nothing. Perhaps it was nothing.

Taking his leave of the great hall, he made his way up to his study to do his least favorite thing. It was something he'd been putting off all month: the books. It was high time he reviewed the accounts of the castle, especially after the wedding. His wife would be fine with Duncan at her side and the men of the village to rally if need be.

When he was done, he would seek out Angus and make a plan to find Berach once and for all.

But he could not get Kenna's words out of his mind. Caitriona's interactions with Duncan swirled in his mind; the first day, when she avoided them both at all costs. The supper where she ripped Duncan to shreds for referencing her past. Even the night he'd brought her home safe and sound, she'd looked at him with an expression Rhys had never seen before.

Just for a moment, she'd looked ready to snap his hand off for touching her. It was gone before Rhys could evaluate it.

He shook his head and went back to tallying up the various columns in his books. But he could not shrug off the feeling he was missing something.

Something important.

RESHAPING THE PAST
Caitriona

Caitriona picked her way along the path, Duncan trailing behind her like a faithful guard dog. Though, she might have felt much safer with a dog than him. Apology or no, she still did not trust him. He seemed contrite, but he'd always been good at manipulating others to see him in a grand light.

A stone wall lined the side of the dirt path, moss growing green and lush around the smooth stones, and daisies bobbing their heads beside. In the morning sun, dew still sparkled on the flowers, and were she not on her way to deliver a bairn, Caitriona might have stopped to enjoy these little pleasures. She adored picking her way through the highlands with no aim in mind, finding shiny beetles and ladybirds, watching the sheep meander in the grass, admiring the dew as it caught the sunlight.

But with her basket heavy on her arm and her skirts kicking about her feet, she carried on. Dorathea's cottage lay a little ways beyond the village, and the sound of children laughing and playing outdoors carried through the air. When she had been here yesterday, she'd been surrounded by Dorathea's many children, all of whom had stories to tell her.

It was much the same when she approached again. Through the wild and beautiful cacophony of vivid snapdragons and hazy thistle, several children ran to her and clamored around. She could only make out snippets as they rushed her forward.

Primroses scattered along the ground and wild roses banked against the walls of the cottage. Dorathea was a gardener, and much like her children, her flowers thrived in a wild sort of way. An herb garden offered up the faint scent of fennel and mint to mingle with the sweet rose and the spice of thyme.

The children pulled her forward past the dog — who gruffed at them but did not rise from his place in the warm sunspot — and to the cottage door. The eldest, a red-haired girl of no more than seven, yelled "Da! The Howdie!"

When the girl turned, pretty freckles dotting over her nose and cheeks, her laugh was infectious. "Ma's havin' the bairn, milady!" she announced.

"Aye?" Caitriona followed the girl in. The cottage was dim but cozy, with herbs and baskets hanging from the beams overhead and a table close to the fire, scattered with wooden dishes and half-eaten porridge.

"I think she's pushed it out already." The girl gestured inside. "Me da's told us nae to come in."

Several low chairs were set up around the fire in the middle of the room, and a long bench welcomed visitors to sit and stay a while.

To the left, the largest bed separated the living space from the sleeping space. Box beds were along one side of the wall for the children, whereas Dorathea was nestled into a big, four-poster bed hung with drapes for privacy.

They were open at the moment.

Dorathea was sprawled out, a squirming bundle on her chest. Scratchy cries filled the air, and her husband Tàmhas was muttering as he attended her. It was obvious the child had arrived only seconds before.

Caitriona did not waste any time. "Have ye passed the afterbirth yet, Dorathea?" She came to the bed, and Tàmhas stepped back with relief.

"Nae, missus. She was born not a minute before ye stepped in. But I can feel the throws coming." She shifted uncomfortably, and Caitriona began to massage her stomach to assist the placenta's delivery.

"Ah yes, just there," she said, checking over the afterbirth when it came, reassured there were no bits left within. She had learned through the wizened Howdie who had trained her, if the tree of life was not complete, it complicated things.

But Dorathea had delivered a healthy baby girl on her own, with nothing to complicate the birth. Caitriona sent Tàmhas out to gather the fennel she'd seen growing, for milk production.

"Now then, what's her name gonna be?" she asked, tying off the umbilical cord once the pulsing had stopped, and clipping it neatly. Most of this was routine she had performed fifty times before, but the newly born child — hair dark and pressed haphazardly against her head — still elicited awe within Caitriona.

"I dinnae ken, milady. We hadnae settled on one yet." Dorathea curled her arm protectively around her newborn and Caitriona tucked the blanket securely around them, having finished cleaning up. "I think perhaps Maisie, if Tàmhas is keen."

"'Tis a lovely name," Caitriona agreed. "A lovely name for a lovely baby."

Dorathea beamed with pride. There was nothing as beautiful as a woman soft in the glow after birth, tired but incandescently happy, arms full of the bairn she had carried within her for nine long months.

A little flutter of anticipation pulled at Caitriona's heart. This morning, after Rhys had departed, she'd counted her weeks and realised her menses were late. They should have come just after she and Rhys had their first night together, but...

She put the thought out of her head. It was still possible she'd come into her womanly time later in the week, but she was not usually late. And she realised with a start she hoped her suspicions were true.

She wanted this life more and more.

※ ※ ※

Several hours later, having stayed to ensure Dorathea had no complications or weakness after birth, Caitriona emerged back into the day. It was after noon by now, and she squinted in the sunlight. Duncan materialized as soon as she came out the door and she smiled at him, a little less wary and a bit more hopeful.

Witnessing the miracle of birth always put her in a forgiving mood.

Falling into step beside him, they took their leave of the cottage and the children, and set off toward the village.

"'Tis a bonny day for a walk," Duncan said, breaking the comfortable silence between them.

Caitriona eyed him. His soft brown hair ruffled in the breeze. "Aye, it is."

Once upon a time, he had asked her for a walk on a lovely day much like this one. And while that particular walk had ended badly, perhaps, if he had not done so, she might not be here today. Falling in love with her life, and Rhys, achieving every dream she'd thought impossible.

Caitriona was loath to bring up the memories, so she shook them away and took a deep breath. "How long do ye plan to stay, Ni— Duncan?"

He shrugged and took her basket without asking, lightening the load on her arms. She clenched her hands, resisting the urge to take it back. This was, after all, a new beginning for them. "A few weeks, I expect."

"Do ye visit Calhoun often?" She trailed her fingers over a tall bunch of daisies, plucking a petal absentmindedly as they passed.

"When it suits me," he said. "And it suits me very well right now."

Caitriona blinked. "Does it?"

"Oh, aye. I've family this way, ye ken?" He plucked a daisy and held it out to her. "A sister, and my mother."

Suspicious, Caitriona ignored his offer of a flower.

With a wry smile, he tossed it aside. "Still excellent at holding a grudge, I see," he said, but his tone was teasing.

Despite her mistrust, Caitriona had to bite back a smirk. Duncan had not lost his charm, even after all these years. "Aye, and dinnae ye forget it," she returned.

"I'll have to warn Rhys never to get on yer bad side." He kicked a stone down the path.

Snorting, Caitriona studied the horizon. Her heart was light, her eagerness to get home to Rhys putting her in a good mood. "'Tis impossible, I have the patience of a saint."

At this, Duncan's laugh echoed through the air. "Do ye now?"

"Aye," she said, relaxing a little toward him. Perhaps they could reshape their past. Perhaps there was hope of redemption, and she would not have to worry that Rhys would find out Duncan was the Niall of her stories.

He had enough to weigh him down without her making an enemy of his old friend.

"And how are ye finding it? Marriage, I mean. Ye seemed eager to find love when...we saw each other last." Duncan hedged around their rocky past with a charm only he possessed, a twinkle in his eye and a grin on his lips.

She hesitated, not quite sure how to put it into words.

It was incandescent, deep; a well that might never run out. Her soul was as inseparable from Rhys as the sun was from the sky. The vast expanse of his warmth encouraged her to be exactly who she wanted to be, and it was a gift she could never repay.

"'Tis better than I had hoped," she said, knowing her answer was feeble at best.

"Rhys is a lucky man," Duncan said, surprising her. "And again, I am sorry."

He seemed sincere. Though his devil-may-care attitude and endless charm were no different, he seemed somehow more rounded; less a conjuring of unpleasant memories and more multifaceted. Human. Prone to mistakes, but perhaps capable of redemption.

Caitriona was about to respond when a dark shape rose from the path ahead. Several men on horses approached them. Their intent was unmistakable. They were Berach's men. A sharp fear ran through her belly.

Slowing her walk, she calculated how swiftly she could run, and to where.

"Duncan," she muttered. He took a step in front of her and held his arm out as if to shield her.

"I see them," he said. "Stay behind me."

The group of men had begun to spread out to circle them on the road. Caitriona slid her hand into her pocket as subtly as possible, and gripped the dirk hidden there. It was not much, but it would have to do.

Straightening her shoulders and lifting her chin, she glared at each and every man, though her heart beat double pace and her hands shook in her skirts. She would never show them her fear. Not after the last time. She was not a rabbit to be chased through the moors, useless and whimpering.

It would not be like the last time.

"Finally," said the man who seemed to be in charge. He was brawny, short but powerful, with dark curls and darker eyes. "The Lady Irving. Ye're a hard woman t' catch."

Caitriona stood her ground, unwilling to move even as one of the men dismounted and came closer, leering. She refused to give him her attention. "Who are you, then?" She addressed the leader of the pack.

"Fergus. Berach sent me to bring ye to his camp. Ye'll come without a fight if ye're smart. And I hear ye're as smart as they come."

The challenge riled her, and she glanced Duncan's way. He was still in front of her, but had lowered his arm to watch the interaction.

The man called Fergus jutted his chin. "Nephew, move away, eh? Ye've brought her to us, finally. Ye're free to go now."

Shock rippled through Caitriona.

Duncan strolled away, shrugging his shoulders. "Aye well, she's a hard woman to get alone," he muttered. "If ye'd come when I told ye the other night, this would be over by now."

Noting the surprise on Caitriona's face, he grinned. "Fergus MacBrighde, at yer service under the soon to be rightful lairdship of Berach Macnammon."

Her stomach twisted into knots. She was outnumbered, barely armed, and betrayed yet again. Regret ripped through her. She should never have trusted Duncan, not even after his apologies. She should have followed her gut. Allowed his actions to prove to her who he was. Words meant nothing if the man had not changed.

Leaving her dirk hidden, she held up her hands. One of the men took her wrists and bound them behind her, yanking her toward his own horse and lifting her up with some effort. For once, Caitriona was gratified to be a larger woman; hearing him struggle was satisfying.

When the man settled behind her, she tried not to shudder. His hot breath was on her neck and his voice was low in her ear. "I'll have ye ken, I mean nothin' but tae take ye where I'm told to take ye."

Caitriona kept her face straight ahead.

"Ye may be the wife of our enemy, but I willnae harm ye," he said. "Unless ye run."

After a moment, Caitriona nodded. "Thank ye."

She believed him. Despite her position, despite his obvious compliance under Fergus' command as they headed north. He did not touch her unnecessarily, only putting a hand on her to stabilize her when the ground grew rougher.

They were in the hills before long, winding through the Macnammon lands and as the hour grew late, Caitriona's heart dropped. It was not an easy place to find. The sun made its way through the sky, passing noon and settling low in the sky by the time they came upon a glen protected by trees, tucked away in the highlands.

It was hidden enough that none would stumble upon their whereabouts.

There were at least thirty men in the encampment, both young and old. Some seemed no older than Aodhán; others sported gray heads of hair. All of them looked up when Fergus rode in.

In their midst was Berach Macnammon. She would have known him anywhere. The piercing eyes and dark hair ran deep within the Macnammon clan, though Berach did not hold the same sway as Rhys.

His shoulders were not as broad, his stride not as confident, his brow not so noble. The dark curls that only added to Rhys's beauty were scraggly and unkempt on Berach.

Caitriona was pulled off the horse and deposited into a nearby tent without a word. Her guard, whose name was Dermid, left her with a grunt and naught but a blanket to sit on. The ties chafed at her wrists as she wondered what was to become of her.

Outside, Berach argued in low tones with an older man who seemed to disagree with Caitriona being captured and held there. Taking in her meager surroundings, Caitriona wondered how long they had been here. The tent was spare; a lumpy pillow and ragged blanket were on the ground, and a kit containing a bowl, mug, and utensils sat beside the tent flap. A lantern was beside it, unlit.

But before she had time to inspect further, Berach entered the tent, his burly frame filling the space. He glowered down at her, disdain in his eyes. Without speaking, Caitriona struggled to her feet.

The man was shorter than Rhys, standing almost eye-to-eye with herself. It gave her confidence to level him with a glare, her height an advantage.

"So ye're the hoor my cousin took as a wife, then?" he said with a snarl. Berach had the voice of a man who was used to yelling. Hoarse and guttural. Cruel.

Lifting her chin, she stood at her full height, shoulders squared, and glared at him. "I am Lady Caitriona Irving of Calhoun Castle, and you will let me go."

"Pish, ye're a loose 'un," he leered at her. "Duncan tells me ye've had yer fill o' men." Without warning, he grabbed her arm and whirled her around, yanking her toward him so hard she nearly fell.

"Duncan is a liar and a coward," Caitriona spat, refusing to show her fear. Anger roiled deep in her belly, mingling with the panic beating desperate wings in her chest.

Berach's whiskered cheek brushed her neck. "A liar, aye. 'Tis why he was the man I sent to find Rhys's weakness. 'Tis only by chance my cousin's pretty new bride happened to be Duncan's old hoor."

The sharp edge of a knife lay cold against her arm, and she started.

"Steady now," he said. "Wouldnae want tae cut yer hand off on accident."

The ropes tying her wrists were sliced free, and she stilled, confusion rife. What was he doing? Did he mean to bed her?

"We'll just need proof ye're with us, ye ken," he said. "Duncan!" he shouted, his mouth still far too close to her ear for comfort.

Caitriona tried to yank away from him, but he kept a firm grip around her wrist. An amused gleam was in his eyes. Raising her hand up, he held his dagger to her wedding ring, nudging it with a sharp point. Then he sheathed his knife and twisted the jewel from her finger with a rough grunt.

Duncan appeared at the door of the tent. "Aye, milord?" His eyes flicked from Berach's hold on Caitriona's wrist, to her face, to the extended ring in Berach's fingers.

"Take this tae Rhys," Berach said.

Misgiving fluttered over the man's face as he eyed his leader. "I didnae expect t' be the one tae..."

"Dinnae forget yer mother and sister, Duncan. A word from me, and their lives are ended," Berach snarled.

Caitriona had never seen an uglier man. Though similar to her husband in looks and some mannerisms, the blackness of Berach's heart spoiled whatever handsomeness he might have had. He was no older than Rhys, but deep furrows in his forehead and bags beneath his eyes belied his surly nature. A shiver ran up her spine.

Duncan was subdued. He met her gaze, and though an apology lingered in the warm brown eyes that had once been so familiar to her, he acquiesced to his master. The lives of his own family were at stake. Caitriona could not fault the man for protecting his own, but she would never forgive him again.

"Take Dermid with ye. And for the love of St. Andrew, dinnae get caught like Gordon and Ian." Berach sent him from the tent, and when he disappeared, fear sliced Caitriona's gut.

What would this beast do with her now? His gaze slid over her, glinting like a wild boar about to charge. "Ye're a buxom lass," he said, and Caitriona wanted to scratch out the eyes that lingered over her figure. "Are ye with child?"

She shook her head. "'Tis too early to tell." Though she had her suspicions, she would never tell the man if she was.

"Well," he said, and before Caitriona could react, his meaty fist slammed into her stomach like a hammer, other hand steadying her by the shoulder so she could not double over with pain. "We'll make sure there isnae a chance." Ruthlessly, he pummeled her again, and when he let go of her she fell to the ground gasping. Without hesitating, his boot connected with her body, ripping a cry from her throat.

Squatting, he grabbed her by the hair at the nape of her neck and forced her face toward him. "Ye dinnae deserve to be Lady of the castle any more than my cousin deserves to be Laird."

Tears streamed from Caitronia's eyes unbidden, and she fought to breathe.

"Milord?" A voice behind Berach saved her from any more pain. The man let go of her hair, and her cheek hit the ground, sending stars into her vision.

"What is it?" he asked calmly, as if he had not just beaten a woman to the ground.

"Ian was followed earlier, and we may be watched." The messenger in the doorway avoided Berach's glare, as if he was afraid he'd suffer the same treatment as Caitriona.

"What makes ye think that?" the bigger man asked, stepping closer to the doorway.

"Our scouts report seeing someone follow Duncan and Dermid, milord. The man seems to have been waiting in the hills."

"And the perimeters have been checked, aye?" her captor asked.

The man in the doorway shrunk back a little. "I...ah...dinnae ken, sir. We wanted to tell ye as soon as possible."

Berach pulled down his shirtsleeves and growled. "I cannae trust ye to do anything yerselves. I'll check the perimeters myself."

He did not spare a second glance her way as he left the tent. As soon as he stepped out, Caitriona began to tremble. It was the second time she had been unprepared for an attack, though she had vowed to never be caught unawares again. Pulling herself over to the lone blanket, she began to go over every lesson she'd learned on where to strike in close quarters.

The dirk was still secure in her pocket, and now her hands were free. She closed her eyes and thought of Rhys teaching her to use the little dagger, his hands covering hers, his voice gentle in her ear. *Stay calm,* he would have said. *Strike upward, strike hard.*

As a midwife, she was familiar with both female and male anatomy as well as any doctor, and knew to aim upward, toward the lungs. It would paralyze her attacker's ability to breathe for a moment, and, though she was loath to cause such a thing, result in death if she were to pierce the lungs. There were many places a knife could cause great damage and be survived, but right now she had to consider the worst.

Aim for the arteries. The lungs. The heart.

Breath ragged, she stood. Her body ached, her stomach roiling and fear pouring through her limbs, threatening to freeze her where she stood. But she fought against it. Placing a hand on her belly, she whispered, "Hold fast, wee one."

A few more days and Caitriona would be firmly past the date her menses should have come. And she would do everything in her power to ensure this would not be another lost child, for Rhys's sake. He had already lost enough.

Through the crack between the tent flaps, she saw the shoulder of the man who had brought news they were followed here. She backed away. Studying the small enclosure, she calculated her choices.

The tent was secure against the ground; no attempt at cutting the side or slipping under its edges would be quiet, and she could be immediately caught. She settled back onto the blanket and took a deep breath. If Berach returned, she would need all of her strength to defend herself.

She would live to see Rhys again. To tell him she loved him. To tell him they would have a child. She would survive this, and she *would* return to her Devil of Calhoun.

FORTY LOYAL CLANSMEN STRONG

Rhys

It was nearing suppertime, and the Rhys was beginning to see double as he stared at the plans before him. He and Angus had spent the better part of two hours plotting how and when to launch their attack on Berach, and now, alone again, he'd been mulling over the blind spots in his head.

They did not know how many men Berach had gathered.

They did not know what kind of weaponry he had.

They did not know if he set up camp permanently, or if he was on the move.

They *did* know he was in the north hills, and had been for some time. This was a small consolation to Rhys, who had executed many battle plans with confidence. He was, after all, the beast of the battlefield. This was not the first time he'd launched an attack.

But this was the first time he was afraid.

Caitriona had not yet returned, but experience told him she was still caught up in the village. Checking on babies, charming his people. The woman was a marvel.

A smile played about his lips thinking of her. When she returned, he was going to sequester them in the bedroom and then...well. Dropping his pen, he was about to close the pages when Callum burst in, worry written all over his face.

"Awright, Callum?" Rhys stood, alarm racketing through him.

Callum shoved his open hand toward Rhys, a small object within. "Yer...yer wife..." he said, but could not finish his sentence. The man struggled to breathe, as if he had been running for hours.

Rhys took the object from Callum's palm. It was Caitriona's ring. Terror curled its fingers into his gut, like winter blanketing its deadly frost over the unsuspecting flowers of spring. He could not move. Could not think. Could not breathe.

"Where is she?" He looked up at Callum. "Where is my wife?"

"Berach has her," his friend said, choking on the words. "Angus spotted them riding through the hills, and then Duncan and one of Berach's lackeys returned. We met them on the moors."

In a burst of movement, Rhys was rounding the desk, scattering papers everywhere. "Duncan? Have they taken him prisoner as well? Is he harmed?"

Not waiting for an answer, he strode out of his study and nearly ran down the hallways, hoping his friend was not in harm's way, ready to storm the stables and ride. Behind him, Callum's steady footsteps followed.

"Rhys, wait," Callum said.

"I hope ye took Berach's lackey prisoner; with ye and Duncan together, 'twould be easy, aye?" Rhys saw red. Someone had their hands on his wife. That man was going to lose his hands.

"Rhys!" Callum grabbed his arm and yanked him to a stop. Rhys turned. Creases of worry dug into his friend's brow. "Rhys, they both went back to the hills. We didnae capture them." He hesitated, eyes growing darker and angrier than Rhys had ever seen the jovial man get. "Duncan is one of them."

"What?" Rhys burst out. "Are ye certain?"

Callum nodded. "From the mouth of Duncan himself...what's left of the MacBrighde clan rides behind Berach."

The MacBrighdes had long since been reduced to a small bit of land and a clan of barely twenty. These days, they paid fealty to the Macnammons, as did many clans in the surrounding lands. In return for taxes, they were protected and cared for when famine hit their crops.

Betrayal ripped through Rhys's chest like a wildcat's claws. He'd known Duncan since they were lads no taller than a frog's knees; their fathers had forged a friendship and they'd continued it. Duncan had been a constant friend, visiting every so often, his cheery nature a stark contrast to Rhys's cloudy one.

"And what did they say of Caitriona?" Sickened, he berated himself. How could he have been so fooled? Years of friendship, tossed aside for what? And how could he not have paid more attention? Caitriona must have known; she'd shown her dislike of Duncan from the start.

Callum shook his head a little, flushing. "I dinnae ken if I should repeat it."

"Out with it, Callum. I ken ye're a good man." He put a reassuring hand on his friend's shoulder. "I need to ken...is she alive?"

The red-haired man cleared his throat, cheeks ruddy with embarrassment and anger. "From the mouth of Duncan — 'yer wife is the...hoor I've always kent her to be, and tonight she'll —'" Callum reddened even more, dropping his eyes. "Rhys, I cannae."

Something in Rhys grew very cold. Every muscle in his body was tense, ready to strike but having no target. "Tell me," he growled, unable to corral his anger any longer.

Lifting his gaze to Rhys's, Callum just barely bit back his disgust. "Tonight she'll make a fine conquest for the clan of Laird Berach Macnammon. Concede, and perhaps her life will be spared."

Everything came to a standstill as Rhys absorbed the words and considered what they meant. What did Duncan mean, the whore he'd always known Caitriona to be? Had Duncan known his wife before now? If so, Caitriona had not let on...or had she?

Reviewing her interactions with Duncan in a very different light, Rhys' stomach dropped. Caitriona's odd behavior, placing herself behind him, disappearing to her rooms the day Duncan had arrived. The way she had loosed her full wrath on him for referencing her past. The argument afterward.

She'd never said a thing, but the evidence was there.

Rhys had been too far in his cups to pay attention, but he had everything he needed to know. That day in the field, in the sunny picnic when she'd laid her past bare to him, she'd told him the name of the man who had ruined her reputation. What was it?

Niall.

Duncan Niall MacBrighde.

He scrubbed his face and stared at Callum. "I've been an idiot, Callum."

"Aye well, it willnae have been the first time, my friend." Callum attempted levity.

Rhys shot him a look. The man was lucky they'd formed a solid basis of trust throughout the years. His stablemaster had become someone Rhys might call a bosom friend. "Are ye with me?" he asked, the news of Duncan's betrayal having shattered some of his trust.

Callum nodded, jaw set, gaze determined. "Always. Me and Jenny and Aodhán are with ye to the death."

Rhys clasped his friend's forearm in a sign of thanks, and then resumed his path toward the stables, a new plan forming. It was suppertime now, the sky shot through with the last of the sunset, but this would not stop him.

He walked out of the castle, shouting orders as he went.

Angus reported Berach was a few hours north, in the hills. They'd taken Caitriona somewhere after noon, her last reported stop being Dorathea's home. She'd left with Duncan, and disappeared.

There was no telling what she would find at the hands of Berach and his clan. Fury roiled deep in his belly at Duncan's callous threats; he would rip the man's throat out. Sever his hands. Destroy all evidence of the blackguard who sullied his wife.

"We cannae wait till morning," Rhys said, addressing the men who rallied around him. "Not when they have Lady Irving." Unexpected emotion burned his eyes, and he cleared his throat.

Callum clapped a hand on his shoulder. "We are all with ye, Rhys." He rarely lapsed to call Rhys by his given name, despite many years of encouragement to do so. It was a small moment of comfort.

Jenny rushed out then in a full rage. "If he so much as lays a hand on her ye just bring him tae me, I'll rip his bollocks out through his throat and slice his —" she stopped when she realised thirty men were staring at her. Taking a deep breath, she held out a parcel. "Bannocks, cheese, a few medicines and herbs and bandages in case..."

Rhys took the package, refusing to acknowledge the implications of her unspoken words. "We'll be back by mornin'. Thank ye, Jenny."

Callum gathered his wife in his arms and placed a sound kiss on her mouth. Behind him, the clansmen whooped. He ignored them. "I love you," he said.

Rhys cleared his throat. "Remind me never tae cross yer wife, Callum."

Jenny scowled at him. "Ye'd best bring my husband back alive, or I'll do the same to ye."

With a start, Rhys realised he believed her. The thunderous glare she gave him was convincing.

Without further orders, his men gathered around them, ready to go. It filled him with pride to know the woman he had married not so long ago already incited deep loyalty amongst his clan. Not one face was reluctant. They muttered expletives toward Berach as each of them mounted their horses, and soon he had forty men at his side, ready to go to war for his wife.

Despite the encroaching night, they would find her. He had explored every part of the Macnammon lands as a child and as a man; he knew every cave and hiding place. In the dark or not, they had the location of Berach's encampment. As soon as the scout had told him, Rhys had known exactly where they were.

Equipped with torches, weapons, and the fiery rage of forty loyal clansmen, Rhys struck out into the darkness to find his wife.

A MAN OF DISHONOR
Caitriona

As the sun sank and darkness overtook the camp, Caitriona's heart followed suit. Every passing moment could bring about the return of Berach to the tent, and her plan was tenuous at best. Surprisingly, his men had brought her more suitable bedding, some food, and a lantern to keep the night at bay. While meager, the meal was filling and she was thankful not to be left starving and bereft of light.

It was more than she would have expected.

She paced the tent, unable to sit still as the hours dragged on. She had always been a woman of action. Any emotion she experienced ended up running her body as well, whether through tidying her surroundings, taking a long ride, or gathering herbs. Her mother had often bemoaned Caitriona's resistance to being still.

Anxious for action, she wore circles into the grass under her feet and considered her options. Would Rhys come in the night? Would she be left alone by her captor? Could she overtake the man who guarded the tent, and escape before the others were alerted?

She knew little of the surrounding lands, and would be lost in the hills without the sun to guide her. There were few trees to offer shelter here. Nothing to hide her from being seen against the gray hills.

All she had was the dirk in her pocket and the swiftness of her legs. If Berach came back to her tent, she would have to try to overcome him; and in that impossible event, what then? There would still be a guard outside; men in the camp to witness her leaving. This tent was near the edge of the camp, but it was not outside of casual observation.

During the day, it would be impossible to leave unseen. But the cover of night might offer some protection.

The horses were kept on the other side of the camp. This much she had seen before they'd put her in here. If she could get a pony, her chances would be far better; she was a confident rider, and even if she aimed in the wrong direction it would be better than being trapped with the enemy.

She scrubbed her face with her hands and straightened her shoulders, forming a plan. Duncan had spread rumors about her even here. If she could get the guard to come in, she could overpower him — he was young, and did not look strong. And if she could defeat him, she might be able to creep from the tent and make her way to the horses without being seen.

From there, she would ride as hard as she could back the way they had come, and hope she was headed in the right direction.

Shaking out her hair a bit, she dropped the blanket from her shoulders and sighed. Men were easily swayed by beauty and temptation, were they not? Removing her arisaid, she took a deep breath, and called out. Her dagger was firm within her grip behind her back.

Outside, the guard grunted. "What's that?"

She positioned herself close enough to the opening to be seen, but far enough away he could not grab her should he suspect anything. "Please, I'm feeling...faint. I dinnae...I need someone. To help me." Fumbling over her words, she prayed he would at least peer in and see her.

After a moment, the flaps opened and a lantern appeared, followed by the young man she'd seen before. He frowned as he looked her over. "Berach'll slit my throat if he catches me."

Caitriona stepped forward and grabbed his lapel with her free hand. "Please, stay."

When he looked her up and down, eyes lingering on the skin left bare by her missing arisaid, she knew her plan would work. "What is it ye want, exactly?"

Loathing the act, Caitriona smiled at him. "I'm sure ye've heard the rumors about me." She was close enough the scent of sweat and smoke rolled over her; Berach's men must not have bathed in weeks.

"They're true then, eh?" A hint of curiosity was in his eyes.

He was taking the bait just as she'd hoped. "I never wanted to marry the Laird Macnammon." She let her eyes drop over him, hoping her act was thorough enough. She had little time to waste. "I need a *real* man by my side."

"Is that so, lassie? Well, there's not much time but there's enough." His answer was cocky.

Part of her felt shame as the young man snickered, fooled through and through by her actions. He was younger than she'd first thought, perhaps nineteen or twenty, and still awkward as he attempted to sidle up to her. She let him slide a hand over her waist, up her side, until he was close enough his hair tickled her cheek.

Sliding her hand from his jacket lapel upward to his shoulder, she leaned toward him, brushing her lips against his cheek toward his ear, and whispered, "I am sorry."

He had no time to register her words as her dagger struck, hard, upward toward his lungs just as Rhys had instructed her.

Caitriona had experienced a fair amount of blood in midwifery and hunting trips. She had attended traumatic births, sewn up women torn by their bairns, and witnessed the most gut-wrenching forms of death. But nothing could have prepared her for the sudden gush of warmth over her hand, the thick way the knife sliced through his flesh, and the hard knock of the hilt against his ribs.

Her fingers were slippery and wet on the handle of the dirk. Warm blood rushed over her hand, soaking into her bodice and sending up its earthy, metallic scent. His eyes wide, mouth open, he could not draw a breath from the shock.

There was no time to feel remorse.

Stepping around him, she slipped from the tent and ducked to the ground. As she had hoped, most of the men were in the center of the encampment around a fire, eating their supper and gossiping amongst themselves. Berach was not among them.

Nobody noticed her as she slunk around the edge of the darkness, stumbling over rocks and cursing under her breath. Her heart beat wild in her chest, her limbs trembling. But she refused to give in to the fear.

She reached the horses undetected.

But then, a cry went up. From her tent, a weak yell rang out, and a few of the men looked that way. One of them guffawed and said something to his companion and they both laughed. No doubt assuming the young man was with her inside, doing everything the rumors said she would do.

When a second yell filled the air, they started to get up. Caitriona utilized their distraction and commotion to grab the reins of the first horse she saw, a mare, untying her from her post and mounting as swiftly as she could.

Her hands were sticky from the blood she had just shed, and she fought against a sick roil in her stomach. The horses were knickering now, restless in her presence, and she kicked the mare's sides, knowing she had precious few moments before they would realize where she was. The animal obeyed her urging, trotting toward the edge of the camp and then bursting into a full gallop as chaos broke out behind them.

Branches whipped her face as they passed the few trees in the glen, and then she was at the opening and letting her horse take the lead through the hills. She did not know which way to go, but her ride sensed her urgency and made its way without hesitation. Wind filling her lungs, Caitriona let the tears stream down her cheeks as they went, hope rising for the first time since she'd been taken.

"Ride, sweet one, ride!" she urged the horse, laying low over her mane. "Take me home, please."

To her surprise, they burst from the hills onto a well-traveled road, and Caitriona guided her mount toward the East, relieved to recognize the way. When she glanced behind, there were spots of light, men on horses with lanterns, and she could hear them shouting.

There was no time to look back, no time to slow down, no time to think. She could only ride under the wide moon, hoping its light would guide her home. Clinging to her horse's mane, she prayed with everything in her being she could outrun Berach's men.

But then, she saw it.

A great hulking shadow on his stallion, heading her off from the right. Berach himself was no more than a horse's length away, staring her down with the fury of hell in his eyes. He kicked his stallion into action and rode ahead of her, angling so she had to either slow down or ram right into him.

Caitriona panicked. She could not go back to camp. There was no telling what he would do to her now that she had injured his man and stolen a horse.

THE DEVIL AND THE MIDWIFE

Without forethought, she reined in her mare and leapt from the saddle into the moors, where the land was soggy and a horse might lose its footing. It was a risk, and one that could get her killed...but didn't. She landed on a mound of grass, rolling down a soft hill and through the mud. There was no time to gather her sense of direction; she pulled her skirt out from under her feet and fled over the marshlands. Toward the cliffs and caves.

Angling for the closest crop of stones, she hoped there would be a cave to hide in. Shouts rang out in the darkness; she was not fast enough. She glanced back just in time for Berach to loom over her, his arms reaching out to grab her waist.

A feral scream erupted from Caitriona, rough and raw and wild. She reared her head back, desperate, and was met with the solid crunch of a nose. It dazed her, but even as she saw stars she twisted and kicked her knee up, aiming for the fragile center. Again, she was rewarded with a satisfying howl when her leg met his body.

His arm loosened just enough for her to drop away, but she was immediately yanked back.

Desperate, Caitriona lurched toward him rather than away, grabbed his leine, and closed her teeth hard on flesh. The tang of blood filled her mouth. All at once, his murderous cry was mingled with the hard blow of something against her head. She went limp, vision blacking out at the edges.

Berach tossed her over his shoulder like a rag doll and trudged back toward his horse and men, who cheered him on. The pain in her head was so great she could not move.

"Tie her hands and feet, ye imbeciles," he roared, dumping her on the road.

Caitriona was still too dazed to resist. Someone trussed her like a deer and two men hefted her up and over the back of the horse she had stolen. Face pressed against the soft coat of the mare, she held back a sob. She could not go back.

Surely, Rhys had realised where she was by now. Surely, Duncan had delivered the message. Their ride back to the encampment was altogether too short, and Caitriona was dizzy from her upside-down position when she was pulled down and thrown over Berach's shoulder again. Blood slid down her skin — her own, trickling into her eye from a wound on her head.

He took her to his own tent, where lanterns were lit and a lush bed of furs and quilts lay in the corner. He dumped her unceremoniously to the floor, eyes fiery, nose bleeding, the clear marks of her teeth on his neck.

"Ye're a lot more trouble than ye're worth, woman," he spat at her, pressing a cloth against the bleeding wound on his thick neck. "I ought to slit yer head and send it to Rhys on a platter."

His hand was on his dirk, and the darkness in his face made her think he would. But he winced and moved the now-bloody cloth from his neck to his face. "Och, ye've broken my nose."

"Good!" Caitriona spat, beginning to get her bearings again. Her hair was wild and falling into her face, and her cheek was bleeding from her swift ride through the glen. Every part of her body ached. She would not give in. Struggling, she sat up as well as she could and glared at Berach.

"If I wasnae a man of honor, I'd kill ye," he snarled.

She believed him, but she did not cower. "What man of honor kidnaps a woman? What man of honor rallies up rebels against his Laird? Ye're no man of honor. Ye're a traitor." The words were unwise, she knew, but she could not stop herself.

Berach knelt before her and took her chin roughly, no mercy in his touch. "'Tis only myself protectin' ye at this moment from the men outside who want between yer legs," he spat at her.

"I dinnae need men like ye to protect me," she retorted. It was unwise.

For a tense moment, he studied her, eyes glittering. And then he shrugged. "Have it yer own way," he said. Walking to the flap of the tent, he opened it and nodded to someone outwith. "Just leave her alive."

He did not look at her as he walked out.

And when Duncan slipped in, cocky smile on his face and violence in his eyes, the last sliver of hope in Caitrioina's chest died.

A FRIENDSHIP ENDED
Caitriona

"I may have lied all those years ago, but after tonight it'll be the truth," Duncan said, leering down at her where she sat tied hand and foot on the furs.

Caitriona was too furious to play into Duncan's inflated ego.

To her surprise, he at least bent to slit the ties around her ankles. If she had been smart she would have put on an act. She could have lured him close, like she had with the young guard. She could have convinced him to untie her. She might have even gotten him to help her escape again.

After all, a man who built his life around revenge for a small rejection was a man weak enough to sway, when the prize was beneath his nose.

But she lifted her chin with defiance. "I swore then ye couldnae touch me, and I meant it."

With a dark laugh, Duncan closed the space between them and dropped to one knee in front of her, grabbing her chin with bruising strength. "Bold words for a woman with no defenses." He crushed her lips beneath his. There was no tenderness in this embrace. No seeking of pleasure. It was pure bitterness, combined with blood and sweat, and left the taste of metal in her mouth when he pulled away.

But if he thought she was going to whimper and break down before him, he was wrong. Caitriona opened her mouth just enough to lure him in, and sank her teeth into his lip, hard.

With a shout, he pulled away and slapped her across the cheek. Her head jerked to the side. She glared at him. Blood trickled from his mouth and he wiped it away, smiling.

"Still fiery as yer hair, I see." A knife appeared in his hands, and he put the tip beneath her chin, pressing enough to break the skin. "I like a challenge."

Before she could react, his blade flicked down and tore through her stays, which gaped open to reveal her chemise, dotted with blood. Her hands were tied behind her back and she could not shield herself, but Caitriona did not show her fear.

"Ye will not touch me, Duncan. No man will touch me but my husband, and I mean to keep it that way."

He snorted. "How did Rhys take it, when ye told him ye were a used woman?"

She narrowed her gaze. "He kens it was a lie made up by a coward." Her husband may not have known Niall and Duncan were one and the same, but at least he knew the rest of the story. Would he figure it out, now that Duncan had sided with Berach?

Gaze darkening, Duncan grabbed her arm and yanked her to her feet as he stood, pinning her against him with a strong arm. There was no dagger hidden in her skirts this time, no way to secretly free herself with the blade, and she suppressed a shudder as he sheathed his dagger and his other hand slid up her back and into her hair.

"I always did have a weakness for red hair," he said, grazing her jawline with his teeth. He tugged her hair hard enough to hurt. "Red hair and a temper to match."

Caitriona held still, knowing a struggle would only excite him. "'Tis a shame ye must lie and coerce a woman to be with ye. No wonder ye're jealous of my husband."

He laughed, exposing sharp white teeth. "Ye try to needle me, woman?" The amusement in his gaze was tinged with something akin to a predator sizing up its prey, and he released her hair only to grip the back of her neck. "It willnae work."

After a moment of silence, she shook her head. "Ye will never be good enough for me."

It was the right thing to say. Rage rose in his gaze and he lost control of himself. In a flurry of action, he ripped her arisaid off her shoulders and shoved her back to the ground. The shoulder strap of her stays fell and exposed skin as her chemise went with it, but these well-made clothes were not as easy to rip as her skirts had been in the past.

He fell on her, pinning her to the ground and crushing the breath out of her as he struggled to get his hand beneath her skirts.

But she was not the Caitriona of years ago, who had frozen with embarrassment under the unwanted advancements of a man she thought she loved. She was not a naive young woman, inexperienced and unsure. She was loved. And the man who loved her was the wind beneath her wings, lifting her up instead of dragging her into his muck and mire.

With a grunt, she jerked her knee into Duncan's unprotected groin, satisfied when he yelped. He rolled off her, groaning, and she twisted away, hoping to find purchase and get onto her feet. With her hands tied behind her back, finding her balance was difficult, but she lurched to stand and started toward the tent flaps.

Not quick enough, for Duncan grabbed the ropes that tied her hands together and yanked her back toward him. She hit his chest and threw her head back, both of them crying out when the top of her skull connected with his cheek. He flipped her around and groped at her body, her face, holding her firm against him and smothering her with another rough kiss.

And then, in the distance, a yell went up in the air.

Someone was approaching the camp. Duncan stilled, glaring at her. "Dinnae think ye're safe yet," he snarled.

The yell sounded again, strangled this time, followed by the beating of hooves and the clang of metal against metal. Duncan shoved her aside and she fell. He burst out of the tent in a flurry.

Caitriona lay on the ground for a moment, dazed, hands still tied. But something glimmered on the furs beside her, and she could have cried with relief. Duncan's dagger lay there, forgotten or perhaps dropped unbeknownst to him. She sat up and scooted toward it, movements awkward. When she got the dagger in her hand, she sat for a moment, wondering how to undo the ties around her wrists.

Carefully, she angled the blade upward until it hit the rope, and she bit her lips. This was not something she had learned in all of her training with Rhys. Still, she knew she could undo the rope with enough friction and patience, so she set about awkwardly rubbing the dagger against the ties, hoping it would be enough.

The first strand snapped as yells outside the tent grew louder. The second gave way as running feet pounded past. Caitriona heard names being shouted; Rhys's voice rang out clear as day, and she huffed a breath, frustrated. When the corner of the tent was struck, flames caught and she redoubled her efforts.

In a few short moments, the rest of the rope gave away and she was free. She leapt to her feet, rushing to the opening, dagger in hand.

Only to barrel straight into the chest of Duncan, who laughed as he caught her in his arms. "Berach has Rhys well under hand. Where do ye think ye're going?"

Caitriona let out a wordless yell and swung his dagger at him, but he was too quick. He smacked the blade from her hand and grabbed the hair at the back of her head, yanking so hard she cried out. Shoving at her shoulder, he flipped her around, pressing her back against his chest and forcing her to look out into fray.

Dawn touched the sky and the camp was in shambles. Several tents were aflame, and men fought all around them.

"See, there, lass?" Duncan said as he guided her vision toward where Rhys and Berach struggled. "Rhys willnae have much fight left in him when he sees ye like this." His tone was cruel, and he yanked at her chemise, ripping it further open over her chest. Her garments keeled open, held on only by her own quick hand coming to stop them falling further.

Fingers digging into her throat, Duncan forced her forward. He had one of her arms twisted behind her. "Time for some fun, eh? I need Berach to win. For the sake of the MacBrighdes."

Caitriona's stomach dropped. Berach pulled back his hand and the glint of a dagger flashed as he swiped it at Rhys. But her husband ducked easily away, smashing his fist into the shorter man's face and holding his own dirk to Berach's neck.

One arm trapped, Caitriona had a choice. Hold up her garments, or grab for the dirk in her pocket. Duncan's grip around her throat and on her other wrist was tight, and he pressed his mouth into her cheek, rough, almost maniacal.

"And then ye'll be a prize for the winner," he snarled into her ear.

"Berach will never win," Caitriona said, quiet and calm. Calculating how much time she had to shove her hand through the opening for a pocket in her skirts, and pull out her blade. How much time it might take her to wrench the weapon through layers of fabric.

How long it would take for Duncan to realize.

Across the camp, Rhys glared down at his cousin with a fury unlike anything she had seen, eyes blazing even in the darkness, face as hard as stone. All around them, men fought. In the darkness, she could not make out who fought for whom, but she knew someone was winning. She hoped it was her clan.

A thrill ran through her. *Her clan.* They were hers, not just Rhys's. They fought for *her*. For both of them. Spotting Angus striking down his enemy, she dropped her chin just enough to see the side of her skirts, where her hand needed to go. She had to pick the perfect moment, when Duncan was distracted, when the fight was nearly done.

But when she looked up again, Rhys was down on one knee, Berach above him, arms rising to strike. Caitriona wanted to scream. Duncan slapped his hand over her lips, silencing the sound. She watched helplessly as Berach's blade slit down Rhys's arm, as her husband threw himself to the side, rolling away, as his cousin advanced.

Her heart stopped.

But then Rhys rose as Berach reached him. Angled his shoulder. Lunged upward, catching Berach in the stomach. The man threw his arms out, trying to protect himself from the hard landing, but they smashed into the ground, Rhys atop his cousin, and the fight was over. Holding a blade to Berach's neck, Rhys carefully rose, nudging Berach to kneel before him.

Without mercy, he slammed his fist into Berach's cheek, and the man went down like a log.

The remaining warriors in Berach's clan had been subdued, most on their knees, hands tied behind their backs, watching as their leader was humiliated.

"Where," said Rhys, not having seen her yet. "Is my wife?" His voice was deadly and calm.

Caitriona understood the rumors now. He towered in the clearing, a head above the rest, his hair dark and wild about his face, his scars glinting as smoke and flames rose around him. Broad shoulders clad in a black leine, his thickly muscled thighs were encased in dark trews and the fury in his gaze could melt the very iron he held.

Berach had not lost consciousness, for his voice was clear from where he lay before his cousin. "I sent my man to slit her throat. Ye're too late, cousin."

Caitriona bristled, and would have yelled for their attention, but Duncan moved first. Shoving her forward, grip a vice around her throat, he shouted. "Macnammon!"

Rhys's gaze cut through the night and settled upon Caitriona, sliding over her with quiet rage. Standing before her old flame, mouth gaping as she fought for air, hair falling around her shoulders and garments in shreds, time stood still.

Her husband's gaze softened, and her heart throbbed painfully in response. He was beautiful, this man she'd married: beautiful in his fury, beautiful in his strength, beautiful in the dust and grime of the battle he'd won to bring her home. Oh, how she loved him.

And then, his attention shifted to Duncan, and the danger in his glare was palpable. Had she been the recipient of such vitriol, she might have surrendered on the spot. It was a testament to Duncan's cowardice that he stood behind her, using her body as a shield and her dishevelment as a trap against the Devil before him.

But then, he'd always stolen his courage from the women of whom he took advantage.

With alarm, she realized Duncan had effectively removed all eyes from Berach, and the man was subtly setting himself to lunge at Rhys. Hands forming into claws, arms tensing, he shifted from his knees to one foot beneath him, ready to ram his body into her husband and attempt to gain the upper hand.

As if trapped in ice, Caitriona could not scream. Berach launched himself at Rhys, taking him down like a ram breaking through an impenetrable door.

Horror flooded her. The time was now. Without hesitating, she let go of her chemise and shoved her hand into her skirts. Her dagger was cold against her palm and she ripped it out of its sheath, slicing through a layer of fabric as she swung it upward and over Duncan's arm. The blade sliced through muscle, and he screamed in response.

She whirled, her only thought to survive.

To get to Rhys.

Duncan's mouth was open in a silent scream, and she did not think. Did not pause. She angled her blade, and rammed it into his side, up toward his lungs, just as he rushed at her, still screaming. They hurtled into the ground, and the breath left her lungs as his weight crushed her.

Warm blood gushed over her hand, which still held the dirk, and she yanked it away. Duncan's cry was garbled, his face warped and unrecognizable with pain, and she shoved as hard as she could, rolling him off of her and scrambling to her feet.

The man who had betrayed her all those years ago lay writhing on the ground, a wound in his side, his arm useless, his mouth half open in silent shock.

"Remember this for the rest of yer sorry days, Duncan Niall MacBrighde," she said, heaving, panic driving her every move, stepping on his good wrist when he tried to grab her foot in a last ditch effort to take her down. Her heart thudded in her chest, and her ears roared. "Ye're nothing without a woman to hide behind."

Home
Caitriona

A dark shadow loomed beside her, and she looked up. Rhys stood there, battle worn but fearsome as he glared down at the man on the ground. The set of his jaw was a steel trap, fire burning in his gaze and a feral wildness in his hair. His shirt gaped open, sliced to shreds. Blood trickled from a wound on his chest.

"Berach is dead," he growled, seeming less like Rhys and more like the Devil of Calhoun every second he stood there.

All of the fight drained from her, and she took her foot off Duncan's wrist, almost stumbling over the rough ground as she stepped aside. "Rhys..." she said.

Relief turned her muscles to jelly, and it was all she could do to hold herself up.

Duncan reached out his good hand weakly to touch the tip of Rhys's boot, unable to even push up from the ground. The wound on his side bled profusely, and his other arm was useless. Caitriona had sliced through a significant amount of flesh on his bicep, and his sleeve was soaked. The pallor in his face belied his loss of blood. It was a wonder he still lived.

Tears leaked from the corners of his eyes, and he begged in a whisper to be spared. "Rhys, old friend, 'twas just a —"

But Rhys kicked Duncan's hand off his boot, cutting off whatever he was about to say.

Towering over him, Rhys growled deep. "I'll rip out yer tongue and feed it to the gulls. I'll cut off yer hands and throw them to the buzzards, and tie ye to a post while yer eyes are pecked from yer head and yer throat is so raw ye cannae even scream. And then, when ye are but a husk of a man, shriveled and keening with pain, I'll lock ye in the dark beneath the castle and let the rats nibble away at yer rotting flesh, until ye are nothing but the shite they digest and excrete on the dungeon floor."

For one frozen moment, the man stared at the dark spectre above him, mouth gaping, gasping for air. Rhys, every bit the Devil in the moment, had sent his threats rolling like thunder through the clearing, ready to end what Caitriona had started.

But he did not have to. Duncan coughed, a gurgle of blood trailing from his lips, and his eyes glazed over. Unfocused. The coughing stopped.

He was dead.

Not looking at Caitriona, Rhys ordered two men to take Duncan's body away. Someone pressed a cloth into Rhys's hand, and he held it to his chest, heaving, his face shadowed and his eyes closed.

Around them, his men rounded up the survivors and the horses. None of Rhys's men seemed to be seriously injured. Though many bodies scattered the encampment, Caitriona was relieved none of them seemed to be of the clan she knew and loved.

"We'll clean up the rest of the camp and then...'tis done." Her husband's voice crossed the sudden silence. The early morning light caught in his black curls like flame upon the coals, turning it into a dark halo. He surveyed the camp grimly. The dark angel presiding over war.

A rush of emotion burned through her, and Caitriona began to shake, pressing her hands to her mouth to stifle a sob. It was this which caught Rhys's attention, and he looked at her.

"Caitriona?" He dropped the cloth he'd been using to sop up blood from his chest and reached for her. But he was not quick enough.

Unable to stop the trembling, the cold so bone-deep her teeth chattered together, she fell to her knees. "Oh, God," she gasped. Her muscles tensed up all over, and she was uncontrollably shaking. Helpless to stop the quivering of her hands, the clacking of her teeth, the full-body shock of it all.

Rhys knelt before her, and his big, warm hands were grazing her all over, searching for wounds. "Caitriona, are ye hurt?" He took her hands, inspected her arms, brushed his fingers over her jaw, wiped the blood from her chest.

She shook her head. Clung to his arms to keep from sinking entirely into the ground. "I s-s-stabbed him," she said, shuddering too hard to get the word out. "I stabbed that — that poor lad I — I killed them both."

It was not just Duncan's blood on her hands, but the young man in the tent, too, who had been lured in by her ruse. She would never forget. The peculiar force of breath pushed out of a man when a knife was sheathed between their ribs. The heat of blood melting over her skin, too warm, too slick. The metallic scent of it filling her nose. And then, Duncan's last breath, a gurgle of blood and violence.

Rhys gathered her to him. "'Tis over now, *lasair-chride*." For a moment, he held her, taking deep, calming breaths to help her find herself again, surrounding her in his warmth, offering her body the heat it was losing in her shock.

Caitriona did not know how long they stayed like that, wrapped in each other, ignoring the men around them who tore apart the camp and readied the prisoners for the long ride home. Angus approached, briefly, to inform them Iohmar, the young guard who had accompanied Caitriona often on her midwifery outings, was dead.

The news settled like a mist, and Caitriona became numb with exhaustion. Guilt. Shame. She lost the contents of her stomach several times, and Rhys held her patiently through it all. Someone wrapped a blanket around them. The sun began to rise above the horizon.

And finally, Caitriona could control her limbs again. Rhys tugged her upward to stand within his arms. When she pulled back to look at him, she realised the dampness on her cheeks was not from her own tears. Rhys's eyes shimmered, and he made no move to wipe away the evidence of his emotion.

Instead, he cupped her face in both his hands, framing her with such tenderness she could barely breathe. "I came tae rescue ye, but it seems ye didnae need me."

A watery laugh escaped her. "Aye, I could have taken all thirty-odd men myself."

The sound that came from Rhys was strangled. Desperately, he pressed his lips to hers. Dragged her into his body again, as if trying to absorb all of the horrors she had experienced into himself. The day-old growth of his beard scraped her skin, his fingers digging into her side, tangling in her hair. He was not gentle; he was not tender.

But then, neither was she.

She pressed against him, wrapped her arms around his neck, clenched her fingers at his collar. They tangled together in a wild clash of soft against hard; his fears letting loose in the way he all but devoured her; her relief producing a frenzied *need* to be close to him. He kissed her lips, her jaw, her brow. Tucked his face into her neck.

And he sobbed.

This big man, who had conquered hundreds of enemies, who led his clan into battle without fear, whose breadth and height made him a veritable beast among men, cried into her skin like a child.

"I thought I'd lost ye. I am so sorry, Caitriona," he said between gasps.

Caitriona's heart welled with emotion, and she dipped her head, brushing her lips and tears against his cheek. "I'm here. Ye willnae lose me." When he pulled back to meet her gaze, she smiled, just a little. "Ye cannae be rid of me that easily."

He shook his head. "I didnae realize who Duncan was."

"Ye had no way of knowing. 'Tis nae yer fault." She smoothed a palm over his cheek.

Dark circles were smudged under his eyes, his beard a little rougher, his hair wilder than usual. He was blood-spattered, filthy, and exhausted. And yet, his first thought was of her. Her safety. Her comfort.

"Why did ye nae tell me? I would never have sent him with ye. Ye would never have been captured." Voice rasping, he traced his thumbs over her cheekbones, back and forth, as if reassuring himself she was okay. "I could have protected ye."

She shook her head a little, trapped as she was between his big hands. "Ye dinnae ken that."

He raised an eyebrow. "Dinnae argue with me, woman."

A laugh bubbled out of Caitriona, borne of exhaustion and relief. "I told ye before, I never listen."

His eyes were warm, still damp, but a small dimple appeared in his cheek. Still, his words were somber. "If I'd kent the man was a rotter, I'd nae have let ye out of my sight. And I'd have thrown him off the walls of Calhoun for his perfidy."

The last statement was both a threat and touched with dark humor.

She chewed on her lower lip. "But if he hadnae succeeded, someone else would have done the job."

He shrugged a shoulder. "Perhaps. But that is neither here nor there, Caitriona. What's more important is that ye didnae tell me when the man who ruined yer life was sleepin' beneath my very roof."

Avoiding his gaze, she studied his bare neck, where his heartbeat thudded beneath the tendons of muscle. "I didnae wish for ye to have tae lose an old friend on my account. Ye've suffered enough. Ye've been betrayed enough. And, 'twas a long time ago. I...I thought I could endure it, for yer sake."

He let out a groan so pained, her throat tightened with panic. "Are ye hurt? Where?" She began to examine him, checking the wound on his chest, which no longer bled; the cuts on his arms. But he stopped her.

"Och, *lasair mo chride,* will ye never learn?" Rhys's hands were gentle as he captured hers, and brought her fingers to his lips. "Ye dinnae have to make yerself smaller for me. Ye dinnae have to hide yer own discomfort for the sake of my own."

The simple words healed a wound Caitriona did not realize she had. The lifetime she had lived, trying to fit in. To be smaller. To wish for less.

To fill the holes people made for her, trying to fit her into their idea of what she should be. A good daughter, diminishing her own future to fulfill her duty in marriage. A good wife, making her dreams smaller to make room for her husband's desires. A good woman, tamping down her passions to fit the ideal of what she should be.

And beyond that, she'd moved through the world with the body she had for so long, she hadn't realised she still held wounds in her heart. She'd always been too much. Too tall to be desired. Too red-haired to be appealing. Too freckled to be pretty. Too curvaceous to be in fashion.

A tear made its way down her cheek, and she swiped it away. "I dinnae deserve —"

He shushed her. Kissed away one tear, and then another. "God help me, there is nae a thing in this world I willnae give ye, if ye ask for it, *mo chridhe*. Ye are the blood in my veins, the breath in my lungs, the light in my very soul. I love ye, Caitriona. I love ye more than my own life, and I willnae live in a world where ye arenae happy."

Her cheeks were wet with tears again, hers this time, but Caitriona laughed. "But I thought the Laird Macnammon had no feelings for his new wife. As I recall," she continued, grinning, "he expected them to live their days apart, a marriage of convenience once the bairn was had."

A loud laugh escaped him, and he rested his forehead against hers, eyes merry. "Ah, Caitriona. The day ye threatened to bed a village man was the day I kent I was truly lost." His tone was full of affection. "I wanted to rip the eyes out o' every man in the clan, so they couldnae look upon ye any more."

She raised an eyebrow. "Ye're not doing much to dispel the rumors, husband. I think maybe ye deserve them."

"Perhaps," he said. "But when I saw ye, ye were a flame I couldnae resist, and I was afraid. After what Iona did, I thought if I let ye in, I'd be lost."

She smoothed her hand over his skin, resting her palm over his heart. "Lost?"

"Oh, Caitriona," he said, brushing his lips against her fingertips. "Did ye not realize? If I let ye in, I couldnae turn back. Ye have enchanted me since the day ye accused me of havin' an affair in the dining hall." He was amused, his blue eyes soft. "Earlier, even. Since the day ye showed up covered in bloodstains and afterbirth, refusing my hand in marriage. I am a fool for ever thinkin' I could marry a woman like you and not be captivated."

"Aye ye are a fool." She lifted up on her toes to press her lips to his. Against his mouth, she said, "And I am a fool with ye. I love ye, Rhys Macnammon. Ye have me forever. Body, mind, and soul."

He tasted of tears and sweat and a future full of everything she had dreamed of. Safe in the circle of his arms, Caitriona ignored her aches and pains, her tattered garments, and the destruction around them. Incandescent happiness shimmered around her soul, which had finally found its twin flame.

"I think 'tis time to go home, Lady Irving," he said against her mouth.

She leaned against him, luxuriating in the safety he exuded. "Aye, I think it is."

Here, in the arms of her devilish husband, she was home. And no matter what happened, she knew she would never want to leave his side.

EPILOGUE

Rhys

Eight Months Later

Watching Caitriona pace around the rooms, her belly rippling with each strong push of muscle, Rhys could not settle. She hummed with calm, but her voice grew louder at the height of each labor pain, and he could not remember what she had told him to do next.

The room was quiet.

Kenna, Maeve, and Aileen were the only other attendants at the birth. Fire stoked, clean cloths ready to catch the afterbirth, and the bed made up with blankets and cushions, everything was ready for the appearance of this child.

His first child to live, God willing.

A short four months ago, during Samhain, Caitriona had gone to stay with her parents, and deliver Maeve's child. Rhys had been a bundle of nerves the entire time, fearful his wife might suffer the same losses Iona had. Coddling her at every turn, shadowing her every step. Smothering her, as she put it.

But she allowed him this time of intense protectiveness, for she understood his fears. When the time had grown near, he had offered to fetch the midwife from the neighbouring clan, or even her mother, and this Caitriona had refused. It was the only time she'd denied him his fussing.

She was confident in her own abilities to deliver.

"I've been training Aileen. She and Kenna will be competent, Rhys," she had said. "I've told them everything that must happen."

Yet, when he'd written a letter to inform her kin of the child, Maeve insisted on coming anyway, despite having a new bairn herself. She had arrived and inserted herself into the flow of the castle without hesitation, husband and children in tow.

The women waited now with endless patience, singing low songs together. He caught the fragments of their lullaby, a song his mother had sung to him as a child. Their voices mingled with the crackling of the fire and his wife's movements, and she sang with them when she could.

And while they stood back and watched, he fidgeted. Tapping his fingers on his leg, crossing from the bed to the window and back again, agitated. Wondering how Kenna and Maeve could be so sedate when a bairn was on the way. Aileen, at least, was fussing with the supplies for the afterbirth.

He dropped into a chair by the fire, knee bouncing.

"Rhys," Caitriona said, voice strained. "I need ye to —" She cut off, another bout of throws rising.

He leapt up and went to her side. "What can I do, my love?"

This time, her humming was mindless, growing louder and louder for what seemed like an eternity. She reached out a hand and wrapped her fingers around his forearm, her grip so strong it might strangle a man. Perhaps she wanted to strangle him for putting her through this pain.

He would take it. If he could take all of her pain onto himself, he would.

This strong, beautiful, determined woman had given him everything, and he would happily live the rest of his life proving he deserved her.

The humming stopped, and she melted into him, exhausted. She had been laboring for seven hours now, and not knowing when it would end drove Rhys mad. How long would he have to watch his wife in pain? How long would he wonder if the child would be born alive and healthy? It seemed this night would stretch on forever.

Taking a deep, controlled breath, Caitriona resumed what she had been saying. "I think I need ye to be with me from now on. My pains are getting stronger."

"Anything," he said, wrapping his arm around her waist. Eager to be of use. Her belly hung low, and she curled a hand beneath it.

"Help me over to the chair; I'd like ye to massage my back." She took the lead, moaning softly when her throws began halfway to the chair. When they got to it, she draped her arms over the back of it and stood, swaying her body through the pain.

Rhys suppressed the panic rising in his chest and placed his hands on Caitriona's back, applying gentle pressure where she'd shown him. Whether it helped or not, he did not know, but she made no sound at all as she swayed. The only way he knew the throws had passed was when she turned her head and smiled at him.

The hours passed thus, slowly moving from the chair to Rhys's supporting arms and then, when the pain came in wave upon wave, squatting before the bed, her face pressed into its softness and Rhys doing everything he could to make her comfortable. Toward the end she did not want to be touched, nor spoken to, and he could only communicate through the hand she'd grabbed hold of and would not release.

Something changed; she let out a loud wail, and she squeezed his fingers so hard the ring upon them left a deep mark when she let up. "'Tis time," she gasped. "Maeve, 'tis time."

As if on cue with her words, a splatter of liquid splashed onto the floor and the three women in the room rushed to her side, ready to assist. The next few moments transformed Caitriona from silent and swaying into a creature of power unlike anything he had ever seen.

She made no sound at first, but after a few moments she let out a feral scream, which Maeve and Kenna seemed to see as a good sign.

It scared the life out of Rhys.

"One more, Caitriona," Maeve said, awe in her tone. "The babe needs one more push."

Gripping Rhys's hand with the strength of ten men, Caitriona took a deep breath and bore down with all her might. The low groan she emitted was otherworldly, filling the bedroom with a pain so ancient it echoed into his soul.

But then, with one last scream, Maeve was moving and Caitriona was leaning back into his arms and the child was in her hands, an impossibly small being with dark hair and chubby cheeks, and it was over.

Tears streamed down his wife's face as she looked down at their child. "It's a girl," she whispered. When the babe began to cry, a watery, hoarse sound, she breathed a sigh of relief.

Kenna and Aileen moved around them, clamping the long cord and then, when it stopped pulsing, cutting it, and Maeve had linen blankets warming by the fire, waiting.

"A wee bonny girl," he murmured in awe. Emotion welled up within him and he realised he was crying. She was the most beautiful baby he'd ever seen. Perhaps a bit red, and her head the odd shape of a newborn, but beautiful all the same. Caitriona tensed in his arms and let out a low huff, and he grew concerned.

"'Tis only the afterbirth," Kenna reassured him. She and Aileen worked to assist Caitriona while Maeve took the bairn and wrapped her.

In his wife's hands was a remarkable organ, the placenta and its sac, where his child had grown for nine months in her mother's womb. Veins on the placenta traced a shape similar to a tree, and Caitriona worked swiftly to account for all its parts. Then she nodded.

Kenna took the organ from her hands, wiped the blood from them, and smiled at Rhys. "Take them to the bed, Rhys," she said, as Maeve handed Caitriona back her baby.

Wrapping his arms around his wife and child he lifted them as Aileen lay a covering over the bed. Caitriona and the baby were settled comfortably against pillows as Kenna rang for assistance in cleaning up. Maids filtered into the room, but Rhys could only stare at his wife and their child, amazed.

There was a glow about Caitriona. She was the most beautiful thing in existence, and she had just given him the second most beautiful thing he had ever seen. Gingerly, he settled himself onto the bed beside her, captivated. His daughter was already noisily suckling at her breast, grunting and nuzzling and making Caitriona laugh with her greediness. He stroked his daughter's cheek, captivated by the downy skin and perfect little features of her face.

She had dark hair, like him, and one little arm waved in the air, searching for purchase. He offered his forefinger. The baby's fingers were so small, they didn't even wrap all the way around his own. But already, his heart was tucked into her small hand.

"What shall we name her?" he asked Caitriona, unable to take his eyes away from the child. *His child.*

"I was thinking Helene," she said.

He smiled. "Helene Macnammon."

"Hmmm, Helene *Irving*-Macnammon," Caitriona replied wryly.

With a laugh, Rhys nodded. "Aye. 'Tis a beautiful name."

Settling his arm around his wife, he pressed a kiss to her temple with a profound sense of contentment. This woman had given him more than he'd ever expected from an arranged marriage to a fiery bride. She'd challenged him with questions that poked and prodded and pained him. But now, there were no secrets, and he was content to keep it that way.

She had known long before him what he had needed and it was a gift. A gift of freedom, of trust, of love.

Heart swelling, he basked in the glow of having a newborn child and a wife who loved him, and the prospect of a life he'd never thought he would have. It was enough to tame him, The Devil of Calhoun, and he would not trade it for the world.

THE END

Acknowledgements

This book would not exist without a plethora of people behind the scenes cheering me on, and while I could never name every single person who influenced making this book happen, I would be remiss if I did not acknowledge a few!

Carrie, Briana, Jessy, Chris, Gwendolyn, Ani, Eudora, Kezie, Amy, Heather, Mandy, Arathi, and Jenny: my fabulous Beta readers, your comments, notes, and occasional all-caps screaming with glee messages made my heart glow.

Emily, exchanging writing excitement, and information as we both go through the publishing journey has been so informative and there are so many things I'd never have thought to do if it weren't for you. Your friendship has made me a better author.

Kayla, your historical, nitpicky input and frank critique pushed this book to be better and better and better. Thank you for sticking with me through the copious voice notes. Your friendship has been a delight from the beginning, and I'm forever thankful to know you.

Brit, my writing wife, you have been obsessed with Rhys since the beginning, and I don't think he'd have been the same without your constant, consistent, and honest feedback. Thank you for (sometimes) yelling at me to get this story out of my head and onto the page. (and thank you for being just as feral for these two as I am.) Your friendship is my favorite.

Stephanie, your friendship is invaluable and irreplaceable. Thank you for listening to the copious voice notes, rants, infodumps, plot spews, workshopping, and everything else, all while not knowing what the heck is really going on because you're not a romance book person. You embody what it means to be a best friend, and I adore you.

Ashton, my kindred spirit, thank you for being the best friend of a lifetime. You have seen me through countless ideas, and celebrated every milestone not only in this journey but in our decade (and more) of being friends. I am blessed by your friendship daily.

To my incredibly talented cover artist, Kina: WOW. You made my dreams come alive with your art, and I am still sobbing over how beautiful and perfect the cover is. Thank you for your patience, and for being a part of making this happen.

To my parents, Tim and Dana: I would never have become the writer I am today if it were not for you both encouraging me from the earliest days to pursue what I loved. Your unwavering support, excitement, unconditional love, and encouragement are everything every child deserves from their parents, and I am so lucky to have you both.

And finally, to my husband: thank you for stepping in when I tapped out. Thank you for being not only an amazing spouse, but also an incredible partner. Without you behind the scenes, washing the dishes and making the meals when I was knee-deep in editing, quietly taking on the tasks which would have otherwise fallen to the wayside in the throes of revisions, and sometimes physically blocking our door so the kids couldn't get me mid-writing, I could not have done this. I love you forever.

And, to my late grandmother, Helen, for whom Rhys and Caitriona's baby is named, I miss you. I love you. I am who I am, because you were so wonderful.

ABOUT THE AUTHOR

Kristina Suko has been a writer since the tender age of seven, when she filled her journals with stories instead of cataloguing daily life like everyone else. She has always been drawn to romance and storytelling. Aside from writing, she is also a full-time content creator on YouTube, a full-time mom of five, and a full-time hoarder of books. She lives in the greenery of the Pacific Northwest with her family, three cats, and the raging signs of AuDHD scattered in every corner of her house. Which probably explains the various new diaries laying around that are all filled with unfinished grocery lists, attempts at journaling again, and half-finished story notes.

If you'd like to see more from her, you can find all of her various platforms and keep up to date with her next book at kristinasuko.com